Where the Love Gets In

Where the Love Gets In

TARA HEAVEY

Macquarie
Regional Library

PENGUIN BOOKS

160824

PENGUIN BOOKS

Published by the Penguin Group
Penguin Group (Australia), 250 Camberwell Road, Camberwell, Victoria 3124, Australia
(a division of Pearson Australia Group Pty Ltd)
Penguin Group (USA) Inc., 375 Hudson Street, New York, New York 10014, USA
Penguin Group (Canada), 90 Eglinton Avenue East, Suite 700, Toronto ON M4P 2Y3, Canada
(a division of Pearson Penguin Canada Inc.)
Penguin Books Ltd, 80 Strand, London WC2R 0RL, England
Penguin Ireland, 25 St Stephen's Green, Dublin 2, Ireland
(a division of Penguin Books Ltd)
Penguin Books India Pvt Ltd, 11 Community Centre, Panchsheel Park, New Delhi – 110 017, India
Penguin Books (NZ) Ltd, 67 Apollo Drive, Rosedale, North Shore 0632, New Zealand
(a division of Pearson New Zealand Ltd)
Penguin Books (South Africa) (Pty) Ltd, 24 Sturdee Avenue,
Rosebank, Johannesburg 2196, South Africa

Penguin Books Ltd, Registered Offices: 80 Strand, London, WC2R 0RL, England

First published by Penguin Ireland 2010
This edition published by Penguin Group (Australia) 2010

1 3 5 7 9 10 8 6 4 2

Copyright © Tara Heavey, 2010

The moral right of the author has been asserted

All rights reserved
Without limiting the rights under copyright
reserved above, no part of this publication may be
reproduced, stored in or introduced into a retrieval system,
or transmitted, in any form or by any means (electronic, mechanical,
photocopying, recording or otherwise), without the prior
written permission of both the copyright owner and
the above publisher of this book

Set in 13.5/16pt Garamond
Typeset by Palimpsest Book Production Limited, Grangemouth, Stirlingshire
Printed and bound in Australia by McPherson's Printing Group, Maryborough, Victoria

A CIP catalogue record for this book is available from the British Library

ISBN: 978-1-844-88209-0

penguin.com.au

To Fran and Frank

Prologue

Sarah squeezed her temples as if she was trying to force the noise out. But still the effect was brutal. Her daughter's screams. The constancy of chaos. She couldn't stand it. She had to get out of this place. But where to? Was there any such thing as escape for the likes of her? She felt guilty for even contemplating it.

And then she thought of the place in the west. That's where they'd go. Mitch could foot the bill. God knew, he owed them. And it would give her head the space it needed, give her body the time to heal. Give her daughter one last chance.

Part I

Chapter 1

The blue roared in Tommy's ears as his feet were knocked out from under him. Nature's washing-machine had him on spin cycle as the foam surged and bubbled over his head. Gasping for breath, he righted himself and retrieved his board. He glanced around for his father. Aidan was several feet away, spitting out water and smoothing back his hair. The two looked at each other and grinned.

This was the closest Tommy ever felt to his father. Not for them the soccer match, the hurling pitch. Why would it be, with the Atlantic on their doorstep? He lay face down on his board and, using his hands, paddled over to his father. 'The size of that one!'

Though they bobbed alongside each other, he'd had to shout – even now, when the water was relatively still. Aidan nodded and smiled back, evidently still out of breath. Then he, too, lay on his belly and they started to drift. Tommy was alone again, allowing the swell to carry him further out. Blue above him and all around him – his entire universe a great, glittering ball of blue. The sun sparkled on his head and he closed his eyes.

What was that?

Nothing.

He closed his eyes again. Drifted.

This time his eyes shot open. Definitely something. Tommy sat up and straddled his board. He looked around for his father. Aidan was further away from the shore now – out of shouting range. A shadow passed under Tommy. He froze.

Something was swimming beneath him. Now around him. Several feet away, a dorsal fin sliced through the water. Tommy heard a strangled cry, which must have come from his own constricted throat. His whole being quaked with panic, as he began to paddle furiously towards the shore. Getting closer now, he half swam, half ran as his feet connected with the ocean floor. He searched wildly for Aidan.

'Dad! Dad!' His voice sounded shrill, childish. And at least half of it was carried away on the wind. 'Get out of the water, Dad!'

He gestured at Aidan, standing as he was now up to his waist in water, gazing out to sea, as if hypnotized by its invisible, unknowable depths.

Finally, Aidan was looking at him, shouting something he couldn't quite hear and gesturing urgently at the water. He could just make out his father's face.

There was no fear in it. On the contrary, it was filled with happiness.

Tommy watched as a massive wave gathered momentum behind his father, so small and insignificant-seeming in front of it. His eyes widened as the wave reached critical mass because there within it, riding the wave, part of the wave – surfing the wave – was a dolphin.

They were home now. Their wetsuits peeled off and discarded on the deck, like second skins. Fiona would kill them when she found them there. But for now she was blissfully ignorant, leaning against the kitchen counter, waiting for the toast to pop. She was listening intently to her son's account of what had occurred, her arms folded tightly across her candy-striped dressing-gown. Aidan could read the intense enjoyment on her face. He could taste its bittersweet nature because it matched his own.

So far, their shared love of the ocean had got him and his son through the worst of adolescence, but seldom nowadays was Tommy so animated. At seventeen, he tended to affect an air of sang-froid. It was only at times like these, when he forgot himself, that the façade crumbled and they glimpsed the boy he used to be. It was a rare and precious sight.

'What a load of crap,' said Alannah.

'It is not!' Tommy half stood up out of his chair, rigid with indignation. 'Tell her, Dad.'

'It was a dolphin, all right.'

'Really?'

'How come you believe him and not me?' said Tommy.

Alannah ignored him and addressed their father. 'Did it come right up to you?'

'I just said it did, didn't I?' Tommy was becoming increasingly irate.

'She did. She circled us both, like a figure of eight.' Aidan demonstrated with a swirl of his hand. 'Didn't she, Tom?' He winked at his son, who sat back down in his chair, enthusiasm restored.

'She did. Dad touched her, didn't you, Dad?'

'Did you?'

'Well, my fingers brushed against her.'

'What did it feel like?'

Aidan leaned back in his chair and appeared to consider the matter. 'Smooth,' he said finally. 'She was smooth, with a hardness underneath.'

'Why do you keep saying "she"?'

Father and son smiled at each other.

'I don't know,' said Aidan. 'That's just the impression I got.'

'Me too,' said Tommy.

'Do you think she's still there?' said Alannah.

'She was gone when we were leaving. Otherwise we'd still be out there.'

'Well, I'm going out tomorrow morning – oh, no, I can't.' Alannah dropped her face into her hands. 'I'll be back in Cork.'

It was the first time she'd expressed dismay at returning to college.

'I'm going out again in the morning.' Tommy was gloating.

'Oh, no, you're not.' It was the first opinion Fiona had offered since the discussion had begun. 'You've got school.'

'I can go before school.'

'You have exams coming up. Do I have to remind you again? I don't want you getting distracted.'

'I won't, Mam. I can swim and study at the same time.'

'Won't your books get wet?' said Alannah.

'Oh, shut up.'

'Stop it, you two. You're behaving like a couple of children.'

Which was, thought Aidan, exactly what Fiona wanted them to be. As did he, if he was honest with himself. He knew he should relish the prospect of spending more time alone with his wife, once the kids had finally left home, but one thought and one thought alone prevailed.

What would he and Fiona talk about then?

As it turned out, Aidan was the one who went out the next morning. Guiltily, after Tommy had left for school. He liked the idea of being on his own in the water with her.

Why 'her'? It didn't make sense.

The sea was quieter this morning, the sky a softer blue. Even after the Atlantic had taken his father he had never lost his love of the water. Out there nothing mattered but the waves, each hungrier than the last, relentless and unstoppable, unchanging but ever-changing. Embracing. He lay on his board and paddled until he was just out of his depth, then waited. Not for waves this time. He had his camera with him, determined to capture her wildness. He rode the swell as if it were an old, familiar horse.

He didn't have long to wait. She swam underneath him at first. Then circled him several times. The same pattern as before. Aidan had to fight down rising panic. Could she tell? He had read that a dolphin could 'see' the adrenalin coursing through a person's veins. And there was something undeniably frightening about being with a wild animal in its natural habitat. Her swiftness, her agility, so superior to his own. If she wanted to, she could knock him off his board and pin him to the ocean floor. But, luckily for him, she didn't seem to want to do that. What she wanted to do, or so Aidan thought, was to satisfy her curiosity. Check him out. She was swimming on her side now, as if to get a closer study of him. He looked her in the eye. And it was at that moment that fear turned to wonder.

Slowly, so as not to startle, he extended his left arm, stretched out his fingers, anticipating her next move. Sure enough, following her pattern, she circled him to his left. He brushed against her. Or did she brush against him?

Her skin felt like silk stretched tautly over pure muscle.

He wondered how he felt to her.

So closely had he been paying attention to the dolphin that he'd forgotten to watch the sea. A large wave loomed above him, ready to cascade. He rapidly turned his back to it and his board to the shore. As he did so, he saw that the dolphin was within the wave, directly behind him. Christ, she was going to plough right into him. How many pounds of pure muscle?

Aidan braced himself for the onslaught as the wave crashed over his head and he was propelled to shore, as if from a catapult. But nothing more dramatic than that happened. He righted himself and looked all around. Of course. She had avoided him easily, with a mastery of water, her natural element, that was alien to him even if he had spent half his life either in or on it. People used to joke that it wouldn't surprise them if he had webbed feet. But this creature made him feel awkward and ungainly.

He'd communed with dolphins before – of course he had. Further out to sea they would ride the bow wave his boat created. But he'd never got up close and personal before. Not like this.

He waded back in again, swam, then was on his board once more and paddling. Sure enough, she came up to him. He fancied she was welcoming him back. Joyously this time, swooping all around, so rapidly and so impressively that he was sure at times he was sharing the water with three dolphins. Could she be in so many places at once? Yes, she could. He was beginning to think she could do anything.

She drew closer to him again, in ever-decreasing circles. Without hesitation this time, he held out his hand and she brushed past him again and again. Then – he must have imagined it. No. There it was. The dolphin pressed her snout into his cupped hand. Aidan stopped smiling inwardly and laughed out loud.

Then she was gone.

He'd forgotten to take a single photograph.

Chapter 2

It didn't take Aidan long to make up his mind to change his trawler to a dolphin tour boat. Not after it became clear that the dolphin was there to stay. He called her Star because it was as if she'd fallen from the sky like a star. One day the ocean was vast and empty, the next it was effervescent with her presence. And she was a star. Much as he would have loved to keep her to himself, she wanted to make herself known – as if craving human company. First she made friends with the surfers. The regulars, wet-suited – young men mainly. Black and slick, they glided between the waves in increasing numbers. She drew a crowd wherever she went.

And she was definitely a she, according to the German marine biologist who had taken up residence in the bay not long after her. Something to do with mammarian slits – it was hard to be sure: the woman's accent could be so obtuse. And it was clearly the same dolphin every time. She had a particular nick midway down her dorsal fin.

Aidan had taken to looking things up himself – books and the Net – until he'd become, he fancied, quite the expert on bottlenose dolphins, although this was not something he tended to broadcast.

Star made friends with the swimmers next – those hardy enough to brave Atlantic waters in April. In the cove, where the waters were calm, her dorsal fin visible and Jaws-like, terrifying the natives at first, then delighting them. She seemed to favour women, although Aidan liked to think that she recognized him. Why wouldn't she? He swam with her every morning.

It was fortunate that he wasn't a man affected by derision because his idea of converting his trawler was met with plenty of it. Mainly from the men he fished with and had known his whole life. Not from Fiona. He had told her over dinner one night.

Her chewing slowed to nothing and her mouth gaped, slightly unattractively. 'You're what?'

'It's a great opportunity.'

'For whom exactly?'

'For everyone.'

She swallowed her mouthful and put down her cutlery. He watched her fold her arms and cross her legs. The vertical line between the brows on her intense little face deepened. He remembered a time when it had appeared only occasionally. Now it was a permanent fixture. Not that he could talk.

'But she could be gone tomorrow.'

'She could. But I don't think so. I think she's here to stay.' Aidan picked up his fork and began eating again.

'You can't possibly know that.'

He shrugged. 'Not for sure, no. But sometimes in life you have to take a calculated risk. You married me, didn't you?' He flashed her a smile, knowing he could win her over. She didn't exactly smile back but her features relaxed a little.

'Would the initial outlay be big?'

'No. A lick of paint and a lot of elbow grease. You could help if you wanted. Keep down costs.' He grinned at her now.

'Oh, no. Wild horses wouldn't drag me onto that smelly boat. Wild dolphins even.'

'Fiona, it'll be great. No more smelly boat. No more smelly me. Something new and different. A proper family business. The kids could help out in the summer and,' this was the clincher, 'if I don't do it, somebody else will.'

She leaned forward, her legs twisted around each other, her

forehead against a bridge she made with her fingers. He watched her line deepen again as she took it all in – processed the information.

'But fishing's been in your family for generations. How can you give it up just like that?'

'It's not "just like that". I've been looking for a way out for a long time.'

'Have you?'

Had he? It was the first she'd heard of it. And she used to be privy to his every thought.

'Yes. There's no future in it any more. Nothing to pass on to Tommy. Over-fishing has seen to that. And I don't want to be part of it now. Part of the rape of the oceans.'

'Isn't that a bit overdramatic?'

'No, Fiona. I don't think it is. Not any more. I was thinking I'd stay fishing for the next few weeks and when Tommy's off for the long weekend we'd get the boat cleaned up in no time.'

She sighed. Deeply and with exasperation. 'All right, then. You have my blessing. We both know you're going to do it anyway.'

He leaned back in his chair and raised his arms to her. 'Come here to me, *cailín maith*. You won't regret it.'

'I'm regretting it already,' she said, as he came around to her side of the table and bear-hugged her. 'Get off me, you big eejit. You can do the washing-up.' But she was secretly pleased. It had been a while since he'd hugged her. 'There's something else I wanted to talk to you about,' she said.

'What's that?'

'This trip we're meant to be taking – it's time we started doing some proper research.'

They had been talking about taking a big trip since the children were small. The promise of it had got them through the worst aspects of infancy and all those times when their friends were raising hell and they were stuck raising babies. When the kids had grown, what wouldn't they do? When the kids were grown, they'd make up for lost time.

And now the kids *were* grown.

'There's no rush, is there?'

'Well, no. But we've talked about it for so long, I just thought it would be good to start making concrete plans.'

He was at the sink now, his back to her, dutifully rinsing the sauce off his plate before putting it into the dishwasher. 'To be honest, Fi,' he turned to her, 'I'm going to have my hands full for the next while setting up this new business. Can we wait till things settle down a bit? I mean, we have the whole summer to make plans.'

'You still want to do it, don't you?'

'Of course I do. Why wouldn't I?'

She shrugged her shoulders. 'You don't seem very enthusiastic.'

'I'm just taken up with this new idea, that's all.'

She nodded.

Yes. That was probably all.

Chapter 3

Sarah had caused quite a stir. Rocked the boat in this one-boat town. Once upon a time she would have welcomed this effect, courted it, even. But everything was different now. Hence the black clothes and the shades as she entered the health-food store, the door uttering a pleasing *ping.* A girl materialized behind the counter, her face widening in surprise. 'I know you,' she said. Then she clamped a hand over her mouth. 'Oh, I'm sorry. What an idiot. I shouldn't have said that. You must get it all the time. Must drive you mad. I'm sure you just want to be left alone to get on with your own business. You don't want to be accosted every time you walk into a shop.'

The words rushed out of her.

Sarah slid the shades halfway down the bridge of her nose. She regarded the girl solemnly over the top of them. 'Are you the town flake?' she said.

The girl flushed slightly, then, seeing that Sarah was smiling at her, laughed nervously. 'I think I must be.'

'I think you must be too. Have you got any of these supplements, please?'

The girl took the list, visibly flustered. 'Oh, look at me, my hands are shaking.'

'I'm not that famous, you know.'

'Are you kidding me? I've been a fan for years.'

'Careful. You'll make me feel old. My fragile ego won't be able to take it.'

'Oh, yeah, sorry. You needn't worry, though. You look fab for your age.'

Sarah laughed. 'Oh, compliments, compliments. I'm glad I came in here.'

The girl was examining the list. 'Some of these are for . . .'

'Yes.'

'They were true, then? Those stories about you.'

'Afraid so.'

'So that's a . . .' She pointed to the woman's head.

'It is, yes.'

'Wow. It looks so realistic. Although I suppose you were able to afford the very best.'

'It was hand-woven at midnight from the hair of seven Peruvian maidens.'

The girl looked for a moment as if she was going to believe her. 'That's a joke, isn't it?'

'It is.'

Sarah continued to look at her expectantly.

'Oh. The supplements. God. I'll go and see what we have.' She turned back one last time. 'You are better now, aren't you?'

'Right as rain.'

'Oh, that's good.'

Sarah selected two herbal soaps and a kiddie shampoo in the time it took for the girl to gather up the pills. 'You've got most of them. I'm surprised. You're very well stocked. I'll take these as well.'

'Here. Have some free samples. They're lovely. And this.'

'Thanks.'

'You are *so* welcome.'

'Well, thank you . . .'

'Valerie.'

'Valerie. You really have made me feel very welcome. I'll be seeing you again soon.'

'Are you staying around here for a while, then?'

'I am.'

'Oh, Jesus, that's brilliant. Wait till I tell my sister. She'll die.'
Sarah laughed again.

'Anything you need. I mean, anything. Just ask me and I'll order it in for you.'

'I might do that.'

'Oh, do. Definitely do that.'

''Bye, Valerie.'

The door had barely *ping*ed shut before the girl was on the phone. 'Bridget, it's me. You'll never guess who was in the shop.'

Chapter 4

Aidan had put the boat to bed. He was the last man in, which was just the way he liked it: the harbour to himself, as silent as it was possible for a harbour to be, save for the intermittent screeching of the gulls, the rhythmic lapping of the water, the rigging hitting the masts. This was where Aidan found his god – out here, among the wind and the waves, where the sounds were not of human origin. For a long time now he had been trying to capture the stillness and peace of such moments with his camera. If he was lucky he got one or two shots a year that lived up to the wonder of what he saw with his naked eye.

This evening he had the camera out again. Crouching on the pier, he peered through the viewfinder to frame the boats and the setting sun in the background.

'It'll never work. Trying to capture the now.'

The woman's voice startled him. He looked up, right into the sun, and clambered to his feet.

'Are you a photographer?'

His laugh was short. 'No. A fisherman.'

'Well, that's even better. Could you bring me out?'

Aidan looked her up and down. He didn't mean to be so bold but the request was unexpected. And from such a source. 'Do you mean out fishing?'

'God, no.' She threw back her head and laughed. Quite a sound. Lyrical. 'I meant to see the dolphin.'

'Oh.' He didn't know what to say. Which wasn't like him.

She smiled at him quizzically, one corner of her mouth

higher than the other, her eyebrows close to her hairline. She was blonde – perfect blonde hair. Her skin was a kind of honey colour, although that might have been makeup. Her accent was posh Dublin. An early tourist?

'You do know about the dolphin?' she said.

'I do.'

'She is still here, isn't she?' Her face clouded.

'Oh, she's here, all right. I just don't think I can bring you out.'

'I'd pay, of course.'

'It's not that. It's a trawler I have, not a yacht. It stinks to high heaven for a start.'

'I wouldn't care about that.'

'And it would be no place for a child.' He inclined his head towards the small girl who had been standing silently at her side throughout. Aidan had attempted to smile at her a couple of times, but the child had continued to stare out to sea, her tiny hand clasped firmly in the woman's. 'A trawler's no place for a child. It's too dangerous.'

The woman sighed heavily and theatrically. 'There must be someone who can bring us out. I can't believe there's no dolphin tour boat around here.'

Aidan smiled: great minds. The smile faded when he saw how disappointed she was, agitated even. 'Tell you what,' he said. 'I have a dinghy. I'll bring the two of you out in that in the morning.'

'Really?' She smiled at him. And it was as if her face had lit from within.

They agreed to meet at half past eight. He watched them as they walked away. He could tell the woman was smiling, even though he couldn't see her face. Her head erect, shoulders back, steps high and jaunty. The daughter had a particular way of walking. On her tippy-toes. As if she was trying to elevate herself to her mother's height. He aimed his camera once more: two black figures against a backdrop of orange.

He watched them walk the entire length of the pier until they were no more than tiny black dots, one tinier than the other.

Aidan didn't hear the woman coming up behind him. The morning felt sacred, so clear and serene, and he was almost in a trance when her voice broke into his reverie. He'd been banking on the little girl alerting him to their presence. If there was one thing children knew how to do, it was how to shatter silence, as his own children had done, once upon a sweet time.

'Good morning.'

He started. 'Morning.'

'I've just realized I don't even know your name.'

'Aidan.'

'Aidan. It suits you.' They smiled at one another. She had an exceptional smile.

'My name's Sarah and this is Maia.' She gestured towards the little girl.

Maia. What class of a name was that? You'd know they were from Dublin.

'Hello there, Maia.' Aidan grinned at her in the winning way he had with children. But Maia seemed intent on staring out to sea. A family trait, perhaps. Shy, he decided. And a beautiful child: four or five, candy-blonde hair, gathered up into a bunch on either side of her exquisite head, huge soft eyes, honeyed skin. A miniature portrait of her mother. Who, Aidan admitted to himself, was no slouch in the beauty stakes either. Something he'd neglected to mention to Fiona, when she questioned his motives in bringing a complete stranger out to sea – free of charge – on a Sunday morning. It wasn't the going out to sea in itself that had baffled her: she knew how he cherished his alone time.

He helped the woman into the dinghy, her hand gripping his, and she in turn lifted down her daughter, a short human chain. Then they were off.

'Are you excited about seeing the dolphin, Maia?'

Again, the child failed to respond. She sat huddled behind her mother, playing with what looked like a piece of string. It was as if she hadn't heard him. Was she deaf? He looked questioningly at Sarah.

'Maia's autistic,' she said.

'Oh.'

Aidan attempted to disguise the pity in his eyes as he glanced from mother to child. So picture perfect on the outside. He grappled for something to say. 'So she can't talk, then?'

'Some autistic children do. But Maia has never spoken. No.'

'And she's, what – five?'

'Seven.'

Aidan tried not to register surprise, but his raised eyebrows gave him away. So tiny for her age. But maybe that was normal for her condition.

'That's why we're here,' Sarah continued. 'I was hoping the dolphin . . .' Her voice trailed off.

'You were hoping the dolphin could help her.'

'Yes.' Her voice was barely audible. 'I suppose you think I'm mad.'

'Not at all.'

'Then you'd be in the minority.'

'I've always found that a good place to be.'

She smiled again. 'Why do you think she came here?'

'The dolphin?'

'Yes.'

'I don't know. Maybe to remind us humans that the ocean doesn't just belong to us.'

Sarah looked at him curiously, as if she was trying to fathom him. 'Do you think we'll see her today?'

'I do.'

'You sound pretty certain.'

'Well, she knows this boat. And, like all women, she won't be able to resist having a nose.'

'Does she know you too?'

'I'd like to think she does.'

'How does she know you?'

'I swim with her most days.'

Sarah stared at Aidan as if she were seeing him for the first time. 'What's it like?'

'What's it like?' His eyes took on a faraway look. 'It's like heaven on earth.'

Sarah closed her eyes. 'Heaven on earth,' she repeated, her voice barely a whisper. 'That's what I thought.'

Aidan shut off the engine and she opened her eyes. 'What's happening?'

'Nothing. This is as good a place as any to see her. Right here in the mouth of the harbour.'

'What do we do now?' Sarah seemed suddenly nervous. Uncertain.

'We wait.'

'Oh.'

So that was what they did, bobbing gently up and down on the water. The morning so perfect – so complete in itself – that maybe it wouldn't even matter if the dolphin failed to make an appearance. For the first time that year, Aidan felt real heat in the sun. So much so that he felt compelled to take off his jumper. With a sense of liberation, he lifted it up and prepared to pull it backwards over his head. He jumped at the sudden high-pitched shriek. Maia had started to scream.

'Put it back on.' Sarah was speaking urgently to him.

He reversed the jumper back down over his face, alarmed.

The screaming stopped as abruptly as it had started.

'What's wrong?'

'It's your T-shirt.'

'What about it?'

'You're wearing a red one.' She laughed at his puzzled expression. 'Maia's afraid of bright red.'

Afraid of bright red? He looked at the little girl. She was huddled into the corner of the boat, rocking slightly. Jesus. Here they were, bobbing up and down like a cork on the Atlantic Ocean, with nothing but a thin piece of rubber between them and the elements, and she was afraid of a red T-shirt? How the hell was she going to respond to a wild animal? Maybe it would be better for everyone concerned if the dolphin didn't show up today. But no sooner had the thought entered his head . . .

Sarah jumped. 'What was that?'

'She's here.'

'Oh, my God.' She gripped the sides of the dinghy with both hands and peered into the water. True to form, Star surfaced on the other side of the boat, spewing spray from her blowhole like a sigh. Sarah switched sides excitedly. 'Maia, a dolphin. Look. Look at the dolphin. Remember? I showed you the pictures.'

Maia was staring fixedly out to sea. If the dolphin happened to surface in that exact spot she'd see her. If she didn't, well, she wouldn't.

Aidan fired up the engine again, hoping Star would swim alongside them. She didn't disappoint: she raced along on her side so that she could peer up at them.

Sarah appeared to be in ecstasy. 'Maia, look,' she kept repeating, over and over. 'The dolphin. Look at the dolphin.'

Aidan's heart was broken for her at her daughter's lack of response. He thought of all the other children he'd seen with Star – those he'd brought out on his boat. The joy on their faces, the squeals of delight. And here was this little girl, locked inside her own private world of darkness.

Star seemed to have disappeared. Aidan knew that this was an illusion. But even he wasn't prepared for what happened next. Because right before his very eyes Star reared out of the water, as if she were standing on her tail, her head level with Maia's. Then she did something that Aidan wouldn't have believed if he hadn't seen it with his own eyes. Star tipped Maia on her forehead. The little girl and the dolphin squealed at one another and the dolphin was gone.

'Did you see that?' Sarah's eyes were full of tears. Aidan nodded, at a loss for words. 'The dolphin wants to make friends with you, Maia. She wants to be your friend. Have you ever seen anything like it, Aidan?'

'No, I haven't.'

'Will you bring us out again?'

'Of course.'

The following week Aidan and Tommy got stuck into Project Dolphin Tours. It was as if the outing with Sarah and her little girl had been a message that he was doing the right thing. His enthusiasm was matched only by Tommy's. As the days lengthened into spring, they scrubbed the fishy smells from the furthermost corners of the trawler, transforming it into a bona-fide boat. Of course, despite what he had told his wife, in the end a damn sight more work was required than a lick of paint. There was the carpentry for a start. The other fishermen were happy to help – in exchange for taking the piss.

'I've a couple of sheep I could lend you there, Noah.'

'I'm telling you, I bet Noah didn't have to put up with half this amount of shit.'

'Noah probably paid his workers.'

'Get away out of that. Didn't I buy you a pint the other night?'

'Last of the big spenders.'

But Aidan's enthusiasm was infectious. And he'd always had a knack for getting people to come around to his way of thinking.

Chapter 5

'I found out who she is.'

Fiona seemed excited as she banged the door of one kitchen press after another. She was often wound up like this after a manic day in the surgery. It didn't always make for relaxing mealtimes.

'Who?'

'Your new woman.' She looked over her shoulder and smiled at him. 'The one you've been taking out in the boat.'

'Oh. What's this?'

'It's a new recipe. Try it.'

Aidan poked at what was on his plate. Not another of Fiona's experiments. He supposed a different man might be delighted to have married such an innovative cook, but his tastes were simple and Fiona's attempts at educating his palate had proved largely unsuccessful.

'She's the actress Sarah Dillon.'

'Sarah. That's right.'

'I can't believe you didn't recognize her.'

He shook his head, raising a fork to his mouth.

Fiona was incredulous. 'She's always on the telly. And she's done tons of theatre.'

Aidan looked blank. He didn't watch much TV.

'She's very attractive. Is she good-looking in real life?'

Aidan shrugged. 'She's okay.' He knew better than to compliment another woman in front of his wife. Fiona knew this about him. She was just testing.

'What's she like?'

'Nice. Normal. Friendly.'

'She had breast cancer, you know. That's why they think she's here. To recuperate.'

He didn't say anything as she sat down opposite him with a satisfied sigh and began to grind pepper over her food. 'Oh.' She got up abruptly and retrieved what looked like a pile of magazines from the counter. She placed them beside him.

'What are these?'

'Brochures. I was in the travel agent's today.'

'I thought we'd agreed we weren't thinking about this trip for a while.'

'No harm whetting our appetites, is there?'

'How did it go this morning, Dad?' said Tommy, as he sat down for his dinner.

'Good. It went well.'

'Did Star show up?'

'She did.'

Aidan had no idea why he didn't tell Tommy about Star's amazing feat. For some reason, he just didn't feel like sharing.

'Perhaps we could have her over for dinner.' Fiona was clearly delighted with herself.

'Who?'

'Sarah Dillon, of course.'

'Well, don't give her this.'

'What's wrong with it?'

'Nothing.' He stood up abruptly, his chair scraping the floor behind him.

'Aidan! Where are you going?'

'Out.'

Rufus, a young, sleek-headed, black Labrador, scrambled noisily to his feet as soon as he saw Aidan heading for the back door and clattered after him, skidding on the tiles in his excitement.

Fiona and Tommy looked after them in amazement, then at each other.

'What's up with him?'

'Don't know.'

Down on the beach, Aidan didn't know what was up with him either. Except that he did. But he was damned if he was going to admit it to himself.

He brought Sarah and Maia out again the following weekend. The wind had picked up and the sea was choppy. 'I hope you don't get seasick.'

'Never. I'm a good sailor. I think I might have been a pirate in another life.'

'Do you believe in that stuff?'

'What? Past lives?'

'Yes.'

'Oh, I don't know. I suppose it's no more fantastical than the idea of heaven. But, then, I don't know if I believe in that either. And I've had cause to give the matter a lot of thought lately.'

He could feel the weight of her gaze. Perhaps she was wondering if he knew about the cancer, leaving space for him to say something. He continued to stare out to sea. He heard her sigh.

'I don't know,' she said. 'Maybe we just break down into our basic components and become one with the earth again. I suppose that's a kind of eternal life. Helping the flowers to grow. Being part of a flower. Or a tree. I guess I wouldn't mind that.'

He was looking at her now and she smiled at him. 'I suppose you're going to have your ashes scattered out at sea.'

'That's the plan anyway.'

'Is that what they did with your father? Didn't you say he was a fisherman too?'

'He was. No, my father was drowned. They never found his body.'

Sarah clamped her hand over her mouth, as if she were trying to prevent the words she had already spoken. 'Oh, I'm so sorry. How awful for you. And your family. Your mother.'

He nodded. 'She never really got over it. I think it was because they never found him. She could never fully accept that he'd gone.'

'Did they love each other?'

Aidan had never thought about it before. 'I suppose they did. They had a lot of respect for each other, that's for sure. My mother was the educated one. She was a schoolteacher. But there was never a question of her looking down on him. They had a very equal relationship – especially for those times.'

Aidan heard his own voice and was astonished at his lack of embarrassment, talking in these intimate terms about his family and his past. It had been a long time since there'd been anyone new to tell.

Sarah was still looking at him sympathetically. 'How many in your family?' she said.

'There are four of us. I have three sisters.'

'Really? You were blessed among women.'

'Maybe I was. I didn't always feel like that at the time.'

'How old were you when your father died?'

'Nineteen.'

'Were you . . . with him?'

'No. I was away at college at the time. Otherwise I might not be sitting here today. He was washed overboard by a freak wave. His name is on the monument at the end of the harbour beside the old boathouse.'

'I've seen it – what was his name?'

'Billy Ryan.'

'I must go look at it again tomorrow.'

Aidan nodded, remembering. He became tangled up in his own thoughts, until her voice brought him back.

'Did it ever put you off becoming a fisherman yourself?'

The question surprised him slightly. 'Not really, no. The opposite, I suppose. It barely occurred to me to go back to college after the funeral – studying philosophy seemed a bit of an indulgence after what had happened, and somebody had to take over the family business. We had the boat repaired and I took up where my father had left off. I guess it was in my blood.'

'In your blood?'

'My grandfather was a fisherman too. And his father before him.'

'Really? Here in Clare?'

'Right here in this very village.'

'How incredible to have such a sense of rootedness in one place.'

'We're not a very ambitious lot.'

She smiled. 'No, I think it must be lovely to feel that you really belong somewhere. We moved around a lot when I was a child and I didn't like it one bit. Although, with hindsight, it helped me.'

'How?'

'Well, having to reinvent myself in every new school I went to was good training for being an actress.' She grinned at him. 'You do know I'm an actress, don't you?'

'I just heard the other day – small-town gossip and all that. You can't keep much quiet around here.'

'No. I don't imagine you can. Just as well I'm not planning to get up to anything while I'm here.'

He looked away.

'So you didn't know anything about me when you brought me out before?'

'I didn't.'

'I hope you're not going to treat me any differently now that you do know.'

'Well, I'd been planning to throw you overboard but I'll probably give it a miss now. It'd only show up in the tabloids.'

She giggled, and he had a brief impression of how she must have been as a young girl. He could see her in Maia too, huddled in her customary position, rocking gently to the rhythm of the boat.

'Do you think she'll show today?'

'She's taking her time. Some days she's just not interested.'

'But you seemed so sure she'd come to us the last day.'

'Ah. That's what you have to say to the rich tourists. Keeps them sweet, you know.'

'Ah, well. I'll be disappointed if she doesn't make an appearance. I had such high hopes after last time, but there's always next week.'

'I'll take you out in the morning, if you like.'

'I couldn't ask you to do that.'

'You didn't ask. I offered.'

'That's really kind of you, Aidan. But are you sure?'

'I'm positive.'

'But you must have something better to do.'

Their eyes locked briefly. They looked away. The silence became oppressive. He was grateful to the wind when it picked up again and gave them something to focus on. Maia whimpered as the dinghy careened up and down. She was like a tiny china doll in her massive life-jacket.

'Hold on tight, ladies. We're heading for home.'

He glanced at Sarah. Oh, no. Should he tell her? He had to. He couldn't let her walk around the town like that. 'Sarah.'

'Yes.'

'You might want to do something with . . .' He tugged at his hair.

'What?' Her hands shot up to her wig, which was tilted at a decidedly odd angle.

'Oh, God.'

He averted his eyes as she adjusted it. No wonder her hair was always so perfect.

'I suppose you know about the cancer too.'

'I did hear something.'

'Of course you did. And if you didn't already know, that would have been a bit of a giveaway.'

They started to laugh, and her momentary irritation dissolved before his eyes.

'Are you better now?' he asked.

'Oh, yes. It's gone.'

'Congratulations.'

'Thanks. Only my hair doesn't know it yet. It's growing back curly.'

'I've heard that can happen.'

'It's very odd. I never had a curl in my life before now. That's if you don't count a couple of bad perms back in the eighties.'

'I remember those. My youngest sister came home one day looking like a poodle. We crucified her.'

They were back in the harbour now. Maia in her arms, Sarah stepped up onto the pier and looked down at him. 'Same time, same place tomorrow?'

'I'll be here.'

Chapter 6

Fiona had put on a suit that morning – a skirt and jacket. She wasn't sure why. Just that it was in her wardrobe waiting to be worn. She was regretting it now. She felt stupid and exposed, as she always did when she revealed her calves. They remained her most childish feature – spindly. When she walked, they didn't quite match in their movements. 'Bambi legs', an old boyfriend had called them. It maddened her that however confident and together she was from the knees up, her fragility was plain for all the world to see from the knees down.

'Who's next, Betty?' She held out her hand for the file.

Instead of passing it directly to her, Betty stood up behind her desk and whispered in her ear. 'It's her,' she hissed excitedly. 'The actress.'

'Oh.' Something to brighten up this dull afternoon of flu symptoms and lower back pain. She went out to the waiting room. 'Sarah Dillon,' she called.

As her next patient ushered a little blonde-haired girl to her, Fiona realized that she was wearing a wig. Nobody's hair could be that perfect. Not on a day like today, the sea breeze whipping up a frenzy. Fiona's own hair had always been a mad cap of wayward curls. Shiny and chestnut – enhanced, these days. She pushed them behind her ears as she sat at her desk. She crossed her traitorous legs and leaned forward, her elbows on the armrests of her chair as the other woman led the child into the room and settled opposite.

'What can I do for you?' The words she had uttered twenty times a day for the last twenty years.

'It's Maia. She hasn't been well. I think she might have this flu that's been going around.'

'Okay. Let's have a look at her.'

'Um, I'm afraid she doesn't really like being touched. She's autistic.'

'I see.' As she said it, it was immediately apparent to Fiona that there was something not quite right with the child. It was as if somebody had flicked on a switch. The agitation. The lack of eye contact. The way she was worrying a piece of string in her tiny fingers. 'Can you describe to me her symptoms, then?'

Fiona was half listening, half on autopilot. 'That sounds more like a cold. I really am going to have to look at her, though. Is there any way we can distract her?'

'Maybe try one of those little torch things you use for examining. That worked one time.'

It did today. When they were almost finished, Fiona said, 'I believe you've been seeing a lot of my husband.'

'I beg your pardon?'

'I'm Aidan's wife.'

'Oh, of course. He told me his wife was a doctor. I never made the connection. You're . . .'

'Fiona.'

'Fiona. That's right. Pleased to meet you.'

'Likewise. Can you get her to hold still there for one minute? Thanks. So how are you finding village life?'

'Oh, I love it. Could stay here for ever.'

'You're not, then?'

'Unfortunately, no. I'm due to start a new job in September. But to take this amount of time off – I've never done it before. It feels so strange. As an actor, you feel you have to say yes to every role that comes along in case it's your last. So that's what I've been doing for years now. Back-to-back jobs. Don't get me wrong, I love it, but you do need a bit of balance in your life. Well, I don't have to tell *you* that, you being a doctor.'

Fiona smiled in acknowledgement. Sarah Dillon was nice. Not the tiniest bit aloof. Unexpected.

'Life has taught me a lot of lessons lately. About slowing down. Taking better care of myself.' Sarah adopted a thoughtful expression. Fiona couldn't tell if she was looking into the past or the future.

'Would you like to come for dinner on Friday night?' The words tumbled out of Fiona in a spontaneous rush of warmth. She watched Sarah's face closely. The other woman's eyes widened in surprise. Had she overstepped the mark? 'I mean, only if you'd like to. We wouldn't want to intrude . . .'

'No, no. That would be lovely. You just caught me off guard. You don't expect to visit the doctor's and leave with a dinner invitation. Pills, perhaps.'

Fiona laughed. 'No, I suppose not. Look, if Friday doesn't suit you . . .'

'Of course it does. My social diary isn't exactly bulging. I'll have to bring Maia.'

'Of course. I meant the two of you.'

'Well, then, thank you very much, Fiona.'

Fiona smiled at Sarah, then to herself. Something told her she could be friends with this woman. And that wasn't a feeling she had every day.

'I'll need you home Friday night, Aidan.'

'Yeah?'

They were in their bedroom, getting ready for bed.

'I've invited Sarah Dillon for dinner.'

She was watching his back as she wriggled out of her skirt. It stiffened slightly and he hesitated for a few seconds before he pulled his top over his head.

'You met her, then?'

'She came to the surgery today.'

He half turned to her. 'Is she sick?'

'No, no. Her daughter has a cold, that's all. You never told me she had an autistic child.'

Aidan shrugged.

'That must be so hard. A single parent with an autistic child. And the cancer on top of all that. My God. You read about these people and imagine they lead such charmed lives but, Jesus, far from it. We're so lucky, aren't we, Aidan?'

'We are. Does she realize you know so much about her?'

'I don't know. Probably. I'd say she's used to it.'

'You're not going to ask her for her autograph, are you, on Friday night?'

Fiona giggled. 'Of course not.'

'Or sneak up behind her and take a photo of the two of you together? You with a silly grin on your face, she with a startled expression.'

She laughed some more.

He came around to her side of the bed and placed his hands on her shoulders. 'You're not going to start stalking her, are you?'

She tipped her face up to his and he smiled at her. 'You're an awful eejit sometimes – but a nice one,' he said, before he kissed her on the forehead and softly on the lips. Then on the neck.

Afterwards, Fiona lay contented but also puzzled. There was something going on with her husband that she couldn't put her finger on. The slagging before they'd come to bed: that was the old Aidan, but he hadn't teased her like that for ages. She missed it. The sex too – normally she could read when he was going to make a move but tonight it had come out of the blue. Yet he seemed – she struggled with the word that kept coming into her head. *Sad.* He seemed sad. He'd clung to her as if he was afraid to let her go. It just wasn't like him.

Her mind wandered back to their first meeting. Right from the start he'd been the most self-assured person she'd ever met. His confidence, unlike hers, was real. It was one of his most arresting and attractive qualities.

That night she'd been out with her classmates, celebrating their qualification as doctors. She had reached a point in the night where she didn't know any longer if she was happy or deflated. It was as if the elation had peaked and now had nowhere to go. It may have been the depressant qualities of the alcohol – her hangover starting already. She annoyed herself sometimes, she really did. Why couldn't she be just plain and simple happy, on tonight of all nights? She – Fiona McDaid – a doctor. Dr Fiona McDaid. She allowed herself a little smile. *Dr McDaid to A and E, please.* That was better. She had peered at herself one last time in the cloakroom mirror and tucked a stray curl behind her left ear.

Back out in the corridor, she had encountered a man puking his ring up. The direct result of a build-up of toxins in the liver, she thought merrily. She was feeling better already. She pushed through the door into the nightclub and was slammed by a wall of sound. Madonna. Feeling positively buoyant now, she began searching for her friends through the forest of variously jerking and swaying bodies. She liked it. The body heat, the sweet, damp smell of sweat, the closeness and intimacy of all those humans. The weird cosiness. A quality she often lacked in her personal relationships.

The men's heads turned to appraise her as she moved through the crush. Then, abruptly, the music changed. Oh, God: a slow set. Not the time for a lone female to be on the dance-floor. She quickened her pace, searching for an escape route, but bodies were blocking her. She thought she spied a gap and headed for it, but that was blocked again. By, of all things, a jumper. Or, more accurately, what her country granny would have called a gansey. It happened to encase a broad expanse of chest.

'Are you busy?'

She looked up into a pair of wild eyes. Blue, she thought, but she couldn't really tell in the dark. 'Busy?' she said, feeling slightly stupid.

'Do you have time for a dance?'

Fiona examined the extraordinary face that was gazing down at her. The impression she had was of a pair of intense shining eyes above high cheekbones, a crescent moon of glistening teeth, and luxuriant reddish-brown hair on his head and in his beard. She surprised herself by nodding. What the hell? It was the end of the night. It would pass the time until she could locate her friends.

The grin broadened and she found herself gathered into a kind of bear-hug. She draped one wrist delicately around his neck. The other hand she rested on his triceps. She closed her eyes briefly, feeling herself smaller than usual – feeling herself tiny. He didn't say anything, just continued to stare at her and grin. It was beginning to make her self-conscious. Should she kiss him to avoid the small-talk? She'd never kissed a man with a beard before. No, that was ridiculous.

'Aren't you hot?' she asked.

'Hot?'

'In that jumper.'

'I'm grand.'

A culchie. Small wonder. 'Where are you from?'

'County Clare.' He announced it proudly, as if he hailed from Buckingham Palace itself. 'You?'

'Stillorgan.'

'What's your name?'

'Fiona.'

'Fiona.' He repeated it, savouring each syllable, as if it pleased him enormously.

'And you?'

'Aidan.'

Not a terrible name – for a culchie.

'And what do you do, Aidan?'

She didn't care what he did. She was only asking him so she could tell him she was a doctor.

'I'm a fisherman.'

'A what?'

'A fisherman. You know. I catch fish.'

'You're kidding?'

'No. I have a boat and nets and everything.'

'Well, I didn't think you used your hands.'

He laughed gratifyingly at her lame little joke, and she felt something catch unexpectedly in her solar plexus. Over his shoulder she could see Cali and Ruth staring at her. She gave them a little smile and a wave and Cali did the same back. Ruth pointed at her watch and widened her eyes. Wondering, no doubt, what her friend was doing, moving in slow circles with this dancing bear of a man.

'Why the surprise?'

'At what?'

'That I'm a fisherman.'

She looked up at him again. The eyes were definitely blue. Maybe greeny-blue. Aquamarine, she decided. 'It's just the beard, the jumper. Everything. If someone was going to a fancy-dress party as a fisherman, they'd look like you.'

He threw back his head and roared with laughter. A great sound. She grinned back at him. She was funny. He made her feel funny. And safe, in a weird way. He made her feel herself, but a new self. She loved the way he wasn't insulted. She was so sensitive that the opposite in another person was appealing. She could enjoy this man, if only for a short while. He was so different from the men she knew. Especially David. Sweet, serious, earnest David, who was going to make such a great doctor. With his milky white skin. His lily white hands. His distinct lack of triceps.

'And what do you do, Fiona?' He swirled each syllable of her name around his tongue.

'I'm a doctor.' There it was. She looked at him archly, from underneath her lashes, to gauge his reaction.

'Get away out of that.' He was dismissive.

'I am.' She was indignant.

'But you're only a child.'

'I am not.'

'What are ye? Nineteen? Twenty?'

'Twenty-four.'

'Excuse me.'

'How old are you? Forty?'

He laughed again, as she'd hoped he would. 'Twenty-eight.'

'Well, you look twice that at least. You should shave off your beard.'

'I've thought about it, but don't you think it gives me a very manly, craggy look?' He rubbed his chin and winked at her.

She rolled her eyes and grinned at Cali and Ruth. They continued to stare. 'What were you doing asking me to dance if you thought I was only nineteen? Are you some sort of perv?'

'I liked the look of you.'

His frankness disarmed her and she lowered her lashes. His shoulder seemed welcoming and she was tempted to rest her head there. But – not a good idea. It was a bit worrying, though. How were her future patients meant to take her seriously, feel safe in her hands, if she looked like a child?

'Maybe you should grow a beard,' he was saying.

'What?'

'It'd make you look older.'

'Stop.'

He gave her waist a friendly squeeze. She found she didn't mind.

'Do you have a boyfriend, Dr Fiona?'

She amazed herself by being tempted to lie. 'I do, yes.'

'Pity. I'll have to use the sack, then.'

'The what?'

'The sack. First I put it over your head. Then I sling you over my shoulder, bundle you into the back of the van and drive like hell back to Clare.'

She giggled. It was sort of a compliment, she supposed.

'Oh, I'm not joking.'

Their faces were almost touching and he had stopped smiling. He was going to kiss her. And she – was she really? – was going to let him. Their lips connected. A warm fuzzy softness, with an undercurrent of something dark and exciting. Beneath her closed lids, Fiona could feel Cali's and Ruth's eyes expanding into saucers.

Chapter 7

Fiona had pulled out all the stops. The best china, the linen tablecloth. She'd even spent a fortune on fresh flowers, daffodils at first. Then, with last-minute horror, she remembered their association with cancer and swapped to tulips. What was she thinking? About the flowers and about everything? After the initial excitement had worn off – having a 'star' over for dinner – the panic had set in. It dawned on Fiona that Sarah must be accustomed to eating in the very best restaurants, and in the homes of other famous people who had housekeepers and chefs and the like. Fiona did have a cleaner, a silent, resentful local woman, but she'd always done her own cooking. Of course she had. And that was another thing. She hadn't asked Sarah if she had any dietary requirements. Not to mention the child. They could be vegetarian for all she knew. Although surely Sarah would have said. Sweet Jesus, Aidan was right. She was an eejit.

That afternoon she worked herself into a frenzy, yelling at Tommy when he tried to make a sandwich as she was preparing the veg. She spent almost as long deciding what to wear as she did what to cook. Monkfish, as it happened. And a simple shift dress. Blue. Her colour.

Aidan avoided her as much as possible, hating it when she was in this mood, eye-rolling the height of his communication. He turned up for dinner, just – five minutes before mother and child were due to arrive. 'You look nice.' He approached his wife with caution.

'Could you open that bottle of wine over there? Let it breathe for a while. They'll be here any time now.'

She scurried past him to the other side of the kitchen. He knew better than to offer to help with the food. Such approaches were invariably misconstrued and led to trouble.

She glanced at him. 'You look nice too. An actual shirt – we're honoured. It only took you four months to put it on.'

She'd bought it for him at Christmas in her annual attempt to smarten him up and, as she'd once put it after a few glasses of wine, 'showcase his fantastic physique'. He'd teased her about it mercilessly – he was just her bit of arm candy, he said – but he tried to make the effort when he knew it mattered to her. Tonight, however, he wasn't sure whom he was making the effort for.

He uncorked the bottle and strolled into the dining room. The table was spectacular – they could have entertained royalty. No wonder Fiona was so wound up.

'I could use some help in here.' Disembodied voice from the kitchen. Testy. He hastened back inside. 'What can I do?'

The doorbell rang.

'Oh, Jesus.' She ushered him out again. 'They're here.'

'That's what happens when you invite people over for dinner.'

'Oh, stop being such a smartarse and open the door. Why couldn't they be late?'

'It's ten past already.'

'Aidan!'

'I'm going, I'm going.'

Seeing Sarah standing in his doorway, smiling at him like that, completely threw Aidan.

'Are you going to let me in, then?'

'Sorry, yes.'

He opened the door fully and stepped aside. She walked into the hallway, Maia so close to her that she might have been surgically attached to her mother's leg. The little girl's eyes darted towards Aidan's, then away again, and he saw that he had been recognized.

'Can I take your coat?'

Sarah shook off a cape-like garment and handed it to him. Then she removed the anorak from her daughter's rigid form.

'Go on in.' He couldn't hang the coats up quickly enough.

'Oh, wow!'

He loved to witness people's reactions as they walked into the dining room for the first time. It was a glorified viewing point, glorying in its panoramic view of sea and sand.

'It's breathtaking,' she said. 'You're so lucky to live here. The sea literally *is* your back garden.' She turned to him and smiled. 'You have a dolphin in your back garden.' She scanned the walls and zoned in on a group of black-and-white photos.

'Did you take these?'

Aidan nodded.

She examined them in silence. 'They're stunning,' she said quietly.

He beamed. Felt himself ridiculous.

'He's sold a few, you know.' Fiona came in and the two women kissed on either cheek, like a couple of Dublin luvvies.

'Fiona, your home is beautiful.'

'Thank you. Aidan, will you pour Sarah a glass of wine? And what about Maia? Will she have some juice?'

'I have her drink with me, thanks. This table is magnificent! Where on earth did you get it?'

Aidan watched his wife glow as she absorbed Sarah's flow of compliments. Neither woman noticed when he left the room to get the wine.

Tommy was at the kitchen table, his arms crossed, a sullen expression on his face as he tilted his chair precariously on its two back legs. 'I'm supposed to be at Kevin's gig.'

'I know. You can go along afterwards. Just keep your mother sweet. It's easier in the long run.'

Tommy scowled, his whole body tense with impatience and frustration. Aidan could almost hear him thinking: Next year.

Fiona bustled back into the room, multitasking as she went. She righted Tommy's chair onto its four legs as she passed. 'Aidan, would you ever bring the woman in her wine? And entertain her for a few minutes. Dinner will be in five. You, too, Tom.'

They knew better than to argue. Much better just to get out of the way.

Aidan, bottle in hand, led the way into the dining room, Tommy trailing unenthusiastically in his wake. Sarah seemed tiny, seated at the top end of the massive oak table. She was hunched over, talking earnestly to Maia. She pulled herself upright as they came in.

'Sarah. This is my son, Tommy.'

Tommy stepped forward and Sarah held out her hand for him to shake, guessing correctly that he wasn't a kisser. Tommy wiped his hand self-consciously on the thigh of his jeans before placing it in hers. Then his demeanour changed. 'Hey, you're famous. You used to be Tabitha.'

Sarah's and Aidan's eyes met and they laughed. Aidan was relieved – Tommy's behaviour had been so unpredictable of late, vacillating wildly between adult maturity, adolescent obnoxiousness and childlike enthusiasm. The latter seemed to be at the fore right now – Tabitha was a character from his favourite children's programme – and that suited Aidan just fine. He watched them as Tommy chattered and Sarah listened graciously, her head inclined, a smile playing on her lips. She must get this all the time.

'And what about that eejit who played the dodgy wizard? Was he that bad in real life?'

'No, not at all. He was lovely. He *is* lovely. A really intelligent guy, in fact.'

Aidan stood beside her and poured a little wine into her glass. 'Would you like to try it, madam?'

Sarah giggled. 'I'm sure it's fine. You can pour away.'

Tommy continued to talk as if his father wasn't there.

Fiona entered, carrying Sarah's and Maia's plates. She laid Sarah's monkfish before her with reverence – whether for the food or the woman wasn't clear – but there was definitely a sense that they had an honoured guest in their midst. Then she put down Maia's tomato soup with toast soldiers. The little girl shifted backwards in her chair and shoved the bowl as far from her as it would go.

'Oh, God, I'm sorry.' Sarah was on her feet.

The Ryan family watched open-mouthed as Maia commenced blocking her ears and screaming.

'It's the soup,' said Sarah. 'She's afraid of anything bright red. Ridiculous, I know, but it's one of her things. I'm really sorry. I should have said.'

She handed Fiona the offending plate. Fiona carried it back into the kitchen. Aidan caught a pink spot on each of his wife's cheeks.

'It's all right. It's gone now. It's gone.' Sarah coaxed her daughter's hands back down. Then she sat heavily beside her and hid her eyes with a hand. 'Oh, Lord. Poor Fiona.'

'Don't worry about it. It's not important.'

'But her dinner party, all the trouble she's gone to. It was stupid not to tell her. I never thought.'

Fiona came back into the room, her smile strained. 'What would Maia like to eat?'

'Don't worry about it. I've got plenty of snacks with me. I've learned to come prepared.'

'I could make her a sandwich.'

'There's no need. She'll be grand.'

'Are you sure?'

'Quite sure.'

Fiona looked relieved. Panic over.

Once the dinner had begun, there was no danger of a lull in conversation. Tommy saw to that, particularly after the small glass of beer he was permitted, which seemed to travel directly to his vocal cords. Fiona deemed it necessary to cut in, when Sarah seemed about to be overwhelmed by his constant deluge.

'So, what brought you to our little one-horse town anyway, Sarah?'

'Oh – this is delicious, by the way. You're not doing your home town justice, Fiona. You possibly don't see it as I do because you've lived here for so long. But it's a stunning location. Do you hear me? Location. What a twat. You'd swear I was shooting a film here. Although why somebody hasn't done that already, I really don't know. But no. The real reason I came here was Star.'

Fiona's face remained blank. The only thing that sprang to her mind was the *Star* newspaper. Was Sarah being hounded by the tabloids?

'She means the dolphin, Mam,' said Tommy.

'Oh.' Fiona lowered her eyes and took a sip of her wine. 'You like animals, then.'

'Well, yes, I do. But that's not it. It's for Maia, really.'

'Maia's the animal lover?'

'No. Well, yes. It's – you're a doctor. Maybe you've heard of dolphin-assisted therapy?'

Aidan looked out of the window. The moon was rising. It was as if it was floating on the water. He didn't like the way this conversation was going. Sarah had told him this and it had sounded perfectly reasonable in the boat. But now, well, he already knew what Fiona would make of it and he felt embarrassed for their guest.

'I've heard of it, yes.'

'Do you know much about it?'

'Not really, no.'

'Well, it's quite a new thing. It's really only been practised in America so far.'

'America. I see.'

'They think that interaction between dolphins and children like Maia can really help the children. There've been cases of some kids speaking for the first time.'

The words came out in a rush and Aidan felt her awkwardness. He had personal experience of how even the greatest enthusiasm could flounder when it encountered the steel wall of his wife's scepticism. He examined Fiona closely as she played with the stem of her glass. He knew her casual demeanour was illusory. She suddenly looked up sharply, in the way she did when she was dealing with a patient. Enter Dr Fiona.

'Would you not be better off seeking professional help?'

'I've been seeking professional help ever since Maia was diagnosed, and she still can't talk.'

'All I'm saying is that there are plenty of charlatans out there, dying to exploit desperate people.'

Aidan cringed. He knew his wife's intentions were good, but she sounded so patronizing at times.

Sarah straightened her back, perhaps trying to recover her dignity. 'I can assure you that I'm not the slightest bit desperate, Fiona. On the contrary, I have a lot of hope. And so far Star hasn't charged us a single cent for her services.'

'Dessert,' said Aidan, his voice over-loud and abrupt. 'What's for dessert?'

'It's cheesecake,' said Fiona. 'I'll go and get it.'

'More wine, Sarah?'

'Please.'

'Can I have another beer, Dad?'

'No.'

'But you always let me have –'

'Not in front of your mother.'

'But –'

'No.'

The remainder of the evening passed without incident. Nobody brought up the dolphin again, and if Sarah had taken umbrage, she hid it well. The post-mortem took place later, in the bedroom. Fiona kicked off her high heels with obvious relief and lay on the bed, legs crossed at the ankles, hands clasped behind her head. She looked content. Satisfied. Smug, even. 'Well, I think that went really well, don't you?'

'I do.'

'She's an interesting woman, isn't she? A little airy-fairy, perhaps.'

Aidan could see where this was going and didn't like it. 'Hmm.'

'What do you think of her?'

'She's nice. Yeah. Seems like a nice woman.'

'*Nice.* Is that the best you can come up with?'

'Oh, for fuck's sake, Fiona. Would you ever give it a rest? You're so . . .' He trailed off, instantly regretting his outburst.

Fiona raised herself up on her elbows and glared at him. 'So what?'

'Nothing. Forget it.'

'No. I don't want to forget it. I'm so *what*, Aidan?'

'You're so – harsh sometimes. So exacting.'

'This is the way I've always been.'

'No, Fiona. You never used to be hard.'

'How can you say that to me? I spend all day every day helping people, only to come home and take care of my family.'

She spat out the final word as if it were a sick joke. He felt her weight rising off the bed and heard her unzipping herself out of her dress. All her movements were angry, loud and exaggerated. The pulling out of drawers, the slamming of wardrobe doors. He knew she wanted to punch him quite badly. He wished she would. He thought he would feel better if Fiona punched him.

'You can finish clearing up.' Her voice was muffled.

She was in bed already, a rigid lump under the covers, several curls sticking out ludicrously at the top of the duvet. She was a parody of their daughter in her younger days, taking to her bed in a strop.

It wasn't like Fiona to retire without removing every last trace of makeup and scrubbing and flossing her teeth. He'd go downstairs and give her the chance to do it without losing face. It would kill her to lie there with a face full of caked-on makeup and a sugary coating on her incisors.

He closed the bedroom door calmly behind him. He knew the very act would annoy her, that she would see it as him trying to assert his moral authority, but he told himself that wasn't why he was doing it. Downstairs, he stood at the door to the dining room and surveyed the scene of carnage. It was like the aftermath of a battle. Chairs pushed out at every angle, discarded napkins like so many bandages. Red wine spillages – drops of blood. He walked around slowly to the end of the table and sat in the place where Fiona always seated their guests. It had the best view of the ocean.

There was no need to turn on the light. One forgotten candle still flickered unevenly and the moon was now high in the sky. He'd missed its meteoric rise tonight but he was glad to see it now, hanging suspended from an invisible filament. He fancied he could see the Sea of Tranquillity and felt he wouldn't mind being there.

The clouds were moving swiftly, obscuring the moon's face at intervals and dulling the silver ripples on the water. Then they were gone and it was revealed again in all its startling luminosity.

Aidan poured some wine into the glass closest to him and brought it to his lips. The liquid was almost black in the darkness. He sipped it thoughtfully. But it wasn't his wife he was thinking about.

Fiona lay in bed, tears seeping out from the corners of her eyes, wondering how she had managed to get it so wrong. She had thought that things were starting to get back on an even keel with Aidan but now it was all ruined. Aidan could read her like a book and he'd known she wanted to let off steam about Sarah and the dolphin therapy. More to the point, he knew she wanted reassurance that what had happened over dinner would be okay, that she hadn't ruined everything with Sarah. Normally if something was bugging her, he was a willing audience. He seemed to enjoy her passion. Other times he challenged her assumptions and made her see things in a different light. But he was always on her side, and he helped her to figure out what to do on those occasions when she really had put her foot in it. This was the first time he had ever acted as if he despised her.

What was really tormenting her was the suspicion that she had brought it on herself. That Aidan was right and she was too harsh. Would she ever learn to shut up and let things go? She wanted to be friends with Sarah – she thought she was great: really warm and smart and, unexpected this, admirable – but when she'd heard her coming out with that mumbo-jumbo about dolphin therapy she'd felt she had to make the point that it was neither scientific nor monitored. Even when she was saying it, a part of her knew that she sounded like the stereotypical arrogant doctor. Did she honestly think she was going to change Sarah's mind? Wouldn't it make more sense to get to know her, then guide her to something more suitable for Maia?

Why, oh, why couldn't she play along as she did when she was out and about being Dr McDaid, a woman of standing in the community? She knew how to smile and nod and be pleasant to people who didn't matter to her that much: she saw it as an extension of her professional duties. But as soon as she wanted to bring people into her world, she seemed to lose her footing, particularly with women. She'd never quite understood her trouble with making female friends. Was it because she'd had only brothers – not enough practice with girls when she was growing up? Or was it because she was just like her father, well-meaning to a fault but her own worst enemy?

With a heavy heart she heaved herself out of the bed and went into the en suite. She took in her blotchy face, red eyes, hair like a stack of hay. She attacked her face with a cotton-wool ball soaked in cleanser as if she was angry with her very skin. She reached for her electric toothbrush. She'd figure out what to do in the morning.

Chapter 8

The boat was finally ready and Atlantic Dolphin Tours officially opened for business. They had a launch and everything – a bottle of fake champers smashed against the prow. Everybody came, even Sarah. People stared at her with unabashed curiosity, the women dissecting her outfit and the men, no doubt, imagining the body underneath. Did they, Aidan wondered, imagine her with only one breast?

The maiden voyage was free to all comers. The family were aboard – Alannah, her father's pet, was home for the weekend. He hugged her as if she was five. Aidan couldn't deny his nervousness, as he steered his vessel to the mouth of the harbour. Was it just a joy-ride he was giving these people? Doubt stabbed at him.

But how could he have doubted her? Star rose beautifully to the occasion by not only appearing but doing a series of jumps and leaps worthy of an Olympic champion.

'Look at her, Dad. She's showing off.' Tommy had come up behind him, his face open and boyish. 'She knows we're all watching her and she's showing off.'

Sarah agreed that it certainly seemed that Star liked an audience. And she should know.

Aidan was grateful for the distraction of all the outer activity because never before in his life had he experienced such inner turmoil. He had always been such a definite man, his moves positive and dynamic. True, he had lived his life slightly out of kilter with society but that was because he'd always been so sure of himself and what he wanted. And now, perhaps for the first time in his life, he found himself floundering. Was he having some kind of mid-life crisis?

He paced the beach that night, his feet bare, his trousers rolled, Rufus snuffling a few yards ahead. Where was the peace of mind this activity always engendered? Why did it constantly evade him?

He knew why. He could avoid it no longer. He sat down heavily on the shoreline and sighed.

It was Sarah.

Always Sarah.

Always in his head, wherever he went. He loved it and he hated it, loved her and hated her too. For doing this to him. Wrecking his head. Wrecking his marriage. Except he was doing that all by himself, with his ridiculous schoolboy crush. Constantly comparing his wife with Sarah. Being angry with her because she wasn't Sarah. How could she be? It was so unfair. And stupid. So fucking stupid. To think that she – a famous actress, such a beautiful woman – would be interested in the likes of him. He was no fool – not most of the time anyway. He had mirrors. And he'd never even finished his degree. She had been to RADA, for pity's sake. He needed his head seeing to.

Although, thank God, nobody could see inside to the thoughts within. What a shock they'd get. The images alternately rose-tinted and pornographic.

'Sarah.' He said her name out loud. It felt delicious on his tongue.

'Sarah.' He said it again, louder this time. Tasting it. Feeling he could possess part of her at least. There was no one to hear, only Rufus. The dog stopped and stared at him for a few seconds, before resuming his panting.

Aidan looked out to sea. He'd be taking her out in the morning. The thought thrilled him. He could pretend to himself that they had a date. These weekly voyages were all he thought about. He was only truly present when he was with Sarah. The rest of the time he was elsewhere. Absent from his wife and from his life. Each seven days felt like seven years. He was addicted and he knew it. He didn't have a clue what he'd do when she went back to Dublin.

Chapter 9

The first time Sarah had seen the bay she was convinced she'd come to the right place. As her car rounded the bend, the sun had come out and illuminated everything, and she had felt somewhere deep in her soul that, even if the dolphin proved a phantom, she had found a fitting home for herself and her daughter. She had come to believe that even if you were in a place for just a short while, it could still be your home if you wanted it to.

The lack of associations was a blessed relief. There was nothing to remind her of her old life. Except, of course, the mirror. So she avoided it. She also avoided all forms of media. She didn't want to hear the news or read the theatre reviews or find out who was shagging whom. Or, worst of all, find out what they were saying about her. It was somehow imperative that she should cut herself off from as much of the noise and the mayhem and the chaos of everyday life as was humanly possible. It seemed to be the only way she could find out what was real and true to her. And her illness had taught her that this was something she really needed to know. And right here, at the very edge of the Atlantic – the edge of the world, it felt like – this seemed the very place to discover it.

She would stand at the edge of a cliff and gaze out at the ocean. It was all she could see. It was so soothing to watch the waves and nothing else – nothing made by human hand. She fantasized that she was the last woman on the planet. And she felt her infinitesimal smallness, which didn't faze her because the cancer had already shown her how tiny she was. How little she mattered to God.

Then she would feel Maia's hand in hers and it would pull her back into the present. Into her life. Where she had to stay. Where she wasn't alone. Where she wasn't insignificant to the wholly enigmatic creature who relied on her so completely.

Sarah had never planned to be a mother. Indeed, when she'd met Maia's father, Mitch, she'd never thought she would be, and although that made her sad, it didn't disturb her unduly. She had plenty of happy thoughts with which to replace it: her career was going well and there was talk of a run in New York for the play she was in. She had met Mitch in the same way that she had met all the significant men in her life – through work. None of those significant men had been father material – but he was the least likely candidate of all. No wonder they had made a singular child.

Mitch had spent most of the run of the play angling for a date. One evening after the show there had been a knock on her dressing-room door. As usual.

'Come in.'

Of course it was him. Sir Twitch-a-lot. She suppressed a smile. 'Hello, Mitch.'

'Sarah.' He parked himself on her dressing-table, touching her chair with his tightly wound legs. Everything about Mitch was tightly wound. He was a mass of nervous energy, fuelled mainly by nicotine. He dragged deeply now on his ever-present cigarette.

'Great performance tonight,' he said.

'And you.'

'No, I really mean it.'

'So do I.'

He allowed a cautious smile, attractive lines appearing at the side of his mouth.

Robert Mitchell was one of the new, up-and-coming actors. He hadn't quite reached leading-man status but he was well on his way. Sarah thought him very talented. And he was bound to develop a strong female following. His write-ups tended to describe him as 'brooding' and 'intense'. Something to do with that floppy black hair. And those eyes – great eyes. Greeny-hazel with extra-dark lashes. He'd be well cast as a vampire.

Sarah was pleased she couldn't take him seriously. She seemed immune to his charms, which was probably why she interested him so much.

'Are you hungry?' he asked.

'I could eat.'

'Want to get something together?'

'Why not?'

Why not indeed? Although she doubted he'd be able to sit still for the duration of an entire meal. He was like a toddler with ADHD. Maybe he'd manage a main course. He chose somewhere simple and local. Good. She'd be home at a decent hour, she thought, as the waiter seated them. And it meant he wasn't trying too hard to impress her. Although possibly he couldn't afford to impress her. She knew what that was like and felt sympathetic towards him.

'So, Mitch.'

'Want one?'

'Why not?'

She took a cigarette and he made a show of lighting it for her with his fancy Zippo. Then he flipped it closed and put it back in the pocket of his leather jacket.

She laughed. 'You've done that before.'

'Might have.' He was examining her closely. She didn't care. 'You don't take me seriously at all, do you?'

'Do I need to?'

'It would be nice if you did.'

'Why is my opinion so important to you?'

'Because I like you, Sarah.'

She was taken aback by his intensity. And now it was her turn to examine him. *Did* he like her? Really? Rather than viewing her as just another conquest? She sighed. 'I like you too, Mitch. You seem like a really nice guy. And you're a fine actor.'

'Don't patronize me.'

She'd angered him. He flicked the ash from his cigarette and began tapping his foot and looking about him.

'I'm sorry. It's just, well, you're very young.'

'I'm twenty-eight.' He was indignant.

'And I'm thirty-two.'

'So?'

'Well . . .'

'You always go out with older men.'

'Well – yes, I do. I don't seem to be attracted to men my own age. I think it's got something to do with losing my father so young.'

'Bullshit.'

'Excuse me?'

'You just need to give us younger guys a chance.' He leaned in closer to her, giving her the full force of those paranormal eyes. 'Isn't it time you swapped those saggy, wrinkly arses for one like mine?' He winked at her. 'Did you see the review it got in the *Independent* last Saturday?'

A few seconds passed – then Sarah exploded into laughter. Mitch sat back in his chair, evidently pleased with himself. She felt herself flush and brought her hands to her cheeks. The nerve of him. He was funny, she'd give him that. The waiter brought the garlic bread and she crunched into a slice to buy herself a little time. But Mitch wasn't giving her any.

'Well?' He leaned forward again.

'And I had you down as shy.'

'How wrong can you be?'

'Very, it seems.'

'So?'

'You want me to decide right now?'

'No time like the present.'

'Well, Mitch,' she wiped her fingers on her napkin, 'I guess I'd be willing to give your arse a try.'

'Tonight?'

'Don't push your luck, Sunshine.'

Their romance followed a classic storyline. She allowed herself to be wooed like an old-fashioned heroine. He bought her flowers and dinner, whenever his finances could stretch that far. She listened as he expressed his feelings; she was gracious, he was ardent. It was as if they were playing a time-honoured courting game. He even kissed her hand on occasion – but slyly, sensuously. Not like a true gentleman. She finally succumbed and tried out his arse. She found it worth the wait and the publicity it had garnered. And he didn't withdraw once the prize was in his grasp, as she had half feared he would. He seemed genuinely smitten and, she had to admit, she was too. The more secure he felt with her, the more he relaxed. She understood now that he had come across like a hyper-active kid because he'd been so nervous around her. Starstruck as well as lovestruck. He was still just a little bit twitchy but she learned to like that about him. To find it endearing.

They went to all the parties together, were regularly featured on the society pages. It did neither career any harm, and Sarah wondered why she had resisted as long as she had. Still, that had been part of the fun.

Were all young men so passionate? So intense? So urgent

in everything they did? She had to admit that it was very flattering and a soothing balm to her fragile, actor's ego.

Shortly after starting her relationship with Mitch, she'd bumped into Peter, a former boyfriend, who had directed her first two plays. And how old, how grey, how drab he seemed to her now. How lacking in vitality beside her current lover. She loved the way Mitch could flip her over in the bed into any position he desired. Peter would have done his back in if he'd tried. It seemed kind of sick to her now, made her uneasy just to think about it. Had she been using him as a surrogate father figure? Had she been his trophy girlfriend? Was that all they had been? Mitch was certainly at pains to convince her of it.

And she was so willing to love him, so in love with love, that she overlooked any fleeting moments of immaturity. They paled into insignificance beside the passion. And, in those early days, she had to admit to being a little less than mature herself. You could even say they gloried in their shared immaturity. Their lives consisted of work, pub, friends, restaurants and parties. And that was it. That was enough. Sarah was having such a good time, in fact, that she barely noticed she had skipped a period.

When it dawned on her that she might be pregnant and should buy a test, she did so with a reasonably light heart. It wasn't the first time she'd taken one and because they'd always been negative before she somehow convinced herself that this one would be too. It was the immaturity again. When it was positive she took another in case the first was faulty. But there was no change. And suddenly all the weird symptoms she'd been having made sense to her. They weren't the result of too much partying after all.

She couldn't look after a baby. She was only thirty-two. She heard an odd whirring sensation in her ears – which might have been the sound of her world crashing down around her.

She couldn't work out when it had happened. It might have been after any number of boozy nights out. She was on the pill but sometimes forgot to take it. The guilt pressed down on her. All that drink. Those fags. What a start in life. The baby was probably irreparably damaged. Still, she had to tell Mitch.

The big reveal happened on the way out one night when she was looking her best, if a little pale. She had to do it. He'd want to know why she wasn't drinking: a course of antibiotics only lasts so long.

'Sit down a minute. I have something to tell you.'

'The others will be waiting.'

'Never mind the others. This is important. Come on.' She patted the seat beside her. 'It'll only take a minute.'

He sat down impatiently.

She took an enormous breath and the words rushed out on the exhalation. 'I'm having a baby.'

'You're what?'

She took this to be a rhetorical question, and instead tried to decipher the emotions fighting for precedence on his face. Shock. Fear. Good stuff too?

'Bloody hell.' He sank back in the chair, as if in need of the extra support.

Sarah, unable to control her agitation, got up and walked to the kitchen, pretending she needed a glass of water. She stood with her back to the door, resting heavily against the sink. He came up behind her and turned her around to face him. He was smiling. Thank God.

'It's great news.' He cradled her face and kissed her lightly on the nose. Then he knelt on the kitchen floor, put his arms around her waist and kissed the fabric covering her taut belly. They both laughed and Sarah felt a lightness she hadn't experienced in days. She thought she might cry with the relief.

Mitch was back on his feet and holding both of her hands in his own. 'Now let's go to the pub,' he said.

After that she stopped going. The smoky air nauseated her. Merely opening the door to their local made her feel sick. So Mitch went alone. It didn't make sense for both of them to miss out on the fun. 'Pity you can't come,' he'd say to her, on his way out of the door.

Pity you can't stay, she thought, on her way to the remote control.

But the thought never seemed to occur to him.

Then he'd come home, long after she'd gone to bed, stinking far worse than the pub. On those nights, her boyfriend's very breath made her want to heave.

Neither of them spoke about marriage. They were both too Bohemian for that kind of malarkey.

Then, all of a sudden, she didn't mind Mitch going out: on one of those nights, alone on the couch, she felt a faint ripple inside her belly. She was no longer alone, and Mitch's antics ceased to matter. She had this secret life inside her and her worries became nothing but a background hum: her figure, her weight, how she was going to continue to work and yet care for the baby. She'd already had to turn down two parts. She amazed herself by not caring. She was far too involved with her own divine collaboration.

Maia came into the world screeching, all six pounds of her. A tiny wisp of a girl. China doll perfect. Eyes massive. Toes and fingers tiny. Mitch was there for the birth. He remained at the top end – they'd agreed: the other end was far too real. He arrived back the next day, festooned with flowers and pink balloons. They cuddled the baby and each other and everything was great.

Three days later Sarah and Maia were let back home. Mitch brought Sarah breakfast in bed. Then he went out to rehearsals. She didn't hear him come in, but she knew that he had because when she fed Maia at two in the morning he was sleeping beside her, on top of the covers, oblivious to the baby's cries. It won't always be like this, he promised, when confronted by her tearful remonstrations. Once this play was over . . .

But Robert Mitchell's star was on the rise and play followed play followed play. And each rehearsal, each performance, was followed by drink. It wasn't obligatory, but to Mitch it might as well have been. Sarah confronted him many times, but her protests fell on deaf ears. He accused her of being jealous and, of course, he was right. She admitted it freely, to herself and him. How could she not be? Stuck at home with no one to talk to, no one to appreciate her. Sarah Dillon, the actor, a figment of her past. Her star had tumbled from the sky more rapidly than she had ever imagined possible. On a really bad day, she would leaf through old press cuttings to remind herself of who she truly was. But it was as if it had happened to another person. The glowing girl smiling back at her bore no relation to the drudge she had become. She knew logically that she was suffering from a chronic lack of sleep and that it couldn't last for ever. But she couldn't feel that. And she knew she'd never be the same again.

It wasn't all bad. On the occasions when Maia settled Sarah would spin them into the silk cocoon of her love. But Maia rarely settled. She seemed to object so strongly to everything – her nappy being changed, her hair being washed. She cried constantly, and often nothing soothed her. And the more Maia cried and the more Sarah needed help, the more Mitch felt the need to escape and the more Sarah felt like a single parent. Both of them were hanging on by their fingernails – to sanity and each other.

One evening, when Maia was almost eighteen months old, Mitch brought a group of friends home. Sarah had been complaining – as usual, he said – that he was always out at parties so he had brought the party home to her. At first she was pleased by this welcome distraction. But soon it became clear that most of them were off their faces, Mitch included. He dragged his daughter out of her cot and brought her into the sitting room to show her off. Because, difficult though she was, Maia was undeniably beautiful. Then someone turned the stereo up full blast.

'The baby!' Sarah's scream was buried under sound.

But then she fell silent.

Because Maia hadn't flinched.

The tests began. Was Maia deaf? No, that wasn't it. What was it, then? Mitch was dragged along for the diagnosis, reluctant and shifty-looking, hung-over.

'I'm afraid your daughter is autistic.'

The words hung in the air. Sarah was overtaken by an overwhelming urge to grab Maia and run full tilt out of the hospital. She looked at Mitch. For guidance? For reassurance? For what? He was dumbstruck. They held hands loosely.

'There must be some mistake,' said the father of her child.

But Sarah knew there was no mistake. It all made a perfect, horrible sense.

They drove home in silence, Mitch behind the wheel and a wall of his own troubled thoughts. Sarah's own thoughts were garbled. Some made her cry while others, bizarrely, gave her hope: she was thinking of facing the future with Mitch now that they had this diagnosis, something concrete to build on. It might change their relationship for the better.

The silence continued when they got home. Mitch sat on the couch, his head lowered. Sarah knelt down beside him and gently but firmly took his hands in her own. 'It's going to be okay. We'll get through this.' She attempted a watery smile.

Mitch stared back at her, his expression bleak. She didn't like what she saw. She liked even less what she heard.

'I've been offered a pilot in the States.'

Sarah withdrew her hands and sat back on her heels.

'I'll be flying to LA next week.'

She continued to stare at him.

'I was waiting for a good time to tell you.'

'And you think this is it?'

He got up and stood a few feet away from her. 'You know how long I've been waiting for an opportunity like this. If it comes off it could be huge.'

'How long will you be gone?'

'A few months.'

Sarah got up and went over to the couch where Maia was sleeping. She looked down at her daughter's angelic, oblivious face. Then she gathered her up and walked towards the stairs. When she was halfway up, she called to Mitch over her shoulder, 'Don't bother coming back.'

He didn't.

Chapter 10

Fiona had noticed that Aidan's absence had become total. He was still in their bed, beside her at night, but his thoughts were elsewhere. He would lie on his back, hands clasped behind his head and stare into the blackness. She could tell by his breath that he wasn't asleep, and he must have known that she wasn't either. But they didn't speak.

One night she had snuggled up to his rigid form. 'What is it, Aidan? What's wrong?'

He hesitated for a few seconds. 'Nothing. Go to sleep.'

Then he turned his back and she fell away from him. Who needed words when you had body language like that – speaking volumes that you didn't want to hear? She marvelled at how alone you could feel sharing a bed with another person, a person you thought you knew inside and out. But the Aidan of late had impenetrable depths that she hadn't even known existed. It occurred to her that thinking you knew another person was nothing but an illusion.

Fiona lay motionless on her side of the bed. It felt lonely and desolate. And this was so unlike Aidan, her tactile, affectionate husband. She was the one who was meant to be cold, the dodger of embraces, sexual or otherwise. And yet here she was, rebuffed. Now she knew how he must have felt. She vowed she would never do it to him again.

The first time Fiona slept with Aidan, she felt as if he'd brought the sea – the whole outdoors – into the bed with them. She imagined she could taste the saltiness on his skin.

His body was well muscled and taut, roughly a third bigger than her own. A thing of wonder. He inhabited it completely, probably because he worked with it. David had only ever inhabited his mind.

She felt small and pale and feminine the first time she woke up in bed with him. She found him watching her with an expression of unaccustomed seriousness.

'What's wrong? Did I snore?'

He shook his head. 'Breakfast?'

'I'll get it.'

'Let me. You stay right there. And, whatever you do, don't get dressed.'

He sprang out of bed, his casual nakedness mildly shocking. He cast his eyes about the place and grabbed her pink towelling robe from the back of the door. She suppressed the urge to laugh as he secured it around his waist. 'You don't know where anything is,' she said. They were in her flat.

'I'm sure even I can figure out tea and toast.'

He closed the door behind him, leaving her to regard the bedroom ceiling. She found she didn't want to be on her own in the bed. She craved his warm presence beside her. Yes, that was the word: *craved.*

He had astonished her with his gentleness. His reverence, even. She wanted more. Maybe a little less gentle this time. She stretched out sensuously, her toes and fingertips reaching out to their utmost limits. Then withdrew them abruptly. What if he didn't want more? He seemed very quiet this morning. Not his usual friendly self. Maybe he was preparing to dump her. Oh, God, she knew she shouldn't have ended it with David. What had she been thinking? But then again, he was making her breakfast, wasn't he? But maybe he was just being a gentleman and trying to lessen the blow. At least she was in her flat. She wouldn't have to slink off home in last night's smoky apparel with a bad case of panda eyes, bed head and a massive dose of rejection. If he did discard her, she could curl up on her couch, wrapped up in her own duvet, eating chocolate biscuits and slowly dying inside.

He came back in, a plate and a cup in either hand. She was yet to own such a thing as a tray. He placed them on her bedside table and sat on the edge of the bed.

'I can't take you seriously in that robe.' She tried jokey.

He smiled, a little wanly. 'Not my colour?'

'Not your size either.'

He fell silent again, watching her intently as she sipped her tea self-consciously. He had given her the mug she used for storing thumb tacks and paperclips and the like. She decided not to mention it. Irrelevant, as he was about to dump her anyway. She began inventing reasons to hate him. A fucking fisherman. What did she think she was doing? And she a doctor. A muck savage, for God's sake. How dare he pursue her and woo her just to dispose of her like so much fish gut once he'd got what he wanted? Then there was the beard. She'd never liked men with beards.

'You really should shave off that beard.' She could feel the spite building within her, as she searched for a really biting insult.

'I will if you marry me.'

A pause.

'What did you say?'

'I said, if you marry me, I'll shave off my beard.'

'You're not serious.'

'I'm deadly serious. Look at my face.'

His face was indeed deadly serious.

'But we barely know one another.'

'You can't tell me you don't feel it too, Fiona. I know you do.'

Yes, she did feel something. But what exactly? Lust?

Infatuation? Yes and yes. But was there anything of substance underneath all of that? Fiona might have been young, but she wasn't stupid.

'My feelings for you are . . . very strong, Aidan. But I need more time.'

'How much time? Another week?'

'No . . .'

'Two weeks?'

He was smiling at her now. She smiled back in relief, the tension broken.

'I don't care how long it takes, Fi. I've got the rest of my life and I'm not going anywhere. I'll do anything it takes to show you my feelings are real.'

'You can start right now.' She sat up in bed, exposing her breasts. His face darkened as he took off her robe. This time he was less gentle.

Her parents were horrified. Their darling girl with this uncouth creature. Her mother might have found him charming in other circumstances, but not in these. Not when he was engaged to her daughter.

Bitter words were exchanged between Fiona and her father.

'I didn't spend all that money on your education for you to run off with some – buffoon.'

'Aidan is no buffoon. He's the most intelligent man I've ever met. He went to university, you know.'

'What did he study?'

'Philosophy.'

'So he has a degree, then.'

'Well . . . no . . .'

'You mean he's a drop-out. He couldn't even finish a bull-shit degree like philosophy. What does he do? Quote Plato to the fish?'

Fiona felt a surge of righteous indignation. 'He had to leave college when his father died.'

Her father looked fleetingly ashamed.

Fiona continued to fume. 'Look,' she said. 'Aidan is the man for me and I'm going to marry him.'

'Jesus Christ. What about your career?'

'I can still have a career. I'm going to set up a practice in Clare.'

'A GP. But you always wanted to be a surgeon.'

'No, Daddy. You always wanted me to be a surgeon, so you could boast to your friends in the golf club.'

'I didn't raise my daughter to speak to me like that.'

'No. You raised me to have a mind of my own, and now that I have one, you don't want me to use it.'

'You manage to twist everything, don't you? You should have been a lawyer, not a doctor.'

But he'd stopped shouting at her. And she knew he loved her too much to deny her anything. Furthermore, Fiona's father believed that if he withdrew his resistance his daughter would tire of her rebellion. That did not happen. As a consequence, both parents attended the wedding and the reception afterwards in the Shelbourne. It was a high point in the Dublin social calendar, her parents pushing the boat out, trying to ignore the suspicion that they were the laughing stock of their friends.

Aidan was all set to honour his promise – shave off his beard for his wedding day. But Fiona stopped him. 'I don't want you to,' she said.

'But I thought . . .'

'I want to be able to recognize you when I walk down the aisle.'

'I'll be the one in the monkey suit.'

'All the men will be wearing monkey suits. I don't want to marry the wrong one by mistake.'

He gathered her up to him and held her close. 'I wouldn't let that happen, Fiona McDaid. You were carved out for me and me alone.'

And that had been nineteen years ago. And now she was forty-three. And none of her patients worried that she was too young any more. God be with the days.

The children had come along immediately, much to her parents' initial horror, then delight. Alannah was a honeymoon baby and Tommy arrived less than two years later. She had the perfect set, girl and boy, salt and pepper. It had been their intention to have children young – to be young themselves when their children were reared. To have a wealth of life left to them, to enjoy each other exclusively again.

She had loved every second of motherhood, throwing all her youthful energy and enthusiasm into it. None of her contemporaries had given birth so young. She sensed they pitied her, considered her early fecundity somehow working class, befitting a woman who had chosen to marry beneath her. Without exception, they had married professionals – doctors mainly, with the odd barrister or bank manager thrown into the mix. David had married a pharmacist – a mousy girl – and they lived in Blackrock, where he was a consultant in the clinic.

If Fiona had ever felt the odd pang, she had refused to entertain it. She presumed everybody felt this pull in life – the tension between reality and what might have been. But for her the road less travelled had not been a particularly bumpy one. And so what if many of her doctor friends had more money than her? How many of them woke in the morning to the roar of the Atlantic, to see the sun rise like molten gold over the eastern horizon? How many could step barefoot out of their front doors and be on a beach in a matter of seconds, walking a demented black Labrador along the line where the foaming sea met the sand? When she had moments of doubt, she comforted herself with these thoughts.

It was seven or eight years – in some cases more than a decade – after she'd had Alannah and Tommy, before her friends from medical school began to reproduce. It had been a solitary time as a young mother. She had tried to make connections with the women of the village, on those rare occasions when she made it to the school gates, but her attempts were unconvincing, to either side. She couldn't delude herself that she had much in common with most of those women and they, in turn, clearly saw her as an authority figure: the local GP, someone with whom they were obliged to discuss embarrassing physical ailments, not a person with whom they could share coffee and laugh freely. She was the snooty one from Dublin – would always be the snooty one from Dublin. She'd been assigned this label before she'd even arrived. She also had the suspicion that the local women didn't understand how a man as charming as Aidan could have fallen for as cool a customer as her. Perhaps a few had even set their caps at him before she'd come on the scene. *Damn Dublin girls coming to our town and stealing our men.* For whatever reason, the women had subtly closed ranks. And she had closed her heart to them, pretending it didn't matter.

Fiona had never been introspective and through all the years of her marriage, until recently, she had been too busy to spend time brooding about her lack of close friends. She had taken the view that not having an aptitude for friendship was just one of those things, like not being musical or good at languages – it would have been a nice attribute but it was no big deal. She valued quality over quantity and she had one fantastic friend, Yvonne, the pharmacist in the next town. And, of course, Aidan, her best friend. But in the last year Yvonne had married and moved to Dublin. And now, it seemed, Aidan had left her in all but body. She didn't know where to turn.

Chapter 11

Aidan knew he was being unfair to his wife. The guilt crushed him. The thought of hurting this diminutive woman, who had always stood by him – because, harsh though she could be, Fiona was as staunch as they made them. She didn't deserve what he was contemplating. But then again, he considered, as his thoughts did another flip-flop, he was only contemplating. He hadn't so much as touched the woman and he hadn't confessed his thoughts. She knew, though. He knew she knew. How could she not? She must think him ridiculous, mooning around after her, staring at her as if he was transfixed. To imagine he was in with a chance. He shook his head, as if to jolt out his thoughts. He visualized them pouring out of his ears, his mouth, his nostrils, leaving his mind clear at last. Free of the obsessive notions he'd been torturing himself with.

Fiona had nothing to worry about. Sarah would laugh in his face when he told her. Because he'd made up his mind that he had to tell her. Tomorrow morning. It was the only way.

He waited at the boat for a full forty-five minutes. That was how long it took him to realize that not seeing her wasn't an option. He had his camera with him, ostensibly to photograph the dolphin but secretly to impress Sarah.

He went to her house. She was renting one of the old fishermen's cottages on the quayside. She hadn't told him this; Fiona had mentioned it in passing. He pep-talked himself along the way. A part of him was genuinely concerned that she had failed to show up for their usual outing, but most of him knew that wasn't it at all.

A developer from Ennis had bought the row of cottages several years back and done them up. Not bad, although a bit quaint for Aidan's tastes. He had to knock twice before he got an answer. She looked different. She was still in her dressing-gown and it was as if the wig had just that second been plonked on her head – it was slightly off centre. Mostly she just looked distraught. 'Oh.' She put her hand to her mouth. 'I'm sorry. We weren't able to make it.'

'Is something wrong?'

A loud, shattering sound came from the sitting room, as if something quite large was being smashed.

'Oh, God.' Sarah turned and disappeared. After a moment's hesitation, Aidan followed.

The room was in bits. He was about to ask Sarah if she'd been burgled when the architect of the destruction became apparent. Maia was in the furthest corner, flinging herself repeatedly against the wall. Aidan watched, appalled, as Sarah rushed over and grabbed her from behind, pinning her arms to her sides. Maia kicked and flailed and began to scream – an unbearable, high-pitched sound. Then she attempted to bite chunks out of her mother. Sarah shifted her position continually, deftly avoiding her daughter's tiny white teeth, and it was clear to Aidan that she'd done this a thousand times before.

He stood awkwardly, a large part of him wishing he hadn't come. 'Can I do anything?'

Sarah shook her head without looking at him.

Maia began to scream again and Aidan turned away. Not only did he feel he was intruding, it was also hard to watch. It was like driving onto the scene of a serious car accident. Shocking and unexpected. The sympathy he felt for Sarah was like a pain in his chest. He wandered into the kitchen, trying to act casual, and stared unseeingly out of the window. Not knowing what else to do, he filled the kettle and switched it on. Then he sat at the table and focused on the flowers: a jam-jar was half filled with water and crammed with bluebells and stitchwort. Little blue bells and tiny white stars. After a time, the screaming subsided. He could hear Sarah murmuring to her daughter. He stood in the doorway, looking back into the sitting room.

Sarah was laying Maia on the couch and covering her with a crocheted blanket. The little girl, her head resting on a cushion, closed her eyes and appeared to find sleep instantly. Sarah got up immediately and, without making eye contact, brushed past Aidan into the kitchen. She sat down heavily at the table, looking for all the world like a woman defeated. Aidan felt at a loss. Small-talk was of little use in a situation such as this. So he made them tea.

'Get that down you,' he said, sitting beside her.

'Thanks.' But she didn't touch it. She was hunched over her mug, her forehead resting in her hands.

'Is she like that a lot?'

'Not often. It's my fault for bringing her here. I've unsettled her. Maybe I should go back.'

'No.'

The vehemence of his reply shocked them both. There was no doubting what it meant. They looked at one another long and hard. Sarah spoke first. 'You can't possibly be interested, Aidan. Not after that.'

'But I am. I'm not sure why but I am.'

'In a one-breasted woman with no hair and a demented child?'

'When you put it like that . . .'

They smiled at each other. Her smile was tired. His was cautious.

With the heavy sigh that Aidan had grown to associate with her, Sarah slid her wig off her head. It lay on the table between them like a dead animal. Aidan picked it up and hung it over his left hand. It was still warm from her body heat and the moment was oddly intimate.

'Haven't you got enough hair of your own?' she said.

'I wasn't planning on wearing it.' He spun it around on his fist. 'It's very realistic.'

'No, Aidan. It's a lie. This is what's real.' She pointed to her head, her expression mutinous, willing him to look at her.

He did. The crown was covered with little wisps of soft, white-gold hair, so thin that you could see the shell-pink scalp shining through in places. He felt as if he was seeing her naked. 'You're beautiful,' he said.

She gave a half-laugh and looked at him incredulously.

It was true. Without the hair, her eyes seemed huge. Luminous. And her bone structure was revealed in all its fragility.

'Here. I'll prove it to you. May I?'

He gestured to the camera around his neck. She shrugged her shoulders slightly. He directed the lens at her.

'I feel an overwhelming urge to put on my wig.'

'Don't. It's much better like this.'

He took several shots as she stared candidly at him.

'Done. I'll print them out for you so you can see for yourself.' He knew that, even though she didn't believe it to be true, she believed him. That he was telling his truth. And that was enough for now.

'Thank you,' she said quietly.

'You're welcome.'

'Will we leave it for today, then?'

'We will.'

Chapter 12

Sarah had tried to ignore it for so long: big, sexy, lovely – married – Aidan drawing her in. Just like he had drawn in the shoals of silvery fish with his nets. She had felt herself getting caught up, like a mermaid. Or maybe it was she drawing him in, like a siren, to where he and his boat and his marriage and his life would get smashed on the rocks of lust and betrayal and heartbreaking hurt. She had decided she couldn't do it to him. Or to Fiona. Or to his family. She'd stay well away. She would go about her business as quietly as possible. She would leave when the summer or her lease ran out, whichever happened sooner.

But that other day in her house, his total acceptance of her, his wanting of her in spite of everything . . . She'd never thought she'd experience that again – had never even bothered seeking it. Yet here it was. Here *he* was. Offering himself on a platter. All she had to do was reach out . . .

After Mitch had left, Sarah had hit an all-time low. She stopped going out, stopped getting dressed, stopped getting washed. Except when Maia had a medical appointment. On those occasions, she would drag herself along and do her best to appear normal. God knew how long she would have languished in such a state, had she not had an unexpected visitor one afternoon.

She toyed with the idea of not answering the door. She often didn't and most people went away eventually. But this caller was persistent. She eased the door open a crack and peered through the gap with narrowed eyes.

'Oh, it's you.'

She immediately relaxed and extended the gap to person width.

Peter Berkeley walked into her apartment. Her director friend, who'd once been a lot more than a friend. Who, throughout the ups and downs of their relationship, had remained a friend.

'I came to see how you were.'

'I'm fine.'

'You don't look fine.'

The honesty of his response shocked her into silence. He clearly wasn't here to exchange pleasantries. Oh, God. She hoped she wouldn't start crying.

'I heard that Mitch had buggered off to the States.'

'Well. That's what buggers do, I suppose.' She tried to keep her tone light, but it came out bittersweet at best. 'Coffee?'

'No, thanks.'

'Tea?'

'Look, Sarah, I didn't come here for a hot beverage, I came to help.'

'That's really kind of you, Peter, but I'm fine. Really I am.' A tremor was creeping into her voice but she fought to keep it out. Damn Peter anyway. He was weakening her with his kindness.

'Sarah, my darling, you look far from fine. Have you seen yourself in the mirror lately?'

'I've been avoiding mirrors.'

'I'm not surprised. I've never seen you so wretched. You actually look sick. You're not sick, are you?'

She shook her head miserably and stared at the carpet. Don't cry.

'And you've lost a ton of weight.'

She laughed humourlessly. 'The up-side of depression.'

Since she would no longer meet his eye, Peter vacated his armchair and sat beside her on the couch. He pulled her into him. This finished her off and a big fat tear rolled down the cheek closest to him. He gave her arm a squeeze, and it was as if he was squeezing all the other tears out of her.

He let her cry until they were used up, which took a while. Then, after copious nose blowing, she began to speak. About what had happened with Mitch but mostly about Maia. It was the first time she'd told anyone except family. And although Peter was silent throughout, she knew he was sympathetic. Knew he didn't blame her as she blamed herself for driving away her man, for making her daughter sick. Even though she'd been told repeatedly that she was not responsible for Maia's condition, the guilt still seeped through the gaps, mostly at four in the morning, alone and in bed, her thoughts compulsive and corrosive, with no one there to talk her out of them and make her see sense.

Peter listened to it all. Patient and egoless. He didn't try to speak until she'd run out of words.

'First of all,' he said, 'I'm very sorry that this has happened to you.' He gave her another little squeeze, which nearly set her off again.

'Second, Robert Mitchell is a piece of shit who doesn't deserve having two such special women in his life.'

'That's Maia's father you're talking about.'

'He doesn't deserve the title, Sarah. Real fathers don't walk out on their families.'

'He's not a bad person, Peter. Just weak.'

'Why are you defending him?'

'I don't know. Maybe I'm trying to convince myself that I didn't make such a stupid choice in the first place.'

'Anyway, bad or weak, it doesn't make much of a difference. It's just not bloody good enough.'

Sarah was silent, absorbing his anger. Peter was right. Mitch's actions had been reprehensible. *His* actions, not hers. She was feeling a little better.

'And third,' said Peter, 'about Maia.' His tone softened. 'How on earth can you think you're responsible for a medical condition she was born with?'

She knew it sounded mad but there was still a niggle. She decided to confess the root cause of her guilt. 'I didn't realize I was expecting for a long while and I just kept living normally, which involved, well, quite a lot of alcohol.'

'And you think you gave her autism.'

'It can't have helped.'

'Sarah. That's the most ridiculous thing I ever heard in my whole life. What does your doctor say?'

'That it had nothing to do with it.'

'There you are, then.'

'But how does he know? They don't really understand what causes autism.'

'The way I see it is this. You can waste all your time and energy beating yourself up over something that's not your fault and that you can do nothing about, or you can take all that time and energy and put it into Maia. You're not going to be able to do both effectively. And your daughter needs you, Sarah. You're all she's got in this world. You can't let her down.'

Of course, that set her off again. But his words had got through.

'How did you get to be so wise?'

'Ah, you know, us old guys.'

'I should have stuck with you old guys. I would have been a lot better off.'

'You can't beat us baldies.'

He'd made her smile, which was his intention.

'Don't torture yourself about the alcohol, Sarah. My first wife, Penny, was a complete dipso. She had at least one glass of wine a day every day she was carrying Mark, and sometimes a hell of a lot more, and he turned out okay, didn't he? Apart from a complete lack of direction in life and terrible taste in women. But you can't really blame that on the booze.'

'Mark will find his way.'

'Oh, I know he will. Anyway, I didn't come here to talk about my son. I want to help you.'

'Peter, just seeing you has been a tonic. Thanks for the pep-talk. It's really helped. I promise I'll get my arse off this couch and start moving again.' She wiped the last of her tears away.

'I'm delighted to hear you say that, because I have a proposition for you.'

'You don't want *another* wife?'

'Oh, no, thank you, dear. I've had quite enough of them.'

'What is it, then?'

'I'm directing a new play.'

'Oh?'

'And there's a part with your name written all over it.'

She examined him closely for several seconds. 'This wouldn't be your version of a charitable donation, would it?'

He affected an expression of indignation. 'Have you ever known me to cast anyone who was anything less than perfect for a role?'

'Well, no, I suppose not.'

'So?' He was leaning back in the couch now, legs crossed, posture relaxed, as if he had all the time in the world to wait for her response.

'Would I have to sleep with the director?'

'Absolutely not. Unless, of course, you were overtaken by an irresistible urge and couldn't stop yourself.'

They smiled at each other like old, old friends between whom sexual tension was a thing of the past.

'In that case, thank you. I'd love to take a look at the script.'

'I'll make the necessary arrangements.'

'Only . . .'

'What?'

'Maia.'

'You'll need childcare, of course. Let me sort it out.'

'What?'

'You heard me.'

'I couldn't possibly let you do that, Peter. That really is going above and beyond.'

'Nonsense. We both know I'm loaded. And if it's the only way I can have my favourite actress in my play, then I'm happy to do it for as long as it takes you to get back on your feet.'

Sarah snuggled into him and hugged the arm closest to her. She felt as if she was cuddling her dad.

Sarah's life improved instantly and dramatically. A nanny, no less, trained to care for children with special needs, had been appointed: she would accompany Sarah to rehearsals so she could be with Maia on breaks. But the best thing was being back at work.

It was as if her blood, hitherto sluggish and stagnant, had begun to flow through her veins again, pumped by pure joy. She had the sensation that things she hadn't even known she was missing were being returned to her – her love of life for a start. The quality that gave her that elusive sparkle. And the biggest surprise, in some ways the best, was that she didn't miss Mitch at all. Not one iota. She realized what a burden their relationship had become – the constant insane drama coupled with the ever-present disappointment that he wasn't pulling his weight, that he wouldn't – couldn't – be the man she needed him to be. She felt angry on Maia's behalf. That he had rejected her as soon as she was proven to be less than perfect. And she despised his weakness. But mostly she didn't think about him at all. Felt glad to be shot of him.

He sent them money from time to time, which suited her. But he never called. That suited her too.

The reviews were gratifying. The play's success led to further work and she was a player again. Except everything was different this time around. She had Maia now. And her child consumed her as her acting once had. Did every parent feel such passion? Would she feel such passion if Maia was 'normal'? She had nothing with which to compare the feeling. Nor did she want for anything. She had no desire for another child, nor did she ever think she would have one. Maia was everything to her. She took up the whole of Sarah's heart. She would stroke her daughter's exquisite cheek while she slept.

'We were meant for each other, you and I,' she would whisper.

But Maia never whispered back. Even when she got older and went to a special-needs pre-school. Then a special-needs school. The words just never came. And Sarah was left to fathom the mystery behind the eyes that would barely meet her own.

So consumed was she with her daughter that she almost forgot herself. Her life was work and Maia, Maia and work, and nothing in between. She avoided relationships like the plague she believed them to be. And she maintained her physical appearance for professional reasons and for the modicum of pride she retained.

Then one day she was in the shower. She lifted her arm to wash beneath it and felt something that hadn't been there before. That was when her life changed all over again.

Chapter 13

It was later in the day in Sarah's house and all was calm, on the outer level at least. She had given Maia her tea and Maia had responded normally. Sarah felt weak with relief that this particular cycle of tantrums had ended. Maia sat quietly in the doorway out to the hall, moving the door slowly back and forth, gazing in fascination at the mechanics of the hinges. The phone rang. Sarah put down the pot she'd been washing and dried her fingers on the tea-towel. It was probably her sister. She usually rang on Sunday evening.

'Hello.'

'Hi, Sarah. Fiona McDaid here.'

There was a deadening sensation inside Sarah. As if a lift in her belly was rapidly descending to basement level. 'Oh. Hi, Fiona.'

'I hope I haven't got you at a bad time.'

'No. Not at all.'

'That's good. Listen, the reason I'm ringing is that there's an art exhibition on tomorrow night in the village hall and I thought you might like to come with me.'

'Um . . .'

'It's by a local artist. She's terribly good. There'll be wine, canapés, that sort of thing. I thought it would be a good opportunity for you to get to know people.'

'It sounds lovely. But Maia . . .'

'You don't have to worry about Maia. Aidan can babysit.'

The conversation was feeling more and more surreal. Sarah had difficulty getting the words out past her heart, which was resting now in her throat. 'And he's agreed to that?'

'I haven't asked him yet. But he won't be doing anything on a Monday night. And it's perfect because Maia knows him from your little boating trips. Either he can go to you or you can bring Maia to our house. Whichever suits you best.'

'Well, here would be better.'

'Your place it is, then. We'll call for you at eight.'

'Okay.'

''Bye.'

Fiona put down the phone. Sarah slowly lowered hers to the counter. What had just happened? Had she actually agreed to that? Had she had a choice? Fiona was truly a force of nature when she set out to do something. A pocket rocket ready for blast-off. Sarah had believed herself to have become better at saying no, especially since the cancer. But it seemed as if she was still as pathetic as before when taken off guard. And the circumstances *were* exceptional. An unexpected invitation from the wife of her potential lover. Except today it had gone beyond mere potential.

A horrible thought struck her, making her feel slightly ill. What if Fiona knew and was luring her into a trap? A twisted honey-trap. It seemed unlikely but she'd be on her guard, just in case.

'You're not doing anything tomorrow night, are you, Aidan?'

'What's tomorrow? Monday. No. Why?'

'I told Sarah Dillon you'd babysit.'

'You did what?' Aidan was unable to keep the annoyance out of his voice. He turned to his wife. She was sitting at her dressing-table, rubbing cream into her face, in rapid concentric circles.

'I didn't think you'd mind. It's only for a couple of hours.

It's for Noreen Dwyer's exhibition. I've asked her to come with me.'

'And she's agreed?'

'Of course.'

'I mean to me minding Maia.'

'Why wouldn't she?'

'You know why, Fiona. Maia's not exactly your average child.'

'But she knows you better than anyone else in the town, apart from her mother. And you wouldn't deny Sarah the chance of a rare night out, would you? She's barely been out since she got here.'

'She didn't come to socialize.'

'I know she didn't. But everyone needs a bit of fun once in a while.'

Fiona's tone was wheedling now, which was even more irritating to Aidan than her former strident one. To avoid blowing his top, he had to remind himself that he was in the wrong, not his wife.

'I'm just surprised she's agreed to it, that's all.'

'Well, she did,' said Fiona, not a little defensively, making Aidan suspect that she had railroaded the other woman into it. The other woman.

'So you'll do it, then?'

'I'll do it.'

'Excellent.'

It meant he'd get to see her again.

Now that the truth was out, there was no taking it back. A blessed peace descended on Aidan and he felt sure he'd done the right thing. The sea seemed to confirm this to him, echoing his inner calm. He'd gone out by himself that morning, right after he'd left Sarah. He killed the engine as soon as he could and lay down flat in the boat. He stared up into the blue stillness and absorbed the sensation of floating weightlessness. No sound. Peace, inner and outer, at last.

Why should this be so when he'd gone one more step towards complete unfaithfulness to his wife? Surely he should be suffused with panic. But the opposite seemed to be the case. He thought he knew why. If it was just sex he wanted from her, it would have felt sordid. *He* would have felt sordid. But there was more to it than that. Although, God knew, he longed to taste her.

The connection he felt to Sarah was like nothing he'd ever experienced. Or if he had felt it before, he certainly couldn't remember it. Yet he knew that in their early years he and Fiona couldn't get enough of each other. He had to be honest with himself about that. Yet he couldn't remember it being as strong as this. Which left him free to delude himself, perhaps. But Aidan didn't care if this was a delusion. He was sure he'd never felt so alive in all his life.

Sarah headed them off at the front door before they had a chance to ring the doorbell. 'I've just got her off to sleep,' she whispered, by way of explanation.

Fiona nodded and entered the house, her movements typically quickfire. Aidan strolled in casually behind her. He nodded at Sarah too, before switching his eyes to his wife. He watched the back of her head as it moved swiftly from side to side, absorbing every detail of Sarah's home. He hadn't told her he'd been here before.

'What a lovely place,' she was saying, from a few feet ahead of him.

Aidan followed them into the sitting room, where Sarah was already putting on her coat. She turned to Aidan, her expression anxious, which might have been for any number of reasons. 'She shouldn't wake,' she said, 'but if she does, call me straight away.' She handed him a piece of paper with a number written on it. He took it from her, careful not to let their fingers touch.

'We won't be long anyhow . . .' Her voice trailed away and, to Aidan, she looked thoroughly miserable.

'No, not at all,' agreed Fiona. 'Two hours tops.' She was smiling broadly and seemed, thank goodness, completely oblivious to the strained atmosphere.

'Help yourself to anything you like. A snack. Cup of tea . . .' Sarah's voice trailed away again. Doubtless she was remembering that he already knew where the kettle was.

'Let's go,' said the innocent railroader.

With one last look at Aidan, Sarah pulled the door closed gently behind her.

He watched their forms morph through the mottled glass, heard their voices fade, leaving him in a silence that seemed immeasurable.

He began to move slowly through the rooms, not to nose but to familiarize himself with Sarah's space. This was where she sat to sip her morning brew. This was the window she looked out of. Every mundane thing seemed sacred, infused as it was with her presence. Aidan sat on the couch she curled up in at night. He sighed as he let himself sink into it as deeply as he could and ran his hands over the material.

All of a sudden, he no longer felt alone. Not knowing why, he turned and looked behind him. Standing at the top of the stairs that opened out into the sitting room was Maia.

Sarah doubted she'd ever felt more like a turd in her entire life, even at the height – or depth – of chemotherapy, her body annihilated by nausea. At least she hadn't made herself feel sick. But to sit in a car beside this pleasant, well-meaning woman who wanted nothing more than to be friends with her was pure torture. And she deserved to feel tortured, to have Fiona unknowingly rub her nose in her own guilt, every time she mentioned her husband's name. Even though she and Aidan hadn't done anything, they might as well have. Their intentions were bad and that was what mattered.

Sarah had never had an affair in all her romantic life. There had been directors and leading men. There had been those who had accused her of sleeping her way to the top, mainly less successful actors who were jealous of her. But it had never been the case. And neither, to her knowledge, had any of her men been involved with other women. She was just drawn to men who shared her passion at any given time. And she had been fickle. She could admit to that.

They were at the place now. She felt like fleeing. Someone offered to take her coat and she handed it to them. She looked down at herself, at the red top she was wearing. She'd had to wait for Maia to fall asleep before she could put it on. Scarlet. How fitting. Someone handed her a glass of wine. That was red too.

Shit. What if she freaked out on him? Aidan continued to stare at Maia, as she continued to stare into the middle distance. She started to descend, one step at a time. Bump. Bump. She looked for all the world like a little ghost in her long white nightdress, her eyes vacant and saucer-like. Aidan felt afraid of this little scrap of humanity who barely came up to his thigh. How ridiculous. She was tiptoeing over to him now, in that peculiar way she had. The first time he'd seen it, he'd thought it was charming. As if she was practising to be a ballerina. But now he knew it to be a feature of her autism and it merely added to her strangeness. The eeriness. If only she would speak, like a normal child.

She was beside him now, continuing not to look at him. She held out her hand. Her fist was closed and Aidan could tell that there was something in it. He held out his own. She dropped something into it, then tiptoed away again. Aidan looked down. Nestling in his palm was a tiny blue ceramic dolphin.

The women were voracious in their desire to get a piece of her. That was how it felt to Sarah anyhow, but she might have been more sensitive than usual. Fiona introduced her all around, charming and gracious, making sure that she was never alone. Ironically, all Sarah wanted was to be alone. But she didn't want to insult these people and their genuine interest in her, so she chattered aimlessly and answered their questions. She didn't want to insult Fiona either – she seemed so pleased and proud to be the one introducing her. And Sarah owed her. You should be flattered, she told herself. Flattered and grateful.

They were all expecting her to buy a painting – she had known they would before she arrived. Because she was on the telly, people expected her to be rich. It was funny, really: she, a single parent who hadn't worked in a year due to her illness; she, who was financially crippled, paying for Maia's therapies and her own medical bills, and had to depend on hand-outs from her errant ex. He was the only reason she could afford the rent on the cottage. She was afraid she was going to have to disappoint them. She looked down at her phone for the thousandth time, keeping it as she was in her hand. No messages. Thank goodness for small mercies. Maia must still be asleep.

Aidan watched the child, fascinated. She was sitting in the corner now, surrounded by spinning tops. She had five on the go. Whenever one slowed, she would start it up again, her whole world a continuous spin. She was mesmerized and so was Aidan. By the tops and by her. What secrets were locked inside that little brain? Then, abruptly, she stopped. As if the tops no longer existed for her. She got up and headed towards Aidan again. He felt his body stiffen, forced himself to relax. He remained motionless, in the position he'd been in while he was watching her: sitting forward on the couch, his elbows resting on his knees. She was beside him now, looking up. Not into his eyes but into his face. He froze as her tiny white fingers touched his beard. She was stroking it now, feeling it. But she wasn't feeling him. It was as if he wasn't there. She was interested in his beard, not him. This went on for several minutes, then stopped as abruptly as it had begun. Maia tiptoed away from him, across the room, up the stairs and out of sight. Aidan stayed sitting for five minutes or so, then followed her up, trying, but failing, to minimize the creaks.

Upstairs was even pokier than it was down. Aidan felt huge and ungainly. There were three doors ahead of him, all ajar. He tried the first. A bathroom. Small and blue and white and functional. He closed the door silently. The next, straight ahead of him, he pushed open. There she was, tucked up in her bed, her back towards him. Now it was his turn to tiptoe until he was standing over her, looking down. She was asleep all right, her eyes tightly shut, her breathing deep and regular. As if the last half-hour had never happened. Aidan backed out of the room and closed the door, feeling as if he'd succeeded in his babysitting duties, even if that success had been down to chance.

There was one more door. He couldn't resist. He pushed it open. Sarah's room was dominated by a small double bed, covered with a pretty bedspread. Everything in the room was pretty. Feminine. There was no room in here for a man. Aidan sat on the edge of the bed and looked around him. It felt forbidden. He felt himself to be an intruder. Although something inside told him Sarah wouldn't mind. His eyes rested on a chest of drawers. He was ashamed of the impulse to open it. How crass that would be, to rummage around in her underwear. His eyes travelled around the rest of the room and landed on a chair. Several of Sarah's garments were draped across the back of it. He got up and picked up the item on top. He recognized it as the blouse she'd been wearing yesterday. He pressed it into his chest, then buried his nose in the folds of fabric. He inhaled her and a slight moan escaped his lips. Oh, God, he was in serious trouble.

They were back home now. Sarah couldn't get the front door open quickly enough. She all but ran into the sitting room, half expecting carnage. But everything was calm. Nothing but big, comfortable Aidan sitting on her couch, as if he'd always been there, waiting for her.

'How was she?'

'She was fine.'

'She didn't wake, then?'

'She did.'

The two women listened as Aidan recounted the events of the evening, Fiona, calm and detached, perched on the arm of the chair, Sarah, coiled and tense, sitting unconsciously close to Aidan, caring only about what he had to say of Maia. She shook her head in wonderment. 'I can't believe it,' she said. 'She's been so difficult lately. I thought she'd have a fit if she woke up to find me gone.' Her body relaxed a little. 'Maybe I'm not as essential as I like to think I am.' She smiled tightly and got up. 'Coffee, anyone?'

'No, thanks.'

'Yes, please.'

Aidan and Fiona spoke at the same time.

Coffee it was. Sarah went out to the kitchen.

'How was it?' Aidan addressed his wife.

'Great.' She was glowing, clearly delighted with how the outing had gone.

Aidan just wanted to get out of there. Or, rather, he corrected himself, he wanted Fiona to get out of there so he could be alone with Sarah. He chastised himself for the thought and spent the rest of the time avoiding looking at her. He barely trusted himself to speak to her. Luckily Fiona talked enough for the three of them combined. The other two heard barely a word she said.

Chapter 14

Star was spreading her wings. Or, at least, extending her flippers to the cove where people swam and it was calm, right up to the shallows where the children played. Where Maia could go.

It was a bright morning in early June when Aidan broke the news. He thought Sarah ridiculously excited but said nothing. He loved seeing her like that. He loved seeing her any way. Their sojourns in the dinghy had proved fruitless. Star showed up all right. She would swim alongside the boat and execute her little dolphin flips and turns, but Maia would seldom engage. She was aware of the dolphin, that was clear, but after that all was blank.

He provided wetsuits for mother and child – an old one that had belonged to the kids – and they embarked on the next stage of their animal odyssey. Maia entered the water cautiously. Some other children were in there already. A little girl ran splashingly over to her. 'Are you here to see the dolphin?'

Maia stared straight ahead and swirled the water with her hands.

'She was here earlier on.'

The little girl spent a few seconds peering curiously into Maia's face, before splashing off again whence she'd come, back to her friends. Aidan glanced across at Sarah. He could have sworn he'd just heard her heart break.

'Come on,' he said. 'Let's get in and see what happens.' He fought the urge to take her hand as they waded, side by side, into the water.

The cove was small and sheltered, surrounded on either side by an intimidating wall of sheer black rock. Maia walked a few steps ahead. She seemed fascinated by the texture of the water. Aidan was continually amazed at how the littlest thing could frighten her at times while other scenarios didn't bother her at all. Such as this. She was reaching her arms now, high above her head, and gazing up into the perfect blueness, as if drawing it down on top of her.

The relative quiet was invaded by the squeals of the assembled children.

'She's here!'

Star came slicing through the water in her seemingly neverending quest for human company. Aidan had never seen her interact so closely with children before. The water bubbled with their mutual delight, Star swooping and swerving, the children splashing and screaming. She seemed undeterred by their high-pitched noise and undisturbed by their quick movements. More than once, a child lunged at her, attempting to hug her. She'd slide from an embrace like quicksilver, yet still go back for more.

Maia was in her mother's arms, having taken fright at the dolphin's sudden appearance. Sarah stood up to her hips in the sea, Maia's legs wrapped tightly around her waist, the child's eyes fixed on Star's undulating form. It was impossible not to smile at the dolphin's meanderings, the children's joy. Impossible for everyone, it seemed, except Maia. Star was coming closer to them now, customary as it was for her to investigate all who shared the water with her. Maia's gaze became more intense, the closer the dolphin got. She was circling them now, looking up at them, recognizing them.

'Oh, my God,' Aidan heard Sarah say. He looked at her and grinned, knowing his expression was childlike and uncontained. It was impossible to be any other way in the presence of this creature. He also knew what a very different experience it was to be in the water with her instead of being in a boat. They were more vulnerable, and it was scarier.

She was inches away now and swimming right in front of them. Without warning Sarah swooped Maia down, right above the surface, and the little girl held out her hand and ran it along the dolphin's back. Aidan and Sarah laughed and cheered. Maia looked as if she'd just woken from a deep sleep and didn't know where she was. Star swam away then, to play with the other children.

'I think I'll take her out,' said Sarah. 'I don't want her getting cold.'

'Okay.'

They set off to wade back to the shore, Maia still in her mother's arms. She began to struggle and look behind her.

'What is it, Maia?'

The child wriggled around, clearly agitated, then pointed out to sea. 'In.'

Sarah peered into her daughter's face. 'What did you say?'

'In. In. In.'

The word and the intention were unmistakable. The laughter bubbled out of Sarah as she spun Maia around in her arms. Then she squeezed her child until she squealed. Maia wriggled out of her mother's embrace into the water and the mêlée of children, dolphin and surf. The water was alive with flailing limbs, bubbles and fins. And Maia was in the centre. Not on the edge. Sarah stood close by and watched, alternately crying and laughing. Aidan waded over to her.

'She's in there,' she said, not bothering to wipe away her tears. 'I always knew she was in there somewhere, my little girl.'

Aidan hugged her to him, not caring if anyone saw them. Enough people did.

* * *

That night Aidan told Fiona about Maia and the dolphin. At last he had an explanation for his elation. Fiona listened intently, perched on the edge of her seat, head inclined, as was her habit, looking vaguely birdlike. He came to the end of his story and waited for her reaction. 'Isn't that incredible?' he said, peeling off his jumper.

'It is, I suppose.'

'You suppose?'

'Well, obviously I'm delighted Maia spoke and that she seems to be making such good progress.'

'But?'

'But there's absolutely no proof that it had anything to do with the dolphin. Maia's been getting speech therapy for years, hasn't she?'

'Yes, but it's never worked.'

'These things can take a long time. It could be that something's just clicked into place for her.'

'So you think it was just a coincidence that Star happened to be there when she said her first word?'

'Absolutely. It was coincidental.'

'Right.' Aidan's tone was resigned as he sat on the bed to pull off his trousers.

'Oh, come on, Aidan. She's an animal, not a therapist.'

He couldn't be bothered trying to convince her. Didn't want another fight. And if he was completely honest with himself, he was glad she was taking her usual sceptical approach. It strengthened the argument in his head that he was with the wrong woman, that it was Sarah he belonged to.

'Anyway, forget the dolphin.' Fiona was beside him now. It had been weeks since she'd watched her husband undress. His tendency of late had been to slip into bed hours after her. She didn't know what he was up to. Probably pacing the beach like a madman.

'I haven't seen these thighs in a long time.' She laid her hand on the one closest to her, her fingers reaching down to the inner curve. Aidan froze for a second, then resumed folding his T-shirt. Undeterred, Fiona kissed the ear-lobe closest to her and nuzzled his neck. Aidan shot to his feet, spilling his clothes on the floor.

'What's wrong?'

'Nothing's wrong.'

'But you've been acting so strangely.'

'I'm sorry, Fiona. I don't mean to.'

'Don't apologize. Look, I think I know what's been bothering you.'

'What?' He turned to her.

'Come and sit down.' She patted the bed beside her.

Aidan looked uncertain. Wary.

'Oh, for God's sake, I'm not going to try and jump you.'

He sat down.

'That's better. Now. It's very common for men of your age to go through this sort of thing.'

'What sort of thing?'

Aidan dropped his forehead into his hand and rubbed it harshly. He looked to Fiona as if he'd rather be anywhere than with her at that moment. She persevered: 'Aidan. There's nothing shameful about erectile dysfunction.'

'Fi . . .'

'Many men your age have difficulty getting an erection. It's incredibly common. Nothing to be embarrassed about.'

'Fiona . . .'

'We see it all the time at the surgery. You should come in and get a few tests. It's important because it could be a sign of blocked arteries. You don't have to see me if you don't want to. Pop in to Chris. He'll sort you out. You can mention my name if you like. He might do you a good deal.' She threw in this little joke at the end, nudging her husband and grinning at him.

Aidan was silent. He had seen a way out, a temporary reprieve.

'That's it, isn't it? I'm right, aren't I?' She peered into his face.

He hesitated a few seconds before he nodded.

Fiona smiled and exhaled. 'So you'll go and see him, then?'

'Okay. Well, I might go to the doctor in Lahinch instead.'

'Whatever. As long as you get it seen to.' She kissed him once on the cheek and patted him twice on the thigh. This time her touch was companionable rather than seductive. She was up now and halfway to the door. 'I fancy a cocoa. You want one?'

'No, thanks.'

'All right so.'

He watched her bounce out of the room, delighted and confident that she'd got to the root of his problem and weeded it out.

If only it were that simple.

He needed a pint. He put his clothes back on and headed downstairs. 'I'm going to McSwigans.'

'At this time of night?'

'I should make last orders.'

'I thought you were going to bed.'

'Change of plan.'

'See you later so.'

He'd known she wouldn't mind: she'd be in such a good mood following her successful diagnosis she'd be agreeable to anything.

It felt good to be out of the house. He found it nigh on impossible to breathe the same air as Fiona, these days, her very existence a constant reminder of his own deceit.

Noel Higgins was in the pub, holed up in their habitual snug.

'How are you going?' Aidan placed a fresh pint of stout in front of the other man and brought his own to his lips. He took a long draught, then wiped the foam off his moustache with his bottom lip before setting the glass on the table. He sighed. 'That's better.'

'Always is.'

He'd known Noel Higgins since school. They'd suffered under the tyranny of the same Christian Brothers. 'Were you out this week?'

'I was.'

'Good catch?'

'Good enough, thank God.'

Aidan nodded, and the two men lapsed into silence.

'Look, Aidan, we go back a long way.'

'We do, Noel.'

'And you know me. And you know I'm not one to be listening to idle gossip.'

'I do.' Aidan took another gulp of his pint.

'Well, I've heard something and I think you should know about it.'

'Go on.'

'That actress one you've been taking out in the boat.' Noel looked across at Aidan, who was staring at his pint. 'Well, there's been talk.'

'What kind of talk?'

'Ah, you know what kind of talk. You don't need me spelling it out for you. That you've been carrying on together.'

Aidan cupped his chin in his hand and pulled at his beard. 'What are they saying exactly?'

'They say you were seen cosying up to her this very morning down at the cove.'

'Oh, that.' Aidan almost laughed with relief. 'I just gave the woman a hug. Her daughter had spoken for the first time and she was a bit emotional.'

'Is that the feeble-minded young one?'

'She's autistic.' Aidan felt an irrational surge of anger towards the man he'd known almost his whole life, towards his ignorance, as if he'd been insulted personally.

'Autistic. That's it.'

'Do you really think that if I was carrying on with the woman I'd be canoodling with her in broad daylight in front of a bunch of kids and their parents?'

'Aidan, I don't think anything at all, but you know how people talk around here.'

'I do. They've little else to be doing in this godforsaken shit-hole.' Aidan drained his pint in one angry gulp – as if he'd been wrongly accused. They'd leave this place, the three of them, start a new life in Dublin. Or somewhere else entirely different, away from prying eyes. His own kids didn't need him any more. They were grown-up now anyway. He looked at Noel. His friend was regarding him strangely. Curiously. With a monumental effort, Aidan composed himself. He put down his glass, sat back in his seat and folded his arms. 'Thanks for telling me, Noel.'

'Not a bother. I was afraid you might shoot the messenger.'

'Not at all. Why should I? Sure, you're only looking out for me.'

'That's right. Giving you a chance to nip it in the bud. The rumour, I mean.'

'Exactly. It's fucking ridiculous.'

'That's what I said. Sure, what would a looker like that be doing with a big yoke like you?'

'You said it, Noel.'

'The likes of her could have her pick of the crop. Still . . .' He took a thoughtful sip.

'What?'

'You should probably steer clear for a while.'

'You think?'

'Ah, yes. Give the rumours a chance to simmer down. The last thing you want is Fiona getting wind of them.'

'You're right.' He had no intention of steering clear. He couldn't have done, even if he'd wanted to.

Chapter 15

They were out picking bluebells, Sarah and Maia, the last of the season. In fact, this little enclave had no real business being there this time of the year. Many were shrivelled now, shrunken and indigo. Sarah had to climb ever higher into the hedges to find the choice ones – the plump, the luscious, the life-filled ones. Their little blue heads, the way they nestled into the palms of her hands, bowing low, as if expressing sorrow that their springtime had come to an end.

She tugged at the stems with vigour and enthusiasm, handing them back to her silent daughter. The bluebells were shallow and yielding. It was a challenge not to pull them up by the base of their stalks, which were white and sap-filled, dripping with the lifeblood of the plant. Sarah squeezed some of the sticky substance onto her hand and rubbed it in. Then she shivered as she was gripped by a premonition, awful in its vividness, that she'd never pick bluebells again. It was as absolute and vague as that. She didn't know where it had come from – maybe the smell of the rotten undergrowth reminded her of decay. She climbed down the bank and gathered up her daughter, trying to calm herself.

The terror didn't subside until she was back at the cottage. Even then, remnants remained, clinging to her entrails. It was this sensation that was to make up her mind for her, once and for all. She picked up the phone.

'Sarah rang while you were out. She wants to know if you'll babysit again.'

'Oh?'

Aidan's insides churned. It was surreal. A man in his forties being asked to babysit by the woman he was in love with. The wife innocently taking the call and encouraging him to accept. In normal times the call would be for Alannah – to mind the children of local families for extra pocket money. Or, more accurately these days, drinking money.

'What's the occasion?'

'She didn't say. Just that something unexpected had come up. You'll do it, won't you?'

'I will, of course.'

'I'll ring her back and tell her.'

Aidan went out to the deck while she made the call. He tried to gather his thoughts but they scattered to the four winds.

He arrived at Sarah's alone this time, looking presentable but not too obvious, he hoped. To either woman. He'd never been a man concerned with his appearance – until now. He'd showered and his clothes were clean. He'd trimmed his beard and had even toyed with the idea of aftershave – a last-minute Father's Day present from one of the children a couple of years ago. It had caused much hilarity at the time. It had probably gone off. He didn't think he'd be able to tell the difference and it would be a dead giveaway anyhow.

His heart was palpitating as he stood on the doorstep. He was way too old for this. She opened the door, a vision in white, dressed up to go out. He wanted to tell her how lovely she looked but the words wouldn't come. He stepped inside and fought the jealousy. Was she going out with a man? The thought hadn't occurred to him until now. He felt almost sickened.

'Thank you for coming at such short notice.' She led him inside.

'Not at all. I know it's not easy, getting someone to mind Maia.'

She smiled. 'Maia's asleep.'

'That's what we thought last time.'

She laughed. 'Yes, we did.'

He stood there awkwardly, not knowing what to do with his hands, his eyes, his words. He, Aidan Ryan, who had always been so comfortable in his own skin.

'Won't you sit?' she said. 'Have a glass of wine with me.'

'Don't you have to get going?'

'Not right away.'

'Okay. Just the one, then. I don't want to be drunk and disorderly in charge of a child.' He felt pleased. More confident. She wanted to spend time with him.

He sat where he had before, in the centre of the couch, taking up half the space with his large frame. Sarah handed him a glass of wine and settled in the arm-chair opposite. He was a beer man, really, but he'd drink methylated spirits if it meant spending time with her. He watched her knock back half her glass. 'Don't you have to drive?'

'No.'

'Taxi?'

'No.'

He looked searchingly at her. 'Someone picking you up?'

She shook her head.

'Then . . .' He looked blankly at her. Not daring to believe . . .

'I thought I'd stay at home instead. Have dinner. Would you like to join me?'

Many quickened heartbeats passed.

'Yes, I would.'

And suddenly Aidan's crush was no longer a crush. It was

reciprocated. A two-way thing. It had life outside his own interior. It was real.

'Shall we?' Sarah got up and led him to the kitchen.

The table, normally so humble and rustic, had been carefully set. The room glowed with candlelight. She indicated where he should sit and he followed her instruction, as if in a dream.

'I made fish pie,' she said, filling the silence. 'I couldn't figure out if being a fisherman all these years would mean that you'd love fish or couldn't stand the sight of it.'

'It's my favourite food.'

'You're only saying that.'

'Would I lie to you?'

Each fell silent, prey to the same thought: they were lying to his wife.

Sarah busied herself with the pie. Aidan drank more wine. He'd have eaten curried fish guts if Sarah was serving them up to him. The food was irrelevant.

He could tell she was nervous, and the knowledge gave him hope. Made him stronger. He took charge of the conversation. 'You look lovely tonight.' He could say it now.

'Oh.' She rolled her eyes and grinned. 'This old thing.'

'Is it new?'

'Bought it today.'

They both laughed, delighted to be sharing a joke, the tension between them dissipating.

'There you are. Get that down you.' Sarah placed a heaped and steaming plate in front of him.

'My God, woman. It's only me you're feeding, not the five thousand.'

'I might have gone a bit overboard.'

'Might?'

'But you have to eat it or I'll have leftovers for a week.'

'I'll do my best.'

He hadn't thought he'd be able to eat, but his stomach co-operated. Sarah nibbled delicately beside him, their knees almost touching. It was delicious. So was the food.

As Sarah rose to get the dessert, she felt wobbly. Good. No, bad. She needed her wits about her. Just not too many wits. Because if she really and truly thought about what she was about to do, she wouldn't do it. And she wanted to.

It felt so natural and right to have Aidan here. So much so that she could almost fool herself into thinking that it *was* natural and right – locked inside this cosy little love nest, the rest of the world shut firmly out. It had been a stroke of evil genius, she thought, to arrange for Aidan to babysit, then forget to go out. If she allowed herself to think about it, she felt deeply ashamed. So she didn't. She ignored her thoughts and focused instead on her feelings. As the dinner drew to its natural conclusion, the tension rose again.

'Coffee?'

'I'm okay with the wine, thanks.'

No activity to disappear into. Nothing to do but sit with him. Wait.

The mood, hitherto light, became more intense. Sarah felt as if she'd laid her emotions on the table along with the food. Would they be so easily devoured? Would she? She felt horribly vulnerable and exposed and never in her life so nervous prior to physical contact. And never before had she felt her missing breast so keenly. Aidan enclosed her hand in his own, covering it completely. She felt a jolt throughout her body, delicious yet almost sickening in its intensity. They looked into each other, deep into each other, as if searching for missing pieces of themselves. They were both old enough to know better.

He had turned her hand over now and lifted it to his mouth.

Soft kisses on her palm. Then her wrist. The delicate veins on her wrist, which transported the sensations around her body. She half rose in her chair and he pushed back his own. Somehow she ended up on his lap, sitting across him as he feasted on her. There was nothing he didn't want to do. Nothing she wouldn't allow. Garments were loosened and pulled over heads. The whole universe constricted into those two bodies, possessed with desire for one another. And then the room turned to liquid and melted down its own walls.

They ended up in Sarah's bed, it being ultimately more comfortable than the kitchen chair. They were no longer encased in twenty-something bodies, after all. Contrary to sexual stereotype, Aidan lay awake while Sarah fell asleep. It was as if she could relax at last. Her head rested on Aidan's chest. He could see her scalp gleaming through the curls. She looked so fragile. He kept one hand on her hip, the other cupped behind his head as he stared up at the ceiling. He felt elated. Not triumphant – not as if he'd scored a goal, or anything like that. It was the elation of longing fulfilled. He had tried to imagine how he would feel once his lust was satisfied. Would he be assailed with the age-old masculine desire to run? But he felt closer than ever to her, wanting more, wanting to stay. Neither had he been daunted by her lack of a breast. To him, her scar only magnified her beauty. Her perfection thrown into stark contrast. He stroked her hip, the rise and fall, the swell. The silky smoothness under his fingers.

His hand froze as the door opened. Just a crack, then further. He remained motionless as Maia climbed onto the bed, as if he could be invisible in his stillness. She crawled up beside him, directly above her mother's head and stared. Thank God he was covered from the waist down. Her little fingers reached out and touched his beard again, as if it was some disembodied teddy bear. He lay like a corpse until she was done – a full five minutes. Then she clambered down again, her mother still sleeping, and disappeared out onto the landing. For the first time, Aidan felt glad she was autistic. He also felt glad that she couldn't talk.

Chapter 16

Though the affair had begun, they shied away from the word. It screamed wrongness when what they had seemed so loving, so whole. Of course, the outside world would deem it wrong. Of course, if discovered, their outer worlds would be destroyed by this inner world. But while the inner world remained secret, their outer worlds could remain intact.

Still, Aidan felt he should tell Sarah about his conversation with Noel in the pub, that people had been talking about them even before they had done anything. He felt he should warn her, just in case. In case of what, he didn't admit to himself. He went to see her the next day. It was noon, a little before he was due to take out his first batch of tourists. He'd never felt so exposed, walking down the high street of his own home town, the place that had nurtured him his whole life. He was one of its sons and now it was turning on him. That was how it felt to Aidan that day in early summer. The sky was overcast and so was his mind. He'd never before succumbed to such paranoia. Then again, he'd never had reason to, never violated the mores of the society in which he lived and breathed. Who were 'they' – the people who spoke of him in scandalized whispers behind closed doors, out of the corners of their vicious mouths, watching him out of the corners of their jaundiced eyes? They could be anyone. Everyone. He nodded at those he knew, stopped to exchange pleasantries with one or two. But everything was forced. False. He was trying to decipher the real meaning behind their words and the real expression at the back of their eyes.

On Sarah's doorstep he looked about him. No one around, just a bandy little dog peeing against a car tyre. Then Sarah was standing in front of him, making it all worth it. Her face expanded in pleasure and surprise. 'Aidan! I wasn't expecting you. Come in.'

He stepped wordlessly inside and she read the worry on his face. 'What's wrong?'

He took her face in his hands and kissed her deeply. Like an alcoholic taking his first drink of the day. He felt her yield beneath him, felt his own being relax. They held each other in a long embrace. Aidan felt he was drawing his strength from her. Sarah felt cherished. They separated reluctantly.

'Let's go inside.'

They sat together on the couch, bodies touching at several points. Sarah looked up anxiously into Aidan's face. 'What is it?'

'There's been talk.'

'About?'

'You and me.'

'Oh.' She withdrew slightly and leaned back in the couch. 'Does Fiona . . .?'

'She hasn't heard anything yet.'

Sarah got up and walked to the other side of the room. She stood with her back to him at the window. The tide was coming in. 'Then we should put a stop to this now before she does hear something.'

He was at her side immediately. He took her shoulders and turned her around to face him. 'You don't mean that.' His voice was urgent, his expression fierce. He looked as far as he could into her eyes. She couldn't really mean it.

'Of course I mean it.'

Of course she didn't. She'd only said it because she knew he wouldn't agree.

'It's the right thing to do,' she said. Sarah felt she was playing a role. That this was all part of some half-forgotten play. She hated herself for it.

'How can it be the right thing?' said Aidan.

'You know how. You have a wife. Two children.'

'My children are practically grown-up.'

'You really don't think for a second that they wouldn't be affected by this?'

They both felt the truth of this, Aidan like a pain in his chest. He sat down on the edge of the couch, as if the wind had been knocked out of him. Sarah watched him with utter sympathy. She didn't say anything. What could she say? She just felt an inestimable sadness washing over her and taking with it all her strength. She sat down beside him, linked her arm through his and laid her cheek against his shoulder. They sat like that for a long time. What to do?

'You don't really want to end it, do you, Sarah?'

'Of course not.'

'Then why say it?'

'It's the logical thing to do.'

He nudged her gently. 'And you're such a logical person.'

Her laugh was gentle. 'I didn't say that. But, Aidan, you know it's right.'

'It doesn't feel right. I only feel right when I'm with you.'

'But you're betraying your wife. We both are.' Sarah couldn't bring herself to say Fiona's name. The guilt was already too enormous. 'And she doesn't deserve it. She's a good person, Aidan. Not like us.'

'Don't say that. You radiate goodness.'

Her laugh came out like a snort. 'I'm the world's first virtuous mistress.' She got up again and stood a few feet away, her arms wrapped protectively around her torso.

'It's not your fault I met the wrong woman first.'

'That's bullshit, Aidan.'

'It's not.'

'It is. It doesn't matter how often you try to justify it to yourself or in how many different ways. It's a betrayal, pure and simple.'

He looked up at her beseechingly, his eyes filled with pain. He reminded her of an animal caught in a trap.

'But I love you, Sarah.'

The room was filled with his declaration and its silent aftermath. Sarah turned her head to hide her joy. Her misplaced joy, because how could she have this happiness at another woman's expense? She'd always thought of herself as a feminist. What a joke. This was hardly an act of sisterhood. And yet . . . Aidan. This lovely man. Who seemed prepared to give up everything for her. It appealed to the romantic in her. It also appealed to the part of her that was addicted to drama, in her personal as well as her professional life. And she knew herself to be absurdly flattered by his attention. She understood now that she had given up hope of a man thinking of her in this way again after everything that had happened to her body. And, God, she got so lonely at times. So sick and tired of coping with everything on her own. She liked to tell herself that it was just her and Maia against the world, that they didn't need anyone else, but that was mere pretence. She saw it now. Fighting talk because she didn't have anyone. She had no choice.

It had been the same throughout her illness. There had been friends, of course. Some great friends. And her sister. But to have no partner at a time like that . . . She realized now that she had resigned herself to coping alone for ever, had steeled herself against the prospect. And here was Aidan, offering his shoulder. And what a shoulder it was.

He came and stood beside her. 'Do you love me?'

Her voice was soft. 'We've only just met.' Someone had to be the voice of reason.

'But that doesn't seem to matter, does it?'

No, it didn't. But still . . . 'It could be nothing but a crush. And while it's very flattering to my ego to be inspiring such passion, these feelings could fade very quickly and I'll be left with a shattered heart and your life will be in tatters. Is it really worth the risk?'

He took her hands in his and turned her to face him. 'Yes.'

His intensity. His certainty. She wasn't strong enough to resist. Or, rather, she'd been too strong for far too long and now she was ready to submit. Let someone else be strong for her.

'Okay.' She sighed. 'But we're going to have to be very discreet. You shouldn't be here now in broad daylight. For all we know, somebody saw you come in. The bush telegraph could be in operation at this very moment. Fiona might already know. This conversation could be a waste of time.'

'I don't care.'

'What do you mean, you don't care?'

'I'm going to have to tell her sooner or later.'

'Don't say that.'

'It's unavoidable.'

'Okay. Oh, God. I don't want to talk about it now. I've had enough trauma for one day.'

He nodded and held her quietly for a while, stroking the back of her neck, her shoulders. 'So. Do you, then?'

'Yes, Aidan. I love you.'

'That's what I thought.'

'It must be great to be so sure of yourself.'

'It is.' He hugged her close and she stared unseeingly over his shoulder.

She was definitely going to hell.

Chapter 17

For Sarah their affair was less consuming than it was for Aidan. Because, for her, other matters were more pressing. On the day her daughter had spoken for the first time she had enlisted the help of a speech therapist in Ennis. Her home was now full of flash cards and wall charts, with which she badgered the child relentlessly. Maia appeared wholly uninterested. All she wanted to do was play with Star. They went down to the cove every morning. On rare occasions, they had the dolphin to themselves but mostly they had to share. Sometimes Aidan would join them but Sarah convinced him to stay away, if he could, as part of Operation Discretion, of which she was by far the more strict observer.

Although Maia had yet to utter another word – she hadn't even said 'in' again – Sarah sensed a change in her daughter. An opening up. Maybe something that only she could notice, but definitely something. Maia's eyes were less blank. She even had some colour in her cheeks – although that could be put down to the time spent outdoors. Whatever it was, it was good. And Sarah wasn't stopping. She put the end of the summer out of her mind. She put a lot of things out of her mind. This didn't always work.

One day she opened the front door to find Fiona standing there. So unexpected was she that Sarah had no time to compose her features. Consequently, her dismay was evident. The other woman picked up on it immediately. 'I hope this isn't a bad time.'

'No. Not at all.' Now, why had she said that?

'I was just passing and I thought I'd drop in and say hello.'

Fiona sounded more uncertain than usual. But apart from that, all seemed normal. As far as Sarah could tell, she didn't know. And she didn't appear to be concealing any sharp weapons. 'Come in.' She stepped aside to allow her access. Thanks be to Christ, Aidan wasn't there – he might have been.

She put the kettle on as Fiona sat at the kitchen table. She seemed more subdued than Sarah had seen her before.

'These are nice.' Fiona gestured to a jam-jar crammed with pinks.

'Yes. Aren't they lovely? I couldn't resist. And there are so many of them right now.'

'I never think of doing things like that. I guess I've been looking at them so long, I've stopped appreciating them. I didn't know you were an artist too.'

'Pardon?' Sarah was mystified.

'This.' Fiona gestured to the table.

'Oh. I didn't do that. Maia did.'

They were looking at a drawing of a dolphin.

'I don't believe it. Really?'

'Really.' Despite the strained and surreal circumstances, Sarah's face broke into a grin.

'But this is astounding. How old is she again?'

'Seven.'

'Seven! This looks like it was done by an adult. And a normal one at that. Oh, I'm sorry, I didn't mean . . .' Fiona rushed to correct herself.

'That's all right. I know what you meant.'

'I thought autistic children had problems with motor skills.'

'Most of them do. A lot would have trouble even holding a pencil. But not Maia. She's always liked to draw. But, lately, she seems to be . . .' Sarah smiled again '. . . inspired.'

Fiona shook her head. 'Very impressive. I remember reading

an article about this. They call it "twice exceptional", don't they? When a child has an ability as well as a disability.'

'Yes, that's right.' Sarah nodded emphatically, and wished for the umpteenth time that circumstances were different, that she could spend more time with Fiona. She placed a mug of coffee in front of her and put the drawing aside. 'So,' she said, 'how come you're not in work today?'

'I've always taken a half-day on Thursdays – ever since the children were small. Of course, they don't need me any more.' Fiona took a sip of her coffee.

To Sarah, she looked incredibly sad. She thought it best to change the subject. 'I really enjoyed the exhibition that night, by the way.'

'Did you?' Fiona looked pleased and perked up again. She launched into a who's who of everyone who had been there. Not only that, but she was animated about the work they had seen and gave Sarah a detailed run-down of what was going on in the local visual-arts scene. These were sides of Fiona that Sarah wouldn't have expected: she was sharp and funny and really passionate about art.

'Yes. It was a lovely night and I liked Noreen's work. What was her second name again?'

'Dwyer. Noreen Dwyer.'

'Oh, yeah. That was it. She was so funny.'

'Yes. She can be quite a character when she gets going. Been through a hard time lately, though.'

'Oh?'

'Her marriage is on the rocks, apparently. I heard that her husband is on the verge of moving out.'

'Poor woman.'

'Yes. Well, not that I can talk. My own marriage isn't in much better shape right now.'

Sarah froze. This wasn't happening. Fiona confiding in her

about the state of her marriage? Sarah groped around wildly for something appropriate to say. 'I'm sure that's not true.'

'It is. Aidan has no use for me any more. Not for talking. Not for sex. He can't even stand to be in the same room as me half the time.' She was looking thoroughly wretched, sitting there, warming her small, capable hands on her coffee mug, needing the warmth, even though the day was mild.

Sarah knew a response was required of her. 'Maybe he's just preoccupied with the new business.' She was panicking now.

'No, it's not that. I told myself it was at first, but there's more to it. I even convinced myself for a while that he had erectile problems, but that's not it either.'

Sarah had gone scarlet and was immobile with mortification. For another woman – a woman she didn't even know that well – to be discussing the intimate details of her marriage, and for Sarah to know only too well that Aidan had no problems in that area.

Fiona was looking at her. 'Oh, I'm sorry. I'm making you uncomfortable.'

'No . . .'

'Yes, I am. I always do this. Part and parcel of being a doctor, I'm afraid. You get used to talking about physical things that most people find embarrassing in a very matter-of-fact way.'

'That's no problem, Fiona.' Sarah felt so bad for this woman, who was clearly reaching out to her in friendship. And she had nothing to give her. She *was* the problem.

The irony was that she was always the one her female friends came to in times of man trouble. And here she was, not with a well run dry but one stagnated with guilt. 'Maybe he's having a mid-life crisis.'

'Maybe he is. Maybe I am. I don't know. I'm not certain about anything any more. There was a time when everything seemed so clear. I had a good marriage. I loved being a mother, loved being a doctor. Now the kids have no need for me any more. And as for the medicine, I just feel so jaded by it. I used to have all the time in the world for my patients. Now I can't get them out of the door quick enough. I've even found myself questioning my motives in becoming a doctor in the first place. Did I really have a calling for it, or did I just choose it because it had the highest points, because I was so driven to succeed at something – anything?'

The doorbell rang.

'I'm sorry, Fiona. I'll have to get that.' Sarah practically ran out to the hall. Saved by the bell. She tugged the door open.

'Hello.' There stood Aidan, soppy grin on his face. 'I had an hour to spare between sailings. I thought I'd drop in to see if my . . .' His smile failed as his wife materialized in the hall behind his mistress. '. . . if my wife had time to join me for a coffee.'

'How did you know I was here?'

'Tadgh Brennan told me he saw you calling in here a while ago.'

'I didn't see him.'

'Ah, he must have been passing down the other end of the street.'

'Must have been. Yes, I'd love to.'

Sarah glanced at her. The smile of pure pleasure on Fiona's face made her feel physically ill.

'I'll just go and get my jacket. It's in the kitchen.'

As Fiona disappeared, Aidan and Sarah looked at each other in dismay. Aidan stepped into the hall.

'What –'

'Not now, Aidan.'

Her words, her tone, her demeanour, all silenced him.

'Here I am.' Fiona was back in the hall again, adjusting her jacket and her hair. 'And look who I brought with me.'

Maia, who had been playing in the sitting room, stepped out from behind her. Without looking at anyone in particular, she walked up to Aidan and took his hand. Aidan looked back at Sarah involuntarily as Maia led him into the house. The two women followed them into the kitchen. Maia stopped at the table and looked up into Aidan's face. 'Dar,' she said.

Sarah was on her in an instant. 'What did you say?'

Maia ignored her. She continued to gaze up at Aidan. 'Dar,' she said again. Then she looked down at the table.

'There. Are you trying to say there, love?'

'I think she means the drawing. She's trying to show me the drawing.'

'"Draw" – is it "draw", Maia?'

'Is she trying to say Star?' said Fiona, from the other side of the table.

'Dar, dar, dar.' Maia repeated the word over and over, flapping her hands in an agitated fashion, clearly excited.

'It is Star! Oh, Aidan, she said "Star".'

Sarah descended on Maia, an all-encompassing embrace that broke the child's connection with Aidan.

'Dar,' she said again.

'Yes, darling, that's Star – oh, well done.' She hugged her daughter fiercely and began to cry, tears flowing thick and fast, snot unchecked. This was full-scale, ugly, don't-care-who's-watching crying.

Fiona walked around to the counter, tore off a square of kitchen towel and handed it to her. Sarah took it wordlessly and, continuing to sob, balled it up in her hand.

Maia stood motionless – emotionless – beneath her mother's heaving body. 'Dar,' she said occasionally.

Sarah eventually managed to compose herself. She dabbed her face dry and blew her nose noisily. 'I'm sorry.' She addressed Fiona.

'Oh, no need to be. It's perfectly understandable. Now, would you like us to stay?'

'No, no. I'll be fine. We'll be fine. More than fine. You go.'

'Okay, then. See you soon.'

They all walked back to the front door, Aidan a few paces ahead. Fiona grabbed Sarah urgently by the arm, startling her. 'You won't let on to Aidan what I was saying earlier?'

'Of course not.'

'Thanks. Right.' She raised her voice to a normal level. 'We'll be off, then.'

Sarah watched them walk away. Fiona looked back at her and smiled. Then she linked her husband and they disappeared around the corner.

Chapter 18

Fiona was once again in possession of that most dangerous emotion – hope. That Aidan would deliberately seek her out to spend time with her when he didn't have to. Part of her realized how pathetic she was, grateful for the crumbs he'd swept off the table of his affection. Nevertheless, she was still smiling next lunchtime as she browsed through the stalls at the weekly food market.

It was new to the town – people's desire for locally grown produce had increased. Furthermore, these markets were fashionable now. Fiona didn't care too much about that. She was just glad it was there. Today, as she ran her eyes over the myriad shapes and colours on the fruit and vegetable stalls, and considered the vast array of weird and wonderful breads she could take home, it seemed to her that the world was once again alive with possibility and abundance. It helped that the sun was high in the sky, beaming down on the shoppers. Fiona reached out for a plaited loaf, sprinkled with poppy seeds, at exactly the same time as another hand. She laughed when she saw whose it was. 'Tadgh Brennan! Get your hands off my loaf.'

'Fiona McDaid! As I live and breathe.'

'Haven't seen you for ages, Tadgh.'

'Haven't seen you either.'

'You have so. Yesterday afternoon. Aidan told me. Why didn't you call out to me?'

Tadgh's eyebrows knitted and he seemed genuinely puzzled. 'Yesterday afternoon?'

'Yes. When you saw me going into Sarah Dillon's house. You told Aidan. Remember?'

Tadgh looked searchingly at her for a few seconds too long. 'Oh, the actress. That's right. I remember it now.' He tapped his temple with two fingers. 'Must be going doo-lally in my old age. Anyway,' he said, with a hunted look, 'you take the bread. I'm supposed to be laying off the carbohydrates anyway, after what you told me on my last visit.' He patted his ample belly fondly. 'Talk about being caught in the act. Take care, Fiona.'

She watched as he merged with, then disappeared into the crowd. Caught in the act, indeed.

She brought it up over dinner that night, her tone carefully casual. 'By the way, I ran into Tadgh Brennan today.'

'Oh, yes? How's he doing?'

'You should know. You spoke to him yesterday.'

Fiona's tone was sharp as her eyes pierced the top of her husband's head. It remained bent over his plate, although he appeared to stop chewing for several seconds.

'I did, of course. Sure, I only spoke to him for half a minute. We didn't have an in-depth conversation.'

'Nor did we. Not after it became clear he didn't have the foggiest idea what I was talking about.'

'Ah. He's probably just losing his marbles in his old age.'

'That's what he said.'

'There you go, then.'

'He's not even fifty.'

'Look, Fiona.' Aidan put down his knife and fork, as if he was defeated by his dinner, the conversation they were having and life in general. 'It really doesn't matter any more. I'm going to bed.'

'Bed! It's barely seven.'

‘I just need to lie down for a while.’

‘Are you sick?’

‘Just tired.’

Fiona sprang up, ready to prod and examine him.

Aidan held up a hand. ‘Leave it, Fiona. I’m grand. At least, I will be. I just need to rest.’ His tone was uncharacteristically weary.

Fiona frowned. ‘All right. I’ll see you when I come up.’

His nod was barely perceptible. She listened to his footfalls ascending the stairs, slow and heavy, also uncharacteristic. Maybe he *was* coming down with something. He’d been remarkably subdued this evening. It was incredible, really. You could be married for years, think you knew your partner, when all of a sudden he presented you with a whole new set of moods to decipher. She sipped her glass of water. No answers came to her. Just more questions.

Aidan lay on his bed, gazing up at the ceiling. He seemed to have been doing a lot of that lately. He knew every hairline crack. Every secret spider’s web. He screwed his eyes up tight. It was too bright and would be for hours. He longed to be enveloped by thick, blank darkness. Longed to sink into it. The darkness seemed softer, more forgiving. It exposed less. He shielded his eyes with his forearm, this time to block out not the light but the images, the words – the dreadful occurrence of that afternoon.

He had gone to see Sarah. He’d known she wanted him to stay away, but he’d had to speak to her after what had happened with Fiona. She wouldn’t answer his calls and he was going out of his mind. He had known it was a mistake, but he’d gone anyhow, as if propelled by some inner self-destructive compulsion.

‘What are you doing here?’ she hissed. She poked her head

out of the door, looked left and right, then rapidly ushered him into the hall.

'I had to come. You wouldn't answer my calls.'

She regarded him coolly. A fist of ice gripped his heart. Wordlessly, she turned her back on him and walked into the sitting room. He followed her like a dog. She sat upright on the armchair, not inviting closeness. Her knees were pressed together and her hands were clasped tightly on her lap. It was as if she were trying to hold herself together. Maia was in her corner, playing with a toy car that Aidan had given her just a few days before, when everything was different. It was an old one of Tommy's he'd found knocking around. Maia acted as if she hadn't seen him. She was holding the car in the air and, with one tiny finger, spinning a back wheel repeatedly. Aidan had seen her do this before. She could keep it up indefinitely. He forced his eyes back to Sarah. He didn't like what he saw. She was deliberately avoiding his gaze and it was clear she wanted him gone.

'Sarah. What happened yesterday. It was a one-off.'

'She thinks I'm her friend.' She almost yelled it. He'd never seen her like that before. It shocked him. Sarah got up and paced the room, her composure shot to pieces. 'I'm not doing this any more, Aidan. It's wrong.'

'But we've been through this before . . .'

'I don't care. I'm not doing it any more. Not doing it to her. It's wrong.'

All he could do was stare at her in desperation. It wasn't as if he could deny that she was speaking the truth. She stopped and turned to him, her eyes unnaturally bright, her wig lopsided, her body trembling. She'd clearly worked herself into quite a state. 'Don't you care about your own wife? Are you really that heartless?'

'Of course I care about her. It tears me up inside, the thought of causing her any pain.'

'Well, you needn't feel torn up any more because I'm ending it now.'

'Sarah . . .'

'Now, Aidan. Now.'

Aidan cradled his head in his hands. They were quiet for a while, she hugging herself and looking out of the window. He spoke to her back. 'This is just your guilty conscience talking.'

She rounded on him. 'Too right it's my conscience and too right it's guilty. So it should be. And so should yours.' She let out a short, humourless laugh. 'You know, I used to consider myself a feminist. I went on marches to support women's rights, for fuck's sake. What about Fiona's rights?'

'What about our right to be happy?'

'Can you really build your happiness on somebody else's misery? Because I can't. You and Fiona were perfectly happy before I came along.'

'That's a matter of opinion.'

'Well, it's my opinion. And it's also my opinion that you can be happy again once I'm out of the picture.'

'You're not leaving?'

She sighed. 'No, I'm not. Although I've thought about it. It would be a lot simpler if I did. But how can I leave now that Maia is making such good progress?'

'And have you thought about Maia in all of this?'

'What do you mean?' She seemed unsure of herself for the first time.

'You know what I mean. What about the bond she's formed with me?'

'She hasn't –'

'You know she has, Sarah. Yesterday when she took my hand – has she ever done that with anyone else?'

'She –'

'Apart from you?'

'No.'

'Well, then.'

'Look, it's unfortunate. But that's the way it's got to be. I'm warning you, Aidan. Don't make me take Maia away from Star. Not now.' She locked eyes with him, her gaze challenging, her meaning clear. If he didn't back off, she'd leave.

Aidan felt an unfamiliar hot, prickly sensation at the back of his eyeballs. He made one last-ditch attempt. 'And what about my feelings? Don't they count for anything?'

Sarah looked out of the window again.

'What if I leave Fiona anyway?'

'Then you'd be leaving her for nothing.'

'But I love you, Sarah.'

She turned back to him. Her features were set in stone. 'Your love for me is irrelevant.'

Aidan slumped back on the couch, the fight gone out of him. He couldn't believe what he'd just heard. Couldn't believe that Sarah was capable of such coldness. Yet she'd said it. And, by the look of her, she'd meant it. He rose to his feet. He didn't say anything – didn't have anything left to say: he'd exhausted every argument, gone down every avenue and each one a dead end. He left the house silently and closed the front door carefully behind him.

Sarah watched Aidan retreat down the street. Only when he'd disappeared around the corner did she allow herself to crumple to the floor. The tears came instantly, as if a dam had burst. As she scrunched herself up in the foetal position, she was aware that she had just given the performance of her life.

Maia crossed the room and hunkered down beside her. She put a finger to her mother's cheek. Then she lifted it up to her own face and looked at the tear that was now wetting her own skin. Then she sucked her finger solemnly and walked back to her corner. She knelt down on the floor, picked up the car and commenced spinning the back wheel.

Part II

Chapter 19

It was like some watery nightmare from which he couldn't wake. He was out day and night in the boat, waiting for a body that the ocean wouldn't yield. His mother's features, stricken with grief. His sisters' faces, looking to him. As if he and not the sea had all the answers.

And the end of the search. The surrender to the inevitable. The simple ceremony. Flowers strewn on the waiting water. His father's name hewn in the slab of stone, space left beneath for the ones to come. For whomsoever the sea demanded as her sacrifice.

His name on the stone.

For years Aidan had had this recurring dream. He would wake up saturated, his sheets twisted. It was only when he'd met Fiona that the nightmares had subsided. And now the dream was back and a gnawing sense of loss haunted his nights as well as his days.

The night after Sarah had dumped him, Fiona had found him sitting on the edge of their bed. She switched on the light as she entered the room. 'What are you doing, sitting here alone in the dark?'

Aidan didn't reply. He was trying to disguise the fact that he'd been crying.

Fiona sat down beside him. 'What is it, Aidan?' She peered up into his face. 'Have you been crying?' She was amazed. Her husband wasn't a weepy man. His tears came hard and slow. The last time he'd cried was at his mother's funeral. That had been more than four years ago. And before that? His father's funeral, most probably. And Fiona had always been there to pick up the pieces, as she was now. Aidan covered his eyes with his hands, but the tears seeped out through his fingers. She hugged him with her whole body, completely encompassing him with her arms. She sat there rocking him until he'd stopped.

'I don't know what the hell's wrong with you, Aidan, and I know you're not going to tell me. But whatever it is, we're going to get through it. If it's depression we can get through it. It can be fixed. If it's a mid-life crisis, that can be fixed too. Even if I have to buy you a shiny red sports car and watch you zooming around the town, your beard blowing in the wind.'

This elicited a small smile. But there was no happiness behind it.

'Whatever it is, we'll get through it together. I promise. Have I ever let you down?'

'No, never. You've never let me down, Fiona.'

She kissed him on the cheek, laid her head on his shoulder and stroked the back of his head. Aidan's eyes welled again, but he managed to quell the flow this time. The knowledge of how little he deserved this tender treatment nearly killed him. His wife never failed to surprise him, not least in her capacity to believe that everything could be fixed, her pragmatic approach to every problem, every ailment.

He went about his business as best he could. Literally. He was doing four or five dolphin trips a day and Star always obliged, coming along for the ride, although the level of her interaction varied widely. Sometimes she'd barely show her blowhole. At others she'd breach full out of the water, thrilling the tourists with her giant, splashy leaps.

He somehow found the energy to put the next part of his business plan into action: hiring wetsuits and offering people the chance to swim with her. Properly. Under water. In her element and not their own. He moved seamlessly between the two worlds, as he always had, and this at least gave him some semblance of calm. Not that he had the energy to be agitated. He'd never had such a sense of the life force being drained out of him. Never in his life had to drag himself out of bed, to force himself to do things that normally came naturally. Did anyone notice? Fiona, of course. He sensed her watching him all the time and tried to pull himself out of it for her sake. But, luckily, his teenage children were, by their very age and nature, far too self-centred and preoccupied with their own magnified problems to see the change in him. This sea-change.

Alannah was home for a couple of weeks, resting and regrouping between her end-of-term exams and an extended trip to London where she planned to work for the rest of the summer. Aidan felt absurdly proud of her as they walked arm in arm along the beach. She was such a complex blend of him and Fiona, with a large dollop of herself thrown into the mix. She was taller than her mother but, thankfully, not as tall as him. She had his family's colouring – vibrant blue eyes, reddish-brown hair. She still retained a smattering of the freckles of her childhood, which nowadays she tended to cover with makeup. She was so like his own mother at times that it was uncanny. It reminded him that life was one continuous loop.

She was unusually quiet today. They walked silently to the sound of breaking waves and the cry of a lone gull. But he knew she was building up to something. Something large. He could almost see her mind working beneath her furrowed brow.

Finally: 'Dad.'

'Yes, love.'

'How do you know when you're in love?'

The question shocked him. Yet, on another level, it didn't.

He squeezed her arm gently. 'Is that what has you so quiet, Alannah?' He liked to say her name, which was in itself a term of endearment. And for Aidan the very utterance of that name was an expression of love for her.

She looked up at him enquiringly. 'How did you know you were in love with Mammy?'

Her face was open and not yet fully adult. She was half girl, half woman, but lately he'd noticed the balance tipping towards the latter. And now this.

'What's his name?'

Alannah's cheeks grew pink and her eyes dropped to her bare feet, planting at regular intervals in the sand. 'Ross.'

'What class of a name is that?'

'It's a lovely name.' Her head shot up again, her voice and eyes defensive.

He grinned at her and felt her relax. 'Is he the reason you broke up with poor Jimmy?'

Ross wasn't Alannah's first boyfriend. Aidan was used to the concept. She'd been seeing Jimmy Kelly since she was fourteen. He'd been in her class at school and Aidan had known his parents since the year dot. Still, all childish things must come to an end.

'Kind of.'

'And I thought you and Jimmy were destined to be married.'

'Dad!'

He'd embarrassed her again, reminding her of the time she had come to him, shortly after getting together with Jimmy, and announced that she was marrying him as soon as she turned eighteen. Well, eighteen had come and gone and she was still single, thank God. 'I'm sorry. Go on. Tell me all about this Ross. Is he in your class?'

'He's in second year.'

Not too much older. That was good.

'He's tall, Dad, even taller than you.' His daughter's face glowed as she talked about the faceless youth.

'Never mind that. Is he any use with a hurl?'

'He played for the county youth team.' Her pride was evident.

'Did he now? And what county would that be?'

'He's from Cork.'

'Oh, Christ, a Cork man. That's all we need.'

'Dad!'

'Does he say "yarra" before every sentence?'

'No. He does not. He's lovely, Dad. You'd really like him.'

'Hmm. Are you going to bring the lad home so we can have a look at him?'

'God, no. It's way too soon for that. I don't want you lot frightening him off. We've only just got together.'

Aidan dreaded to think what 'got together' meant. He put it out of his head.

'So. You didn't answer my question.'

'What question?'

'How do you know when you're really in love?'

He sighed and his pace slowed. It was as if his feet had grown heavier. 'I don't know why you're asking me, Alannah.'

'Because you're so old. You must have picked something up along the way.'

'Cheeky article.'

They laughed. Then his face grew serious again. What to tell his daughter? This girl on the cusp of life who trusted him implicitly. He who deserved no trust placed in him. This girl, who adored him completely, saw him in such a simple, one-dimensional way. She wouldn't adore him if she knew the truth of what he was, what he had done. The thought sickened him and, for the first time, he felt relieved that he was no longer with Sarah.

'You know you're in love when you can't think of anything

else but that person. When you eat, drink, sleep that person. When you feel as if you can't exist for one single second without them.'

He glanced at her. She was wearing a dreamy expression. That wouldn't do. 'But that doesn't mean it's real.' He saw her jolt out of it. 'It could just be lust. Infatuation. Nature's way of making us procreate. So I don't want you doing any of that procreation. You have your whole future ahead of you.'

'I won't, Daddy.'

'Good. Because you don't really know if you're in love until you've faced a few obstacles together. Time will tell you what you need to know.'

'Is that the way it was with you and Mammy?'

His nod was barely perceptible. He looked out to sea. A few trawlers were coming in. 'And you can tell that Ross fella that if he so much as harms a hair on your head, I'll wrap that hurl around his neck so fast he won't have time to say yarra.'

Chapter 20

Sarah had found a babysitter, now that she could no longer avail herself of Aidan's services. She had been in the health-food shop one day, and Valerie's chatter hadn't been quite as aimless as usual. She had a sister – Bridget – a special-needs assistant, who was saving to buy a house, didn't have a full-time job and was looking for some extra cash. Would Sarah be interested in her childminding services? Sarah uttered a silent hallelujah. Maia had taken to Bridget with an ease that had been absent with new faces in the past – all part of the great unfolding of Maia Mitchell. She came to the house three mornings a week, leaving Sarah free to do as she wished.

Those empty hours were a guilty pleasure for Sarah, who had never been in the habit of allowing herself the gift of time. But she was learning as her daughter was learning. The high drama of recent weeks had taken its toll on her already depleted reserves. She was emotionally spent and knew she had to do something to recover from this complete and utter exhaustion.

She found her cure in the water. She discovered a quiet time – an in-between time – when she had the cove to herself. In the morning the dolphin drew the children and the water was alive with their antics. Then, at about eleven every day, Star disappeared. To sleep? To hunt? Her mystery remained intact. And she didn't appear again until early afternoon, when she entertained the tourists on Aidan's boat. So Sarah felt as if she was alone in the water, which she knew to be an illusion. But if she thought of all the creatures with whom she was sharing it – from plankton to whale, from jellyfish to shark – she would have run out screaming. So she didn't think. Not too much anyway. She just tried to empty her mind.

This was what found her, one glorious morning in July, swimming solo as usual, doing her best to abandon her thoughts. It was hard for a woman with a tendency to over-think everything, but she drew on what she could recall from yoga classes as she floated on her back. The sensation was delicious, her skin hot with the sun. She knew she should be more careful: since the chemo, she burned so easily. But she couldn't bring herself to get out and put on more lotion. This must be what it was like in a flotation tank: this feeling of weightlessness, of total peace and calm. And all for free.

Then her eyes snapped open: she was no longer alone. She could scarcely take in what she was seeing. High above her head, a perfect glittering arc, as Star soared over her. Her body went rigid with shock and she sank beneath the surface. She came up coughing and spluttering, then looked all around her. Nothing now above her but the golden globe of sun; nothing below her but her feet treading water. All around was still. Silent and deserted.

And then a fin was slicing through the water, coming at her, swift as a silver arrow, now launching over her head again. Sarah didn't know which emotion to feel. There were so many to choose from: fear, panic, elation. If the dolphin was to land on her . . . But she wouldn't. Sarah trusted in Star's agility, her aerodynamics, her perfect timing.

And here she was again, quicker this time, right over her head.

She was playing with her. *Star was playing with her.* Sarah laughed like a child.

The dolphin jumped again.

And again.

And again.

Sarah chose her emotion. The emotion she chose was joy.

Chapter 21

Fiona was going out on a date with her husband. She examined herself in the full-length mirror. She'd bought a brand new little black dress for the occasion. She turned and looked over her shoulder, checking her rear view. Arse not too big. Just right. There was no point in asking Aidan what he thought. He'd only lie or grunt.

Their marriage had been undergoing something of a renaissance of late. She didn't know what had changed but something had. It was as if Aidan had come back into himself, dragged himself out of the strange funk he'd been in for such a long time. She'd stopped analysing it and decided to be grateful. She took the stairs cautiously in her new three-inch heels. The occasion required some elevation.

'Ready.' She stepped into the hall, smiling broadly.

He turned to her. His shoulders were slightly hunched and his hands were in his pockets. But he attempted a smile. 'You look nice. New dress?'

'Thanks. Yes. I got it today.' She gave him a twirl. Then a beam. 'And I love that shirt on you.' She came up to him and adjusted the collar. 'I haven't seen you wear it since the night Sarah Dillon came to dinner.' Her face clouded. 'She never did invite us back.'

'Let's go.' He pulled away and opened the door.

'I haven't seen her lately. Have you?'

'No.' He was walking rapidly down the driveway, several steps ahead of her.

'I wonder what she's up to, these days. She wouldn't have

gone back to Dublin without saying goodbye, would she?'

'I don't know.'

Fiona half hoped Sarah had gone away so she could put the memory of her embarrassing revelations about her marriage behind her. She regretted unburdening herself to the other woman, who hadn't seemed all that interested in pursuing a friendship. Yet again she had misjudged. Thankfully, things were getting back on track with Aidan, so she had decided to give Sarah no more thought. The great confession was a moment of weakness, best forgotten.

He clicked the car open and held the door for her.

'Oh,' she said, irrationally pleased. 'Thank you very much.'

She settled her bum into her seat, her mood lifting all the time. Aidan got in beside her. As he turned on the ignition, his Leonard Cohen CD blasted its lyrics into the car. Fiona turned it off instantly. 'I'm not listening to that miserable shite again. Let's just talk, shall we?'

Aidan nodded as he pulled out of the driveway.

It was a beautiful evening. Fiona chatted about this and that but after a time, weary of Aidan's lack of response, she stopped talking and took in the scenery instead. A warm breeze rippled through the open window and ruffled her curls. She was used to Aidan being subdued and it didn't bother her. It was impossible to feel anything less than upbeat on such a night.

They were going to a new restaurant in Spanish Point. There was an unspoken agreement between them that they needed to try somewhere different – something different – away from their home town and the people they knew. Somewhere new and fresh and neutral. Their new start demanded nothing less.

The waiter pulled out Fiona's chair and placed the napkin on her lap. It was that kind of place. She could see that Aidan was uncomfortable already.

'A bit much, isn't it?' he said, when the waiter had gone.

'Well, I like it,' she said, determinedly bright. She examined his face. 'You trimmed your beard.'

He brought his hand instinctively to his chin. 'Well, you know – didn't want to let the side down.'

'You could never do that, Aidan.' She reached out and clasped his hand across the table, so happy to have him there. *Really* there. 'It's been too long since we did something like this,' she said. 'I can't remember the last time we ate out together, just the two of us. Can you?'

'That place in Doolin.'

'You're right. That was before Christmas. Last November. Let's not leave it so long again.'

'We won't.' He was inspecting the menu. 'Sea bass in Guinness batter with hand-cut fries and pea compôte,' he read out. 'That's just fish and chips and mushy peas. Why can't they say so?'

'It's called presentation, Aidan.'

'It's called trying to justify their prices.'

She willed him not to spoil things for her, but when the waiter came back to take their order he was politeness personified, and she knew she could relax. Her husband might look out of his element in a smart restaurant, but he was far from being a Philistine. And he was so secure in himself – she didn't think she'd ever seen him adopt a macho position in his life. He just didn't feel the need to prove anything. Aidan was kind and sensitive and decent. She sighed without realizing it. Now, if only he'd look at her the way he used to . . .

The starters had arrived, but when she'd finished hers he still hadn't touched his. 'What is it? Don't you like it?'

'No, it's fine. I just wanted to say something.'

'What?' She was on the edge of her seat. The edge of her breath.

'The trip.'

'What trip?'

'You know, when Tommy's gone off to college.'

'Oh. What about it?'

'We should start making plans for it.'

'I thought you weren't interested any more.'

'Well, I am.'

'Okay, then. I'll go to the travel agent tomorrow. Get some more brochures. And I'll look on-line too.' She took a sip of wine and grinned. 'I fancy the Far East. How about you?'

'Wherever you like. And another thing, Fi.'

'Yes?'

His face grew serious. 'I wanted to say sorry.'

'For what?'

'For everything. For the way I've been lately. I know I haven't been easy to live with.' He looked at her for confirmation.

Fiona shrugged.

'And I wanted to let you know that from here on in – from this night on – everything's going to change. You don't deserve the way I've been treating you, Fiona, and I'm so sorry.'

She didn't say anything for a few moments. Then she raised her glass. 'To a new start.'

He touched his to hers. 'A new start.'

They both drank and she smiled at him. 'You know I'd forgive you anything, don't you?'

He doubted it.

Chapter 22

Market day had come around again. Sarah and Maia were wandering through it having spent an uneventful morning splashing around in the cove. Uneventful in that Star, although present, had decided to keep her dolphin self to herself. Sometimes she did that, chose not to interact, and Sarah kind of liked it. It meant that when she did come to them, she did so of her own free will. She was her own dolphin. Her own special creation.

The dichotomy between the calm of their morning and the chaos of the market couldn't have been greater. Sarah questioned the wisdom of bringing her daughter with her but to hell with it. She was in serious need of a treat. And in spite of the improvements Maia had been making, restaurants were still not a good idea. They were fraught with opportunities for tantrums and other antisocial behaviour. The market was the lesser of two evils.

Sarah was starving after the morning's exertions. She longed for the soft, warm comfort of fresh bread, the succulence of ripe fruit, pastry so newly baked that it dissolved in her mouth. She longed for closeness with other human beings as well. The loneliness was getting to her, the novelty of her own company wearing thin. She missed Aidan with a terrible ache and wanted to be crushed up against other people, to hear human voices, busy and urgent. The sights, sounds and smells of the market – she needed them to fill her emptiness. That day, she was willing to take the risk of sensory overload to her child.

She was trying to negotiate her way to the bread stall, with

Maia clinging ferociously to her leg, holding her back. She realized the problem: to get to the bread, they had to pass the fruit stall – a stunning display vibrant with colour and life. The trouble was the pyramid of tomatoes stacked high at the far corner. Maia wouldn't pass them so Sarah brought her around the back instead. That worked. She was just congratulating herself on her ingenuity when someone said hello to her. She was in dire need of a friendly voice, a friendly face, and this face was so friendly. But it was the wrong face.

'Fiona.'

'Sarah. Long time no see. It must be over a month. We were beginning to think you'd left town.'

'Oh, no. Still around. Just living the quiet life. You know how it is.'

'How's Maia?'

The child reacted clearly to her name, but chose to look away.

'She's great. Never been better.' Sarah's smile was genuine.

'I think she's taken a stretch.'

'Do you?' Sarah resolved to measure her daughter the second they got home.

'Yes, I definitely do. She looks considerably taller to me. And her skin. She's lost that unhealthy pallor.'

'Yes, I've noticed that too.' Sarah beamed.

'Whatever you're doing, well done, because it's working.'

'Oh, I can't take any credit for it. It's all down to Star.'

'The dolphin?'

'Yes.'

Fiona's thoughts were clearly mirrored by her expression. Her cynicism. Her incredulity that Sarah was still hanging on to her daft notions about Star. Which was, perhaps, why she changed the subject so abruptly. 'Hey, why don't you both come back to our house for lunch?'

Sarah felt panic rising. 'I can't.' She thought quickly. 'We have an appointment with the speech therapist in Ennis at half two. We'd have only just arrived and we'd have to go again.'

'That's a pity. Well, we must get together again some time soon. I mean that. You call me and let me know when's convenient for you.'

'I'll do that.'

'Make sure you do. 'Bye for now.'

''Bye.'

Sarah watched Fiona walk away. She breathed a sigh – of disappointment rather than relief. Regret, too, and yearning. Because, irony of ironies, there was nothing she would rather have done that afternoon than have lunch with Fiona. It was exactly what she needed and wanted – the company of such a woman. But she was the wrong woman. And it was Sarah who had made her wrong – by her own foolishness, her weakness, her disgusting behaviour. *Disgusting*. Yes, that was the word. She felt the full shame of what she had done wash over her. She had been trying to hide from it but she couldn't any more. She was the one who had brought the relationship with Aidan to the next level. She had invited him over, knowing how he felt about her and knowing full well the inevitable outcome. There were no two ways about it: she had seduced Aidan, not the other way around. Not only that, to get him into her bed, she had exploited his wife's kindness and trust. She had asked Fiona to send him over and Fiona had obliged, thinking she was doing her new friend a favour.

Sarah shuddered. It was right that she should suffer from the fall-out. She was lucky it wasn't a damn sight worse: they had taken such foolish risks – only good fortune had stopped them being caught. Head bowed, she walked on, her only wish now to get home, the market having suddenly lost its charm.

Chapter 23

Aidan was out at sea, the only place he felt at home these days. He barely felt at home in his own body. His soul didn't seem to fit any more. It had expanded when he was with Sarah. Now he couldn't get it back into his old body, his old life.

It was Saturday afternoon and the boat was heaving with tourists. Tommy had come along to help out, as he did most days – Aidan never had to insist. The boy came voluntarily and with enthusiasm, Star apparently lighting him up just as she seemed to do with everyone. Aidan reflected on how much he owed this wild animal. She was allowing him to spend so much time out at sea, on his boat, with his son. And she'd brought him Sarah. Although look at where that had got him.

Tommy came and stood beside him, the tourists temporarily taken care of. 'I've been thinking, Dad.'

'I don't like the sound of that.'

'The business. It's doing really well, isn't it?'

'It is, son, it is.'

'And it's a big help to you when I come out on the boat.'

Aidan glanced briefly at his son. 'You're handy enough, I suppose.'

'Well, I was thinking. There's really no need for me to go to college at all. I could stay here and help you run the family business. "Ryan and Son – Atlantic Dolphin Tours".' He framed his hands as if seeing the words before him. 'I could paint it on the side of the boat.'

His suggestion was greeted by silence.

'What do you think?'

'What do I think?'

'Yes.'

'I think a lot of things.' Aidan fell silent again.

'Come on, Dad.'

'All right, then. It's entirely up to you what you do when you leave school, Tommy.'

Tommy waited for more words but none were forthcoming. 'Is that it?'

Aidan shrugged and they sailed along in a silence punctuated by intermittent whoops whenever Star surfaced.

'Then again,' said Aidan, eventually, 'it'd be a terrible pity to miss out.'

'On what?'

'College life, of course.'

This time it was Tommy who failed to respond.

'I mean, there's all those clubs you can join for a start. New friends to make.'

'I have plenty of friends here.'

'And half of them will be going away to college. Kevin will be going, won't he?'

'I suppose.'

'And then there's all the girls.'

Tommy's face changed, just a little.

Aidan extended his right arm. 'Girls as far as the eye can see.'

Tommy laughed, embarrassed.

This was clearly a consideration. 'How will they be able to resist a surfer dude such as yourself?'

'What if I don't get the points?'

He'd finished his exams several weeks beforehand.

'Do you have reason to believe you won't?'

'I don't know, Dad. I'm not a swot like Alannah.'

'You don't have to be. You're two different people. You have your strengths and she has hers.'

'But I might not do as well as her.'

'So what?'

'You really wouldn't mind?'

'Not at all.'

'But Mam would.'

'Your mother would only be upset if you got a place and you didn't take it.'

They both knew this was a partial lie, but decided to go along with it.

'And if you did that, she'd make your life a living hell. Not to mention mine.'

'She would, wouldn't she?' Tommy sounded glum.

'So, why not give it a go anyway? You can always drop out if you don't like it.'

Tommy appeared to be absorbing this. Aidan knew his son was no quitter. If he started something, he liked to see it through.

'Besides,' Aidan added, 'I thought you couldn't wait to see the back of us.'

Tommy kept staring straight ahead and Aidan knew that fear was at the heart of all of this. Fear of the unknown. Fear of the future unfolding before him to God knew where. 'You know we're not going anywhere, don't you? That we'll still be here for you? You can come home every weekend if that's what you want. Like Alannah used to do in the beginning. Then you'll probably meet some girl, the same way she's met this Ross eejit, and we won't see you for dust.'

Tommy smiled. 'You know why he won't come here, don't you?'

'Who?'

'Ross.'

'Why?'

'Because he's terrified of you.'

'Me? Sure, I'm just a big teddy bear.'

'Lana told him what you said about wrapping the hurl around his neck.'

Aidan threw back his head and laughed. It was the first time in ages that either of them had heard the sound. 'Good enough for him,' said Aidan. 'Now, that lady over there has gone a bit green. Be a good lad and get her to move to the centre at the back.'

'All right, Dad.' Tommy sprang into action, still the same boy he'd always been, when you got down to the root of him. Aidan felt better than he had in weeks, his son confiding in him. He had always been the one his children talked to. The more touchy-feely one, Fiona always said. She, for all her good intentions, tended to be a little too harsh, too pragmatic. And a little too inclined to try to mould them into the image she held for them. Aidan had always been more willing to allow them to grow into the people they were destined to be, to let them develop their own preferences, consciences, ideas. And, every now and then, he was rewarded with moments such as this. He smiled again.

The breeze was warm, the air clear. The people on the boat looked to starboard as Star jumped clear out of the water. She remained suspended, and it was as if time stood still for several seconds. Then she began her descent, showering everyone with silvery rainbow droplets when she landed.

Chapter 24

Star had many faces, many personas. That was how it seemed to Sarah. At times, she was perfect elegance, a magical, mythical creature. Other times, she was playful, comical, even. Her permanent smile was clearly a trick of nature, yet somehow so convincing. And there were times when she was almost an alien – her face so odd from certain angles. And it was, as Aidan had told her once, as if she had fallen from the stars. Especially when she emitted one of her strange clicks or cries. The first time she did it, Sarah had almost jumped out of her skin. But she was used to her now. And, she fancied, Star was getting used to them.

That morning there were many other children in the water. Sarah wished they'd all go home but she knew in her heart that was wrong. They had the right to this experience. As did Star, who seemed to delight in weaving in and out of all the wriggly little bodies, feeding on their excitement. It never failed to amaze Sarah how the animal tempered her actions to suit whoever was in the water with her. Her style of play when interacting with an adult male was completely different from the way she responded to children. She was far more gentle with them, as if she sensed their vulnerability.

Sarah was lost in a daydream when the level of childish screams reached a new height. Something had happened. Maia was tugging urgently at her arm. Sarah looked down – her daughter's eyes were huge and she was flapping her hands like mad.

'Aid,' she said.

'What did you say, Maia?' She had to be sure.

'Aid.'

She was sure. This was Maia's name for Aidan.

Sarah's blood stopped moving around her body. Was he here? She looked in the direction of the commotion and saw Aidan's dog, Rufus, in the water, mingling with the children, his head slick and black, panting. Sarah's head turned automatically towards shore. But it was only Tommy, standing with his hands in his pockets. He took one out and waved at Sarah. She waved back. But where she had expected relief, there was only disappointment.

She returned her attention to the water, where she saw something she'd only heard about before. The dog and the dolphin were swimming and playing together. Every so often, Rufus would be caught up on a wave and yelp, but he showed no inclination to stop until Tommy whistled and he paddled back to shore. Once on dry land, he gave himself a massive shake, drenching a group of little girls who were standing close by, causing them to scream. Then he trotted after Tommy, who waved once more at Sarah before disappearing.

Sarah felt deflated, all the energy gone out of her. She hadn't seen Aidan since that horrible day at her house. He'd doubtless been avoiding her, staying away from places he thought she'd be. She'd been keeping a low profile too. She allowed herself to think about him now. Her thoughts weren't good.

It was the following Saturday and Sarah felt gloomy. She didn't know why. She had been looking forward to this morning since she had booked Bridget mid-week. She should have been celebrating her increasing sense of freedom. That had been the plan. The miracle that was Maia's transformation had continued and now she was willing to go just about anywhere with Bridget. The first time Sarah had left her daughter at Bridget's house, she had walked down the garden path in dread, sure that she would be returning to collect her within minutes because the child had freaked out. But it had gone just fine. Bridget knew exactly how to handle Maia. So, this morning had been about treating herself to some long overdue self-indulgence. She was going to go for brunch, browse in the boutiques, get a manicure. She was going to be Sarah Dillon, woman in her own right, instead of Sarah Dillon, mother of an autistic child.

Was the end of her love affair the only reason for her unhappiness? She hadn't been feeling all that great lately – maybe that was part of it too. A strange, bloated feeling in her belly, as if she'd eaten something a little off. Or maybe she was coming down with a bug. Of course, it might be that she was missing work, the Dublin theatre scene. She had been a bit antsy of late so maybe it was time to get back to her real life. But to leave Star behind, to take Maia away now . . .

Whatever it was about today, even the brilliant sunlight couldn't penetrate her gloom. She decided a decent coffee would sort her out. She pushed open the door and went into the Melting Pot, the best café in town. It took her eyes a few seconds to adjust to the darkness inside. Then her heart did a double back flip and she wondered if she could make it out of there before she was seen.

Aidan, who was facing the door, was staring right at her. They locked eyes. His expression was unbearable to her, not because it held recrimination but because it was so completely and utterly sad. And she knew that she was the cause of it. It wasn't too late. She could still walk right out. He'd understand. He'd probably thank her for it.

'Sarah!' But now Fiona had seen her too and she was waving at her, looking at her expectantly, waiting for her to come over.

Feeling as if she was walking in slow motion Sarah put one foot in front of the other towards their table. Her heart was like a clock ticking in her ears.

'Sarah. You remember Alannah, don't you?'

'I do. Nice to see you again, Alannah.'

The girl smiled broadly at her. Aidan's smile.

'And you know Tommy, of course.'

'Yes. Hi, Tommy.' She was amazed at how normal her voice sounded. That it hadn't come out as a croak.

Tommy gave her an adolescent nod before casting his eyes downward again, his surf-dude hair flopping over his eyes and hiding the worst of his acne, as it was designed to do.

'Why don't you join us? We've only just ordered.'

'Oh.' This was like a nightmare she couldn't wake up from. She thought fast. 'I only came in for a takeaway. I have to get back to Maia.'

'That's a shame. How is she?'

'Good. Doing very well, thank you.'

'Any new words?'

'A few.'

'You must give me the name of that speech therapist. She's obviously worked wonders. I have a few patients I wouldn't mind referring to her.'

Her name is Star.

'I'll do that, Fiona. Anyway. Lovely seeing you all again. I'd better head. 'Bye.'

''Bye, Sarah. Don't be a stranger.'

Sarah turned her back on Aidan's family and walked over to the counter. The girl took her order immediately. It still wasn't quick enough. She could feel Aidan's eyes boring into her back, like a pair of blue-green lasers, just as they hadn't left her face the whole time she was at the table. Aidan and his family. Tears tickled the backs of her eyes. Thankfully, the girl was quick. As she placed her order in the paper bag, Sarah picked out Fiona's voice. She was whispering – or, at least, Fiona thought she was: 'Honestly, Aidan. You didn't say a single word to Sarah. Even Tommy's better than you and he's a teenager. The woman must think you don't like her.'

Sarah bolted and raced down the street. She had practically come out in a sweat.

'Sarah!'

Christ! It was Fiona. Why was she following her?

Sarah stopped in her tracks and turned slowly, hoping she didn't look as terrified as she felt. Fiona seemed oblivious, though, as she came to a halt, heaving for breath. 'You're some mover, you know that? I thought I was going to lose you.'

Sarah wondered what on earth was so urgent she'd had to run after her.

'You forgot this,' said Fiona, handing her a small leather wallet.

'Oh,' said Sarah, and relief flooded through her. She smiled at Fiona. 'Thank you. I'll forget my head one of these days. If you hear rumours of a headless woman walking around the town, you'll know who it is.'

'Actually, I'm glad I got you on your own. There's something I've been wanting to say to you for a very long time.'

Sarah's interior froze again, but she hoped she was maintaining a veneer of normality.

'That day in your house – you know, when Aidan called in for me.'

Sarah nodded.

'You were so kind, letting me go on like that.'

This was excruciating.

'I know we only met each other a short time ago, but I just thought, I don't know, that you'd be a good person to talk to. I mean, my friends around here, they all know Aidan too. Some of them have known him longer than they've known me. It just didn't seem appropriate to go to them. Whereas you – you barely know him. And I suppose I was looking for a fresh perspective. Someone neutral.'

Sarah felt incapable of making a sound.

'The funny thing is, that day was a turning point for me and Aidan. I don't know what shifted, but something did. And ever since then things have been getting back on track. Slowly but surely, as they say. Maybe I'd been keeping things pent up for so long that letting them out made me more relaxed so things got better at home. I feel like – somehow – it's partly, indirectly, down to you. I wanted to say thank you.'

'You don't have to –'

'Yes, I do. I'm sorry for bending your ear that day. And thank you for the result.' Fiona's grin faded. 'Are you all right? You look a bit – shook or something. I know it's not exactly a medical term.' She laughed.

To Sarah, Fiona seemed one hundred per cent happy. She felt a deep sense of yearning. Was it always necessary for one person's happiness to be at the expense of another's? She forced a reply. 'I'm okay. Just coming down with a bug, I think.'

'Well, you know where I am if you need a doctor.'

Yes, I know where you are. Living with Aidan. Sleeping with Aidan.

Suddenly the guilt that Sarah was accustomed to feeling around Fiona morphed into resentment. She gave the other woman a tight smile. 'Thanks for the wallet. I'd really better go.'

'Of course, I'm keeping you. Goodbye, Sarah.'

'Goodbye.'

Sarah walked away, feeling rude, unfriendly, small-minded and petty. She didn't like herself very much.

Their marriage was back on track.

That was good.

That was what she had wanted.

Chapter 25

The only time she didn't feel lonely was when she was in the sea. That had become her truth. The loneliness had sneaked up on her and taken her by surprise. She had always had so much going on in her life that she'd never been lonely. Even when Mitch had walked out, even when she'd been in the chemo ward – both times when she'd felt desperate and frightened and alone – she had never felt lonely. But now loneliness seemed almost constant. It was in her bones and the only time it seemed to lift was when she was in the water. Maybe it couldn't swim. She imagined it was her familiar, a cat that padded right up to the shoreline with her, watched her in the water, waited patiently until she was done, then resumed its position as her constant companion once she was on land.

The water was also where she was most able to ignore what was staring her in the face, the signs she was choosing to pretend weren't there. But the worry was still sneaking in through the back door, gnawing away at the furthermost reaches of her mind. The nausea. The constant desire to pee. The heartburn. And, most of all, the ongoing, debilitating tiredness, which made it so hard to cope with Maia at times and robbed her of some of the joy of watching her daughter progress. The last time she'd felt like this was almost eight years ago. Denial was the only thing that stopped her spiralling into complete panic so she was clinging to it for dear life and swimming. Swimming a lot.

As she walked along to the cove one morning she distracted herself by trying to figure out exactly what the dolphin did for people. She came to the conclusion that a large part of it was that when you were with her you forgot about everything else. You were forced into total present-moment awareness, unable to focus on anything but this incredible encounter. And in that experience you got a brief holiday from your thoughts – whatever incessant, obsessive thoughts happened to be driving you mad at that particular time. It wasn't the only thing but it was part of it. And that was the part Sarah was embracing right now as she forgot everything that had ever gone wrong in her life and entered the water – entered the present moment – with Star.

She wasn't the only one in the water that day. There were lots of people. Holidaymakers, most of them. Some had come to see the dolphin. To others she was a magical surprise. There were lots of children flapping around. Sarah estimated her chances of getting near Star today as practically zero. Star always gravitated towards the children when they were there, and that was as it should be.

Sarah drifted along on her back, some distance away from the hullabaloo. She was gifted with the sun, its beams resting gently on her face. She closed her eyes and revelled. The good thing about floating was that if you didn't relax you sank. A kind of disciplined relaxation. Which made her think again that she really should try meditation. But something always stopped her.

She was amazed at the whooshing sensation around her. Amazed because it meant that Star had come to see her when there were so many new friends to make. She lifted her head, lowered her legs and trod water. She could see Star's dorsal fin a few feet away. She was swimming towards her, slowly enough. Sarah couldn't see her but she knew she was doing that thing she did, that barely perceptible side to side movement of the head. Then the fin disappeared and Sarah waited to see where she'd resurface. It could be anywhere. But what happened still took her off guard. Star had come up beneath her and tapped her belly with her snout. Had she imagined it? She took a deep breath and put her face under the water. Star was close by, as if watching her. To Sarah's amazement, she did the same thing again, swam up to her slowly, head wagging from side to side, and gave her stomach a gentle head butt. Then she swam back towards the crowds.

Sarah watched her tail retreating. Aidan had told her about how dolphins could 'see' inside you. It was their ultrasound. Like when you had a scan. Like when you were having a baby.

Sarah bought a test on the way home because she was no longer able to escape the truth, even under water. She peed on the stick, flushed and adjusted her clothing. Then she washed her hands and picked up the stick again. Nothing was happening. She looked at her watch. Give it another minute. She did. She frowned. It was negative.

She had thought that a positive result would be the worst possible outcome. She had thought wrong. Negative was even more negative. She had time to go to the doctor before Maia came home. Instead she chose to vacuum the house from top to bottom, tidying as she went. She knew she wouldn't have the energy afterwards. And if she could at least get her house in order, it would be some defence against the chaos that was threatening beneath. She wouldn't be overwhelmed. She refused to be. She looked at her watch again. Too late to go to the doctor's now. She'd have to leave it. Maia would be home soon and that was more important. That was her priority.

That night she lay awake, staring unseeingly into the darkness, her two hands clamped against her belly, holding down the rising tide of panic. This proved a full-time job. She couldn't let go for one single solitary second or it would all come flooding through and she would drown.

In the morning she was still holding on. Just about. She knew she had to go to the doctor. But not Fiona. God, no. She'd go to the other woman doctor in the surgery. What was her name? It didn't matter. She'd find out when she got there. She watched Maia nibble the cereal on her spoon. She didn't have the heart or the stomach to eat anything herself. She got them both ready and left the house.

The morning was cold. At least, it seemed so to Sarah, whose bones felt so exposed and vulnerable to every stray breeze. Maia tiptoed along beside her. The surgery was quiet, just one old woman and herself: it seemed that most of the bugs had left town for the summer. She and the old woman were the same. Sarah felt that instinctively. The woman stared into space, as if unaware of or uninterested in their presence. She was in another realm, past caring. Sarah knew how that felt.

She spoke to the receptionist – Betty or Beth, something beginning with B. Could she see the doctor who wasn't Fiona? She didn't put it like that. No, she couldn't. It was Fiona who was on duty today. Sarah nodded vaguely, easily defeated, and sat down again. The old woman went in. Sarah sat there. Maia played with her piece of string. The old woman came out. Sarah was called. Maia played with the string. It was all part of a dream. Fiona was part of the dream. Her words couldn't break through.

'What can I do for you today?'

Sarah felt her own words, buzzing outside her head.

'Pop up there on the couch.'

'Pop'. Doctors were forever wanting you to pop up onto things.

Fiona palpated her belly. Sarah stared at the hairline cracks in the ceiling. Then at the frown lines on Fiona's forehead as her hands travelled back over Sarah's belly, feeling again, kneading again. Sarah was a piece of dough. Ready to be rolled out.

'You can get up now.'

Sarah sat on the edge of the couch, her legs dangling childishly. Her head had righted itself but her thoughts stayed jumbled. She looked at Fiona.

Fiona's worried, she thought dispassionately. *Poor Fiona.*

'I can feel a mass in your abdomen. You need to get it checked out right away.'

A mass. Sarah thought of a priest at an altar. Lifting up his hands as he preached to a congregation of tiny people in her stomach.

'There are tests I could do, but it's much better if you go directly to a gynaecologist. I'm going to give you a referral letter.' Fiona was writing furiously on a piece of notepaper. She stopped as abruptly as she'd started. 'Fuck it. I'll ring her.'

Sarah slipped silently off the couch and into her chair like a blob. Maia was under the couch, fascinated by its workings. Fiona dialled, her legs coiled around themselves, her jaw tense.

'Dr Patel's secretary, please.' She looked at Sarah and smiled tightly. 'Oh, hello, Fiona McDaid here. I'd like an immediate appointment, please, for one of my patients.'

Sarah registered the garbled sounds at the other end.

'Yes, it is.' Fiona sounded so reassuring. No wonder Aidan had married her.

'Oh, yes. That would be wonderful, thank you.' Fiona put down the phone, wrote something and handed it to Sarah. 'She'll see you tomorrow morning.'

Another night like last night. Sarah folded the paper without looking at it and put it into her wallet, like a receipt.

'She's excellent, this woman. One of the best.'

Sarah failed to do her part to fill the silence.

'It could be nothing,' said Fiona.

Sarah got up. She had told lies to Fiona. It was only fitting that Fiona should now tell lies to her.

They walked home slowly along the pier. They came to the bollard where she'd first met Aidan. Sarah sat down and watched the midday sun. She stared directly into it. Inadvisedly. As if she didn't need her eyes any more. Then she watched Maia playing on the sand. Round and round her daughter spun, her arms outstretched, her face tilted skyward. The sun spinning around on her axis. Sarah wanted to join her, wanted to be her. Wanted to be anyone but herself. To shed her skin. Shed her body. Maybe she was about to.

Stage four. Was that better or worse than stage one? It was the same with third-degree burns. She could never remember if they were better or worse than first degree. These were the irrelevancies that were crowding her mind, crowding out the thought that she was going to have to think. There was no mistaking, however, the look on the consultant's face.

'I'm so sorry. I'm sure the tests will confirm my diagnosis.'

How many times a week did she have to say that? Extend her sympathy, part professional, part human. That was what she'd do. She'd focus on the other woman for a while. How difficult for her to have to impart such dreadful news.

Sarah found she was developing goose pimples all over her skin. Her peripheral vision seemed to have vanished and only a tunnel remained. She felt it was good that she was sitting down. The consultant sat down beside her. Put a white, sterile arm about her shoulder. She'd been so busy concentrating on her breast that she'd forgotten all about her ovaries. Had never given them a second thought.

Presumed they were just sitting there doing what ovaries did best. Not rotting themselves and her other organs.

'Is there someone I can call for you?'

Sarah shook her head, then said, 'No. A taxi.'

The woman nodded and made the call. She had beautiful caramel skin and thick, shiny black hair in a long rope down her back.

When she'd finished, Sarah spoke, her voice sounding very far away. 'How long?'

'No time at all. There's one waiting outside.'

'No. How long?'

'Oh. Not long, Sarah. You really should have someone with you.'

'I'm all right. How long?'

'A couple of months. Probably less.'

'Okay.' She got up.

'I'll walk out with you.'

'There's no need.'

'I don't think you should be on your own.'

'I'm used to it.'

Sarah walked out of the office on unknown legs, following the signs to the exit. The consultant shadowed her at a discreet distance. After watching her get into the taxi and being driven away, she went back to her office and rang Fiona McDaid.

Chapter 26

Aidan's mobile rang as he was getting out of the shower. He'd just been for a swim and he was feeling fine. The phone slipped out of his hand on its third ring. It skidded across the tiles. He chased and retrieved, feeling like Rufus. 'Hello.'

'Aidan, love, it's me.'

'Fi.'

'I need you to do something for me.'

'What's wrong? You sound funny.'

'Oh, Aidan, I've just heard the most terrible news.'

'What?'

'It's Sarah Dillon.'

His blood stopped flowing, just for a second. 'What about her?'

'She's got stage-four ovarian cancer.'

The seconds ticked by.

'Is that . . .'

'Terminal. Yes. She has only months to live. Weeks, maybe. Poor Sarah. Did she ever speak to you about her family?' She paused. 'Aidan!'

'Sorry. She has a sister in the States.'

'Right. That's not much good to us. Look, I need you to go directly to her house. She's on her way back in a taxi as we speak. Just be there when she gets home, won't you? If she sends you away, so be it. But just so she has someone. I'd go myself but I've got back-to-back patients for the rest of the day. I'll call in later. Are you still there?'

'Yes.'

'You'll do it, then?'

'Yes.'

'Thanks, love. I'll call you in a while. See how you got on.'

Aidan moved around the bedroom like a man in a trance. He got dressed. Then he packed a small bag. He knew he wouldn't be coming back.

The taxi man kept staring at her. Was it because he recognized her or because she looked as strange as she felt? She didn't think she was crying. She touched her cheeks to make sure. No. Completely dry. Maybe she was talking to herself. She kept saying the same words over and over in her head. She might have said them aloud without realizing. I'm dying. I'm dying. Did it make it any more real?

'I'm dying.' This time she did say it out loud, as a kind of experiment. The man's eyes widened in alarm and snapped away from hers. She laughed, ever so slightly. Then she stopped. She looked out of the window. Everything seemed different. Even the sky had a surreal orange tinge. A sense of foreboding was everywhere, lurking behind every tree, every crowd, behind every smile. Her body began to shake. Oh, God. An incredible fear overcame her. There was nowhere to hide. No escape. Then the feeling went away. Because the thought was impossible to comprehend. At least she wouldn't need chemo. She laughed at her own black humour. Wouldn't need it because there wasn't any point.

The taxi-driver was asking for directions now. She told him where to go as if she was normal – as if everything was the same as it had been when she had left the house that morning. Suddenly they were outside her home and there was Aidan. What was he doing? He shouldn't be there. He was paying the taxi man, talking to him, opening her door, unstrapping her seatbelt, holding out his hand to her. She wasn't surprised to see him. Although he shouldn't be there. It was like being in a dream. You were living in a house, except it wasn't your house. You were living with a man, except he wasn't your husband. Somehow he had her key and he was opening her door. He had his other arm around her waist and she kind of fell against him. He half carried her over the threshold and into the sitting room where he deposited her on the couch. Sarah automatically curled her legs up beneath her. Aidan crouched in front of her, his eyes level with hers, his hands on either side of her legs. 'What do you need?' he said.

'Whiskey.'

'Whiskey. Right.' He got up decisively and began to search the house for a bottle. Sarah wanted to call out and tell him it was in the press above the fridge, but she couldn't find her voice. He discovered it in due course and brought her a shot in a wholly unsuitable glass. He handed it to her and sat beside her on the floor. 'Get that down you, girl.' He rubbed her calf as she drank. 'Is Maia with Bridget?'

She nodded.

When she'd finished the whiskey, he took the glass from her and stood it on a side table. Then he got up on the couch and wrapped his arms around her as tight as they would go.

Sarah slept for a good two hours. Even the doorbell didn't wake her. Aidan gently disentangled his limbs from hers and got up to answer it, straightening out the kinks in his body as he went. It was Bridget and Maia. Bridget turned her surprise into a tactful smile. Maia, who hadn't seen him in a good month, walked right past him as if he were a constant feature in the house.

'Look, Bridget . . .' he started. He kept his voice quiet. He knew her, of course, had done since she was a kid. Just like he knew everyone in this town. 'Sarah got some bad news today.'

'Oh?'

'So she might need you to mind Maia more than usual over the next few weeks. How are you fixed?'

'Yeah. That should be all right. Is there anything I can do?

Bridget craned her neck past him into the hall, as if trying to garner a clue.

'We're grand for now, thanks. I'll be in touch.'

He closed the door on her surprised face. She was doubtless wondering what it had to do with him.

Back inside, he found Maia attempting to wake her mother, shaking her by the shoulder. He watched Sarah come to, the glazed expression overtaken by the automatic delight at seeing her daughter. Maia was clutching something in her hand. She thrust it at Sarah. It was a single buttercup.

'Fower, Mama.'

Sarah sat forward. 'Did you just call me "Mama"?'

'Mama.'

'Oh, good girl, good girl.' She laughed and tried to hug her, but Maia stood rigid. And that was when the first tears fell.

Aidan rocked Sarah well into the evening. It must be evening by now, he thought. He couldn't see the clock from where he was lying and he didn't want to move for fear of disturbing her. But the time was getting closer. Several messages had beeped onto his phone. He hadn't got up to check them. Eventually Sarah went to lie down on her bed for a while. Aidan sat downstairs staring into space.

The bell rang. Aidan got up to answer the door. His wife stood in front of him. 'So you *are* still here. The boys said you hadn't taken the boat out. Is she in a bad way?'

'Not at the minute. She's upstairs resting.'

Fiona bustled past him and straight into Sarah's sitting room. 'Why don't you go home and get yourself some dinner?

There's a lasagne in the freezer. I'll take over here.' She was unbuttoning her jacket as he followed her in.

'No. I'm staying.'

'It's very good of you, Aidan, but there's really no need. She could probably do with a woman to talk to. And she might have some medical questions. Did she ring her sister yet?'

'She hasn't, no.'

'Did you ring her?'

'No, I –'

'Well, she's going to need someone looking after her.'

'She will have someone.'

'Who?'

'Me.'

'You?' Fiona stared up at him, not taking it in.

'I'm really sorry, Fiona.'

'For what? What are you talking about?'

'I'm going to stay here and look after Sarah. Move in.'

'But that's ridiculous. Sure, we hardly know her.'

Aidan looked down at his feet. Though he had known he'd be having this conversation with Fiona ever since he had taken her call, he had not prepared for it. All he could think about was Sarah. And in all the times he had thought about leaving Fiona when he and Sarah were together, he had never imagined how he would tell his wife. He was burning up with shame.

The downward look was all it took. He could sense Fiona becoming dangerously still.

'Have you been having a . . . Is there something going on?'

He raised his head and looked her in the eyes. The time for subterfuge was over. 'Not lately. But there was in the past.'

'Oh, my God.' Fiona fell into a chair, covered her face with her hands, bent over at the waist and started rocking. 'I can't believe this. I can't believe this is happening. Oh, God, oh, God, oh, God.'

'Fi, I'm . . .' He reached out to touch her arm but she swiped his hand away.

'Don't touch me.'

Aidan put it back into his pocket and stood there meekly, allowing his wife's wrath to find its voice, knowing he would deserve everything that was coming to him.

She stopped rocking, stood up, walked behind the chair and gripped the back, as if to create a barrier between herself and her husband. 'And to think I sent you over here today. What kind of fucking fool does that make me?'

'You're not –'

'Shut up.'

'I don't –'

'I said shut up,' she growled, and in the silence that followed, they regarded each other in mutual horror.

'I can't believe this,' she said, and began pacing in circles. 'All those times. All that time you were acting so strangely. That was it, wasn't it? You were seeing her.' She stopped to look at him and he nodded. She paced some more and then stopped in front of him. 'You're really staying?' Her voice was soft now.

'Yes.'

'I won't even have the satisfaction of kicking you out.'

'I'll collect the rest of my stuff tomorrow.'

'The rest of your stuff. You mean you already have some things with you?'

He nodded again.

'Do you have any idea what you're doing?'

He didn't say a word.

'You're willing to throw away everything we have for a woman who's going to be dead in a couple of months?'

'I love her.' His words were quiet. Firm. Shocking. He hadn't expected to say it, but now she knew.

'I thought you loved me.'

'I do, Fi. But this is different.'

'What the hell is that supposed to mean?'

He hung his head.

Fiona stepped right up to him and hissed, 'Do you really think she'd look twice at the likes of you if she wasn't sick?' She walked out of the house, then faced him as she stood on the doorstep. 'You're really going to stay here?' She was incredulous.

'This is something I have to do. I can't explain it.'

She shuddered and turned on her heel.

Fiona's sandals click-clacked efficiently along the pavement, as if nothing was wrong with the rest of her. She kept expecting Aidan to follow her, for her own footsteps to be joined by those of her husband, for him to run after her and tell her it had all been a terrible mistake. A sick joke. But that didn't happen. She walked as fast as her maverick legs could carry her, relieved that she'd brought her car and didn't have to walk the whole way home, bumping into people who might want to stop for a chat on this pleasant summer's evening. It happened now.

'Lovely evening, Dr McDaid.'

She set her face in smile mode and quickened her pace as her patient slowed down, probably preparing for a speech about her bunions. It was all she could do to stop herself breaking into a run. Just one more corner and her car would be in sight. She rifled in her bag for her keys, praying she wouldn't meet anyone else, her entire being focused on getting to her car. Made it. Her Renault was now in sight. She was close enough to click the locks open.

'Fiona!'

Somebody called her name from across the square. She raised a hand in salute, without turning to see who it was. She all but lunged at her car and bundled herself into the driver's seat, her mask slipping rapidly. She couldn't let it go just yet – she was still in public and it was broad daylight. This should be happening on a dark November night. The person, whoever it was she had snubbed, would get over it. They'd soon find out the reason for her odd behaviour anyway. Soon the whole town would know.

Fiona reversed the car in a dangerous arc, blessed that no one was behind her, and sped off in the direction of home. Her breathing became ragged now. She forced herself to slow it down, the doctor in her overtaking the patient. It was good in a way to have something to focus on, something as fundamental as her breath. It stopped her thinking. There were two sets of traffic-lights between where she was and where she wanted to be – her own front door – and both were red. She drummed her fingers on the steering-wheel. 'Come on, come on.'

There was one car in front, between her and the lights. They turned green. The other car failed to react straight away.

'Come on!' she screamed, a whisker away from blasting the other driver out of it with her horn. Not a good idea. A neighbour.

The car moved off and she trailed its snail's pace. Until home. *Oh, thank God.* She could feel this terrible thing building up inside her and soon it would be impossible to contain. Tommy was out, staying at a friend's house. Thank God. Thank God. Thank God. She repeated this as she walked up to the front door. She opened it. Closed it behind her. Leaned her back against it. And screamed until there was no breath left in her body. There was nobody to hear her, only Rufus, who pricked up his ears and wondered when Aidan would be back to take him out for his walk.

Chapter 27

It was the middle of the night. Aidan woke up and didn't know where he was. He'd been having a dream. The sea levels were rising. He was with Fiona and the kids, except the kids were still small. They were all going to drown. He remembered where he was and sat up in the dark. He groped around on the bedside table and found a glass of water. He took a couple of deep gulps as his eyes adjusted to the darkness. The first thing he noticed was the lack of rhythmic breathing. Then he saw that one half of the bed was empty. As his eyes adjusted further, he discerned a dark shape at the window. Sarah was seated on the windowsill, partially obscured by the curtains. Aidan positioned himself on the edge of the bed closest to her. He was still fully clothed. He felt like shit. But that was irrelevant. He wanted to say something. How are you? How are you doing? Something like that. But the words seemed hopelessly inappropriate and inadequate. Instead, he stood up briefly, stroked the side of her arm and sat down again.

Sarah didn't move. She didn't speak either. Not for a long while. Then she said: 'What are you doing here, Aidan?'

He looked through the darkness at her. Unsure. Trying to make out her features. 'Just being here with you.'

'I know that. But why aren't you at home?'

'Because you need me more.'

'What did you tell Fiona?'

'That I'll be staying here.'

'As my nurse?'

'No, as your . . .' He trailed off. And for the first time it occurred to him that she might not want him.

'Did you tell her about us?'

'Yes.'

'Oh, Aidan.'

He couldn't see, but he had the impression that she'd covered her face with her hands. 'What's wrong?'

'What do you mean, "what's wrong"? You know what's wrong. You've only gone and ruined your life.'

'I don't see it that way.'

'Well, you should.'

They were quiet for a while. Sarah seemed numb. He grasped for the right words. 'You need me.' It was the best he could come up with.

'So does your wife.'

'Not as much as you do.'

'I'm going to be fine.'

'But, Sarah . . .'

'I'm going to get a second opinion and I'm going to continue taking my supplements and I'm going to completely change my diet. Nothing but organic fruit and vegetables from now on.'

Aidan didn't reply – he couldn't. He was struck dumb by the unexpected level of her denial. Was it possible? Hadn't Fiona said . . .? 'But stage four. That's . . .'

'Oh, my God. You think I'm going to die, don't you?' And with that she burst into a fit of loud and uncontrollable sobs.

Aidan lifted her off the windowsill and onto the bed beside him. The moon was still behind the darkest cloud. He couldn't see her face properly, not even at this close proximity. Her sobs stopped as abruptly as they had started. She was sniffing loudly and wiping her cheeks with her hands. 'Miracles happen all the time, you know.'

'I know.'

'You hear about these things, don't you?'

'You do.'

She leaned heavily against him and he sensed her relax. 'I'm glad you're here,' she said.

'Me too.'

Tommy had found his mother in the kitchen. The scene was unprecedented: the upper half of her body was sprawled across the table, her face obscured by her hair, her arms lying loose above her head. And a bottle of vodka standing upright. One third full. No glass. Tommy felt the hairs do something strange at the back of his neck.

'Mam.' He shook her shoulder gently. Fiona started and mumbled something incoherent. Then she kind of rolled herself up and blinked blearily. Tommy watched in horror as she wiped the drool from the side of her mouth, and saw her own horror as she registered what she was doing. She sat upright and looked around. Her face was all creased and the light was clearly hurting her eyes. 'What's wrong, Mam?'

Fiona rubbed her face.

'Has something happened?'

'Ask your father.' She scraped back the chair and plodded out of the room.

Tommy knew his father wasn't there. His car was missing from the driveway and, besides, he could feel his absence in the house. He picked up the phone and dialled Aidan's mobile number. Probably switched off. Nothing new there. Aidan hated mobiles and had to be forced to carry one. Where would he be at this hour of the morning? It was barely eight. Maybe down on the beach. But that wouldn't explain the missing car.

Tommy heard the shower being switched on upstairs. God knew, she could do with one. He would have thought he'd be delighted to catch his mother in such a condition – she was always going on at him about the dangers of alcohol. But the reality was something different altogether. Scary. He felt as if his whole world had shifted on its axis. He tried his father's phone again.

Aidan stretched out his body as best he could. He seemed to have kinks and cricks in every joint. He had slept fitfully and awkwardly, cradling Sarah. He thought longingly of the bathroom at home. Sarah had only a crude shower attachment in hers.

His thoughts turning to other matters, he rooted around in his pocket for his phone and switched it on. His jacket was draped over the back of the chair, covering Sarah's discarded clothes. One missed call. Home. He felt a twisting sensation in his gut. He put the phone back into his pocket. Sarah was still asleep. Still in the foetal position that his contorted arm had been trying to support. She'd been sleeping a lot since her visit to the consultant. Her body's reaction to the shock, Aidan thought. Maybe she just didn't want to be awake. He lowered himself back down and turned over to look at her. She was wearing a blue and green oversized checked shirt. Possibly the long-lost property of a long-lost boyfriend. He felt a ridiculous pang of jealousy. It wasn't as if she was likely to leave him for somebody else. He, Aidan Ryan, would be the last man in her life. She had saved the last dance for him. The last dance by default.

It was twenty-four hours – less – since the universe had turned itself inside out. Since the impossible had become possible and the unthinkable thinkable. But not sayable. Not yet. Not out loud. His phone rang. He looked anxiously for a few seconds at his vibrating pocket before fishing it out. Home. Wherever that was. He braced himself before pressing the green button. Fiona deserved an answer. Not to mention the opportunity to abuse him.

'Hello.'

'Dad, where are you?'

Tommy. His stomach back-flipped. This was even worse. 'Tom. How are you doing? I just stayed overnight at a friend's house.'

'I thought that might be it.' His voice sounded relieved. 'Too much to drink?'

'Something like that.'

'You're not the only one. Mam's had a skinful. She's in a right state.' Tommy paused, clearly waiting for a reaction. He didn't get one. 'Has something happened?' And his tone was worried once more.

'Look, Tom, something *has* happened. I can't talk about it over the phone. I need to meet up with you this morning.'

'What is it?'

'You need to give me about an hour.' He glanced at Sarah's sleeping form, thought about Maia in the next room. 'Meet me on the beach. At our spot.'

'Dad, you're freaking me out.'

'Don't worry, Tom. It's going to be all right. Your mother, is she in a very bad way?'

'Well, she's hung-over. Although she could still be rat-arsed. She's after getting through almost an entire bottle of vodka. Mam never drinks that, sure she doesn't.'

She didn't. Then again, it wasn't every day she heard that her husband was leaving her for a dying woman.

In an effort to bring some sense of normality to the situation, Tommy turned on the radio. A familiar programme, familiar voices. Then he opened the fridge door and did his customary ten-second stare. Eggs, he thought. Scrambled eggs. Everything would seem more normal after breakfast.

After a mammoth feed, Tommy went upstairs nervously. His parents' bedroom door was closed. He was tempted to bypass it, go straight to his room, grab his wetsuit and his board, catch some waves before he met his dad. But some innate decency propelled him forward. He rapped gingerly on the door. 'Mam.'

No reply. He knocked louder. Called out louder: 'Mam.'

Still nothing. Feeling slightly panicked, he edged the door ever so slightly open. He could see his mother. She was sitting on the floor, facing him, propped up against the bed. She seemed hardly to notice him. She was wearing her dressing-gown and staring directly ahead.

'Mam.'

He entered the room. Not knowing what else to do – this kind of thing falling right outside his usual remit – he sat on the floor beside her, folding his long body into a more manageable size, extending one leg outward, clasping his other knee with both hands. It was weird, being bigger than your own mother, though the fact remained that this compact little woman still had infinite power over him. He glanced anxiously at the side of her face. She was horribly pale and her features were kind of pinched. As if everything had shrunk and fallen in on itself. He realized with some consternation that she'd been crying. Mam never cried.

'Are you sick, Mam?'

'*I*'m not sick, no.'

'What is it, then?'

She turned to him. 'You haven't spoken to your father, then?'

Why did she keep saying 'your father'? What was wrong with 'Dad'?

'I have. Just for a minute on the phone. He wouldn't tell me what was wrong either. I'm meeting him in a while.'

She looked straight ahead again and paused for a few seconds before speaking. 'He's left me, Tom.'

The words reverberated meaninglessly in Tommy's head. What did she mean, left her? He was only staying with a friend. 'What do you mean?'

'I mean he's left me. Our marriage. Our home.'

'But . . . left? Where? Where's he gone?'

'He's moved in with Sarah Dillon.'

Sarah Dillon? The actress? The words now felt as if they were in his chest – his hollow chest – knocking around inside. 'I don't believe it. Why would he do that? Sarah Dillon? It doesn't make any sense.'

'He says he loves her.'

Tommy thought he was going to be sick. This was way too adult for him. Too real. Then, compounding everything, his mother started to cry. His mother! Right in front of him. He had an overwhelming urge to run out of the room, but his limbs failed to respond. It was as if he was frozen by the horror of it all. His mother seemed embarrassed to be crying in front of him too. She hid her face in her hand and the noises she made were stifled. They weren't full-blown sobs, although Tommy felt they would have been had he not been there. Feeling himself in completely unknown territory, he placed a hand tentatively on his mother's shoulder. Judging by the way she instantly leaned against him, he'd done the right thing. Her crying intensified, though. That wasn't good.

They sat like that for quite a long time, Fiona and Tommy, mother and son, their roles reversed for the very first time. Never before had Tommy had to look after her. A small part of him rose to the occasion and became an adult that day. The rest of him remained downright terrified. Who was going to look after him now? Who was left to turn to? He spoke gently, once his mother's sobs had subsided: 'Can I get you anything?' It was what one said in such situations.

She sniffed and shook her head.

'Cup of tea?'

'I don't think I could keep it down. Oh. There is something. I need you to ring the surgery and tell them I won't be in. Tell them I'm sick and that they'll have to arrange cover for the next few days.'

'Okay. Anything else?'

'No. That's it.'

She was rooting around in her pocket and wiping her nose. She seemed to be recovering herself. Thank God. Tommy slowly extricated himself and unfolded his body. He stood uncertainly for a few seconds before leaving the room, then descended the stairs like an automaton and went back into the kitchen. He called the surgery and told his lies. Then, the numbness pervading his body more completely by the second, he left the house via the back door. Rufus scrambled excitedly to his feet when he saw where Tommy was going and pushed past his legs to ensure he didn't get left behind. He went tearing off down the deck, Tommy stumbling behind him like a man let out of solitary confinement. He took in deep draughts of air, realizing how stifled he had felt inside the house. How the very atmosphere in his home seemed suddenly poisoned.

Tommy was on the beach now. He found his spot and sat down heavily on the sand. A fine drizzle had set in and there was no one in the water. Some of the breakers were magnificent. What a waste. No one to ride them. Rufus ran ahead of him in a zigzag pattern, following his nose, looking up expectantly every so often, wondering why Tommy was just sitting there. Not walking, not running, not throwing, not swimming. But Tommy didn't have the energy to do anything except sit. Sit there and wait for his dad.

Chapter 28

Aidan left the cottage quietly. All was calm within. Sarah and Maia were up and breakfasted, proceeding with the morning as if nothing untoward had happened. The streets were quiet too. He came across a couple of people he knew. They nodded at him. 'Morning, Aidan.' Nobody knew yet. Too soon. He'd get a day's grace. Two at the most.

The sand swirled under him as the wind picked up. He quickened his pace, head bowed, hands in his pockets. He had to get to his son.

He saw his boy from a distance, as a dark dot huddled on the sand. A smaller dot ran hither and thither in front of him. Rufus. The dog noticed him first. He lifted his head and caught his master's scent on the breeze. Then he pricked up his ears and stiffened his body as Aidan came into his view. He bombed down the beach to greet him, as if someone had fired him from a cannon. Aidan saw Tommy's head turn and knew he had been spotted.

He was close now. Close enough to see his son's features. He tried to analyse them. Too late. He was there and Tommy was on his feet. He noticed that his son kept his distance and knew immediately that Fiona had told him. Tommy's face was uncertain, many emotions battling for precedence.

'Has your mother –'

'She says you've left her for Sarah Dillon.'

His son's words shocked Aidan into silence. Was that really what he'd done?

'Is it true?' Tommy's voice contained a tremor.

'Yes.'

This was apparently the confirmation that Tommy had been waiting for. Aidan looked on in horror as his son's features contorted in disgust, then rage. He was unprepared for what happened next. Tommy emitted a strange, anguished howl, launched himself at his father and knocked him to the ground. Aidan lay flat on his back on the sand, pinned down and winded, as the blows rained down on him. He shielded his face with his arms and attempted to catch Tommy's hands with his own. The boy was too strong for him. Too quick. The whole experience was both surreal and awful, his little boy trying to inflict damage on him, attempting to match the pain that Aidan himself had caused. It was like some sick enactment of the wrestling games they used to play when Tommy was a kid. But now his strength was that of a man and it was fuelled by fury. Aidan finally succeeded in pushing Tommy off him. Now he had *him* pinned to the ground. He looked down directly into his son's eyes. What he saw there was horrible.

'You bastard!' Tommy screamed up at him.

Aidan let him go and the two staggered to their feet. Aidan tried to recover himself, bent over with his hands resting on his knees, his breath uneven. Tommy's rage was still out of control. It was as if, Aidan thought, his son was possessed.

'You fucking bastard!' Tommy yelled.

His son never swore at him, but Aidan was hardly in a position to admonish him now. 'Tom,' he said, with some effort, 'I'm sorry.'

'You fucking shit!' The words were spat, screamed out.

'Sarah's sick, Tom.'

'What's that got to do with us?'

'She's dying.'

This seemed to register on some level, and uncertainty clouded Tommy's eyes as he took it in.

'She only has a couple of months to live.'

'So you've destroyed our family for the sake of a couple of months? For someone who's not even going to be here?'

'I haven't destroyed –'

'I trusted you.'

The words sliced through the wind, through Aidan's heart, coating everything with their sickening residue. 'I'm sorry, son. Really sorry.'

'Stop saying that. Just come back.' He started to cry.

'I can't.'

'Why not?'

'It's too late. It's done. And Sarah needs me.'

'Fuck Sarah. We need you. We're your family. Not her. Why can't her own family take care of her?'

'It's not that simple.'

'Yes, it is. Mam's in bits. Come and see what you've done to her.'

Aidan felt a lump in his throat as his son cried with abandon. He'd done this to him. To them all. 'I don't expect you to understand, Tommy. It's just something I have to do.'

'Bullshit. You have to be with us. *We're* your family.'

'I haven't left *you*, Tom. Or your sister. I'm still here for you.'

'You just keep telling yourself that, Dad.' Tommy began to walk away.

'Stay, Tom. Please.'

'Just keep away from me. Keep away from all of us. We don't need you any more.'

The words stung, as they were meant to. Aidan could see Tommy regaining his composure as he strode along, his rage dissipating as he wiped his face with his sleeve. He wanted to shout out to him, tell him to look after his mother, but he didn't dare.

Rufus looked up at him, his head cocked, his tongue lolling, hoping for an extension of this abortive walk.

'Home,' said Aidan.

Rufus's ears rose a notch, while the rest of him remained stationary.

'Go on,' Aidan hissed, his tone urgent. 'Go with Tommy. Home.'

Still the animal stood stock still, his body poised.

'Go,' Aidan roared.

The dog skedaddled after Tommy, giving Aidan one backward, baleful glance as he left. He'd never had to choose before.

Aidan watched his son walk away from him. It was the worst sight he had ever seen.

Aidan let himself back into the cottage with Sarah's key. He'd have to get another cut. But not yet. He followed the voices into the kitchen. Sarah and Maia were sitting together at the table, heads bowed over a drawing that Maia was doing. Another dolphin, no doubt. The walls of the cottage were already plastered with dolphin pictures. Some were stuck to the fridge. Others, the ones Sarah considered the best, were framed and hung. But they were all bloody good. Star in every possible position, at every conceivable angle. Sarah looked up as he entered. Her smile almost made it worth it. 'Nice walk?'

'It was grand.'

'Did you meet anyone?' She was studying him intently.

'Not a sinner.'

She visibly relaxed and turned her attention back to Maia.

Aidan left the kitchen and walked quietly up the stairs. He hesitated before entering Sarah's room and sitting on the bed. This wasn't his room. Should he even be in here? Was he invading her space? Her privacy? All that had seemed so clear, so certain, was now dissolving. He covered his face with his hands and rubbed his eyes. They felt heavy and full of grit. He saw Tommy so clearly – his anguish. Heard his voice, the hurt, the accusation. But he'd done it now. It was done. But far from over.

Back at home, in the kitchen, Tommy dialled a number. It rang three times.

'Hello.'

'Alannah.'

'That you, Tom?'

'You need to come home.'

'What do you mean, come home? Is something wrong?'

'It's Mam and Dad.'

Chapter 29

Aidan sat watching the house for some time. There was no telling who was home, if anybody. No signs of life were visible through the downstairs windows and nothing had stirred when he pulled into the driveway. He had driven, lacking the courage to walk through the streets of the town where he had been born.

He left the sanctuary of the car and went around to the back of the house. The door was unlocked as usual. Rufus clambered to his paws when he walked into the kitchen. It was the only welcome he was likely to receive. Breathing a little easier, he walked through the rooms, marvelling at their familiarity, marvelling at the fact that he didn't live there any more. He walked up the stairs, his ears like antennae, his eyes like radar, scanning for signs of life. There were none. The house was empty.

He walked into the bedroom and took a sharp breath. Husband and wife stared at each other for several interminable seconds. Fiona was still in her pyjamas. She was crumpled-looking.

'Get out.'

'Fi, I –'

'Don't call me that. Get out.'

'We should –'

'I'm not interested in anything you have to say, Aidan. Just get out of my house and don't come back. What are you doing here anyway?'

'I came to pick up a few things.'

'So you didn't even come here to talk to me. I suppose you thought I'd be in work. Bloody coward.'

'Maybe we should talk –'

'Get out!' she screamed at him.

Aidan held up his hands and backed out of the room. Fiona advanced across the floor and slammed the door in his face.

Fiona waited for the sounds: his steps on the stairs, the back door closing, the car pulling out of the driveway. Only when there was complete silence did she sink to the carpet and hold her body tight. She envied Sarah Dillon – not because she had Aidan but because, for her, the pain would soon be over.

She lay there for – she didn't know how long. There was no sun to track across the sky. And her body clock told her nothing any more. Her body seemed to be rebelling against sleep. Well, if it didn't want her to sleep, what did it want her to do? She was damned if she could see the point of all those extra hours to her day. Her days were far too difficult to get through as it was without tacking extra redundant hours to the end of them. Or the beginning of them, depending on what hour of the morning or evening it was.

Her stomach no longer required food. As she was little more than an ear, she heard the car pulling into the driveway, then the voices outside. The voices were on the deck. Now in the house. Downstairs. Now coming up the stairs. Someone opened the bedroom door. Footsteps. In front of her. Someone knelt on the floor beside her.

'Mammy.'

'Alannah,' she whispered. She half sat up and allowed her daughter to engulf her. Tommy was there too, half hugging his sister, half hugging her. The three of them clinging together for dear life.

Sarah's body also seemed to be rebelling against sleep, as if it was trying to steal some extra hours of life to make up the time she was destined to lose. It was an interesting strategy for it to take, loyal, even, although it was a battle it couldn't win. The trouble was that those extra hours inevitably fell in the middle of the night – the darkness closing in on her, her thoughts accelerating, her fears magnifying to atomic levels. Night terrors. Could it really have been only a couple of days since she saw the consultant? It felt like years.

It was then that she reached out for Aidan, his arms engulfing her in his comforting, life-affirming, all-enveloping bear-hug. The only thing that could save her from oblivion. And it was in those moments that she knew she couldn't hand him back to Fiona. That her need was far greater than the other woman's. Even though she herself was the other woman. And if that meant she was going directly to hell then so be it.

There came a morning when Sarah's mood was buoyant. The sun was out and she was happy. Aidan couldn't tell if it was forced or real. She might be trying to keep his spirits up, as he was doing for her. But he doubted it. She seemed genuine. Which was more of a concern. How long was she going to dwell in this state of denial? Aidan didn't know much about these things, but he recalled reading once about the different stages of grief. One was denial, he was sure. Although maybe that applied to loved ones left behind.

'Let's go for a swim.' She beamed at him.

His chest constricted. Going out in public. Together. She was looking at him expectantly. He couldn't disappoint her. 'Okay, then.' Had to happen some time.

They got ready – like a typical family heading out for a typical day on the beach. Picnic lunch prepared. Bucket and spade for the child. Swimsuits, sunhats, sunscreen, sunglasses. Mother and daughter completely oblivious.

Out on the pavement, they began to walk: Sarah and Maia hand in hand ahead, Aidan lagging several steps behind. He felt as if he was going to face a firing squad. Dead man walking.

The town was busy. Cars and people coming and going. He reasoned with himself that it wasn't all that unusual for him to be seen with Sarah and Maia. It had been common knowledge that he used to take them out on his boat.

They were there now, at the cove. Nothing had happened so far. Perhaps he'd been worrying unnecessarily. He scanned the beach and saw no one he recognized. Tourists. They were safe.

The day was so normal as to be surreal. The clouds were high and wispy, the water calm. Mother and daughter collected shells in daughter's bucket. Daughter emptied shells out and arranged them into rows. Aidan watched like some bare-chested guardian, his jeans rolled up, his shorts back at the house – if Fiona hadn't burned them yet or cut them to ribbons and left them out for the binmen. He hoped it had made her feel better if she had.

Star showed up, which was good. It meant that everyone was looking at her and not at them. But it wasn't just that. The presence of the dolphin seemed to raise the bar on everybody's happiness. The laughter of the children. The excitement. Who could fail to be infected by the joy?

Before long Sarah, who'd been in the water, waded out and sat down beside him.

'Is something wrong?' he asked.

'No. Why should something be wrong?'

'No reason. You usually stay in for longer, that's all.'

She shrugged and wrapped a towel around her wet legs.

'Are you cold?'

'No, Aidan. I'm fine.' Her response was terse. But she relaxed again as she watched Maia splash alongside the other children – not with them, exactly, but close enough to create the illusion of normal play.

* * *

It was mid-afternoon and their picnic lunch was long gone. Aidan worried that the temperature was dropping. 'We should go.'

'All right.' Sarah seemed lost in her own private dreamworld. 'As soon as Maia's finished in the water.'

'Okay.'

She came back to his reality. 'You know what I'd love?'

'What?'

'A mug of coffee and a sticky bun.'

He smiled. 'We don't have much food in.'

'No, I meant in a café.'

'Oh.'

'That lovely little place on the harbour. You know the one.'

'The Melting Pot.'

'That's it!'

It was Fiona's favourite too.

'We'll go there.'

Aidan said nothing. If she sensed his apprehension, she didn't let on. It wasn't like her to be insensitive, obtuse, but he could hardly expect her to be her usual self. And he felt ill-equipped to deny her anything right now.

Maia finally emerged and stood impassively as her mother dried her off. She looked better, Aidan thought, better than he'd ever seen her. Less fragile, more sturdy. Less pale, more pink. Less blank, more animated. No wonder Sarah chose to focus on her.

The Melting Pot was hopping, only two tables empty. They sat down at one. Aidan felt like sliding under it. The place was full of people he knew. He felt eyes boring into him. He felt no goodwill, only ill. Was it just his guilty conscience?

They sat for ten, fifteen minutes or more. No one came near them. Sarah was growing progressively impatient, repeatedly trying to catch the waitress's eye. Aidan was developing a severe sense of foreboding. 'I think we should leave.'

'No way. There's a bun up there with my name on it.'

Before he could stop her, she was out of her chair. She walked up to the counter and it seemed to Aidan that every eye was on her, every breath held.

'Excuse me.' Her actor's voice rang out clear as a bell. 'We'd like to order some food, please.'

The woman behind the counter was Mag O'Neill. Aidan had gone to school with her brother.

'We've finished serving for the evening.'

'What? But it's not even four.'

'Sorry. Service is over.' The woman held up her hands as if there was nothing she could do, although she ran the place. Aidan caught her eye – and felt himself turned to stone.

'But that's ridiculous.' Sarah was becoming irate. 'You always serve far later than this.'

'Sarah.' Aidan was behind her, holding her arm. 'We should go.'

'No, Aidan. This place is packed with people eating. They've been serving everyone around us.'

'Sarah.' His voice was more urgent. 'We need to leave. Maia's getting agitated.'

Sarah swung around to look at her daughter. It was true that she was muttering to herself and starting to rock. Sarah scanned the rest of the café in genuine confusion. Every eye was riveted upon her, every diner enjoying the show. Aidan gathered up their things and bundled the three of them out of the door.

They walked along the street in silence, Sarah dazed, Aidan raw, until they got to the cottage. The only place in the whole town where no one could get them. Sarah went straight up to her room. Aidan followed the minute Maia was settled. He knocked gently on the door. There was no reply but he went in anyway. She was sitting on the bed, her eyes cast down. He sat on the floor looking up at her. She shook her head. 'I don't understand it,' she said. 'How could they be so cruel?' She appeared genuinely mystified.

'They've obviously heard that we're together now. That I've left Fiona.'

She stared at him, then nodded briefly. 'So soon?'

'Small-town gossip. You're not in Dublin now, you know.'

'Maybe I should be.'

He didn't know it but his face was grief-stricken. She touched his cheek gently. 'I meant maybe we both should be.'

'Oh.' He relaxed visibly. 'Is that what you want?'

'No. I don't want to take Maia away from Star. But maybe it would be better for all of us. What do you think?'

'I don't know.' He scratched his head, as if trying to make the thoughts come out right. 'They're not going to make it easy for us, people around here. But on the other hand this is where my livelihood is. And it's my home. The Ryans have been here for as long as – if not longer than – any other family. I don't like the idea of being run out of town.'

'Of course not.'

'And I know it sounds strange, but I don't want to leave my family.' He allowed himself an ironic smile and rubbed his eyes with his thumbs.

Sarah stroked the back of his head. 'Maybe it would be easier for them if we weren't here,' she said softly.

He considered this. 'Maybe.' He looked deep into her eyes.

She gazed back into his. 'Why are you doing this, Aidan?'

'I have no choice.' He stated his truth simply.

'There's always a choice.'

'Not for me. Not since I met you.'

'I don't want to be your crucifixion, Aidan.'

'What do you mean?'

'I don't want to be an excuse for you to sacrifice yourself.'

'Why would I want to do that?'

'I don't know. People can be weird.'

'Not me.'

'You don't think you're weird?'

'Watch it.' He smiled at her.

'Seriously, Aidan. It's very romantic and all, and I'm happy you're here with me, but I don't relish the prospect of ruining other people's lives.'

'Their lives won't be ruined. They're hurt, very hurt, but they'll get over it in time.'

'You really think so?' She wanted to believe him.

'I do. And everyone else will get used to it too. And they'll move on to the next hot topic of conversation.'

'It'd have to be pretty good to top this. The actress and the fisherman.'

'The actress and the bishop, maybe.'

'Yes. We'll have to arrange that.'

It was such a blessed relief to laugh.

'So you want to stay, then?'

'Yes.'

'Me too.'

'So that's settled.'

She went to get off the bed but something stopped her. Aidan saw her skin turn to ash. 'What is it? What's wrong?'

'Nothing's wrong. Nothing at all. I think I'll just lie here for a while.' She lowered herself onto the bed as if she was made of porcelain.

'Do you need anything?'

'Maybe one of those painkillers the consultant gave me. They're in the press above the toaster.'

'Okay.' He was in the kitchen before she'd closed her eyes. He located the tablets and took them down. They were as yet unopened. This was the first time. It was starting. So soon?

Chapter 30

It was night-time and Tommy and Alannah were sitting in their childhood kitchen. Everything familiar, yet so unfamiliar.

'At least she got dressed today.'

'Yes, that's something.'

Alannah had managed to convince Fiona to put on some clothes some time around midday. Then she'd coaxed her out onto the deck for a while. That was as far from the house as she could get her to go. Fiona seemed horrified at the notion of seeing or being seen by any of the neighbours. Neither would she answer the phone. Alannah and Tommy had had to concoct a variety of excuses between them. They had spent the day taking turns to sit with her, watching daytime TV mostly.

'Do you think she's in shock?'

'I do.'

They'd kept trying to fill her with hot sweet tea and cover her with blankets. Fiona had grown impatient with them. 'I'm not an invalid, you know.'

Now she was in bed again. Out of her clothes. They presumed the routine would continue indefinitely.

'What are we going to do?'

'I don't know, Tom. I have to go back to London in a few days. They won't keep my job open for ever.'

'You can't leave me here on my own with her.'

'I'm going to have to. You're a big boy now, Tommy.' She had to laugh at his expression. 'Don't worry. Mam will pull herself together. You'll see. She's a fighter.'

'Maybe she'll go around to Sarah Dillon's house and beat her up.'

They chortled briefly at the notion.

'Dad says she's dying.'

'I know. You said.'

The mood was instantly sombre again.

'I could kill Dad.'

'So could I.'

Neither had a problem displaying their anger but the pain underneath – that was better hidden.

'Are you going to meet up with him while you're here?'

'I don't know, Tom. I don't know what to do.'

'I think you should go and see him.'

'Why?'

'See if you can talk some sense into him.'

'What makes you think he'd listen to me?'

'Because you're his pet.'

'Am not.'

'Are too.'

She was quiet. What if she wasn't his pet any more? What if Sarah Dillon had usurped that role? Or Maia. Did he think of the little girl as his daughter now?

'So, are you going to see him?'

'Oh, I don't know, Tommy. Stop pestering me, will you? I'll think about it in the morning. I'm too tired now. Did you say Mam was drinking vodka when you found her first?'

'Yes.'

'The whole bottle?'

'There was some left.'

'Where is it?'

'What – the bottle?'

'Yes.'

'In the recycling.'

'What about the vodka that was left?'

'I poured it down the sink.'

'What did you do that for, you fecking eejit?'

'I didn't want her drinking any more of it.'

'That's a criminal waste of good alcohol.'

'There's some beer in the fridge.'

'Good man.' Alannah went and extracted two cans. She took one for herself and placed the other in front of her brother. She sat down again and they popped the tabs simultaneously. 'Cheers,' said Alannah, and they clinked cans.

It was good for a while, like they were proper grown-ups. Then it started to feel wrong, as if the lunatics had taken over the asylum. They'd never have been doing this if everything was normal. Their mother wouldn't have allowed it if she'd been in the full of her health. But they each had the impression that if Fiona were to walk into the room right now she wouldn't bat an eyelid.

'It's weird,' said Tommy.

'What is?'

'Having to look after your mother.'

'Mmm.'

'I mean, she's not even that old.'

'I know. If she was ninety and wearing incontinence pants you'd think, Okay, fair enough. But . . . Jesus . . . '

They both started to giggle helplessly, like kids again.

'Come on. Drink up. Let's have another.'

Another led to another led to another led to a hung-over Tommy and Alannah the next morning. They moved around the kitchen in slow motion, taking turns to stare vacantly into the fridge and moan intermittently. The empty cans still crowded the middle of the table. They finally settled on dry toast and tea, although Tommy was building up to a full Irish.

'What are we going to do with Mam today?'

'Convince her to get up for a start.'

'Will we bring her out for a drive? If we go somewhere far away she might get out for a walk, some fresh air.'

'Jesus, there you go again with all the questions. Let me have my tea first.' Alannah sat hunched over the table, her head in her hands. Tommy parked himself beside her, leaned back and closed his eyes.

'What's going on here?'

They both leaped, then turned to find their mother framed in the kitchen doorway. She was fully dressed, fully made up and, if not looking exactly like her old self, she was giving a very good impression of it.

'Mam. You're up.'

'I am. And high time by the look of it.' She click-clacked into the room. 'Where did all these cans come from?'

Alannah and Tommy glanced at one another, not knowing whether to be delighted or terrified.

'We thought –'

'You thought wrong. Clear up this mess immediately. I don't want to see either my children or my kitchen in this state ever again.'

'Yes, Mam.' Tommy scooped up an armful of cans and went directly to deposit them in the recycling bin.

'How are you feeling, Mam?'

'I'm fine, Alannah. Why wouldn't I be?'

'Well, because –'

'Is there tea in that pot?'

'There is.'

Alannah sat down in relief as her mother poured herself a mug of tea.

'My God. What have you done with this? It's stewed to oblivion. I'll have to make a fresh pot.'

Alannah watched her mother's compact form move quickly and efficiently around the kitchen. Tommy came in and stood beside her. The two Ryan offspring grinned at each other behind her back.

'Are you going to work today, Mam?'

'I'm not.'

'Oh. It's just that you're all dressed up.'

'I'm going to Dublin.'

'For the day?'

Fiona stopped what she was doing and turned to them, leaning back against the sink. Her face and voice softened. 'No, love. I'm going for a week or so. I haven't decided how long yet. I just need to get away for a while. I think you'll both understand.'

'Of course.'

'I'll be staying with Yvonne. I've arranged for cover in the surgery.'

'Would you like us to come with you?'

'No, you're okay, Alannah. Well, you can if you like but there's really no need. I'm sure you should get back to your job. Not to mention Ross.'

If Alannah's face clouded at the mention of her boyfriend's name, she hid it well. 'Maybe I can drive up with you. I don't have a ticket booked so I can fly from Dublin instead of Shannon.'

'I'd like that.' Fiona smiled for the first time since Alannah's arrival. 'How about you, Tom? Fancy coming along for the ride?'

'I'll stay here if it's all the same with you. Rufus will need someone to mind him.' Free house. Magic.

'Okay. But no parties while I'm gone. You can have three friends back at a time, no more than that.'

'Yes, Mam.' Jesus. When she was back, she was back.

'Right then, Lana. How long do you think it'll take you to get ready?'

'You're going now?'

'No time like the present.'

'Well, I did want to go into town and pick up a few things. And I'll have to pack.'

'Okay, you do that, and I'll book a flight for you while I'm waiting.'

'My God, Mam. Do I have time for breakfast?'

Fiona laughed. She laughed! 'Of course you have time for breakfast.' She went over to her daughter, seated at the table, placed a hand on each cheek and kissed her forehead. Then she went up to Tommy, who was standing a good head and shoulders above her, grabbed his face in both hands, pulled it down to her and did the same to him. 'You're good kids, really.'

Alannah was in a tizz. She'd thought she'd have more time to make up her mind. To see her dad or not to see him. She could always ring him. But she didn't want their first contact to be on the phone. She'd noticed that he hadn't rung her. It hurt but didn't surprise her. For all he knew, she was still in London, oblivious to it all. She hadn't been out of the house much since she'd come home – and he was keeping a low profile, no doubt.

She decided to go and see him. She couldn't believe she had to go to *her* house to see her own father. *That woman*. To think she'd liked her, thought it was exciting and exotic to have Sarah Dillon taking up residence in *their* town. And now she'd taken up with *her* dad. Yuck. It was bad enough thinking about your own parents together, but your father with another woman? Jesus. Alannah felt increasingly disgusted and irate the more she thought about it.

She was there now. At the end of Sarah Dillon's street. She lurked at the side of the last cottage in the row. What to do? Just march up to the front door and ring the bell? She supposed so. But what if the slut answered? What would she do then?

Alannah jumped back as Sarah's front door opened. She waited a few seconds, her breath held, before peering around the wall.

Maia was the first to skip out onto the pavement. She looked different from how she remembered. Bigger. Then Sarah. She looked all right. Not like someone who was dying. She was wearing her wig. Stupid cow. She was fussing around with Maia, bending down and putting a rucksack on the little girl's back. Then Alannah's heart did a little double take as her father stepped out onto the pavement beside them. She watched him shut the door and lock it behind him. He pocketed the key. As if he lived there. Then the two adults positioned themselves on either side of Maia, like they'd done it a million times before, and each took one of her hands in their own. They crossed the street and walked away from Alannah towards the beach, if the bucket and spade her dad was holding in his other hand were anything to go by.

Alannah felt physically ill. They were just like a family. They were a family. There was no way she could go up to him now. She was no longer part of the unit. And for the first time she felt sorrier for herself than she did for her mother. One part of her family had voluntarily removed himself. Could the other parts survive without him? Did her family still exist?

She was still pondering this on the way to Dublin in the car with her mother and the silence. It wasn't awkward. Neither of them seemed to notice it, both absorbed in their own set of thoughts.

They had left the house around midday. Tommy waved them off almost cheerfully. He had his board under his arm and Rufus snuffling excitedly around his ankles. He was about to go surfing for the first time since the crisis had occurred. Alannah could see how delighted he was that the status quo, as he saw it, was partially restored. One parent at least back to normal.

But Alannah could see more readily past the façade. It would be a long time before her mother was anything like approaching normal. How did a person get over something like this? She didn't know if she could.

'How's Ross?' Fiona surprised her with the question.

'He's fine.'

'You don't sound too sure.'

'Don't I? Oh, we had a stupid row before I left. Nothing serious.'

'Really?'

'Really.'

She couldn't wait to get back to him. Apologize for being such a silly cow. After everything that had happened in the past few days, their row seemed petty and insignificant. She vowed that she would never jeopardize their relationship again. It was too precious, and Ross too special. He would never do to her what her dad had done to her mam.

She embraced her mother tenderly at the airport. 'Are you going to be all right, Mam?'

'Of course I am. We all are. You just wait and see.'

'You promise?' She was nine years old again.

'I promise. Now go. You'll miss your flight.'

She felt her mother's eyes follow her in the queue for security. Every time she looked back she was still standing there. Just before she handed over her boarding card she waved at her to go, that she was fine. Her mother turned to walk away, her shoulders slightly slumped. Then, in a gesture Alannah recognized, she straightened up and walked towards the doors with her head erect. Maybe she would be okay, after all.

Part III

Chapter 31

Sarah sat alone on the beach. She wasn't meant to be there. She had promised Aidan she would stay at home. He worried about her being out on her own while he was on his boat earning a crust. But Maia was with Bridget and this opportunity was far too good to miss – the day too sublime, too perfect in all its little details and imperfections. She sat on her folding chair, looking out to sea. She had a blanket over her legs. Like an invalid. She laughed to herself.

The sea moved in. The sea moved out. In. Out. Breathing. As if all the ocean were one gigantic animal. She tried to match its breath with her own. But her breaths were too short, too shallow. She tried to imagine what it would be like to be out there alone, at the mercy of the waves and the sea creatures. She felt scared. She pulled her blanket higher.

She concentrated on the sea's breathing. Gentle. And she relaxed again. She suddenly saw herself as if from above. A lone woman, sitting on a chair: so small and insignificant. The further away she got, the smaller she became. Until the sea engulfed her. In. Out. She was gone. All that was left was the chair. And she saw with a terrible clarity that the chair, this piece of plastic, would outlast her. Shivering uncontrollably, Sarah gathered up her things and went home.

When Aidan got back that evening, the cottage seemed unnaturally quiet. He searched from room to room. No Maia. How odd. He took the stairs two at a time. The door to Sarah's room was ajar so he pushed it open. There was a human-shaped lump in the centre of the bed. 'Sarah?'

He pulled back the covers. She was lying in a tightly locked foetal position. 'Sarah.'

She was crying, her eyes screwed shut, tears leaking out of the corners. She was rocking herself rhythmically, as her daughter was inclined to do when she was scared.

'What is it?' He kicked off his shoes and climbed into the bed beside her, wrapping her body in his own. 'Hey, what's wrong?'

'I'm dying.'

Oh.

He held her tighter, absorbing her grief the best he could as her body heaved.

'I'm dying, Aidan. I'm dying.'

He stroked her hair, feeling the fragile shape of her skull through the wispy curls. She felt so small, so thin. If he squeezed too hard she might disappear like a puff of smoke and he'd be left with nothing. And he was suddenly very glad that he was there. The doubts that had plagued him fell away. It had all been worth it to be with her at this moment.

'Promise me you won't go,' she said.

'I promise.'

'You'll never leave me?'

'I won't leave you. Not ever.' If only he could extract such a promise from her.

Sarah had stopped crying. She was still dying. It was just that she had no more tears left. For now. She sat cross-legged on the bed, sipping the mug of tea Aidan had brought up for her. She hadn't wanted him to leave her, even to go down to the kitchen for five minutes. She felt so vulnerable without him. He was watching her now. Intently. Trying to analyse every nuance of feature and posture.

'I think it's time you told your family,' he said.

She nodded, her resistance gone.

'Will you ring your sister?'

'I'll call her tonight.'

'Good. And your friends in Dublin. They'll want to know. Want to help.'

'I know.'

'Don't deny them, or yourself.'

'I know, Aidan. You don't have to keep going on.'

'Sorry.'

'That's all right.'

They were quiet for a while. She put down her mug.

'I'd better go and pick up Maia.' Aidan started to get up.

'No.' Sarah grabbed him by the wrist and pulled him back down.

'Do you want to go?'

She shook her head.

'What, then?'

'I was wondering . . .'

'What?'

'If you'd consider it ghoulish to have sexual relations with a dying woman.'

'I'd consider it an honour.'

It was one hour later. Aidan had finally been allowed to leave the house but only to pick up Maia. He was under strict instructions to come straight back. He found himself on Bridget's doorstep. The woman herself answered.

'Bridget.'

'Aidan.'

'I've come to collect Maia.'

'I know.'

She knew. Of course she knew. Everyone knew by now. He

tried to gauge her reaction to him. It was measured. Polite. Neither one way nor the other. He couldn't tell if she was indifferent to the relationship or if she was maintaining a professional reserve. Probably wanted to keep her job.

'Look, Bridget, you may as well know that Sarah is very sick.'

'You mean the cancer. She's on the mend, isn't she?'

'The cancer's back.'

'Oh. Is it . . . serious?'

'Yes.'

'Is she –'

'Yes.'

'Oh, Jesus.' Bridget blessed herself. The movement was involuntary.

'So that's why you had Maia for such a long time today. And it's why her hours will probably become more erratic. Are you okay with that?'

'Of course. I'll help out any time I can.'

'Thanks. I'll make sure you're compensated for any inconvenience.'

'There's no need.'

He'd been prepared to buy her loyalty. But judging by her stricken face, that wouldn't be necessary.

A few days later they were having breakfast as usual. *As usual* – funny how quickly the unusual became usual. The three moved around each other with a fluidity that would once have seemed impossible. Aidan made the coffee while Sarah and Maia sat side by side at the kitchen table. Maia was having the exact breakfast she had every morning of her life: two Weetabix with warm milk. Aidan had learned the hard way to heat the milk first and fill the bowl to a certain level so that the Weetabix swelled to the correct size.

He'd done the grocery shopping too. He'd gone to the next town in case he ran into anyone in Dunnes who wanted to take him on. He just wasn't ready for one of Fiona's elderly patients – and, God knew, some of them were devoted to her – to batter him over the head in the frozen-food aisle. He knew he'd forgotten half of what he was supposed to get and Sarah was too polite to say. Right now, she was spreading bright red strawberry jam on her wholemeal toast instead of the usual, and preferred, marmalade. Maia started to make little noises of protest.

'What is it?'

She kept pushing Sarah's plate further away from hers.

'Would you stop, Maia? I'm trying to eat my breakfast.'

She did it again.

'Stop!' Sarah yelled at her.

Maia stared at her mother in open-mouthed fascination – as if she were a door hinge or a spinning top.

'It must be the jam,' said Aidan. 'That's my fault. Here. Give it to me and I'll get rid of it.'

'No. I'm having my breakfast and that's that.'

Sarah recommenced eating her toast. Maia uttered more mewls of protest and began pushing at her mother's plate again. It was apparently the last straw. 'Jesus Christ.' It was a scream. 'Can I not just eat my fucking breakfast in peace?' Sarah rose from her chair and flung her plate with great force across the room. It hit the wall and shattered. There were tiny bits of white ceramic everywhere. Then she picked up the jam-jar and hurled it to the floor. The glass smashed and everybody watched the red gel ooze out. The two adults stood like statues. The child did not. First, she covered her ears with her hands. Then she started to rock. Then the hand flapping.

'Oh, Maia, I'm so sorry.' Sarah bent down to her but Maia flapped her away.

'Why don't you go upstairs? I'll deal with her,' said Aidan. He was looking at her with . . . what? Pity?

'Are you –'

'Yes. Just go.'

Sarah left the room and the chaos behind. She ran up the stairs and, not giving herself time to think, put on yesterday's clothes and grabbed her car keys. She went quickly back downstairs. Maia seemed a little calmer, although still a long way from neutral.

'I'm going out.'

'But I thought –'

'See you later.'

She was on the street, walking. Walking so fast. It felt good. A relief. Just to get away. She walked faster. She couldn't move fast enough to escape herself. To shed this body.

She got into her car. Faster. She'd barely driven it since she'd got there. Just left it parked around the corner. She drove it now. It was slow to start and juddery at first, then smooth. She drove out of town and away – away from Maia, from the house, even from Aidan. She turned on the radio, let the music blare and fill her ears, so loud she thought they would bleed. Then she screamed. With the windows shut and the volume turned up, she could barely hear herself. She pulled abruptly into a lay-by. She was at the cliffs.

She slammed the car door without locking it and headed up the path. No looking back. It was windy up there. She folded her arms across her chest and walked grimly, her head down. The gulls screeched above, wheeling around her. She was at the top now. The wind whipped the breath from her mouth. She stood on the edge. The waves crashed ferociously against the rocks below. All was movement. All was energy. She wanted some. She lifted her arms to the sides as if appealing to the heavens. Then she raised her head upward and screamed until there was no sound left. And somewhere out in the ocean, a lone creature recognized her voice.

She arrived home two hours later. She let herself in, unseen and unheard. Voices were coming from the kitchen. She crept to the door and peered through the crack. Aidan and Maia were sitting at the table. Maia was drawing, with Aidan leaning over her. Sarah felt herself relax and almost smiled. Then she climbed the staircase as if it were her own private Everest. When she reached her bed, she pulled back the duvet and lowered herself onto the mattress. Then she pulled it over her head, drew herself up into a ball and lay there blinking in the half-light. She fell asleep, deeply and dreamlessly. And when she woke up her sister was lying in the bed beside her.

Chapter 32

Aidan was fascinated by Sarah's sister, Helen. He couldn't get over how different they were from one another. Right now he was mesmerized by her arms – plump and freckly: they reminded him somehow of currant buns. But that could have been because she was making a cake, stirring the mixture capably and methodically. Maia looked on solemnly, licking a spoon. Aidan wanted to ask her what had possessed her to make a cake in the circumstances. He was trying to figure out a polite way to frame the question. Eventually he just said, 'What are you making?'

'A cake.'

'I know, I –'

'A Victoria sponge. Sarah's favourite.'

'Oh.'

There was a pause. Helen looked up at him and smiled. 'It relaxes me,' she said.

'Oh, right. I just thought, you know, you only just got here. You must be jet-lagged. I would have thought cooking was the last thing on your mind.'

'It's not cooking, it's baking – there's a difference.' She shrugged. 'It'll be a nice treat for Sarah to wake up to. The smell, if nothing else. And, besides, it keeps Missy here entertained.' She inclined her head towards Maia, who was continuing to lick every last morsel off the spoon. She smiled at her niece.

Aidan thought he saw tears welling in her eyes. The house would be flooded at this rate.

'I've never seen anything like the change in this girl. It does the heart good to see it.' She continued to stir.

'You have kids, don't you?' he said.

'Three boys. Ten, eight and six. Each bolder than the next. You?'

Aidan shifted uncomfortably in his seat. 'A girl and a boy. Nineteen and seventeen.'

'What do they think of you leaving their mother for another woman?'

The question blind-sided Aidan. There was more to Helen, with her mild manner and sensible haircut, than met the eye. 'They're upset.'

'I bet they are.'

The truth was, he didn't know what Alannah thought about him leaving Fiona. He'd left several messages on her phone but she hadn't got back to him. It was more than a week now since that morning with Tommy on the beach. He'd never gone so long without seeing or speaking to his kids and it was killing him. Tommy wouldn't respond to his messages either.

'You know,' said Helen, 'they're at a very difficult age for you to do something like this to them. They'll probably be quite badly affected.'

'You don't have to tell me that.' He was losing the warm feelings he'd had for the woman. He sat in silence for a while, trying to damp down his anger while Helen and Maia transferred the sponge mix into the baking tins. 'So, how long do you think you'll be able to stay?' he said, after a while.

Helen threw back her head and laughed, both hands on her ample hips. 'You mean, how soon will you be able to get rid of me?'

'That's not –'

It was.

'Ten days. That's how long I've been given away from my life.

The boys. My job. And, of course, I'll come back before . . .'

Aidan nodded. The mood was suddenly sombre again. He never seemed to move far away from sombre, these days. Helen was busying herself with the tidying up. Aidan lifted himself out of the chair. 'I'd better be off,' he said. 'The people will be waiting.' It wasn't strictly true. He didn't have to go for a while yet. He just wanted to get out of the house.

'Look, Aidan.' Helen walked rapidly from behind the counter and stood directly in front of him, blocking his exit. 'I'm not your enemy. I don't condone what you did to your wife and kids. If my own husband did that to me I'd be destroyed.'

Aidan flinched. Was the woman trying to make amends or what?

'However, what you've done – what you're doing – for my sister, it's pretty incredible.' She shook her head. 'I can't work out whether you're an arsehole or a saint.'

Aidan laughed, her words taking him by surprise. 'I'd say one part saint and three parts arsehole.'

'That sounds about right.'

They grinned at one another, both feeling now that they might just make an accommodation.

'Aidan.' She became serious. 'You and I are going to have to get on here. This is about Sarah. Not about us.'

'I agree.'

'I'm not trying to usurp your role. She'll need us both.'

'I know.'

'Right then.' She stuck out her hand. 'Friends?'

He smiled and took it. 'Friends.'

She called out to him as he was walking out of the door: 'I'm sorry to be so direct, Aidan.' She came right up to him and lowered her voice, mindful of her sister upstairs. 'It's just that there isn't time to be anything else.'

* * *

Aidan stepped out into the sunshine. He felt a degree of freedom he hadn't experienced in a while. He knew it was because of Helen – someone else to share the load for the next ten days. He was glad to have her as an ally because he wouldn't want her as an enemy. Although he thought a lot of it was front. She was just trying to suss him out and to protect Sarah. That was understandable. He sensed a core of sweetness inside her. Sarah had the same, except hers was more exposed. He could have thought about it all day – talked about it, basked in it. As far as he could see, from the few hours he had spent with her, Helen masked her soft side with a sensible, practical persona. But he liked her, he decided. And it was just as well. Although he had been cut to the quick by her comments about his children. How could he make them see that it wasn't them he'd left?

He thought about them whenever he wasn't thinking about Sarah. He tried to project himself into their future lives. When Tommy was a fully grown man. If he was married. If he then met a woman like Sarah and felt that way about her. That passion. Such overwhelming, all-consuming love. Such a feeling of having to be with that woman at all costs. Would he want his son to leave his marriage for such a woman, such a love? The answer was yes. He would.

But, on the other hand, if someone did to Alannah what he had done to Fiona, he'd kill him. Squeeze the life out of him with his bare hands. It was all so confused in his head. His parents-in-law must hate him. He imagined their conversations about him now, feeling justified in their initial suspicions of him, that they'd been correct all along in their conviction that he wasn't good enough for their daughter. And perhaps they had been right all those years ago. And now in their hatred of him. His mind boggled. The number of people who must hate him now. Aidan Ryan: destroyer of lives.

He walked towards the town, imagining everyone he passed holding a new opinion of him – an opinion he could do nothing to control. The die was cast. He'd been avoiding people he knew, of course, sticking to the beaches and to his boat where it was mostly tourists he met. But now, coming up the street in the other direction, was his old drinking buddy Noel Higgins and he wasn't going to be able to avoid him: they were practically on top of each other. The two men slowed, trepidation on their faces. On Aidan's, because he didn't know what to say – talk about being caught out in a lie – and he didn't know what he'd do if Noel walked by him.

But Noel wasn't going to do that. 'Aidan.'

'Noel.'

They looked one another in the eye for several seconds.

'Well,' said the other man, 'you've really gone and fucked it up this time.'

'I have, Noel, I have.'

They laughed.

'Come on,' said Noel, 'you dirty-looking eejit. I'll buy you a pint.'

McSwigans was blessedly empty. They sat in the snug anyway, just in case someone came in. Aidan didn't approach the bar. He went straight to his seat while Noel got the drinks in. Then they looked at each other and Noel shook his head. 'What were you thinking?'

'It was just something I had to do.'

'As in a man's got to do what a man's got to do?' He shook his head again.

Aidan kept his peace.

'Poor Fiona couldn't even bear to stick around.'

'What do you mean?'

'She's gone to Dublin. Did you not know?'

'No, I didn't. Sure, none of my family will speak to me.'

'Are you surprised?'

'No.'

'Nor should you be. The missus called up to the house a couple of days ago and only the young lad was there.'

'Tommy's there on his own?'

'He is.'

It wasn't like Fiona to leave Tommy unsupervised.

'And Alannah's gone back.'

'Alannah was here?'

'She came home to be with her mother for a few days.'

Aidan felt as if he'd been delivered a blow to his gut. His girl had been home and she hadn't even contacted him. Things were even worse than he'd thought. He leaned forward in his seat and sighed.

'Is she really worth it, Aidan?'

'Yes. She is.'

'Really?'

'Yes.'

'And is it true what they're saying?'

'Is what true?'

'That she's dying.'

He nodded.

'Aidan, I don't know how else to put it, and forgive me if I insult you, but what are you getting out of it?'

'I get to be with her. And know that she's safe. Being looked after.'

'But I hear tell the sister's arrived.'

'Jesus. Is there nothing you don't know?'

'Word gets around. You know how it is.'

'Her sister's here for a week and a half. She lives in the States. What else are they saying about us?'

'What are they not saying?'

'Just give me the general gist.'

'Well. There's a lot of people have sympathy for Fiona. Especially the women.' He chuckled to himself. 'You'd want to keep well away from the women of this town.'

'Don't I know it. Your one in the Melting Pot wouldn't serve us the other day.'

'Ah, I wouldn't mind her. She's an awful hatchet head, that woman.' He took a sup of his pint. 'But then again. There are others who never had much time for Fiona.'

'Like who?'

'Ah – I'll not mention any names. But, you know, those who think she was always a little too far up herself, looking down on the locals, us ignorant bog warriors, that kind of thing.'

'Is that what they thought? I had no idea.'

'Not everyone, mind. Just an element. And those people, they see you as one of their own. You're from here so they side with you.'

'I don't think they're the kind of people I want taking my side.'

'Trust me, Aidan. You need all the friends you can get right now.'

'I suppose you're right.'

They drank in companionable silence. It felt good to Aidan, the male company. He didn't realize how much he had missed talking to a man. Even if he wasn't exactly bringing good tidings. The household he was living in felt one-sided. He and Sarah and Maia – and now Helen. All that oestrogen. At home, he'd always had Tommy to balance things out. Tommy, who was now home alone, with no father to balance things for him. With no one. He'd go and see him and make everything all right. He had to try. Had to find a way back to his children.

Chapter 33

Sarah and Helen were sitting up in bed together, regarding their toes. 'You have Gran's feet,' said Sarah.

'You mean the shape?'

'No. All shrivelled up and wrinkly.'

'The cheek of you.' Helen nudged Sarah with her shoulder, not as hard as she would once have done. Sarah laughed her familiar laugh. Impish. She was back in the role of pesky little sister again. It was fun to feel irresponsible for a change.

'Do you have many memories of Gran?'

'Of course. I was nineteen when she died, remember. You're not that much older than me, you know. You just look it.'

'There you go again.'

They grinned at one another.

Sarah took a sip from the mug of water she was holding. It had been her favourite mug for coffee, but she didn't seem to have much of a taste for coffee any more. Many aspects of herself that she'd taken for granted, identified with, were falling away, which made her wonder who she had been all along. 'Remember how Mammy used to be embarrassed by her?' she said.

'Yes.'

'Poor Mam. Forever trying to be something she wasn't.' As the words came out of her mouth, she wondered how much of her time on earth she had squandered trying to be something she wasn't. The thought made her shiver and she linked her arm through Helen's for comfort as much as warmth. She had noticed a tendency to do this of late. She had an intense longing for physical contact, human warmth, as if she was holding onto life itself. 'What do you make of Aidan, then?' Best to change the subject.

'I don't know.'

'What do you mean, you don't know? He's lovely.'

'What do you want me to say? Tell you how cute I think he is on a scale of one to ten?'

'Cute! You're such a Yank.'

'Stop.'

'But you are. How long have you been over there now?'

'Twenty-one years.'

'Half your life.'

'When you put it like that . . .'

Again, an uncomfortable thought. Sarah had lived what she had assumed was roughly half her life. Turned out that was it. She could feel Helen thinking the same thing. She laid her head on her sister's shoulder. 'Hand us another piece of that sponge.'

'Okay.' Helen did so eagerly. 'We'll get crumbs in the sheets.'

'I guess things like that don't matter any more.'

The two women bit into their respective slices and chewed thoughtfully.

'You know,' said Sarah, 'it's amazing, when you get right down to it, how little actually matters at all. Maia, do you want some more cake, darling?'

Maia lifted herself out of her game in the corner and approached the bed, arm outstretched, eyes eager and saucer-like. She grabbed the cake offered to her and returned immediately to her game.

'Say thank you, Maia.'

'Say tank you, My.'

The words were delivered through a shower of cake crumbs and the two women laughed at the miracle of her response.

'Let's get up,' said Sarah, abruptly swinging her legs over the side of the bed. 'I'll have time enough to be lying here.'

The following day was uncompromising in its magnificence. Sarah was sure of it the second her eyelids flickered open. She moulded her body against Aidan's until the rhythm of his breathing was interrupted and he was awake.

She loved the first moment of his consciousness. The eyes, first dazed and slightly bloodshot, then coming into focus. Then the expression of pure love and joy when he realized where he was, who he was with. He would pull her in even closer and nuzzle his face into the nook where her neck met her shoulder. His beard would tickle and she would squirm, but towards him, not away. And they would lie there, breathing each other in. There was no better start to the day.

'Let's take the dinghy out,' she mumbled into his neck.

He pulled away slightly so he could look at her. 'This morning?'

'Yes. I want Helen to meet Star.'

'Your wish is my command. But not yet.'

He pulled her back into his warm fuzzy closeness and she privately agreed. Not yet.

It was as if God had laid on the day especially for them. *Here, have this special bonus day at the end of your life.* It was Sarah's day, but the others got to share. And she wondered if they saw the colours as vividly, as poignantly, as she did.

They were out now, bobbing along on the open water, the breeze carrying and shunting them along. It felt absolutely right to be there, as if they were in the right place, at the right time, doing the right thing. It was seldom in life that everything drew together in such perfection. Perfect perfection. Sarah glanced from sister, to lover, to daughter. The three people most precious to her on this earth. All gathered together on this tiny little boat. She imagined a gigantic wave, a freak tsunami, gathering suddenly from the ocean's depth and consuming them so they could all go together. So she wouldn't have to travel alone into eternity. But she knew this was selfish and not her true heart's desire. Some pieces of her had to go on. They could be her representatives on earth.

'What?' said Helen.

'I didn't say anything.'

'You're looking at me funny.'

'Sorry – there she is.'

Sarah's finger shot out and they all followed its direction, Aidan with his camera. But she was gone already.

'Keep looking. She'll resurface.'

Sure enough, several seconds later, a few feet from where she was first spotted, a perfect silver arc broke the water and disappeared again, as if it had been a momentary mirage.

'Oh, yes.' Helen jumped to her feet and literally rocked the boat.

'Sit down!'

'Sorry.'

Star came closer to the boat, so close that they could hear the sigh of her blowhole. Sarah had learned to treasure that sound and value it above any other. Life's breath. In. Out. Whether it was Aidan's breath in the bed beside her, her daughter's butterfly breath on the back of her hand when she checked her at night-time, or animals' breath. The other day Sarah had gone for a walk in the countryside. It was a slow walk. She was out gathering foxgloves. Her last time. The thought had caused her to shed a few tears. She came across a clump at the entrance of a field. A group of horses stood there, regarding her solemnly. Then one by one they came over, all six of them. Lacking titbits, she had fed them handfuls of grass, which was lusher and greener on her side of the gate. She had stayed for a while, feeding them and stroking them and hearing them breathe. So comforting. Big animals were best for this, she had discovered. They had the best breath. Cows weren't bad if you could stand the stink. And she liked the sound they made when they munched the grass. She thought a dog would be good. A big old dog. But she had yet to try that one. And then there was Star. A mammal in a world of fish. Living exclusively in the water, but needing the air above it to survive.

'You know the way we started out in the water?' She directed this at Helen.

'How do you mean?'

'You know how we were once fish, then developed legs and crawled out of the ocean onto land?'

'Speak for yourself. I was never a fish.'

'You know what I mean. Evolution.'

'Go on.'

'Well, dolphins did the opposite. They once lived on land but they went back into the sea.'

'Really?' Helen looked at Aidan for confirmation. She was coming to regard him as an expert on all things oceanic.

'She doesn't believe me. Tell her, Aidan.'

'It's true. Dolphins and whales. Well, dolphins are whales, really. They're the only mammals that went back in. Permanently, that is.'

'Really? What did they look like when they went back in?'

'Nobody knows.'

'Tell her about the flippers, Aidan.'

'What about the flippers?'

'If you look at a dolphin skeleton, the flippers are made up of five individual bones. Like the fingers of a hand.'

'And their tails,' said Sarah. 'They're like two legs fused together with flippers for feet.'

'Stop,' said Helen. 'You're giving me the creeps.' She shivered in the hot sun. 'My God. What are they?' She leaned over the side of the boat and said loudly into the water, 'What are you?'

In an explosion of droplets, Star launched herself out of the water and, in a breathtaking stunt, flew through the air to the other end of the boat before disappearing again, drenching them all.

'She heard you,' said Sarah, once she'd stopped laughing.

'Holy shit!' Helen wiped her face with her hands and smoothed back the hair that had been plastered onto her forehead.

'We've been ignoring her for too long,' said Aidan. 'She doesn't like that. Typical woman.'

'Did you get her?' Sarah said to Aidan, gesturing to his camera.

'You must be joking. She's way too quick for me.'

Smiling at him, Sarah stood up in the boat, expertly placing her feet so that she and everything else remained balanced. She lifted her wet T-shirt over her head and discarded it. Helen averted her gaze from the blank space at the top of her sister's swimsuit. She glanced briefly at Aidan. He didn't appear to notice.

'Did I mention,' said Sarah, 'that dolphins have extraordinarily large brains? Much bigger than ours?'

'That doesn't prove anything,' said Helen. 'Men have bigger brains than women and they're far more stupid.'

Aidan laughed.

'I'm going in.' Sarah was peeling off her tracksuit bottoms.

'You're going in?' Helen looked horrified.

'Exactly what I said.'

'Do you think that's a good idea?' said Aidan.

'Best I ever had.'

'I'm not sure you're strong enough.'

But she didn't hear him. She was already diving in, the cold hitting her body like a gigantic slap. And all was quiet.

Star was with her immediately. Sarah could feel her joy. Joy. That's what I would have called you, she thought. They stared at each other for several seconds, two underwater creatures, sharing the moment. Then they emerged together, bursting into the air, Sarah gasping for breath, Star rising and falling like a wave. Sarah smoothed back her hair and laughed with abandon. She turned to find the boat. It was several feet away. Helen and Aidan were hanging anxiously over the side.

'Are you okay?' her sister called.

'Never been better. Come on in. The water's fine.'

'No, thanks. I'll just watch.'

And the two sisters settled into the roles they'd inhabited their entire lives. Helen, the elder, standing on the sidelines, observing wild, young Sarah as she took all the risks.

Sarah couldn't hear them now, but she felt she could.

'She's not well enough.'

'I know she isn't.'

She swam further out. Sarah and Star. Sea and sky. Taking turns to swim on their backs, on their fronts. Echoing each other. Mirroring one another. Had she ever known such ecstasy as this communion with a wild animal? They were the same. Touching each other frequently. Part of each other. Playing together.

Sarah glanced at the boat. It was further away than ever before. Aidan and Helen were more relaxed now, she could tell. They were no longer watching her constantly. They were talking, merely glancing at her every now and then. She relaxed, lying on her back, letting the sun's rays bathe her entire body, relishing the sensation of Star swooping below and around her.

She was almost in a trance when her left leg cramped and went into spasm. She panicked, tensed and her rigid body sank. She flailed dementedly with her arms, kicked her good leg and managed to get herself upright, her head above water. She coughed and spluttered and looked all around her for the boat. Aidan and Helen were totally oblivious to her, deep in conversation. She tried to cry out but her leg spasmed again and all she got was a mouthful of salt water as her head sank below the surface once more. She fought her way up, spitting and gasping. Suddenly she was aware of a presence beside her. The dolphin had positioned herself immediately to Sarah's left, where she remained, perfectly stationary. Sarah draped herself over Star's body and burst into tears. She waved towards the boat.

It was Maia who saw her first. Her little girl stood up and pointed. Sarah couldn't hear the noises she knew she would be making, but the others could. She waved again, and thought of the poem 'Not Waving but Drowning'. Would they know? Beside her, Star breathed evenly. Then she saw Aidan turn his head towards her. As if in slow motion, he stood up in the boat and, without stopping to remove a piece of clothing, he dived into the water. She watched him swimming towards her, closer and closer, a dreamlike sequence. And then he was upon her. She held out her arms and he took her.

Star circled the boat until the humans were back on board. Then she raced off, like a silver arrow shot from an invisible bow.

The fear was gone now. They were back home and Sarah was propped up in front of the computer screen, wrapped cocoon-like in her duvet. It was Aidan who had mummified her in this way. She'd had to wriggle at first to allow her arms to reach the keyboard. He had wanted her to get into bed and rest. Her loved ones were forever trying to get her to rest – as if she wouldn't have enough time for that. Her bed held less and less appeal with each passing day. She associated it with defeat. And while she did feel weak after the incident in the water, she also felt a kind of elation. She had cheated death. Albeit temporarily. This battle was hers. She also felt an intense curiosity that demanded to be satisfied. She was searching for stories similar to her own of humans being saved by dolphins. What she found astounded and delighted her – tales from ancient times to the present day.

There was a recent story of four New Zealand lifeguards who had been out training when a pod of dolphins suddenly approached at great speed. They herded them together and began circling them, slapping their tails against the water. At first the swimmers thought they were being attacked but the dolphins did nothing except nudge them back to shore. Later they discovered that a great white shark was submerged a few feet away and that the dolphins had formed a protective circle. She liked that. Then there was the Japanese soldier who had fallen off his warship during the Second World War. His comrades had believed him lost but he was washed up alive several days later, saying that a pod of dolphins had surrounded and protected him, supported him when he was tired and helped him to get to land.

She read on. There were legions of stories. She was drawn to the word 'psychopomp' and zoned in on it. It came from the Greek, meaning 'guide of souls'. The ancients believed that dolphins accompanied and guided the souls of the dead on their journey across the cosmic sea. And the Etruscans of ancient Italy had depicted dolphins carrying souls to Elysium, the Islands of the Blessed. From time into eternity. She felt elated.

Aidan came into the room. 'How are you feeling?'

'Good. I feel good.'

'I came to see what you wanted to eat. Helen's making lunch.'

'I'm not that hungry.'

Aidan bent down behind her and gripped her upper arms, as if emphasizing how thin she was becoming. 'You've got to eat something, Sarah.'

Did she? Did she really? She had less and less interest in food and only ate to please Aidan or Helen. The process was automatic now, a robotic bringing of food to her lips and swallowing it. 'I'll have a cheese sandwich.'

'Good girl. I'll go and tell her.' Aidan bent down and put his arms around Sarah, laying his head against hers and hugging her from behind. A protective circle.

That night Sarah had a dream. She was all alone in the sea. She was happy, joyful, even. She was swimming with abandon. She was strong and she was masterful, slicing through the water with an ease she seldom felt in real life. In her joy, she swam further out than she had intended until she could no longer see the shore. Suddenly the sea was alive with dolphins. Hundreds of them. Thousands. As far as the eye could see. And she was the only human. Everywhere there were fins and tails and countless silver arcs. Dolphins breaching. Dolphins diving. Dolphins leaping and spinning and dancing. A frenzy of dolphins whipping up the water until it was no longer calm. They were circling her now, leading her, she didn't know where. She no longer had to swim, carried along by a thousand slipstreams: she was buoyed up. Buoyant. Speeding along, faster and faster until the feeling was no longer pleasant, until panic set in. She tried to hold herself back but it was too late: she couldn't break the momentum. Still she struggled against it and was no longer buoyed up. She was sinking and flailing, suffocating and choking.

'Sarah.' In the distance someone called her name. Calling her back to shore.

'Sarah.' Louder.

'No.' She felt herself trying to say it, forcing the word out of her throat.

'No.' She got it out and she was awake.

Aidan was with her, holding her. 'Sarah. You're okay. You were having a nightmare. You're okay now.'

Sarah relaxed. Then she sat up in the dark and groped around for her glass of water. After she had had a few sips, she lay down and sank into the warm, human body that was offered to her.

Chapter 34

A secret part of Tommy wanted his mother to come home. It hadn't been all that great without her. A hangover every morning didn't have much to recommend itself. And the novelty of cold pizza or chocolate-chip cookies for breakfast was wearing thin. Which was why, this morning, he was preparing a breakfast worthy of and reminiscent of his mother – muesli, natural yogurt, orange juice. A girl's breakfast. There was still plenty of that sort of stuff in the house: he'd touched none of it since her departure and chosen instead to use the money she'd left him to buy takeaways and junk. A little more than a week later, he felt nauseated. So junk food *was* bad for you. He ruminated on this as he chewed his muesli. It tasted so bland. He got up, took the sugar out of the press and shovelled a few spoonfuls on top. Much better.

This time alone had really made Tommy doubt himself. When he thought of going away to college, he felt only terror whereas once there had been a mixture of fear and excitement. It wasn't so much the prospect of having to deal with the practicalities of everyday living that bothered him: he didn't know whether he could cope with the loneliness. Mam rang him every day, Alannah every second day, and still . . . the house felt wrong. Like he didn't belong. Sure, he'd have his friends over in the afternoons. But then they'd go home to their own families, their own beds.

He'd taken to bringing Rufus up with him at night. The delighted animal, normally confined to the kitchen or the porch, would clatter up the stairs and land with a satisfied snort on the rug beside Tommy's bed. Tommy would sometimes play the guitar to him and the dog would whine theatrically. His breathing at night was soothing and comforting.

The muesli had proven wholly unsatisfying. He was back at the fridge, trying to decide what next to feed the black hole that was his adolescent stomach.

'Hello, Tommy.'

'Jesus Christ!' He dropped the block of cheese he'd been holding. 'What are you doing here?'

'I came to see how you are.'

'What would you care?' Tommy hated the way it came out, sounding so childish.

His father frowned slightly. He was upset. *Good.* 'I heard your mother's gone away for a few days.'

'So you thought it would be safe to come back to the house and collect the rest of your stuff?'

'No. That's not why I'm here. I really do want to know how you are.'

'I was just fine until you went off with that woman and wrecked our lives.'

'Tommy, I never wanted to hurt you or Alannah.'

'What did you think was going to happen, Dad?' It came out as a yell.

'I know. You're right, of course.' His father pulled out a chair and sat at the kitchen table.

What was he doing? He wasn't staying, was he? Tommy began to feel panicky: this wasn't a conversation he felt equipped to have. He didn't feel strong enough to resist him. When he'd first seen him standing there, his strongest impulse had been to fling himself into his arms, as if he were a little boy. He hated himself for it. He hated his father for making him feel like that. His show of anger was hard to maintain when he felt so taken off guard. If only it wasn't so early and he wasn't so hung-over. His father was looking at him curiously. Tommy had the horrible feeling that he could read his thoughts. He glanced at the kitchen clock. 'Mam's due back any minute, you know.' The truth was, he didn't know when his mother was coming back. If ever.

His father followed his eyes to the clock. 'Those batteries need to be changed again. There's no way it's four o'clock.'

'She's coming home this morning.'

'That's good. Only if I were you, I'd clean up the kitchen before she gets back. She'll have your guts for garters if she sees it like this.'

His father was smiling at him now. Tommy turned away so he wouldn't see the smile on his own face. It felt achingly good to talk to him. Too good. He tried to bring his anger to the fore again as he opened the fridge door and looked blindly towards the eggs. He felt his father come up behind him.

'Here. Let me make you breakfast.'

'No, I don't want . . .'

'It's the least I can do.'

His father took him firmly by the shoulders and led him to the table. 'You sit yourself down. You look like you could do with the rest.'

Tommy felt more and more powerless. His body betrayed him, collapsing into the chair. His emotions were betraying him too.

'What'll it be?'

Tommy didn't reply.

'A full Irish, I think. Best cure in the world for a hangover.'

He felt his father grinning at him but he wouldn't look up. Couldn't betray his mother by doing so. He sat there helplessly while his father busied himself around the kitchen, moving with annoyingly familiar ease. He cooked a mean breakfast and Tommy's tastebuds betrayed him too as the smell of rashers filled the air.

There was an urgent scraping at the back door. Rufus. Tommy had let him out for his pee earlier. It was amazing Rufus had missed his father coming in. But he knew he was here now. Either that or the rashers. Tommy got up and opened the door. The dog went into paroxysms of ecstasy, the entire back half of his body wagging, whimpers escaping from his whiskered lips. His father petted him, knowing exactly how the dog liked to be rubbed. Stupid mutt with his misplaced loyalty. Tommy would never be like that.

This was all so confusing. On the one hand, the scene felt so familiar. On the other, it was completely wrong. Then his father placed his breakfast in front of him and it smelt so right. 'There you go. Just what the doctor ordered.'

Tommy looked his father directly in the eye. He could tell he was a little bit shocked at what he'd just said, that it had just slipped out. There was a split second in which the two nearly grinned at each other, but Tommy looked at his plate just in time. His father sat beside him and they began to eat.

'There weren't any mushrooms,' his dad said, after the first mouthful. 'I suppose they were too much like vegetables to be included on your shopping list.'

Tommy ignored the comment and kept on eating. It occurred to him that he was at an advantage here. That he could actually get away with being rude to his father. For the first time in his life. He'd never have got away with ignoring him like that before.

They ate in silence, soaking up egg yolk and juices with the type of unhealthy white processed bread that Fiona would never have allowed into the house. They washed it down with pint glasses of full-fat milk. That was normally forbidden too. If only the circumstances were different, this would have been heaven.

They were finishing, mopping up.

'I'm really sorry, Tom.'

Tommy couldn't bring himself to look at his father. It wasn't disgust. It was fear. Fear of honesty. Fear of emotion. Fear that he was going to cry.

Too late. The first tears came and he swiped at them.

'Really sorry.'

The deluge began and he covered his face. His father rubbed the back of his neck. Then he moved his chair in closer and hugged Tommy's head into his chest. That distinctive musky smell. Tommy cried with abandon.

'You're all right, Tom. You're all right.'

After a couple of minutes, Tommy pulled his head away and began to recover himself. 'Why did you do it, Dad?'

'Well.' Aidan clasped his hands in front of him thoughtfully. 'You've heard the saying bandied about "You can't help who you fall in love with."' His father looked at him and Tommy gave a slight nod, not that he knew anything about falling in love.

'Well, I always thought that was horseshit. An excuse people used to be . . . unfaithful.'

The word made Tommy cringe and his father seemed pretty embarrassed too.

'But then I met Sarah and it was like the whole world just . . . just . . . I can't describe it.'

Tommy wasn't convinced. 'I thought you loved Mam.'

'So did I.'

What had his father just said?

'I mean, I do. I do love your mother. How could I not love her? She's a wonderful woman. She's kept us in line all these years, hasn't she?' His father smiled at him weakly but Tommy had no intention of going along with this pathetic attempt to get him onside.

'But you can't have loved her. Not really.'

His father looked at him sadly. 'I suppose there are different types of love. Different strengths. Different intensities.'

Tommy believed his father was trying to tell the truth, but it just didn't add up. 'You've turned our whole family into a lie. My whole life.'

'No, Tommy. That was never a lie. That was real. Is real.'

'How can it be?'

'We're still a family. Only . . . altered.'

'Ripped apart.'

'No. My feelings for you and Alannah are exactly the same. You've got to believe that.'

'How can they be after what you've done to us? How do I know you won't stop loving us the way you stopped loving Mam?'

'I haven't and I won't.' His father sighed. 'Look, the love between parent and child is different from the love between a man and a woman. There's a special bond, Tom. It's unbreakable. A parent never stops loving their children. I hope you get a chance to experience that yourself some day.'

'If I ever have kids I'm never going to do to them what you've done to me and Alannah. Never.'

His father couldn't answer that. He just nodded.

'Do you know what Kevin told me?'

'What did he tell you?'

'That everyone knew about you and Sarah. The whole town. Back in June. Everyone except me, Lana and Mammy. He didn't tell me because of the exams. You made fools out of all of us, Dad.'

His father studied the table. 'What does Alannah think?'

'She doesn't want anything to do with you.'

His father sighed again and seemed to slump further in his seat. To Tommy he looked completely crushed, more tired than he'd ever seen him. Old and defeated. He felt something he'd never have expected to feel in this situation – he certainly hadn't felt it over the past few weeks: sympathy. He wanted to say something, but he didn't know what. *He deserves to feel this bad,* he told himself. And yet . . .

'Is Sarah . . .?'

'She's okay right now. Still able to get out. Her sister's here. That's given her a lift.'

Tommy nodded. 'There's something else I don't understand.'

'What?'

'If Sarah's . . .'

'Dying?'

'Yes. Then why couldn't you just be a really good friend to her? You didn't have to leave us. I don't get it, Dad. What's in it for you, when she's only going to be around for a little time longer?'

'What's in it for me?' His father's mouth was grim. 'That I get to be with the woman I love for every second of every day that she has left.' He got up slowly, stiffly. 'I'm going back now, Tom.' He took a wad of notes out of his pocket and put them on the table. 'There you go. Buy yourself a few vegetables. You look like you could do with them. Or at least have them in the fridge for when your mother comes back.'

Rufus got up hopefully as Aidan approached the back door. He bent low and caressed his head. 'No, boy. You stay here.' He paused with his hand on the back-door handle. 'You know, I could really do with some help on the boat.'

Tommy stared at him silently.

'Just think about it.'

Tommy had to resist the urge – the childish urge – to run after his father and fling himself into his arms. Because he wasn't a child any more.

Chapter 35

Fiona let the sea-breeze blow right through her. She lifted her face to it, held out her arms. Not too far out, because she and Yvonne were walking the seafront in Clontarf, and there were many people coming towards them. Thanks be to God, she didn't know a single one of them. The anonymity was so diametrically opposed to the claustrophobia of her home life that it was freeing. She'd miss this sense of expansion when she returned.

Since she'd arrived at Yvonne's, Fiona had been feeling as if she were shedding little pieces of herself. Which pieces she couldn't quite identify, and whether they'd still be missing when she got back, she couldn't be sure. But she did feel she would be returning home a slightly altered woman.

'I'll miss you when you go back.' Yvonne was reading her thoughts.

'It's lovely of you to say so, Yvonne, but you must be sick of me by now. I've been here nearly two weeks. If I have a house-guest for longer than two nights I feel like I'm losing my mind.'

'You must be joking. You're the easiest visitor on earth. A home-cooked meal on the table every evening when I come in from work. Jesus, who wouldn't miss that? Poor Richard will anyway. He's been spoilt rotten since you arrived. He didn't realize how hard done by he was before. He'll be wondering what kind of a wife he got himself lumbered with.'

Fiona doubted it. The two had been married for less than a year and were still very much in love. Fiona had found it almost painful to watch them together, even though she knew they were toning down their displays of affection for her benefit. But even little things, like hearing them chatting in bed at night, were excruciating.

Anyway. This was only an issue in the evenings. Richard and Yvonne worked during the day so Fiona had filled her time with museums and shops, galleries and cafés – bliss in any other circumstances. She'd visited her parents. Of course, she hadn't told them about Aidan or even that she was staying in Dublin. She could imagine what they'd have to say and she wasn't ready to hear it.

'It's not just the meals I'll miss,' Yvonne continued. 'I've really loved our chats – kicking back with a glass of wine in the evening. Life is great here, obviously, but the one thing I really miss about Clare is the great sessions we used to have putting the world to rights.'

'Ah, go on . . .'

'No, seriously, Fiona, you're great company. Never forget that.' Yvonne gave her arm a little squeeze.

Fiona was glad she was wearing sunglasses, so her friend couldn't see the tears in her eyes. She wished she could believe those words to be true but she was acutely aware of her many flaws. It was as if she'd only just begun to see herself clearly and she didn't like what she saw – particularly her tendency to be such a know-it-all at times. She guessed it was because she identified so strongly with her mind and felt her intellect was all she had to offer. When she had been growing up, people had always praised her for being clever and top of every class. Maybe she had fallen so deeply in love with Aidan because he seemed to regard her mind as just one part of an amazing package. She remembered how playful and liberated she had felt around him in the early years of their marriage. But now she saw that over the years, as they had settled into the routines of work and child-rearing, her easy-going side had gone into decline. The two weeks at Yvonne's had made her realize she needed to find it again. Even if her marriage was over, she needed to reinvent herself. She would prove to herself – and everyone else – that she had far more to offer than efficiency and brain-power.

'Are you hungry yet?' Yvonne had stopped walking.

'Yes, I think we've had enough exercise to justify lunch,' said Fiona, pulling herself together.

'How about that pub over there? They do a mean toasted sandwich.'

The two women stood arm in arm at the traffic-lights, waiting for the colours to change.

'You do know, don't you, that you can stay with us for as long as you like?'

'I know that and thank you, Yvonne, but it's high time I got back to my own life. Got back and faced things, found out whether or not Tommy's burned the house down around his ears.'

Yvonne laughed. Fiona smiled at her. 'I've missed the little blighter,' she said. 'Not that he's little any more.'

A picture of Tommy at six, wearing a bright blue anorak, pedalling his bike furiously around the driveway, popped into her head. With it came an extraordinary sensation in her chest. She didn't know what it could be – it certainly wasn't anything medical – but it felt like a desperate need to see her son as soon as possible. She wanted to see him and hold him and touch him.

Dear God, what had got into her? She *was* being sentimental today. Melodramatic, even. Tommy was fine. Alannah was fine. It wasn't as if she'd never see them again.

And then little Maia Mitchell popped into her head.

Clearly this time out with Yvonne was doing things to her

mind. It was all very well vowing to be a better, kinder person but now she was getting silly. As she raced across to the pub with Yvonne, she decided that the sooner she got back to some kind of normality, the better.

Chapter 36

Sarah and Helen were doing everything in their power to make the most of what they euphemistically referred to as Helen's 'holiday'. Only it was really Sarah's time that was running out.

Helen had driven them out to The Burren and the two women had spent the morning wandering on and wondering at its eerie moonscape. They were back now, sitting on their deck-chairs on the beach, while Maia lined up her rows of shells. The day was chilly and they each had a plaid blanket draped across their legs. Like Darby and Joan, Helen said. She was uncharacteristically quiet now. Gazing out to sea as if she was searching for answers. There were none. Sarah could have told her that. 'What's up, Sis?' Sarah nudged her arm.

'Nothing. Just thinking.'

'About what?'

'The past.'

'It's a dangerous place to visit, you know.'

There was an overlong pause.

'And?' said Sarah.

'And what?'

'What did you find lurking around in the hidden recesses of that brain of yours?'

Helen turned so she was half facing her. 'I used to be so jealous of you.'

'You were?'

'Yes. I mean, really badly jealous. I almost used to hate you at times.'

'Helen!'

'I know, I know. It's terrible. But can you blame me? Look at me. Look at you.'

'I've always thought you were very pretty.'

'Come on, Sarah. You were always streets ahead of me when it came to looks. And then there was your talent. Your fame. All the men falling over their feet to get to you.'

'And not one of them stuck. I'm almost forty and I've never been married.'

'Why did you not marry, do you think?'

'Don't know. It just never seemed to happen for me. Maybe I was too busy flitting around from one to another. Could never settle. Then Maia came along.'

'And then there was Aidan.'

'Yes. Then there was Aidan.'

'Do you think . . .?'

'Do I think that if I had a future I'd have it with him?'

'Something like that.'

'I think so. Probably. But we'll never know now, will we? At least I don't have to worry about him getting bored with me. I won't be around long enough to be boring.'

'Sarah!'

'It's true.'

They watched the sea for a while. Rolling in. Rolling out. Taking its giant breaths.

'Soothing, isn't it?'

'Yes. Sarah . . . That's not all.'

'Oh, bloody hell.'

'When I said I used to hate you. I used to sometimes . . .'

'Spit it out.'

'I used to sometimes wish that bad things would happen to you.'

'What kind of bad things?'

'I don't know. Just anything.' Helen promptly burst into tears. Not something she was prone to do.

'So now you think you've given me cancer.'

'Well, I don't know . . .'

Sarah laughed.

'It's not funny.'

'Well, I think it is. When did you stop feeling this way about me?'

'Around the time I met Dave. When I started being happy with my own life. Do you think you can forgive me?'

'Of course I can. You big noodle.' Sarah pulled her in for a hug. Was this the way it was going to be from now on? She having to comfort people who were upset because she was dying? 'I think,' she said, 'I know how to make you feel better.'

'How?' Helen sniffed.

'By getting in on this confession session myself. I've got my own little disclosure to make.'

'What is it?'

'Remember that boyfriend you had? First year of college?'

'Derek.'

'Derek! That was him. Looked like the lead singer from Echo and the Bunnymen.'

'He had the hair and all.' They roared laughing and Helen wiped away the last of her tears. 'What about him?'

'I snogged him once.'

'You did not! When? While I was going out with him?'

'Yes.'

'You bitch!'

Sarah squealed. 'Look who's talking!'

'Oh, yeah. Sorry.'

'It's all right.'

'When did it happen?'

'He called around to pick you up one night. You were taking ages to get ready – as usual. Probably couldn't fit into your ra-ra skirt or something.'

'I'll say it again. You're a bitch.'

'I know. Great, isn't it? Anyway, I was entertaining him in the sitting room and it just sort of . . . happened.'

'What do you mean it just "happened"? Somebody must have made the first move.'

'It was me. I'd never kissed anyone before and I wanted to see what it was like. I wasn't trying to steal him or anything.'

'Oh, well, that makes it all right, then. Jesus. How old were you?'

'I was fifteen.'

'Fifteen!'

'I know. He was practically a child molester. You're not really upset, are you?'

'No. I always knew he was a bit of a shit.'

'He wasn't much of a kisser either. I didn't realize at the time because I had no one to compare him with. But it was like he'd lost something inside my mouth and was trying to find it with his tongue.'

'Oh, stop. I remember now.'

'We should give him a call. Frighten the shite out of him. For the laugh. Do you think he's married?'

'Not unless his kissing technique's improved.'

The two women laughed with abandon. Maia turned to them, then went back to her shells.

They were quiet for a while, watching the waves, the surfers caught up in them, Star riding with them from time to time.

'You'll have to come in with me,' said Sarah.

'In where?'

'There.' She nodded her head forward. 'For a swim. With the dolphin.'

'Oh. No way.'

'I'll get you in there if it's the last thing I do.'

Chapter 37

It was a summer's evening in London. The workers spilled out of their offices, like prisoners on day release, onto the baking hot pavements and down, down, into the sweltering intensity of the Underground. All those people. Not one connection. Just an endless stream of humanity, looking in one direction. All about the destination. Nothing about the journey.

Alannah was among them, temporarily at least. Just one more anonymous worker. In the beginning she would forget herself, make eye contact with someone on the street and nod at them, or smile at somebody on the tube. The reaction was always instantaneous: look away from the lunatic. In this city, friendliness was equated with insanity. But in spite of that she liked it.

She would step outside her office in the evening – the office in which she was virtually inconsequential – and walk into the wall of heat that the tall buildings had retained throughout the day. Then she'd turn the corner and the first thing she'd see was the Houses of Parliament, rearing up magnificently. And she didn't feel inconsequential any more. She felt part of the throbbing history: Big Ben, Westminster Abbey. She would stroll around the Abbey on her lunchbreak, linger at Poets' Corner, marvel at Elizabeth I's tomb. Oliver Cromwell – did the Brits not know what he'd done?

Today she was going directly home, to a poky little bedsit two tube rides away. She shared it with Ross. The previous night had been fantastic. He'd got home before her for a change and opened the front door, naked under a floral pinny. Spag bol. The only thing he could cook. Candlelight and Spanish plonk. She smiled at the thought, then rapidly rearranged her features in case the woman sitting opposite thought she was a psychopath. It wasn't all that difficult to quell the smile, with negative thoughts crowding in on her again. Had her dad done things like that for Mam when they were first together? She remembered him doing plenty of nice things for her over the years. She expelled the negative images. They had no place in her rose-tinted world. Ross would never betray her like that.

When she had come back from her brief visit home, Ross had accused her of 'acting funny'. No wonder, he had said, when she had told him what had happened. She told him with shame, as if what she came from was no longer worthy and that she was no longer good enough. Ross had held her and briefly she'd felt secure. But most of the time, Alannah had felt as if she was floating and didn't know where she would end up. She was glad she was away from it all. Then she felt guilty for having this thought.

She was on her street now, nearing her front door. Her footsteps slowed and then she stopped walking altogether. It couldn't be. She saw something leap in her father's eyes when he saw her. She couldn't tell what her own looked like. She forced her feet to walk slowly forwards and he in turn walked slowly towards her.

They met halfway.

'Dad.'

'Alannah. It's good to see you.'

'What are you doing here?'

'I came to see you, of course. I thought we could talk.'

'What made you think I'd want to talk?'

'I thought it only fair to give you the chance to give out to me in person. I thought you might even enjoy it.'

She looked down at her toenails, painted crimson, poking out of the front of her sandals, looking vulnerable. She wouldn't let him soft-soap her.

'Did you get my letter?' he said.

'Yes.'

She was clearly expected to say something further. The truth was, she hadn't read it. She had carried it around with her in her pocket for two days. When she had finally opened it, she had got as far as 'Dear Alannah' before screwing it up into a ball and throwing it into the bin. After a couple of minutes' intense staring, she had taken it out again and put a match to it. She hadn't wanted to know – wasn't ready to hear. She still wasn't. Yet here he was, forcing himself, his explanations and justifications upon her. She felt angry and sullen and continued to stare at her feet.

'Are you going to let me in at least? Show me where you've been living and what state you've been living in?'

'No.' Her response was urgent and instantaneous. She didn't want him invading this private little part of her. She had a horrifying thought. Did he expect to stay with her? 'How long are you here for?'

'I'm catching a flight later tonight.'

She breathed a little easier. That was something.

She knew it was rude, not inviting him in. It went against her basic nature. But apart from anything else, Ross might be there, resplendent in his pinny. And even if he wasn't there personally, there were bits of him everywhere. His boxers on the bedroom floor where he'd stepped out of them this morning. And while her parents weren't stupid, and they knew that she and Ross were living together, there was no need to rub her father's face in it. It would only embarrass both of them. Then again maybe he deserved it.

'Is there somewhere we can go to talk?'

She sighed in exasperation and defeat. They couldn't stay here in a stand-off all evening. And she could hardly go in on her own and leave him there. She wasn't that cruel. And he had made the effort to come all this way to see her . . .

'There's a café on the next street.' She marched forward. She could hear him a few paces behind. It made her feel important. She knew her way around here and her father didn't. He was a stranger, she practically a native. She wouldn't bring him to her favourite place in case one or other of them made a scene and she couldn't show her face in there again. Besides, he didn't deserve somewhere nice.

People walked by them on the street, typically uncurious. She wondered if her father seemed as out of place to them as he did to her. Like an alien that had just landed from another planet. An innocent abroad. Although, as he had proved lately, not all that innocent.

They entered the café and stood stiffly at the counter.

'Have anything you want,' her father said. 'My treat.'

She swung around to him, quite aggressively. 'You bet it's your treat.'

He smiled at her ruefully and she forced herself not to smile back. Her feelings were so mixed that she didn't trust herself. They sat down with two coffees and two enormous pavlovas, the tension between them equally vast.

'So,' he said, 'how are you liking London?'

'I love it. I'm thinking of staying for good.'

She wasn't, of course. The words were calculated to hurt.

'You mean not go back to college?'

'No,' she countered weakly. 'I mean live here when I've finished college.'

'Oh. And your job?'

'The job's great.'

It was all right.

'Your colleagues treating you well?'

'Ah. They're a bit patronizing towards "the little Irish girl".' She grimaced. 'They're always telling me I'm so wholesome and fresh-faced. Things like that. And there's this one woman and she's always going on about my freckles. Stupid eejit. As if no one in the whole of England had freckles.'

'Surely fresh-faced is a bit of a compliment.'

'No, it isn't. I bet you wouldn't like it.'

He laughed. 'It's a long time since anyone accused me of being fresh-faced, Alannah.'

She looked down at her dessert so he wouldn't see the amusement in her eyes. Damn her father anyway. He had this way of reaching her, opening her up. And she responded like some over-eager puppy. She stabbed at the pavlova with her fork.

'Remember how you used to rub lemon juice on your nose to try and fade your freckles?'

'Mmm.' She was noncommittal, her mouth full of meringue. If he thought she was joining him on a pleasant trip down Memory Lane, he could think again.

He seemed to sense this. 'Look, Lana, as you well know, I didn't come here to talk about freckles.'

She said nothing, gave him nothing. She wanted to know what he had to say yet she was fearful of it.

'First and foremost, I'm sorry. Sorry for all the hurt I've caused you and your brother.'

'And Mam.' She was instantly furious.

'And your mother. Of course your mother. It's just that I'm here today to talk about how this affects you and Tommy.'

She didn't trust herself to speak. She was trying to control the little prickles at the back of her eyes.

'I want you to know that it was my marriage I left, not my children. Never my children.' His voice was low and urgent.

'I've never stopped being your dad, Alannah. Not for one second.'

'You've destroyed our family.' The tears were in her voice now and she despised herself for her weakness.

'It's not destroyed. Just changed. Just different. We'll be a family again, you'll see.'

'You didn't see Mam, what you did to her. How crushed she was. How could you do that, Dad? She didn't deserve it.'

'I know she didn't, love.' Her father looked ashamed of himself and she was glad.

'So why did you do it?' She really wanted to know.

They stared into each other's eyes and Aidan shrugged.

'I fell in love.'

What was that supposed to mean? 'For God's sake, Dad. You're not a teenager. I'm the one who's supposed to be immature, not you. If you were going to have a mid-life crisis, could you not have just bought yourself a motorbike?'

They were silenced, shocked by the incongruity of her words. Then they both started to laugh, helplessly and simultaneously. Alannah was annoyed with herself, but couldn't stop. The situation was so unreal, so ridiculous. Above all, she was glad she hadn't chosen the other café because she wouldn't be able to set foot in this one again. First nearly blubbing, then laughing uncontrollably. She could feel the eyes of the other customers on them. Their waitress was hovering close by with a pot of coffee.

She wiped her eyes with her napkin and blew her nose as discreetly as possible. Her father was looking relieved. That wasn't right. It annoyed her. 'Don't think I've forgiven you or anything.'

'Oh, I don't.'

'It's going to take a lot more than a pavlova.'

'I know.'

'It's not even a very good pavlova.'

'Yes. The meringue should be sticky on the inside. This is all dry and chalky.'

'Serves you right,' she said.

Her father smiled, and gestured to the waitress for a refill. Alannah felt a pull in her chest. If only she didn't love him so much. It made it so hard to be mean to him. She examined his face as he was looking away from her. He seemed older than she remembered. The lines around his eyes when he smiled were deeper.

'Is it true?' she said, when the waitress had gone away. 'About . . . Sarah.' It was hard to say her name.

His face clouded and he leaned forward again. 'Yes, it's true.'

'How long?'

'A month or two.'

Alannah was floored. In all their conversations about the sick actress, Tommy had never explained she was that sick. 'Is that all?' She couldn't keep the words in.

Aidan nodded and looked even more tired.

'So when . . . it's all over, what are you going to do?'

'I don't know. I can't think that far down the line.'

Alannah shook her head. It was incomprehensible to her. Her father – her stable, sensible father – throwing away everything for a woman who wouldn't see Christmas. A small part of her even found it romantic. But she stuffed that bit down to where it belonged.

'I need you to know something,' he was saying to her urgently.

'What?'

'I need you to know that it was never my intention to hurt anybody, as stupid as that sounds. Not you, not Tommy or your mother. And I know that I have hurt you all. Terribly.

But just so you know. It was never my intention. You believe me, don't you, Alannah?'

She looked at him for a few seconds, then nodded. She didn't have to ask herself what Sarah saw in him. She knew. And another thought struck her. A new and wholly surprising one: out of all the people her father had hurt, and after all the upset he had caused, the person who was suffering most was himself.

Chapter 38

Another three days and Helen's holiday would be over. The two women clung to each other like limpets to a rock. This was the day that Helen had agreed to get into the water with Star. Sarah had worn her down as the sea erodes the cliffs.

'But I'm scared of water.'

'We'll go to the cove. There won't be any waves.'

'But I can't swim.'

'You can wear a life-jacket.'

'I don't even like animals.'

'Star's no ordinary animal. You'll like her.'

Helen gave in. She had no choice.

The day was clear and bright. The foursome walked down to the beach, hand in hand, Helen and Sarah in front, Aidan and Maia behind. Their collective emotions were mixed. Trepidation. Expectation. Nostalgia. Joy. They had arrived.

Aidan helped Helen with her life-jacket, her discomfort almost palpable. He felt a little sorry for her. She had made him promise to leave his camera at home. She said she wanted no photographic evidence of herself in a swimsuit.

'Come on, then.' Sarah took her sister's hand and the pair waded in.

'I'm not going further than waist level.'

'You won't have to.'

The water was calm, the life-jacket ridiculous. Star greeted them with a succession of impressive leaps and torpedoed towards them.

'Oh, Jesus Christ.' Helen froze as the dorsal fin sliced through the water in her direction.

Sarah battled Helen's urge to turn and run, linking her arm tightly and propelling her forward. 'Come on. You'll be fine.'

'I've heard of dolphins pinning swimmers down to the sea bed.'

'Not this one. She's never harmed anyone.'

'But it's a wild animal. You don't know what it'll do.'

Maia splashed ahead of them and was joined by the dolphin, sweeping and circling. Helen relaxed slightly as she registered the little girl's lack of fear. 'Maybe I'll just watch for a while.'

Sarah examined her face. 'Okay,' she said, let her go and waded forward a few feet, joining her daughter.

Aidan moved up alongside Helen. 'You all right?'

'I'm fine,' she said, momentarily startled by his bare chest.

They watched mother and daughter in the water. Maia was never so animated as when she was with Star. The two other-worldly creatures squealed at each other as if communicating on some level that only they could understand. Then, as was her habit, Star swam over to investigate the other humans with whom she was sharing her water. She swam right up to a rigid Helen, who screamed with a mixture of fear and excitement. The sound seemed to frighten the dolphin and, to Helen's combination of relief and disappointment, she swam back to Sarah and Maia.

Sarah was holding Maia now, her own body embraced by her daughter's arms and legs. She supported her with just one arm, her free hand trailing lightly on top of the water. Star positioned her blowhole directly under Sarah's hand, remaining several inches under the water. Then she blew bubbles into her palm, a rhythmic succession. Sarah looked down at Star, then back at Aidan and Helen. *Are you seeing this?* Then she brought her attention back to her daughter. Something was coming over Maia's features. Something new and indefinable. Then the child lifted her head and did something she'd never done before. Maia laughed. The sound bubbled up through her body and emerged triumphantly from her throat.

A bowl. That's what it reminded Helen of. A great big bowl of stars turned upside-down over their heads. It was two nights later and Sarah had made them bring her to the beach. 'Let's lie down,' she had said.

So they had. On the sand. Soft and yielding, moulding themselves into it. Aidan, Sarah and Helen, in that order. Sarah said they should drink it in with their eyes and with all of their senses until they were filled with stars, full to the brim. Brimming with stars.

It was like staring eternity in the eye, Helen thought. No getting away from it. She recalled other times in her life when she had looked to the stars. Outside her house in Minnesota at night: on the ground, the suburbs in all their determined ordinariness, and up above the heavens spreading outwards in all their terrifying glory. She had always chosen to duck her head back inside, to the utility room, the TV. She chose banality every time. Chose to ignore that she might be short-changing herself. But out here, with her sister, who had never taken the easy route either in life or out of it, Sarah wouldn't let her get away with it. Would make her look.

'You know we're all made of stars, don't you?'

Aidan's deep voice made Helen jump.

'How do you mean?' Her sister's voice, softer and sweeter.

'The only elements that have existed for ever are hydrogen and helium. All the other elements were created by applying massive amounts of heat and pressure to those two. And the only place in the universe, in nature, where that kind of heat and pressure exists is in the centre of stars. So, if everything on earth, including humans, is made up of those elements, then it follows that we must be made of stars.'

Sarah laughed. 'I like that. We're stardust. All three of us. The whole world. Nothing but stardust.' She stretched her arms above her head and luxuriated in the sensation. A shooting star fell across the sky. 'That'll be me soon.'

Helen froze. Aidan said nothing. When it became clear to Sarah that her comment had been met by a resounding silence, she spoke again. 'We're going to have to talk about it sooner or later. If not for my sake, then for Maia's.'

'I'll take her back with me to America. When it's time.'

'I don't want you to do that, Hel. I want her to stay here.'

Helen lifted herself onto her elbows and looked down into her sister's face. Sarah's eyes were closed. She seemed extraordinarily tranquil.

'I want her to stay here with Aidan.' Her tone was matter-of-fact. As if she were giving instructions as to her grocery requirements. Although how else she could have said it, Helen didn't know. A fanfare of trumpets was hardly practical.

Aidan was sitting up now, his elbows resting on his knees. The star-gazing session was officially over. 'What about her father?'

'He doesn't want her.'

'But he has rights.'

'He's coming to see me next week. We'll sort it out then.'

Aidan and Helen looked down at Sarah, her eyes still closed, then at each other, full of questions.

'Where will he be staying?'

'Don't worry. He won't be here long enough for it to become an issue.' She sounded definite rather than bitter.

'But, Sarah, won't he want some say in his daughter's future?'

Sarah shrugged. 'He's never shown any interest up to

now.' She sat up and moved closer to Aidan. Helen watched as she laid a hand on his forearm and looked up into his face, which was still directed towards the ocean. 'You'll take her, won't you?'

The words were softly spoken, barely above a whisper. Aidan's head moved around and he gazed down at her. Helen was almost jealous of the look he gave her.

'I will.'

Sarah hugged his arm and he pulled her closer. Was there anything he'd deny her?

'And, Helen, I want you to be her other guardian.'

'Have you really thought this through properly?'

'I have.'

'But – I don't mean any offence, Aidan – wouldn't she be better off with family?'

'I want her to stay here, Helen. She's happy here. You wouldn't want to refuse me my dying wish, would you?' Sarah was looking at her intently, one corner of her mouth slightly raised.

'Not another dying wish. You've had at least ten of them since I got here.'

'It's important to know when to press your advantage.'

'It's important to know when not to overdo it.'

'Go on, Helen. Say you'll be her guardian.'

'Of course I will. I just think you should wait and hear what Mitch has to say about it.'

Sarah smiled a placatory smile, satisfied that she had got her way again. 'Now I'm going to make a sand angel,' she announced, and lay down again, moving her skinny arms back and forth, a guardian on either side of her.

Helen's flight was an early one. Aidan drove them all to the airport, the sky still streaked with red. He didn't say much.

And neither, of course, did Maia, who lolled in her booster seat, half asleep. The two women were locked in their own private world. Fingers, memories, souls interlocking.

'Do you remember the first time Daddy called you Sassy?'

Sarah shook her head.

'You were only about five, doing one of your shows in the sitting room. You kept popping out from behind the couch in different outfits. Wearing Mammy's high heels. Gorky shoes, we used to call them. Do you remember? I don't know why we called them that. You'd be doing your little song-and-dance routines. I was jealous of you even then. You were always so much more sparkly than me. And Daddy's face when he looked at you. His little Sassy. I always wanted a name like that.'

'It's just a name, Hel.'

'But it suited you so well. And it's not just the name. It's what was behind it. The affection.'

'Daddy loved you too.'

'I know he did.'

They both thought of their father. One of them wondered if she'd see him again soon. The other hugged into her sister's arm, as if never letting go of her would make a difference.

They entered the departure hall on leaden feet. The women huddled together and spoke to each other urgently. Aidan took Maia to see the planes. She stood at the plate glass, fascinated. 'Pane,' she said, over and over. 'Pane.'

Sarah walked Helen up to the man who checked the boarding passes. He looked away discreetly as they cried all over one another. He was used to public displays of affection, although seldom so uncontained. Then they were separate. And the other travellers walked around Sarah as she took in her sister's every last move. The clumsy way she removed her boots for the security man. The many times she had to walk through the metal detector, successively taking off more bits of jewellery. When it was over, Helen gathered up her belongings and turned to her sister one last time. Then she waved and was gone.

Aidan was waiting for Sarah, hand in hand with Maia.

'Pane, Mama,' said her daughter. 'Pane.'

Chapter 39

The house was still, but welcoming. It felt so good to be back in its familiar arms, among all her things, the colours she had chosen. Her paintings. Their furniture. Fiona ran her fingers around the curve of the dining-room table. Then she remembered the night that *she* had sat there and hastily withdrew to the kitchen, where the memories were of her family.

She'd received no slobbery greeting from Rufus, which could only mean that he was out with Tommy. Fiona moved to the window. The sea was dotted with surfers. On the beach, a black speck zigzagged up and down. Rufus, following his mysterious doggy smells.

Fiona smiled, satisfied. Her son was close by. She kicked off her sensible shoes and replaced them with daft fluffy slippers. Then she opened the fridge to see what crustiness awaited her. Not too bad. No offensive smells. A lot of Coke and too much beer. Many pork products. But considering he wasn't expecting her, the place was in pretty good nick. She began to make herself coffee. Oh, the joy. Yvonne and her husband were lovely, had done everything in their power to make her feel welcome, but they knew fuck-all about coffee. It felt like aeons since she'd had a decent cup. She could have done something about it. Normally she would have done. She wasn't the type of woman who balked at muscling in on somebody else's domestic arrangements. But she hadn't done so and she didn't quite know why. She thought it was a confidence thing. Fiona McDaid – always so sure of herself. Not any more.

It was good to be back beside the sea too. The proper sea. Wild and rough. Not the pathetic little seafront that Dublin had to offer. She'd missed the waves. The rushing. The rhythm. In. Out. In. Out. Odd, how something so powerful, so threatening, could also be so soothing.

She had considered staying in Dublin for good. Thought long and hard about it. It made sense: nothing but an empty nest to go back to. And she wasn't even from the place. God knew, there were plenty of locals willing to remind her of the fact even twenty years on. But she had come to the realization – the surprising one – that no matter what anybody else thought, the town now felt like home. And her house – she loved it. Perched on the edge of the Atlantic. Built on sand instead of rock. Vulnerable to rising sea levels. But she couldn't leave. Wouldn't. It was one of the few good things she had left out of her marriage. That and her children.

She glanced down at her ring finger. It had been blank now for the best part of three weeks. In the beginning there had been a white ring of skin, but that had darkened now, after three weeks' exposure to the sun, and merged into the rest of her hand. So soon.

One of the black dots had stopped bobbing up and down on the ocean and was now walking up the beach, a white board under his arm, the black speck zigzagging rapidly behind him. Fiona stood up and away from her maudlin thoughts. She opened the fridge and took out the packets of rashers and sausages, already partly plundered. She wouldn't normally have approved of such a breakfast. Wouldn't normally approve of having such food in the house, but nothing was normal any more. And Tommy was always starving after he surfed. Besides, she felt like spoiling him. They'd never been apart for so long. And soon he'd be gone permanently. She banished the thought as she positioned the rashers on the grill pan. At least this was healthier than frying. And he wasn't having Coke. He could wash it all down with the freshly squeezed orange juice she'd bought on the way home.

The back door opened and Fiona smiled to herself. Rufus skittered into the room, his tail a blur. It was either Fiona he smelt or the rashers. Either way, he skidded about in a state of high excitement. Tommy walked in stiffly behind him, his face wary, as if not knowing what or whom to expect. Then he saw Fiona and broke into smiles.

'Mam.' He walked impulsively to her and hugged her awkwardly, his board still under his arm.

'You're all wet,' she squealed, as he squeezed her. When had he become a man?

'Sorry.'

'It's all right, but next time take your wetsuit off before you come into the house.'

'I will.'

There she was, reverting to type already, poor Tommy barely in the door. She could hear herself but it was as if she couldn't stop herself. Back in mother mode already, having been in friend mode for the last couple of weeks. She believed herself to be far less of a pain in the arse as a friend than as a mother.

She was aware that part of the reason she was being so bossy now with Tommy was because of how he had seen her before she left. So broken. Helpless and weak. She wanted to dispel that image for ever. For both their sakes.

'Something smells good,' he said.

'The rashers and sausages you've been buying since I've been gone.'

Tommy looked sheepish.

'You may as well finish them up. Get them out of the house. I don't suppose a vegetable passed your lips the whole time I was away.'

'I ate two raw carrots yesterday.' Tommy was defensive.

'Did you? Good man. Go up now and get changed and this'll be ready for you by the time you get down.'

Fiona began to hum to herself as Tommy went upstairs. Her movements were almost jaunty as she set the table for her son. She was feeling so much better now. She'd got her role back. Her groove. She grinned and put on the radio. Something cheery. Happy background noise.

Tommy came down, his hair towel-dried and sticking up wildly. He sat down eagerly at the table.

'Would you look at yourself? What have you done with your hair?' Fiona fussed around his head.

'Stop!'

'I'm just flattening it down.'

'Don't use your spit.'

'I'm not. Don't be ridiculous. My God, Tommy. You'd need a wire brush to get through this lot.'

'Ah, will you stop it, Mam? I'm starving.'

'Always thinking about your stomach.' Fiona assembled his mixed grill and put the plate in front of him, simultaneously planting a kiss on the side of his face.

Tommy began wolfing it down immediately. Fiona sat next to him with her muesli and another mug of coffee. He looked astoundingly healthy for a boy who'd been fending for himself over the last fortnight. She felt a pang that he could survive so well without her – but proud too. No doubt his healthy glow was down to the fresh air and exercise he'd been getting in the surf. She hoped it had been a good life they'd given their children, here, on the edge of the roughest of elements. She thought it was.

'So,' said Fiona. 'The house is still standing.'

He nodded, his mouth full.

'Did you have many people over?'

'A few,' he managed.

Which, thought Fiona, could roughly be translated as ten to twelve. 'Male or female?'

'Mam!'

'Well, a mother likes to know these things.'

'A mother likes to hear what she wants to hear,' said Tommy.

'Cheeky so-and-so.' Fiona pretended to be taken aback, but there was a smile in her eyes.

'I'm glad you're back, Mam.'

'I'm sure you are. Someone to cook for you and clean up after you.'

'Does that mean I don't have to wash up?'

'It does not.'

They smiled at one another, both entirely comfortable now. She took a sip of coffee and ran her fingers over the nicks in the table. 'Did anything happen while I was away?'

'Like what?'

'I don't know. Anything. Did anyone call around? Did you see anyone?'

'You mean, did I see Dad?'

She looked down at the table.

'He called round one day.'

'On his own?'

'Yes.'

'What did he have to say for himself?'

'Lots of stuff. Sorry mostly.'

She nodded. 'Is he still . . .?'

'He's still living with Sarah.'

She nodded again, more vigorously, as if she was trying to get the repellent idea to stick inside her head.

'There's something else I have to tell you,' her son added.

'What?'

'I've started going out on the boat with him in the afternoons.'

'Have you?'

'I have. You don't mind, do you?'

'Not at all. Why should I?'

'Well, for obvious reasons, Mam. I'll stop if you want me to.'

'No, no. Sure, why would you do that?'

'If it upsets you.'

'No, Tom. It's your job. You'll need to get a bit of money together before you go away in October. And, besides, he's still your father.'

'So you're sure you don't mind, then?'

'I'm sure.'

'Definitely?'

'Absolutely. I don't mind.'

She did mind. But she knew she had no right to.

Voices floated in from the deck. Tommy and Fiona looked at one another, instantaneously sharing the one thought. But it wasn't him. The voices were younger and there were several of them. Fiona felt her shoulders relax.

The voices and their owners drifted right into the kitchen. Tommy's friends, Kevin, Paddy and Tim. Their confident swaggers, their overloud laughter, all ended abruptly at the sight of Fiona. 'Boys,' she said.

Kevin was the quickest to compose himself. 'Dr McDaid. We didn't know you were back.'

'You don't say?'

Paddy was carrying a plastic bag. It dangled self-consciously against his elongated calf. With a marked lack of subtlety, he hid it behind his legs, drawing Fiona's attention to the fact that it contained a six-pack of beer. He looked excruciatingly uncomfortable. They all did. Was she really that terrifying?

She stood up slowly. 'A bit early for that kind of carry-on, isn't it, Paddy?'

She watched his Adam's apple bob up and down. 'Here.' She held out her hand. Paddy handed her the bag. 'Now, I'm going to put it in the fridge where it can stay nice and cool for later. In the meantime, why don't you all sit down and I'll fix you some breakfast? Kevin, do you take your eggs scrambled or fried?'

'Fried, please.' Kevin didn't have to be asked twice. He sat down beside Tommy and grinned. The other two, slower and more incredulous, joined them.

Fiona busied herself at the stove. She looked back once at her son and saw his happiness. It filled her.

Chapter 40

Tommy went out that night. Fiona didn't mind. Except she did. She didn't realize how much until after he'd gone. The house was as quiet as a tomb, the clock ticking into the silence, each tick louder than the last. Eventually she couldn't stand it any more. She turned on the TV to drown the silence and opened a bottle of wine to drown her sorrows. It felt both reasonable and appropriate.

The TV was slick, the wine slicker. She wondered what Aidan and Sarah were doing, as she had wondered every night since he'd left. Except now they were palpably close again. She could almost hear his heartbeat on the seat beside her. Feel his breath. Except it wasn't her head on his chest.

So she drank more wine. She knew this wasn't a wise move, that it was making things worse instead of better. But she couldn't seem to stop herself. Just as she couldn't stop herself raiding the fridge and the kitchen presses. Anything to comfort, to anaesthetize. At this rate, she'd be twenty stone and he'd never come back to her. A fat, raving lunatic of a lush, that was what she was turning into. That was what he had turned her into. Her anger began to build. As did her self-pity.

She hatched a plan to go over there. March up to their front door – it was no longer merely *hers* – hammer loudly on it, demand entry. Tell them what was what. Deliver a large piece of her mind. Yet her mind was becoming more befuddled by the minute. More sozzled. Not worth delivering to anybody. She lay backwards on the couch and the ceiling spun. Oh dear. Never a good sign. She hauled herself up and wove her way through the lower part of the house and out of the back door. Fresh air was what she needed. Or did that make you even more drunk? Drive the alcohol deeper into your veins? For the life of her, she couldn't remember. Dr McDaid was firmly off duty.

She stood unsteadily on the deck for several seconds. She knew it was officially chilly out, that she needed a jacket, but she couldn't feel the cold. So, what the hell? She devised a plan to combat climate change. If everyone remained drunk all the time, no one would need to turn on the heating. Brilliant! Even half cut she could save the planet. Except maybe she was fully cut by now. She kicked off her slippers and left them on the deck. She descended into the sand, bare-footed and bare-armed. Bare-souled.

The night felt beautifully cool on her skin, the breeze like a waterless waterfall. Refreshing. The wind blew the clouds across the moon, at times revealing, at others concealing. And the stars disclosed themselves in clusters. Fiona stumbled along in the sand, telling herself that its uneven texture was making her walk like that. But soon she was out of the soft, the deep, and onto the hard and flat. Any further stumbling belonged to her and her alone. She was still clutching the bottle of wine. She'd only just realized it. She must have ditched the glass somewhere along the way. Hopefully in the kitchen. It was a good one. Part of a set. They'd got it for their wedding. Hah. She'd make sure she smashed it when she got back in.

Every so often, she'd take a swig of wine. Trickles would flow from the side of her mouth, like blood. She wiped them lustily with the bare skin of her forearm. How fortunate, she thought, that she didn't have a sleeve. Nothing to stain. Skin just washed clean. She knew the thought was irrelevant, but she had it anyway. Oh, fuck. She wasn't alone. Someone else was on the beach. Two someones. Walking hand in hand.

Walking towards her. She hid the bottle behind her back like a bold child and tried her best to look sober. She walked in an imaginary straight line along the sand, as if a garda had stopped her car and was testing her sobriety. She held her head high as the couple approached.

'Evening,' she said.

'Hi, Dr McDaid.'

It was a local girl. She didn't remember her name. She didn't recognize the boy – although he might have been a child she'd known who had grown up. She'd had that experience a few times of late. She felt them eyeing her curiously as they walked on by, hand in hand. She slyly passed the bottle from her back to her front. A few seconds later she heard the girl's high-pitched giggle.

'... drunk ...' The wind carried the word to her.

Laugh all you want, bitch, thought Fiona. Laugh while you still can. Only a matter of time before he dumps you, cheats on you. In no particular order. Then you won't be so smug.

She took another swig. She supposed it would be all over town tomorrow. Dr McDaid sozzled and wandering pathetically on the beach. Pathetic and alone.

She had reached the sea now. She stood on the division between water and land. Then she crossed the line into the ocean. This cold, she could feel. Like sticking her feet in a bucket of ice. A thrill travelled up through her body and she felt newly exhilarated. The sea was rough, exciting, the waves giddy. She rolled up her trousers as far as they would go and waded in further. She balanced herself with her arms, the bottle in her left hand. She took another swig. Almost gone now. Further she went – up to her pelvis. The waves were roaring in her ears now. Deafening her. If she were to scream, no one would hear. Not the smug, innocent couple. Not anyone. She tried it. Long, lovely and loud. It felt good. She did it again, lifting her arms above her head and stretching her fingertips out as far as they would go. And screaming. At the top of her lungs. Now that was what she called therapy. She should start prescribing it. Good for whatever ails you. Then she got the fright of her life. There was something moving in the water beside her. Something dark and shadowy and sleek. Before she had time to back off, a cloud lifted away from the moon, illuminating everything. A silver arc rose and fell before her in the water. Fiona exhaled as relief flooded her.

'What are you doing here?' she yelled. 'Don't you ever sleep?'

Did dolphins sleep? She had no idea. Her mind grasped at a half-forgotten conversation she'd had with Aidan. Something about dolphins shutting off one side of their brain at a time as they slept. That was it. They had to stay semi-awake because they were conscious breathers. Not unconscious breathers like humans. It occurred to Fiona now that if she had to breathe consciously, she most likely would have stopped three weeks ago, the pain of living having seemed so great at the time. Truth be told, it wasn't that much better now.

The creature continued to swim around her, just as she had swum around Aidan, Sarah and Maia. Which reminded Fiona, who hurled the bottle at Star.

'Fuck off, you bitch.' She was yelling again, slurring her words, wavering unsteadily. 'If it hadn't been for you, she would never have come. And none of this would ever have happened. It's all your fault you – cow!'

She felt ridiculous. Was ridiculous. Knew herself to be, even in this drink-sodden state. Imagine throwing a bottle at a dumb animal. Imagine throwing it into the sea where it could wash up on the shore, smash against a rock and cut some child's feet. She sometimes came across broken glass on the beach and it never failed to incense her. And now, here she was, just as bad as those people who left glass around. Worse.

She moved further into the sea. Further away from the shore. She had to get that bottle back. She wouldn't be responsible for a child hurting itself. She was waist level. Now chest level. The water was rougher out here, the waves more insistent. Logic non-existent. She was aware of a dorsal fin to her left, travelling straight towards her, making her panicky. The speed was uncanny, right up against her now, her heart in her mouth as the dolphin nudged her, before turning abruptly and swimming in the opposite direction. And there was the bottle, bobbing up and down alongside her. It was a split second before she realized that Star had brought it to her. Well, she reasoned, she *was* a bottlenose dolphin. The thought made her laugh. But as she opened her mouth, she let in sea water. Lots of it. Fiona went under.

Panic overtook her as she fought to the surface. She emerged, coughing and spitting. She had to get out. She wasn't a strong swimmer and the water was treacherous. Suddenly sober, she knew this to be madness, but was she too late? She could no longer feel the ocean floor. She looked to shore. It was further away than she had imagined. Fiona began to swim, her arms and legs ineffectual against the drag of the tide. A wave crashed gigantically over her head and she was pulled under. She felt helpless against the force of the water. Felt weak. And then the most frightening thing of all happened. She thought about giving up. Of not fighting any more. Of letting the waves do with her as they wished. Take her where they may. She would submit. Yield. Go with the flow of the ever-changing ocean.

She felt her body go limp. An extraordinary sense of peace washed over her. *The peace of God that surpasses all understanding.* These words ran through her mind. Was this it? Was this what death felt like? Was it her time? The irony wasn't lost on her. But she was only forty-four. This couldn't be her time. She struggled, breaking the surface of the water with her head, drawing in life breath. She began swimming again, harder now, against the full force of the ocean. It was useless. She was losing. One final push. She felt tears in her eyes. Salt water. This couldn't be it. She couldn't let it be.

Gathering her final resources, Fiona sliced at the water with her arms, kicked ferociously with her feet. And just as it was falling away from her, her strength diminishing to nothing, something came up beneath her and propelled her forward. Fiona flew towards the shore, flailing helplessly, until she felt the sand beneath her feet again. Dry land. *Terra firma*. Blessed relief. She stumbled forward, desperate to be out of the water. When she'd cleared it, she fell onto the sand, panting heavily between coughs. She turned and looked back out to sea. Nothing.

But she knew there had been something.

A few days after her drunken swim Fiona went back to work. After that escapade she knew she needed work to anchor her. For her first day back, she put on a trouser suit. She was feeling vulnerable already: why add to it with a skirt?

It was just as well she wore armour because they all came out – the vultures and the voyeurs. They came to gawk at the cuckolded wife. Could you be cuckolded if you were female? She wasn't sure. She decided to look it up some time, if she could be bothered. But the thing was – the crucial thing was – that it hadn't been as bad as she'd expected. As usual, the things in life that she'd wasted precious moments worrying about had turned out not to be worth worrying about in the first place. And the one thing she'd never worried about – her husband leaving her for another woman – had come to pass.

She was sure there was a lesson in there somewhere. She just couldn't figure out what it was.

Her mood was buoyant when she left the surgery that evening and it didn't even dip much when she returned to her half-empty house. Just Tommy and her. Where once there had been four, now there were only two. Soon there would be just one.

A short while ago she would have doubted her ability to cope with such a scenario. But something had shifted in Fiona since the night when she had grappled with death and come out the victor. Now that this second chance at life had been delivered to her, she had no intention of wasting another second feeling sorry for herself. She was no victim and she had proved it. And if she'd had some help in her triumph over the elements . . . Well, she didn't go there. Only in her bed, lying awake through the early hours, did it seem possible. In the pure light of day, it seemed ludicrous – a wave had propelled her to the shore. All else was drunken hallucination. In any case, she felt better than she had ever expected to feel again and that was a pretty good start.

Chapter 41

Aidan and Sarah were in the bath. Sarah hadn't felt up to going out that day, so this was their self-created sea. Aidan had lit numerous numinous night-lights. These were their self-created stars. The bath was tiny and narrow, barely large enough for Aidan alone, yet they managed, sitting face to face, she cradled between his big hairy knees, which rose up out of the water on either side of her like mountains.

Sarah was listless. She appeared to have shrunk into herself. She had been this way since Helen had left. She was sicker too, requiring more painkillers. It was as if the illness had been held in abeyance while her sister was there. As if she had been having a holiday from her illness. Aidan suspected her symptoms to be as much psychological as physical, although the more he observed, the more he became convinced that the two aspects were intertwined, to the point of being indistinguishable.

She was brighter now, however, than she'd been all day. Her features were relaxed. All day long, her face had brightened only when Maia had walked into the room. It didn't do that for him. Which was good, he reasoned. She had to be able to show her pain, her sorrow, to someone. But it did make him wonder about the nature of her feelings towards him. Did she really love him? Or was she just clinging to him in her hour of greatest need? Was he the only port in this ultimate storm? It was so hard to know – the irony being that they probably wouldn't be together now if she hadn't got sick. It was what made every moment they had together so intense in its own bittersweet way. She was staring at him.

'What is it?'

'You look tired,' she said.

'Do I?' Did he? He never really considered it.

'Yes. I'm taking a toll on you.'

'Nonsense, woman. Sure I'm grand. Big, strapping fellow like me. I can take anything you have to throw at me.'

She smiled. But her smile was weak, sad. 'I hope so.'

'I can.'

She sighed then, and appeared to relax a little. 'It suits you, though.'

'What does?'

'Being tired.'

He raised his eyebrows.

'It does, you know. Makes your features more defined. The lines around your eyes are deeper, sexier.'

He grinned at her and she grinned back.

'Like when you smile,' she said.

She placed her hands on her own knees and rested her left cheek against them. The gesture was so childlike, so vulnerable. In his chest he felt such a surge of love for her. As if he just wanted to scoop her up and hold her tight against him. Protect her from everything. Why couldn't he do that? Well, for one thing, the bath was too small. She lifted her head again, her neck reminding him of a stem. 'I bet you have lovely lines around your mouth too. Except nobody ever gets to see them.'

He reached up his hand and touched his beard, transferring bubbles onto it in the process. 'There's a reason for that.'

'I know there is.'

He hesitated. 'You want me to shave off my beard?'

She shrugged. 'It's up to you.'

He threw back his head and laughed. 'Typically female response.'

She merely smiled, watching him with her head inclined.

He thought of asking her if this was another one of her dying wishes. But the mood didn't seem right and that joke was no longer funny.

They both regarded each other seriously now.

'I thought you liked me the way I am.'

'I do. I don't want to change you, Aidan. Just see the real you.'

'This is the real me. I've had this beard for so long, it's part of me.'

'That's fine. It was just a thought.' She rested her face against her knees again, apparently resigned.

Suddenly a tidal wave. The waters shifted as Aidan rose up.

'What are you doing?'

'If it's the real thing you want, it's the real thing you'll get.'

'You don't have to.'

'I want to. I want to prove to you that I'm not hiding anything under here. That I don't have any hideous scars. Or a weak chin.'

'Perish the thought.' She was sitting upright now and laughing at him. He watched her in the mirror of the medicine cabinet. How much brighter she was. 'You'd really do this for me?'

He turned to her. 'You know I'd do anything for you.' He returned to the medicine cabinet and she swallowed, taking him all in. His arse cheeks clenched and soapy.

Aidan rooted around until he found what he was looking for – the packet of disposable razors that Helen had left behind. Hardly ideal but all he had to hand. He lathered his face with soap and began the process, creating little landing strips at first. It wasn't unlike mowing the lawn, which was all he had to compare it with, it had been so long since he'd shaved. Which was one of the reasons he kept nicking himself. The other being the inadequacy of the razor. 'The right tool is the one that gets the job done' – he heard his father's voice in his head. He'd been thinking about him a lot lately, wondering what he'd make of the predicament his son had got himself into. Or maybe he thought of him because he was dead.

It was fast emerging now – the Aidan Ryan jawline. Surprising even him. He'd never let his beard grow into a big bush. It was always well trimmed and had a shape to it. Fiona had told him on several occasions that it enhanced his features rather than masking them, like most beards. He wasn't sure what that meant but if she was happy, he was, and he hadn't given his appearance a thought in nearly two decades. So, getting rid of the beard was like a restoration project, chipping away at the growth to reveal the raw material underneath. As he was finishing, Sarah got out of the bath and stood behind him. They stared at his reflection in the mirror. They ran their fingers along his cheeks and chin.

'Handsome guy,' said Sarah.

'Weird-looking guy, more like.' He peered at himself more closely, viewing his face from every angle. His forehead was normal – tanned and lined – and all the way down to the base of his nose. But underneath that it was virgin territory.

'How long is it since this skin has seen the sun?'

'Twenty-one years.'

'Twenty-one years.' She shook her head. 'Your beard has come of age.'

'Older than Alannah,' he said. And longer in duration than his marriage. 'Don't you think I look like a newly plucked chicken?'

She laughed. 'No, I don't. All you need is a couple of days in the sun and it'll blend in with the rest of your face.'

'It'll take more than a couple of days.'

'Weeks, then.'

'I feel naked.'

'You are naked.'

'Oh, yeah.'

He watched her laugh properly for the first time since Helen had left. And it was worth shaving off his beard. He'd shave his goolies if he thought it would get a laugh out of her. Maybe he'd save that one for the next rainy day.

She shivered suddenly. 'I'm freezing.'

'Let's get back in.'

He turned on the hot water and added more bubbles. She stepped back into the tub. You could almost count her ribs now. He got in beside her, sat behind her, this time with her back pressed into his chest. He soaped down her arms, her swan's neck, her one remaining breast.

'I never thought I'd be able to do this again,' she said.

'Do what?'

'Let a man see me naked.'

'You're beautiful.' He kissed the ear closest to him and watched her cheek rise as she smiled.

'The thing is, I don't care any more whether I am or not. After all the years I spent obsessing about my body, my looks . . . to think I used to be self-conscious about my stretch marks. And then this happened,' she pointed to the place where her right breast used to be, 'and made the stretch marks irrelevant. It's all relative, isn't it?'

'I suppose it is.'

'And now that . . . this is happening to me, well, it just makes me realize that none of it matters. That it's all going to be gone soon anyway, as if it never existed in the first place.'

He held on, more tightly than before.

Next morning they were having breakfast, eating toast off the same plate, their legs intertwined under the table. Sarah craved physical contact and Aidan just wanted to crawl inside her.

They were still getting used to his lack of beard. Sarah would look at him intermittently and laugh.

'Oh, you think it's funny, do you?'

'I do.'

He gave her a crumby kiss.

Maia walked into the room. They had left her sleeping late. She stood in the kitchen doorway and stared at Aidan – at the place where his beard used to be.

'Oh, God. Here we go. Hi, Maia.'

The child continued to stare. Then she began to talk. 'Hi, Maia. Hi, Aidan.' She repeated this several times. Then the hand flapping began, hands rigidly down by her sides, as she walked along on tiptoe. A little penguin. She completed two revolutions of the kitchen table in this way, before sitting in her customary chair, placing her chin in her hand and waiting expectantly for breakfast.

'I think we got away pretty lightly,' said Sarah. She stood up and started preparing the little girl's food. 'If a change like that had happened, say, a year ago, she would have gone nuts.'

'Nuts,' said Maia.

Aidan smiled at her. 'Don't you think you should tell her that her father is coming tomorrow?'

'She wouldn't understand. She doesn't know the concept of a father. She's never had one. Up until now.' Sarah bent low and kissed Aidan on the cheek. He savoured it. And tried to ignore the fact that he was nervous as hell about Robert Mitchell's visit.

Chapter 42

It had been more than a year since Mitch had set foot in Ireland. He only came to visit his mother. But mostly he flew her over to visit him. He liked spoiling her, showing her the high life. Showing off his life. She was impressed. She never said it but he could tell.

And now here he was, in Clare of all places, the rain falling softly, like a cliché. Typical August weather. When he'd left LA it had been in the mid-thirties. He shivered in his shirt-sleeves in the back of the cab that was ferrying him from Shannon to Sarah's place. He could see the driver giving him funny looks in the rear-view mirror. Perhaps it was because of how he was dressed, but more likely it was because he recognized him. He put in his earphones, leaned back in the seat and closed his eyes. He didn't turn on his iPod: it was just a prop to stop the man starting a conversation. Normally his inclination would be to chat away, nineteen to the dozen – it suited his image as the Irish lad made good who hadn't forgotten his roots. Today he just wasn't in the mood. He'd bung the driver a few hundred to pick him up again that afternoon – on condition that no reporters showed up while he was in Clare; he couldn't take the chance that the man wouldn't call one of the tabloids and get the media on his tail.

Ever since he'd had the call from Sarah, an air of unreality had settled into the corners of Mitch's life. He had recognized her voice right off, even though five years had passed since they'd last spoken. She had always had a great voice – rich and creamy. Although there was another element to it now. After the initial surprise of hearing from her, he had felt mostly fear. What did she want from him? More money? Something to do with the child? And then she had told him she had cancer. That it was serious. That she wanted to discuss their daughter's future. That had really put the fear of God into him. He had started to explain his lifestyle but she had cut him off. Just be here, she had said. Sooner rather than later. So here he was. He didn't want to be, but he was.

They were coming into the village now. Pretty enough, he guessed. Quaint. Good sea views. Pity he felt as if he was travelling to his own execution. He repeated the address to the driver, who circled around a few times before he found it. A terrace of tiny cottages. Sarah's was bang in the centre. Again, the word 'quaint' came to mind. It reminded him of the set of a film he'd had a part in once. Scene One: the hero arrives in the windswept, rain-sodden, West of Ireland fishing village. Where were all the men in Aran jumpers? That was what he wanted to know.

Even as he thought these thoughts, Mitch was aware that he was trying to distract himself from his anxiety. He refused to call it by its real name, which was fear. He paid the driver and put him on a generous retainer for the day, subject to his discretion. The man had obviously known who he was – he had called him Mr Mitchell as they drove into the town – but he seemed like a decent sort who wouldn't have needed the extra incentive to keep quiet. Still, it was better to be sure. His heart sank as he watched the cab pull away. There was nothing else for it. He faced the doorway. Faced the music. He rang the bell and waited. Anticipated. Tried to work out how long it had been.

The door was opened by a man in his forties. He had a vaguely intimidating air – Mitch couldn't tell if this was for his benefit or not – and extraordinarily vivid eyes. He wouldn't have looked out of place in an Aran jumper. Rugged type. Well cast as a fisherman. Would need to grow a beard first, though.

'Come in,' he said.

Good voice too. Rich. Authentic. He didn't ask Mitch who he was, presumably because he already knew. Mitch held out his hand. 'Robert Mitchell.'

The man took it. 'Aidan Ryan.'

Mitch followed him in, taking in his surroundings as he went. The place was charming, earthy. Ordinary. A far cry from his condo in LA. There was a woman standing in the kitchen. He did a double take. She gave him a slight, wry smile. 'Do I look that different, Mitch?'

'Sarah. No, of course not. I'd recognize you anywhere. How the hell are you?' Even as the words passed his lips, he cursed them. He moved forward and kissed her on each cheek. Jesus Christ. She was vaguely like Sarah. She had her eyes. Her voice. His initial crazy thought had been that she must be Sarah's sister or some other relation. But it was her, all right. A much emaciated version. She was wearing a short, skimpy sort of skirt. Her legs stuck out of the bottom like two sticks with knobbles in the middle for knees. Her thighs were actually narrower than her knees. The Sarah he knew had always had killer legs. And the hair. Where was the lustrous golden hair? She had short, wispy curls now, reminding Mitch somehow of a lamb. It must have fallen out. But there was still a kind of beauty. In her eyes. Which were huge now. And her smile.

When she had said those words on the phone – *I'm dying* – he hadn't known what to think, but he'd thought he'd managed to process the information. Now he realized he hadn't. Not really.

'I'm off out, Sarah.'

The man had walked into the kitchen behind him.

'Nice to meet you, Robert.' He looked him directly in the eye. There was a warning in there somewhere. He turned his attention to Sarah. 'Will you be all right?'

'I'll be fine,' she said. Mitch saw the look that passed between them. Saw that they were in love. Poor bastards.

The man left and he missed him instantly. He also had an overwhelming urge for a cigarette.

'Why don't you sit yourself down, Mitch? I'll make us some coffee. That's presuming you haven't gone all LA and decaff on me.'

'Fuck, no. Still on the hard stuff.' He sat down in one of the kitchen chairs and allowed himself to relax a little. She was being nice to him at least. Didn't appear to have a major axe to grind.

She pulled out a chair and sat beside him. She leaned her elbows on the table, her face in her hands and smiled. 'So,' she said. 'Tell me all about your life in Lala Land.'

She was inviting him to talk about himself. His favourite subject. Of course, she knew that. 'What do you want to know?'

'Anything and everything. Are you really going out with that girl who co-starred in your last movie?'

'No, not really. It's just good for publicity for us to be seen out and about together.'

'But you have slept with her?'

'Of course.'

'And she likes you?'

'Seems to.'

'You always were a shallow git.' She'd said it matter-of-factly, without a trace of rancour in her voice or on her face.

He grinned at her. 'Sure – you know that's always been part of my charm.'

'Oh, I know all about your charms, Robert Mitchell.'

She grinned back, looking in that moment almost like her old self. Except her skin was a funny colour now. Not honeyed. Not the way he remembered it. 'We had fun, though, you and me,' he said.

'Oh, yes. It was great fun being left to raise an autistic child on my own.'

There was nothing he could say to that.

She got up to pour the coffee. The atmosphere was a little bit tense but not too bad.

'Where is she anyhow?'

'Maia is . . . here.'

A little blonde girl walked into the room. She went past Mitch, directly to the sink, picked up a glass of water and proceeded to drink it.

'Hello, Maia,' said Mitch.

She ignored him. Sarah didn't immediately correct her, like the mother of an ordinary child might have done. 'Maia. This is Mitch. He's come for a visit.'

The child appeared not to have heard. She was opening a drawer beside the cooker. She took out several pieces of paper and a pencil case and sat down at the kitchen table opposite him.

'Are you drawing a picture, Maia?' he said.

Again, she failed to react.

'I thought you said she could speak now.'

'She has some words. Maybe she just doesn't want to talk to you.'

'Oh. I almost forgot.' He fished around in the pocket of his jacket. 'I bought her some sweets in Duty-free.'

'Thanks.' Sarah took them out of his hand and placed them directly in the press above the fridge. 'She's on a sugar-free diet, but thanks anyway. It really makes up for the last six years.'

'I sent you money, didn't I?'

'You were always generous, I'll give you that. When you had it, that was.'

'Yes, when I had it.'

'And now you have it all the time. How does it feel?'

'Fucking brilliant.'

'Can you please not curse in front of the child?'

'Sorry.'

'I bet it does feel brilliant.' She smiled at him. 'I'm happy for you, Mitch. For all your success.'

'Are you?'

'Of course I am. Is it everything you expected and more?'

'Ah, you know. You couldn't exactly call it a meaningful kind of existence. I'm hardly saving lives. And there's only so many clothes you can buy, fast cars you can drive, hot women you can fu– sleep with.'

'So it suits you down to the ground, then?'

'Basically, yeah.'

They both laughed. It was funny how easily they'd slipped back into the old familiar patterns.

'What do you think she's drawing anyway?'

'It's a dolphin.'

He inclined his head, trying to see upside-down. 'How can you tell?'

'She always draws dolphins. That's all she ever draws.'

'Is that normal?'

'For an autistic child, yes.'

He watched Maia for a while, her little white-gold head bent, her face intent. 'She's gorgeous, Sarah. Just like her mother.'

Sarah smiled serenely, accepting the compliment. And he saw that she was proud.

The picture was starting to take shape.

'That's really good. Who taught her to draw like that?'

'No one. She taught herself.'

'That's very good, Maia,' he said, his words loud and over-enunciated, as if he was talking to a deaf person.

Maia carried on drawing.

'Jesus, that's brilliant. You could sell that.'

'I suppose you're going to tell me she gets it from your side.'

He laughed. 'I wasn't, actually. I was going to ask you if all autistic kids can do this.'

'No. It's pretty rare, but not unheard of. Most have trouble even holding a pencil.'

'Why won't she look at me?'

'Because children with autism don't do eye contact. Jesus, Mitch, do you know nothing about the condition?'

'How would I?'

'Well, did it never occur to you to Google it or something?'

'I saw *Rain Man* once. Years ago. Can she do that thing with the counting?'

Sarah shook her head. 'You're an awful fecking eejit, you know that?'

Mitch was startled. He had been living on the west coast of America for such a long time now that he wasn't used to these uniquely Irish insults any more. Here to call someone a fecking eejit was almost a term of endearment. Because that was the way she had said it to him. Without any trace of anger against him. Against the world. He imagined that if he were dying at such a young age, he'd be seriously pissed.

'How old are you, Sarah?'

'I'll be forty on September the twenty-third. You can come to the party if you like.'

The words stayed hanging in the air between them. She looked him in the eye and he looked away. Did she believe she'd still be alive by then? Did he? Embarrassed and horrified, he turned his attention back to Maia. 'Why dolphins?'

'Because there's one living here, in the bay. That's the main reason we came. Would you like to see her?'

'What – now?'

'Why not? It's stopped raining and you've finished your coffee, haven't you?'

He had. She hadn't touched hers, he noticed.

'All right.' He stood up tentatively. 'If you're sure you're up to it.'

'I'm not about to keel over, Mitch. Come on. It's not far.'

'How do you know the dolphin will be here?' he said, as they walked towards the beach.

'I don't for sure. But she's here most mornings, playing with the surfers. Either here or round at the cove.'

Mitch lifted up his face and let the breeze flow through him. It was invigorating. Welcome after his long night of travel and the worry about what he'd find once he got here. His reception. So far so good.

'I always wanted to live beside the sea,' said Sarah.

'I remember,' he said, surprising them both.

'Do you?'

'Yes, I remember quite a lot.' He slowed down a little in his walking and looked at her. 'It wasn't all bad. Was it, Sarah?'

'No, Mitch. It wasn't.'

He took her by the hand and they recommenced walking, Maia wandering along ahead of them, collecting sea shells in a bucket.

'Oh, Lord,' she said. 'We'll be starting another scandal.'

'How do you mean?'

She gestured at their interlocking fingers. 'This.'

'You don't have to if –'

'No, I want to. It's nice.'

She gave his hand a squeeze.

After a while he spoke again. 'What do you mean, "another scandal"?'
'Aidan left his wife for me.'
'The guy I met earlier?'
'Yes.'
'Is he one of the reasons you came here?'
'No. I met him here.'
'Fuck. That was quick work.'
'It just sort of happened.'
'These things always do.'
'Mmm.'
'It's a small place. It must be awkward as hell. Where does his wife live?'
'See that house over there?'
'The one with the wooden deck?'
'That's it.'
'Jeez. You like living close to the edge.'
'I just like living.'
Sarah stopped walking and turned to the ocean. She pointed with her free hand. 'There she is.'
Mitch faced the same direction. Sure enough, the dolphin was visible, her whole body encased in the length of a wave. 'Oh, yeah. I see it.'
'Her. She's a female. Her name is Star.'
'What's she doing?'
'Surfing.'
He laughed. 'So she is.'
There were only a few surfers out that morning, the majority having been kept away by the early rain.
'Ever tried it?' said Mitch.
'Tried what?'
'Surfing.'
'Oh. No. You?'

'Once, yes.'

'Never had you down as the sporty type.'

'Well, when in California . . . '

'Were you any good?'

'Nah. The spray kept putting my fag out.'

She giggled – in the way he remembered.

'No, seriously, I was crap. Couldn't stay up on the thing at all. I don't know how they do it. Some of those guys make it look so easy. Like poetry.'

'Have you given up smoking?'

'Pretty much. You don't have a choice over there. You can't even smoke outside in some places.'

'*That*'s what's different about you. I couldn't put my finger on it. You're not smoking. And you're not as twitchy either. And less skinny.'

'Careful.'

'I mean that in a good way. Not as scrawny. You probably work out all the time, do you?'

'Kind of have to.'

'And your teeth are whiter too.'

'That would be the veneers, my dear.' He tapped his front teeth with his forefinger.

'Dar,' Maia shouted, and pointed.

'Yes, darling, it's Star,' said Sarah.

Mitch's head whipped around. 'She spoke.'

'Told you.'

The little girl stood silently watching. The two adults watching her.

'Have you ever heard of dolphin-assisted therapy?' said Sarah.

'I have, as it happens.'

'Really?'

'Again, California. They go in for that kind of thing over there.'

'Of course. Well, Star's been working with Maia – on an unofficial basis, of course. But she's really helped her come out of herself.'

Mitch nodded noncommittally. His natural cynicism didn't allow for such possibilities. But he wasn't about to insult her. And what right had he to question what did and didn't work for the daughter he'd abandoned? He looked at Maia again. So perfect on the outside. If he had known this was how she'd look . . .

'Let's sit down,' Sarah said.

They settled alongside each other on the sand, Mitch trying not to look at Sarah's emaciated legs. They said nothing for a while. Eventually Sarah broke the silence. 'Why so serious?'

'Oh, I was just thinking. You have every right to be angry with me.'

'I know I do.'

'So why aren't you?'

'What's the point?'

'If I were you, I'd be seriously pissed. With me. With life. With what's happening to you.'

'I was at first. But I haven't the energy to feel that way any more. It takes a lot out of you, being angry all the time. It's downright exhausting, in fact. I need to put all my energy into Maia and into trying to keep myself well. Make it to my big birthday bash. And as for you, my darling, I made my peace with that a long time ago.' She turned her head and looked directly at him. 'I know you're not a bad man, Mitch, just a weak one.'

He was ashamed, knowing in the pit of his soul that she was right.

'And more than anything else I feel sorry for you.'

'*You* feel sorry for *me*?' Mitch couldn't keep the astonishment out of his voice. Who could possibly feel sorry for him?

Robert Mitchell, movie star, with his good looks, his money, his career, his car – she hadn't seen his car, of course, but if she had, she'd be seriously impressed. Above all, he had life. An abundance of it. Yet this dying woman was saying *she* felt sorry for *him*.

She laughed gently, and he knew she'd guessed his thoughts. 'I know that must sound strange to you,' she said, 'but I do. Because you're missing out on your daughter's life.'

As if on cue, Maia approached Sarah and handed her a shell. 'Oh, thank you, my darling. It's beautiful.' She caressed the mother of pearl with her fingertips. Maia had already walked off again, not even waiting for her mother's response. 'You don't know what a blessing she is.'

Mitch watched Maia doubtfully. The child had walked to the water's edge and had started to twirl, her head tilted to the sky, her arms out by her sides. Again and again, spinning like a top. 'What's she doing?'

'She likes to spin.'

'She reminds me of . . . What do you call those men in Turkey?'

'Whirling dervishes.'

'That's it. Why does she do it?'

'I imagine she likes the sensation.'

Mitch nodded, recognizing his avoidance of the moment he'd been dreading. She was going to ask him now, and that would be the end of this pleasant morning.

'So I really think, for your own sake more than anything else, that you should make every effort to keep in touch with her after I'm gone.'

'You mean . . .?'

'You thought I was going to ask you to take her.'

'Well – yes, I guess I did.'

'I wouldn't do that to her.'

‘What do you mean?’ Mitch’s initial relief was temporarily taken over by indignation.

‘I couldn’t uproot her from her life and send her off to a foreign country to live with a total stranger who,’ here she looked pointedly at him, ‘knows absolutely nothing about autism. Why? You weren’t going to offer to take her, were you?’

‘I . . . Well, I’m never home and I . . .’

‘No. I didn’t think so. Don’t worry, Mitch. I never expected that of you.’

This time the relief entered his limbs and relaxed his whole body. ‘Where’s she going to live, then?’

‘Right here. With Aidan.’

‘With your boyfriend?’

‘Yes.’

‘Are you sure that’s a good idea?’

‘Yes.’

‘But you’ve only known him for . . .’

‘A little over four months.’

‘And he’s not even related to her.’

‘And you are. Look how useful you’ve been.’

This silenced him.

‘Mitch, I don’t mean to insult you but Aidan is the closest thing she’s ever had to a father. He’s incredibly good with her and she’s really taken to him. She’s going to need some stability in her life when I’m not around any more.’

‘What about that sister of yours? What’s her name again?’

‘Helen.’

‘Helen. That’s the one. Fuck, she really hated me.’

‘Still does. Thinks you’re a waste of space.’

‘Thanks very much.’

‘What can I say? The truth hurts. I thought of Helen, of course, but she lives in the States too and it would be such an upheaval for Maia. And Helen's already so busy with her boys. No. The best thing for Maia is to stay right here. There's a good special-needs school close by. I've enrolled her for September.'

'And he's agreed to take her?'

'He has.'

'Fuck.' Such an act was completely outside the perimeters of Mitch's understanding.

'Please, Mitch. Watch your language.'

'Oh, yeah, sorry. What's he like, this Aidan fella?' He watched her face as she stared off into the middle distance.

'He's the most remarkable man I've ever met.'

He experienced a surprising pang of jealousy. 'What? Even more remarkable than me?'

She laughed, her expression affectionate. 'Even more so. Believe it or not.'

Her honesty was surprisingly refreshing. He'd got used to LA, to his movie-star status, everyone pandering to his ego, telling him what he wanted to hear. Was this why he'd been avoiding Ireland, where the natives had no trouble bringing you back down to earth with a resounding bang? 'You don't think he has any . . . ulterior motives, do you?'

'How do you mean?'

'Well. How can I put this? He's a man. She's a pretty little girl.'

'No, Mitch. I don't think he's a paedophile.'

'All right. I just had to ask.'

She inclined her head in acknowledgement.

'So,' he said, 'what *do* you want from me?'

'Money.'

'Oh, I see. Is that all I'm good for?'

'No. But it's seriously expensive to look after an autistic child. And the money you've sent me over the years has come in very handy. But mostly I want you to promise me that you won't cause any trouble.'

'What kind of trouble?'

'Aidan and Helen will be her guardians. They have to be allowed to get on with caring for her as they see fit.'

'They won't get any interference from me.'

'Good. Thank you. But by all means, Mitch, come and see her every now and then. For your own sake. She's taught me the meaning of love, this girl. Maybe she can do the same for you.'

Mitch was silenced again, touched. He looked straight ahead at the surfers drifting up and down. At the dorsal fin, appearing and disappearing in the water. At Maia as she walked towards them – towards him. She held out her hand to give him something, then looked him in the eye for the first time and dropped a shell into his palm.

'Fuck,' she said.

'Now look what you've done.' But Sarah was laughing. She grabbed Maia's face in her hands and kissed her forehead. 'You learned a new word, Maia. Well done.'

Mitch laughed with her. Some role model he was. He stood up, brushed the sand off his jeans and held out his hand to Sarah. 'I'm starved. Where does a person go to get some food around here?'

Their walk into town was memorable, Mitch creating quite a stir. It was the young girls who recognized him first. Sarah grinned at him as they nudged one another and giggled. 'It's nice not being the one getting stared at for a change.'

'Don't you like people noticing you? You used to.'

'Did I? Yes, I suppose I did. I guess I'm past all that now.'

'What about this place?' Mitch stopped outside the Melting Pot.

'Oh, no, not here.'

'Why? What's wrong with it?'

'Nothing. It's just that I'm barred.'

He was incredulous. 'You? Barred? For what?'

'For being a scarlet woman.'

'Oh, that.' He laughed. 'We'd better find somewhere else, then.'

Privately he thought Sarah so pitiful-looking that the chances of someone kicking her out were slim to none. As slim as she was.

They settled for a quieter café at the edge of the pier. Even there, Mitch attracted undue attention. The waitresses got themselves in quite a tizz. One had Mitch autographing a napkin. Another posed for a photo with him, which a third took with her mobile phone. By now he had calmed down about the prospect of tabloid photographers turning up; he realized he had been overwrought before, nervous about seeing Sarah and his daughter. Now he felt back in control. If any showed, he'd be able to fob them off with his usual charm.

They were finally left alone to eat.

'So, Mitch – does anyone call you Mitch any more?'

'Only you. And people from the old days the odd time I hear from them. Although half of them stopped talking to me after I left you.'

'What do they call you in LA?'

'Robert. Or Rob.'

'Which do you prefer?'

'Rob. It's more manly.'

She laughed at him.

'How are they all anyhow?' he said. 'The old gang.'

'All well – as far as I know.'

'As far as you know? I thought you were thick as thieves with them.'

'I was until recently.'

'You mean they don't know?'

'No. And I don't want you shouting your mouth off either.'

'I won't. It's just . . .'

'What?'

'I'd have thought you'd want your friends around you at a time like this.'

'I'll invite them to my birthday party. How about that? Come on, Maia. You have to eat something.' And she commenced cutting Maia's food into tiny pieces.

They went back to the house to wait for Mitch's taxi. Aidan stood up to meet them.

'What are you doing back?' said Sarah. 'Why aren't you out on the boat?'

'I wanted to make sure you were okay.' He looked at Mitch as he said this.

'I'm fine.' She embraced him, and Mitch watched them sink into one another.

There was a beep outside the window. He ducked his head and peered out.

'Cab's here.'

'Already?' Sarah disengaged herself from Aidan and turned to the father of her child. 'Do you have everything?'

'I didn't bring anything. Just my handsome self.'

She smiled. 'That was a very short visit.'

'I would have arranged to stay longer if I'd known you didn't hate me any more.' His face grew more serious. 'Thank you for not hating me any more.'

'You're welcome.'

He looked at his daughter. ''Bye, Maia.'

'Say 'bye, Maia.'

''Bye, Maia.' The little girl said it to no one in particular.

He nodded to Aidan. 'Nice to meet you.'

Aidan nodded back. Then Mitch took a few steps towards Sarah. He held out his arms and they hugged each other. 'I'll be seeing you, Sarah.'

He spoke the words into her neck so he didn't have to look her in the eye.

Part IV

Chapter 43

Aidan felt increasingly helpless. Sarah was so listless. Her body was one thing but her spirit was another, and he couldn't stop it sinking. It didn't help that it was late summer, the natural world preparing for its own demise, autumn's chill unmistakably in the air. He brought her out for a drive one day and turned on the radio, looking for some music to distract or inspire. It was the end of the news, the hay-fever update. The danger had passed, the young girl informed them. Everything that was going to bloom had already bloomed. With a quick sidewards glance, he changed the channel. This time he found music – 'Enjoy Yourself, It's Later Than You Think'. He turned it off. Sarah hadn't reacted, not outwardly, but he could feel her deepening gloom. And it took every ounce of his strength to avoid being sucked into it.

Everywhere there were reminders. They couldn't escape for one moment. They walked through the town and felt the dearth of tourists. They walked through the country and every tree they passed seemed to shed a single orange leaf. They went to the shops and the signs were everywhere: 'Back to school. *Get your uniforms, your bags, your books.*' But there was no new term for Sarah.

Maia started at her new school, a modern, well-run special-needs facility in a nearby town. Access to a good school had made Sarah all the more certain that she'd made the right decision in electing to leave her child in this place. It was some distraction from the inescapable fact that the endless summer had come to an end. But once Maia was settled into her routine, there was no rousing Sarah. It was as if she was finished now. Aidan tried various strategies to distract her, but the time for distraction was over. He just hadn't faced up to it yet.

One day he sat on the edge of the bed – she had just woken from a nap. 'I've been thinking,' he said. 'The musicians we hired for Alannah's eighteenth. They might be good for your birthday party. I could –'

'Stop it, Aidan.'

'Stop what?'

'There isn't going to be a party.'

He felt as if she'd kicked him in the solar plexus. 'What do you mean, there isn't?'

'I'm not going to make it to my fortieth birthday. It's as simple as that.'

They stared long and hard at each other, their respective breathing audible in the darkened room.

'I won't have you giving up on me, Sarah. You have to have something to hang on to.'

'No, Aidan. Not any more. It's time to let go.'

Her words horrified him. He sat, rooted to the spot, as she lay down again. 'I'm tired,' she said. 'I need you to leave now so I can sleep.'

'But you've only just woken up.'

She didn't respond, just closed her eyes. He stayed by her side until her breathing had established a rhythm. Then he wandered out to the landing, his eyes adjusting to the relative brightness there. He felt alone and completely unequipped for what he was dealing with. He needed to talk to someone. And the someone he needed to talk to, above every other someone on the planet, was Fiona. He smiled grimly at the irony. Fiona would know what to do. Fiona, with her unflinching ability to tackle situations head-on. Yet she was the one person in the world he couldn't talk to and that was entirely down to him. He hoped she was doing better than he was. This seemed likely in the circumstances. He knew she was back – Tommy had told him – and that she was working. Which was a sign that she was piecing together the life he had blown apart.

He was downstairs now, sitting on the couch, his face in his hands. Everywhere there was pain. Everywhere he turned, everywhere he looked. Some of it of his own making. Some of it not. Psychological pain. Physical pain. He didn't know which was worse. But he knew he couldn't deal with it all on his own.

Sarah's handbag was on the seat beside him. He stared at it for a few seconds before dipping his hand inside. He quickly found what he was looking for: her address book. Small and flowery and tattered. Sarah was a pen-and-paper girl. He searched for names that sounded familiar, then began to make calls.

Sarah was staring at a rectangular patch of sunlight on her bedroom wall. She wondered at the source, then realized she hadn't closed her curtains properly. A gap shone through. The patch of light danced with the leaves of the tree outside her window. The breeze picked up and the leaf shadows moved in a frenzy. She even saw a bird. It landed briefly on a twig, then off again, its tiny wings reflected. She had sound effects too. A rustling. She must have left her window open a crack. She watched for as long as she was allowed to – until the delicate filigree of leaves had faded and the sun had gone in.

There was a knock on her bedroom door. She considered feigning sleep. It would be Aidan, trying to cheer her up again. She was finding it increasingly wearisome. She closed her eyes and turned on her side. She heard the door open, felt the new air enter the room. She was aware of another presence. She felt eyes on her.

'Hello, Sarah.'

She sat up slowly. 'Peter?'

'The very same.'

'What are you doing here?'

'I came to see you, of course.'

'Who told you? . . . Aidan.'

'He's only looking out for you.'

'Why did he bring you up here? I would have come downstairs to meet you.'

Peter smiled. 'He didn't think you would.'

She sat up and fluffed the pillows behind her. 'I would so have come down. Look at me in this ratty old nightgown and not a screed of makeup on me. Honestly. The room is probably all stuffy too. Throw that window wide open, would you, Peter? And you may as well draw the curtains back while you're at it.'

Peter obliged and the room was illuminated. He turned back to her and she read the shock on his face. He tried to hide it. But his mask had slipped for a couple of milliseconds. This was exactly why she hadn't wanted to see her old friends. She had no desire to see herself reflected in their eyes. The horror of what she had become. Dead woman walking.

His mask back in place, Peter sat on the bed beside her. He took one of her hands in both of his. 'How are you?'

'I'm dying.'

'I know that, darling, but Aidan thinks you're depressed.'

'Wouldn't you be?'

'Probably, yes.'

How many more of these ridiculous questions was he planning to ask her? And she couldn't bear to see the pity in his eyes.

'I brought you some things.'

Peter got up and retrieved a bag he'd left by the door. It was useful for him, she supposed, to have something else to focus on. He sat down again and took out the first item. 'A box of chocolates to tempt your tastebuds, my dear.'

'My favourites. Thank you.' She placed them on her bedside table. Maybe Aidan would eat them.

'And a bouquet of flowers for the patient.' He pulled out a posy in yellows and purples.

'Lovely. I'll get Aidan to put them in some water.'

'And these are from Jessica.' He handed her a stack of books.

'Jessica's sending me gifts? I guess she doesn't hate me any more. No longer perceives me as a threat.'

'Jessica never hated you.'

Sarah shot him an arch look.

'She just wants to help, Sarah. We all do. If you'll only let us.'

'Who's "all"? Who else knows?'

'Pretty much everyone. Brace yourself for some visitors.'

Sarah leaned her head back on the pillow. The very thought of visitors exhausted her. She picked up the books and began to read out the titles. '*The Tibetan Book of Living and Dying.* Jesus, is she trying to finish me off altogether? Tell her she needn't bother.'

Peter kept his counsel as she went through the books. They were all spiritual in nature, a few about death.

She placed them on the table next to the chocolates. 'Tell her thank you very much. She's made my day.'

'You don't really mean that.' He was teasing her now.

'Oh, I absolutely do. I didn't think it was possible for me to feel more depressed but she's just proved me wrong. Congratulations, Jessica.'

'But surely seeing my handsome face has cheered you up no end.'

'Not your face. Your cravat, maybe. Did you get dressed in the dark?'

'I did, as it happens. I didn't want to wake Jess. And I wanted to get down to you as soon as I could.'

'In case I popped my clogs in the meantime?'

'Sarah, Sarah, now you're being unfair.'

She knew she was. But it was better than being depressed.

There was another knock at the door and Aidan popped his head in. His stubble was growing back. She liked the effect, but it hurt her when he kissed her – her skin had been so sensitive lately.

'Just wanted to see if anyone would like some tea. Or coffee.'

'Come in here, Aidan Ryan. I have a bone to pick with you.'

Aidan stood sheepishly in the doorway.

'What do you mean by showing Peter directly up to my room? A woman has her pride, you know.'

'I thought it would be a nice surprise for you.'

'You did all right. I'll have tea. Two sugars.'

'Peter?'

'Tea would be lovely.'

'Let's have it downstairs,' said Sarah, swinging her legs over the side of the bed. 'I've had enough of being an invalid for one day.'

The two men vacated the room to give her space to get dressed. They descended the stairs, one after the other, and regrouped in the kitchen. Aidan turned to Peter, just in time to see the other man's face collapse.

'Oh, my God,' he said, staring out of the window, trying to compose himself.

'I'll get you that cup of tea,' said Aidan. He had to walk

around Peter, who stood stock still, the thumb and middle finger of his left hand pressed to the corners of his eyes. 'You should be pleased,' said Aidan. 'This is the first time she's been up in three days. And me calling you without telling her and showing you up to her room has really pissed her off. Which is good too. It's invigorated her. I'd much rather see her angry than depressed.'

Peter didn't reply. Because he couldn't. Aidan came up to him and gave him a manly pat on the shoulder. 'It's good that you came.'

Peter nodded, his eyes still squeezed shut. 'I have to get out of the house for a few minutes. Go for a walk or something. I don't want her seeing me like this.'

'Of course. If you go out the front door, turn left and walk for about five minutes, you'll come to a cove.'

Peter moved towards the door. 'Thanks.'

'No problem.'

'I won't be long.'

'Take your time. We're not going anywhere.'

Peter walked like a man in a trance, his only thought his destination. All others were held in abeyance until then. He found the cove without any trouble and stepped gratefully off the street. There were a few swimmers at one end. He went to the other where he positioned himself between two giant rocks and sobbed himself dry.

'Jesus Christ.' He blew his nose noisily, the sound obscured by the waves as they collided with the rocks. He felt marginally better. At least he'd be composed when he got back.

He'd been dreading seeing Sarah. Turned out his dread was right on the mark. Peter was a kind man, but not the best at dealing with harsh realities. He had led quite a cosseted life, he knew. Of course, his dear parents had died, but they'd both had the good grace to do so suddenly and conveniently, his father instantly of a heart-attack and his mother seven months later in her sleep. None of this hanging around and reminding everyone of their own mortality.

Sarah's appearance had shaken him deeply. He doubted he would have recognized her on the street. Where was the laughing, vibrant girl he'd known and loved? He'd seen glimpses. Like when she'd made fun of his cravat. That was the old Sarah. But her golden skin was now almost lilac – the blue veins shockingly visible. And her hand when he'd held it – a collection of bones encased in a fragment of skin. The bump under the covers that represented the rest of her body had been barely visible. And her legs when she had swung them out of the bed – that was the worst.

He took a few deep breaths and made his way back towards the house, confident he'd be able to keep his composure. Nice place, he reflected, as he walked through the town. Not a bad place to spend your last days.

Aidan let him in and the two men nodded wordlessly at one another. Sarah was sitting at the kitchen table, her two hands clasping an enormous mug from which steam was rising. Peter guessed it was being used as an agent of heat as much as anything else. Sarah was dressed for January, layer upon layer of wool. She looked up as he entered, her face a series of hollows.

'Ah,' he said breezily. 'The lady has arisen.'

'Where did you go?'

'Down to the cove. I took the opportunity to look around while you were getting ready.'

'I thought it was me you came to see.'

'It was, my dear.' He sat beside her and gave her hand a little squeeze. This tetchiness was new. Aidan placed a mug in front of him. 'Tell me, how is young Miss Maia?'

Her expression softened and opened out as she told him about her daughter and the progress she had made. 'Will you keep coming to see her?' she said, anxiety creasing her forehead. 'She's at school right now but it would be good if you could visit her from time to time.'

'I will.' Peter looked down at his mug.

Sarah's expression brightened. 'Aidan, did you know that Peter and I were together for three whole years?'

'No, I didn't,' said Aidan. 'Maybe you could give me some advice on how to handle her.'

'I always found it best to keep her on a very short leash.'

Sarah laughed. 'The cheek of you two.' But she looked fondly from one to the other. Her two favourite men. 'You know, it seems so strange now,' she said. 'I can't believe that we were ever together in that way.'

'It doesn't seem strange to me.'

'Does it not? I mean, being here with you now, you seem so much more like a . . .'

'Father figure?'

'Well. Yes.'

'Well, I am terribly old.'

'I used to worry about that when we were together. That if we ended up getting married or something, you'd die so much earlier than me and I'd be left on my own. Funny that.'

Peter looked down at his tea. He didn't think it was funny at all.

Chapter 44

It seemed to be working. The almost constant influx of visitors from Dublin had brought Sarah back to her old self. She would hold court in her bedroom or downstairs, impossibly stylish and smiling broadly. She'd even bought some new clothes from the local boutique. She tried them on happily in front of the full-length bedroom mirror, avoiding her half-naked reflection, only looking at herself when she was dressed. Aidan lay on the bed and evaluated each outfit. He took random photos of her as she posed like a fashion model. Their mutual favourite was a long floral dress. The skirt reached her ankles, the sleeves were long enough to cover her knife-like elbows, while the crimson base colour lent her complexion some much-needed warmth. She twirled in front of the glass and examined herself from every angle. 'Not bad,' she said. Then her expression altered. 'I want to be laid out in this dress.'

Aidan didn't say anything.

'Okay?'

'Okay.'

She nodded, apparently satisfied, and went back to admiring the dress in the mirror. 'It was even on sale,' she said. 'Make sure everyone knows it was a bargain.'

She was trying to make light of the situation, he knew. But he still couldn't handle it, her talking this way.

The other day, when she had been putting on makeup in preparation for one of her visitors, she had asked him if he thought it was in bad taste. Like putting makeup on a corpse. He hadn't replied to that, had merely left the room. He concentrated these days on minding the visitors, getting them drinks, on keeping Maia happily in her routine, on making sure Sarah's every whim was catered for. In other words, attending to everyone's needs but his own.

He was touched by Sarah's visitors, although many of them were rather eccentric for his taste. He found little common ground with them. But they were kind and they buoyed her up. One woman played the harp for Sarah while she dozed. Another gave her a full manicure and pedicure. Someone else massaged her aching bones. And there was no end to the gifts.

Her buoyancy sometimes extended into their absence and he would make the most of these times with little trips into town. Today they were going to the market, hand in hand, three in a row.

'Are you trying to tempt me into eating again?'

'I might be.'

'But I have no appetite.'

'That's no excuse. You have to try.'

She smiled at him and walked on. They had reached the first stalls. Sarah lingered at the soaps.

'Food, woman,' Aidan urged. 'Forget about soap.' If he couldn't tempt her here, he couldn't tempt her anywhere. He bought her a selection of mini baklavas. She nibbled at one like a chipmunk. He put his arm around her and they pressed on to the pies, the preserves – the fruit stall. He was looking around, taking it all in, when he realized that Sarah had stopped walking. He looked down at her, then at what she was looking at. Or, rather, who. A few feet ahead, as if frozen in time, was Fiona. All three stood in horrified silence. Then Fiona fled.

'Go after her,' said Sarah.

'I can't leave you alone in the middle of the market.'

'She shouldn't be left alone either.'

'Okay. Let me take you home first.'

And so it was that Aidan deposited his mistress at home and went to talk to his wife.

Fiona stood in her kitchen and cursed herself. She had rehearsed so many times what she would say if she bumped into them. How she would be. So proud, so strong. So dignified. She would not hare off in the other direction like a frightened animal. Like a coward. She was no coward but she had never faced anything like this before. And never in her wildest dreams had she thought she would have to.

She began to make tea. It was the calming ritual she was after rather than the beverage. When it was ready, she sat down at the table and laced her fingers around the mug. Her fingers were still trembling. She clasped it tighter and willed them to stop. She was stronger than this. Better than this. Better than the two of them put together. She wouldn't allow them to do this to her – wouldn't let them best her. You can't control what happens to you but you can control your reaction. She repeated the words several times, like a mantra. She had read them in a book that Yvonne had given her. She didn't usually go in for all that self-help crap but, these days, she needed all the help she could get.

Her fingers had steadied a little. That was good. You couldn't be a doctor with shaky hands. And then she noticed that she hadn't cried. Tears hadn't occurred to her body or her mind. And that, she thought, was a victory of sorts. Her emotions had been visceral, the shock of being confronted with what she knew was reality: Aidan with his arm around Sarah. There was nothing like being slapped in the face with it.

But something else had been equally shocking: Sarah Dillon's appearance. She hadn't seen the woman since the day she'd found the lump. And since that time Fiona had been going through such turmoil herself, such a maelstrom of emotions, that she hadn't stopped to think – really think – about how close Sarah would be to death by now. She was knocking on its very door by the look of her.

Fiona stopped herself wondering what would happen after Sarah was gone and concentrated instead on the image that was still so strongly at the forefront of her mind: Sarah with Aidan's arm around her; Sarah with her arm around Maia.

There were footsteps on the deck outside. She straightened her back and prepared her smile for Tommy. When Aidan walked in, it was everything she could do to stop herself collapsing into a heap. On the inside, that was. On the outside, she held herself perfectly straight, her face – she hoped – impassive. 'What are you doing here?'

'I came to talk.'

'I want you to leave.'

'I'm not leaving until you talk to me.'

'Get out of my house.'

'It's my house too.' He pulled out a chair and sat down beside her.

Fiona eyeballed him furiously. 'If you think,' she said, 'that I'm going to sit here and listen to you trying to justify yourself . . .'

'I don't think that.'

'Well, that's good, because I won't.' She looked at him sharply. 'You shaved off your beard.'

He instinctively cupped his chin with his hand.

'It's ridiculous.'

'I know. I'm growing it back.'

'She ask you to do it, did she?'

He didn't respond.

'Well, I never would have married you if I'd known what you looked like underneath. Just like I never would have married you if I'd known what you *were* underneath. What you were capable of.'

'Well, I'll never regret marrying you, Fiona.'

The words knocked her temporarily off balance, but she was back up again in an instant. 'That's because I didn't destroy you, Aidan Ryan, the way you destroyed me.'

'You look as if you're doing pretty well.'

'In spite of you, Aidan.' The words were spat out. 'In spite of you.'

His face might have been made of stone for all the impression her words were making on it. Her anger rose and swelled. And she made it her mission to hurt him. '"You were carved out for me and for me alone". Do you remember saying those words to me right before our wedding? Do you, Aidan?' She thought she saw him flinch. 'I suppose Sarah was carved out for you too, was she? And how many other women?'

'There were never any other women.'

'Oh, just the one, was there? Well, lucky me.' She looked at his bowed head and struck again. 'You're just another deluded, middle-aged man, Aidan. Do you think she would have looked twice at you if she hadn't had the cancer? If she hadn't needed someone to look after her?'

His head snapped up. 'Let's just leave Sarah out of this.'

She rose from her chair, rigid with fury. 'Oh, I'd love to, Aidan. I'd just love to leave Sarah out of this. But *you* brought her into it. Remember? You bastard.' The last word came out in a snarl and Fiona collapsed into the chair again, as if deflated. She sat in silence for a full minute before turning to him again. 'And how about "I do"? Do you remember that? In sickness and in health? *My* sickness, Aidan, my health. Not somebody else's. Not some other woman's.'

Aidan stared fixedly at the table, betraying no emotion. This was more than Fiona could bear. She picked up her mug and flung the contents violently in his face. The tea was only lukewarm now, more's the pity. Aidan sat stock still and blinked several times, the liquid trickling from his hair and chin. Silently, he pushed back his chair and walked over to the drawer where the tea-towels were kept. He took one out, wiped his face, left the towel on the counter, returned to the table and sat down again.

'Have you got nothing to say for yourself?' she said, her words dripping with disgust.

'Sorry,' he said. 'Sorry is what I've got to say.'

'And that makes it all okay?'

'No, of course it doesn't. But it's all I've got.'

She shook her head. 'You're so fucking reasonable, aren't you? So fucking morally superior. You make me sick. I don't know how you can live with yourself after what you've done to this family. Why did you come here anyway?'

'I told you. To talk.'

'Well, I really don't want to talk any more.' She sounded as drained as she felt.

'I thought it was important to communicate on some level. For the kids. And for us.'

'There is no "us" any more.'

'There'll always be an us, Fiona. If only as parents.'

Aidan was waiting for a response, but she was damned if she was going to give him one. Let him stew. Eventually he seemed to make up his mind that she was finished and stood up.

'Is that it?' she said.

He sat down again. 'Tell me what you want from me.'

'*Tell me what you want from me.* What the hell is that supposed to mean? Do you think you're doing me a favour here? Is this some kind of therapy session for my benefit? Don't make me laugh. Okay. I'll tell you what I want, shall I? I want you to leave Sarah. Then I want you to walk around the town with the words "I am an unfaithful bastard" written on your chest in scarlet lipstick. How about that for a start?'

'I'm so sorry, Fiona.'

'Don't look at me with that pathetic, hangdog expression. And don't say sorry as if you had no choice in the matter.'

He looked away.

'That's what you think, isn't it? That you had no choice in the matter.'

'Fi, I . . .'

'If you tell me, Aidan Ryan, that you can't choose who you fall in love with, then I swear to God, I'll take that teapot and crack it across your skull.'

Aidan avoided her stare and this time, at least, she knew he was ashamed. There was no need to say anything else. She could think of plenty more – really mean stuff about Sarah. But how could she say any of it in the circumstances? What kind of person would that make her?

'You can go now,' she said.

He stood up again, as if he'd had as much as he could take too.

'I'd like to say it was nice to see you but it wasn't. It was shit.' She laughed mirthlessly. 'You know, you've really made things impossible for me. I can't hate Sarah because she's dying. Half the town has sympathy for her instead of me because she's dying. And here I am, feeling jealous of a woman who's dying.'

He regarded her with an annoying amount of sympathy.

'How could you leave me for her?' Her voice almost broke. 'Why would you hurt me like that? I thought we were happy.'

Aidan looked stricken. 'We were happy. It wasn't a lie.'

'You've made a mockery of everything I've ever believed in.'

He came cautiously towards her.

'Don't.' Her voice was urgent. 'Don't you touch me. Don't you even come near me.'

He held up his hands and backed away, as if he were trying to placate a cornered animal. Then he left the house quietly, his footsteps fading on the deck outside until . . . silence. Only when Fiona was sure of it did she allow herself some tears. And officially exempted herself from the rest of the day.

Chapter 45

Sarah was waiting anxiously for him. She scanned his face as he walked into the kitchen. Another woman, another kitchen. 'Was it really grim?'

'It was pretty bad, yes.'

'She's bound to be very angry.'

He nodded.

'Is it raining out?'

'No.'

'Your hair's all wet.'

'She threw tea over my head.'

Sarah laughed nervously, then stopped herself. 'Was it hot?'

'No. But it might have been. I don't think that would have stopped her. I was just lucky it had cooled down.'

She breathed deep. The laughter gone out of her. 'It was brave of you to go and see her like that.'

'I'm not brave. I'm a coward. I should have gone to see her long ago instead of waiting till we bumped into her.'

'Well, at least it's done now. You've got the first meeting out of the way. Perhaps it'll get easier from now on.'

'Perhaps.' He sounded unconvinced.

She pulled her chair up closer to him and put her hands on his shoulders. 'You know,' she said, 'I don't think I'll ever get over what you've done for me. Even if I live to be – oh – forty.'

'Is that your idea of black humour?'

'Yes. Do you like it?'

'Well, it's better than no humour, I suppose.'

'I've been reading this book. One Peter brought me. And now I know what you are to me.'

'What do you mean?'

'Have you ever heard the term "*anam cara*"?'

'*Anam cara*.' He repeated the words, his expression thoughtful. 'Soul friend,' he said.

'That's right. I never knew you had good Irish. I suppose there are lots of things I'll never know about you and now I won't have the time to find out.' She looked momentarily sad. 'But, yes. You're my soul friend, Aidan. When I first met you, I had a feeling we were meant to be together. Live together. I think you did too.'

'Yes, I did.'

'But now I know we were never meant to live together – not long term anyway. But you were meant to be with me as I died. God sent you to help me.'

Aidan looked away. She knew he didn't believe in God.

'There's a really good chapter in the same book about death. You should read it.'

'Some other time, perhaps.'

'Yes. You're worn out now, I can see that.' She kissed him on the cheek. 'So, *anam cara*, how about a nice cup of tea?'

When he woke up the next morning, the bed was empty beside him. He could tell from the light it was later than his usual getting-up time – that, and the sounds and smells emanating from the kitchen. Someone was playing opera quite loudly. He eased himself up on one elbow and rubbed the corners of his eyes. Then he looked at the clock. It was after nine. He got out of the bed with some urgency. He never slept this late. The perpetual fisherman, he usually woke around five – even as a young lad, going out on his father's boat. You just became accustomed to it. He didn't know what had happened this morning. He dressed himself rapidly in yesterday's clothes and went down the stairs barefoot.

The kitchen was in uproar. Sarah was right in the eye of the storm, moving from pot to pan and singing obliviously. She eventually spotted him, her smile incomparable. She walked up to him and took both his hands. '*Madame Butterfly*,' she said. 'She dies in the end. Tragic but beautiful. Come on, sleepy head, I made you breakfast.' She led him to the table.

'Why didn't you wake me?'

'I thought you deserved a lie-on.'

'Where's Maia?'

'I asked Bridget to take her to school this morning. There you go.' She laid a plate in front of him. 'Bacon and eggs. Just the way you like them.'

Aidan couldn't help thinking that it should be the other way around, him helping her, him serving her. But it was good that she was feeling up to it. Great, even. And so was the food. He realized how ravenous he was, hours after his usual breakfast time. 'Won't you sit down beside me?' he said.

'Just give me a minute to check the food.'

She fluttered around the cooker, tasting and stirring. Then she sat down beside him with a satisfied sigh.

'What are you cooking?'

'Different things. I've done a casserole and a lasagne and I've divided them up into smaller portions.'

'What for?'

She looked at him anxiously, as if worried about his reaction. 'I'm going to put them in the freezer so you can have them after I've gone.'

Aidan dropped his knife and fork with a clatter. 'Well, you certainly know how to put a man off his food.'

'Sorry.'

'Why would you do that, Sarah?'

'You won't have time to cook. There'll be the funeral to sort out, Maia to cope with, people coming and going. It'll be hectic – and handy to take one of these meals out of the freezer, pop it into the microwave and hey presto.'

He looked miserably at her.

'And I like the idea of being able to do something for you after I'm gone. To be able to nourish you when I'm no longer here.'

Aidan sat in stricken silence. Sarah took his hand in hers and laid it against her cheek. 'Look, Aidan, I know you find it difficult when I talk this way but I have to talk about it with someone and you're all I've got. It's asking a lot of you, I know it is, when I already ask so much. But I need it so badly, I really do. If I don't talk about it, it'll get bottled up and I'll be depressed again. And I don't want to waste one more precious second being depressed. I've accepted it now. I'm going to die and that's the beginning and the end of it.'

'Sounds like giving up to me.'

'It's not giving up. It's accepting. Surrendering to what is. This book I've been reading –'

Aidan got up with an angry scrape of his chair. 'Not those bloody books again. I've a good mind to burn them all.' He dropped his plate into the sink.

'They help me, Aidan. I've found some of the ideas so inspiring.'

Aidan was leaning heavily against the sink, staring out of the window. She came up behind him, encircled his waist with her arms and laid her cheek against his back. He didn't have it in him to respond – his body remained rigid. She let him go and stood at his side, gazing imploringly into his face. 'Aidan, the Buddhists have this concept of a happy death and that's what I want for myself. I want to die well. I've made lots of mistakes in my life, done many things badly. I don't want my death to be one of them. I want to do it properly. I want to die beautifully. I want my death to be an inspiration. But I don't think I can do it without you.'

She watched closely as all the different emotions fought for dominance on his face. She could see the clouds reflected in his irises. As if there was a miniature sky inside each eye. She could feel the resistance draining out of him as he relaxed and turned to her. 'Okay, Sarah, I'll help you. I'll help you die beautifully. As beautifully as you've lived. As beautiful as you are.'

She hugged him again, a new lightness infusing her. 'Thank you.'

Aidan looked over her shoulder, wondering how the hell he was going to make it through the next few weeks.

The next morning the doorbell rang. Sarah looked up from her book. 'That'll be the soul midwife. Let her in, Aidan.'

Aidan did as he was told. What new madness was this?

A woman in her fifties stood at the door. She had blonde hair and kind eyes. Quite normal-looking. 'Hello, I'm Sheila. You must be Aidan.'

He held the door open. Another woman. That was all he needed.

They entered the sitting room. Sarah smiled and made to get up from her duvet cocoon on the couch.

'Please don't move,' said Sheila, sitting down beside her. 'It's lovely to meet you, Sarah.'

'And you.' Sarah smiled at her new best friend.

Aidan found he couldn't watch. 'Would you like some tea?' he found himself saying.

'No, thank you. I'm sure you do nothing but make tea for visitors. A glass of water would be lovely, though.'

Aidan went through to the kitchen. He gazed out of the

window as he filled the glass. That was where he wanted to be. He went back into the sitting room and handed the glass to Sheila. 'I have to go out. I'll leave you to it.'

'But I wanted you to hear what Sheila has to say.' Sarah's face was a picture of disappointment.

'Sorry, I can't. I have to source a new part for the boat.'

'Oh, all right. See you later, then.'

He nodded and was gone. Soul midwife! What next? Thank God he had Tommy – another male – to talk to on the boat each afternoon. He'd go mad otherwise. He looked at his watch. Still a few hours to go. There was only one place in the world he wanted to be and that was the pub.

He snuck through the door in the early hours, hoping in vain to go unobserved. But Sarah was waiting. 'Where have you been?'

She sounded exactly like a wife.

He walked past her, avoiding eye contact, and headed straight for the kitchen. There he stood unsteadily by the sink, filling a pint glass with water and swaying ever so slightly.

'Tommy called here about five times. He was frantic.'

Tommy. Shit.

'And so was I, Aidan. Where on earth have you been?'

She was standing by his side now, her hands on her hips. Classic fishwife pose. He said nothing, instead knocking back the water.

'Are you . . . drunk?'

He paused after several gulps. 'Yes, I am, thanks be to God.' He continued slugging the water down, impervious to her glare. When he'd finished his glass and looked down, she was gone. Good. Bloody woman. Trying to control him. Telling him how to live his life. Aidan belched and the sound reverberated around the kitchen. He felt great – for several seconds.

Then he didn't feel so great. He walked out of the kitchen, placing each foot in front of the other with elaborate care. He took one look at the stairs, knew in his drunken wisdom that he'd never make it, and even if he did, she'd probably kick him out. He collapsed on the couch.

Aidan came to slowly and painfully. Something was poking at his face. He tried to swat it away but it didn't work. He finally realized it was Maia, playing with the new growth on his beard. He attempted to sit up, shielding his eyes from the midday sun with his forearm. He groaned, as only half the contents of his head seemed to sit up with him. It was as if someone had loosened his brain while he was asleep. Everything was thudding.

'Here.'

He removed his arm from over his eyes and blinked. Sarah was standing above him, holding out two white pills in one hand and a glass of water in the other. He took them from her. Sarah giving *him* painkillers. This was a first. She left the room and he swallowed the pills with all of the water. Then he sat up properly, placing his feet on the carpet and his head in his hands. He was still in his clothes. He could actually smell himself – seldom a good sign. There was no point in putting it off. He raised himself to his feet and walked gingerly into the kitchen. Sarah was playing with Maia and studiously ignoring him. He sat down again, this time at the table, and awaited whatever punishment she was to bestow. He felt somewhat blasé: it wasn't possible to feel worse than he already did. He jumped when she spoke to him.

'There's coffee in the pot.'

He mumbled his thanks and pushed himself up again, using the table as a support.

The coffee was strong and rich and vaguely nauseating on his empty stomach, which gurgled as the coffee met the beer remaining in his system. Sarah sat down next to him and he found he couldn't look at her.

'Fun, was it, getting yourself in that state?'

This time he did look at her. 'Best fun I've had in months.'

She nodded, her eyes hard, her lips set in a straight line. 'I was worried sick about you.'

'Yeah, well, now you know how it feels.'

'Is that why you did it? To teach me a lesson?'

The line of her mouth wavered and she made to get up. He grabbed at her arm and pulled her back down again. 'No. I don't know why I did it, really. Just that I needed some kind of . . . release.'

'You could always try talking to me or to someone else. There *are* people available to talk to in these kinds of situations.'

These kinds of situations. Was it actually possible that somewhere in the world, somebody was in the same situation as him? If there was, he felt sorry as hell for the poor bastard.

'I had to put up with so much of this shit from Mitch and I swore I'd never do it again.'

Aidan said nothing. There was no need. They'd both had the same thought at the same time: that she wouldn't have to put up with it for much longer.

'But it's not just that, Aidan.' She gripped his forearm with both hands. 'I need you – really need you. More than I've ever needed anyone.'

Aidan stared at the table.

'What if something had happened to me and I couldn't contact you? You didn't even have your phone with you.'

'I don't know where it is.'

'It's on the boat. Tommy found it.'

'Oh.'

'I mean, I understand. I really do. At least, I'm trying to put myself in your position. You must feel like shite.' She looked at him for confirmation but she didn't get any. 'I need you to open up to me, Aidan. The only way we're going to get through this is by being completely honest with one another.'

The shame was worse than the hangover. 'I know. I know you're right.' Although there were so many things he couldn't tell her.

'I'm scared, Aidan.'

'I know you are.'

'Not of dying – I'm afraid you're going to leave me.'

'Oh, Jesus. Come here to me. Of course I'm not going to leave you.' He scraped his chair closer to hers and engulfed her with his body.

She began to cry. 'I didn't think so before. But after yesterday . . .'

'Yesterday was a one-off. It won't happen again.'

'You promise?'

'I promise. It's out of my system now.'

'And you won't go off again without your phone?'

'I'll staple it to me if I have to.'

She giggled through the tears.

'That's better.' He squeezed her tightly. What was left of her. 'I'll never leave you, Sarah. Not ever. You have my word.'

Most of the guilt didn't set in until later, when all the alcohol had left his system and his fluids were replenished. His body was fortified with stodge and he felt almost human again. It was overrated, he decided, being human. Too many conditions attached. Too many obligations. Too many feelings.

Sarah was as bad as he had ever seen her and he knew that this was down to him. He tortured himself with the knowledge. She smiled at him to reassure, a little crescent in a moon-white face. But he wasn't reassured – not one bit. How could he have been so stupid and selfish? He raged at himself, punching pillows when she wasn't around. Her total forgiveness made it almost worse. There was no anger for him to resist.

She woke up that night and wanted to talk. She didn't always wake him. Not on purpose, at least. But he knew she went downstairs in the middle of the night. She would sit at the kitchen table, pour herself a glass of wine and sob her heart out. He had sat on the stairs and watched her once, through the crack in the doorway. There was something in her that needed to do it so he had left her to it.

But tonight she needed his company. He forced himself out of his stupor and sat up in bed beside her. The darkness was almost complete, which led to a rare kind of intimacy. 'We never got to talk about the soul midwife,' she said.

'What do you want to tell me about her?'

'Well, I'd rather you asked me some questions.'

'All right, then. How much does she charge?'

'Aidan! Not that kind of question. A proper one. Anyway, you don't need to worry about that. Mitch gave me a big fat wad of cash before he left.'

'Isn't he marvellous?'

'Now, now. No need to be jealous. I'm well aware that it's the easiest thing in the world to throw money at a problem – so long as you have it, of course. But his money has come in very handy over the years. Anyway. He owes me and he knows it. So why shouldn't I hire a soul midwife?'

'No reason at all. Good on you.'

'Next question so.'

'Oh, right. How does one qualify as a soul midwife?'

'Are you taking the piss?'

'No.'

'Well, Sheila worked for years as a hospice nurse. But this is more on the holistic side of things.'

Holistic. One of those bullshit words he detested.

'Soul midwives come on the scene when there's nothing else that can be done medically. Typically in the last few weeks of a person's life. To help the dying person and their loved ones.'

He still couldn't get his head around the matter-of-fact way she now spoke about her death. Could she really be that accepting? Or was this just some grand delusion destined to crumble? He suspected and feared the latter. One of his legion of fears.

'You should be pleased, Aidan. You won't have to do it all on your own any more.'

'I'm coping.'

'Oh, is that what you were doing last night? Coping?'

He had no answer for that.

'I was thinking of asking Helen to come back earlier than she'd planned to help you out. But she has the boys and she's already taken time off from her job. So I thought, Why not hire a professional? I have the money. There are no pockets in a shroud, as my granny used to say. Anyway. Next question.'

'How do you know she's any good?'

'I've seen her references.'

He wanted to tell her that dead people couldn't give references, but he couldn't bring himself to say the D-word. She read his mind anyway. 'Not from the dead people, smartarse. From their families.'

'Look, Sarah, I don't mean to be cynical . . .'

'Then don't be.'

'It's just that you're in a pretty vulnerable position right now. I don't want people taking advantage.'

'She's not like that. You can see for yourself tomorrow. She's coming in the morning and you can ask her as many questions as you like.'

'Maybe I will.'

'Good. Now snuggle down with me here. I want to be held from behind.'

'Like this?'

'Yes. No. Just move your arm. That's it. Perfect.'

And that was how Sarah fell asleep. Big spoon, little spoon. In perfect harmony.

Chapter 46

A wasp lay dying on the windowsill. Every so often, it buzzed pathetically. Aidan didn't know whether to help it on its way or leave it to its own devices. Once upon a time, he would have rolled up a newspaper and thwacked it without a moment's thought but now he questioned everything. Especially himself. The doorbell rang. It must be her.

She had this annoyingly serene way about her, as if she knew something he didn't. As if she knew better than him. And she didn't even know Sarah. But it was good that she used to be a nurse. He was prepared to concede that much. 'Sarah's still sleeping,' he said. 'Do you want to come back later?'

'That's okay. I don't mind waiting.' She stepped inside and Aidan followed her into the sitting room. 'Besides,' she smiled, 'it gives us a chance to talk.'

'Yes.' Aidan looked around him uncomfortably, as if she lived here, not him. 'Can I get you . . .?'

'I'm fine, thank you.' She sat down on one end of the couch and looked at him expectantly.

Someone else expecting things from him. He sat down on the other end, politely masking his reluctance.

'Aidan,' she began, 'it's important you know that I'm not here to take over in any way. My job is solely to support. And my presence does not in any way imply that you're not doing beautifully by yourself.'

It was as if she'd read his mind. More likely she'd been talking to Sarah.

'I'll be calling in every few days, or whenever either of you wants me here, until God decides to take her home.'

'Your God has a lot to answer for, if you ask me.'

She gave him a look of intense sympathy. He found this incredibly annoying.

'Why would he take a woman in the prime of her life, the mother of an autistic child, a woman who has so much to give, and make her suffer so much?' To his absolute horror, his voice broke. He wasn't, was he? He wasn't going to cry? He was. Oh, Jesus. He covered his face with his hands as the sobs came and his body heaved. Sheila's arm was instantly around his shoulders, stroking his upper arm as if he were a boy. It was awful at first, his uncontrollable display of emotion in front of a total stranger. He'd never had an experience like it in his entire life. But after a while it was as if he began to let go, get into it almost. In a way, he had no choice. The involuntary reactions of his body were betraying him, emotion spewing out of him as if he were spontaneously erupting. A volcano. Or, better, a mighty geyser. Letting off steam. Releasing all the pressure that had been building up inside him. He'd hardly even known it was there. But Sheila seemed to be taking it in her stride. Behaving as if it were completely normal to embrace a total stranger on a Thursday morning and let him sob and heave all over her. Perhaps, for a soul midwife, it was just another day at the office.

He was starting to collect himself. The embarrassment was closer now. He found a fresh hanky and blew his nose. 'Sorry about that,' he said. 'I don't know what happened to me.'

'Don't apologize. It's perfectly understandable. You're going through so much.'

'But you're meant to be here for Sarah, not me.'

'I'm here for whoever needs me. Now, let *me* get *you* a cup of tea.'

He didn't protest as she disappeared into the kitchen. He couldn't believe what he'd just done. Aidan Ryan: man's man, father and fisherman, protector and provider, crying like a baby in the arms of a woman he'd hardly met before. She came back in and sat down beside him as she waited for the kettle to boil.

'Sarah doesn't have to know about this,' he said.

'You have my absolute assurance that she won't.'

He nodded, relieved. He was amazed at how good he felt. As if a storm had passed. He sank back into the couch. There was something to be said for this crying. No wonder women did it all the time.

'Did Sarah tell you what we're going to be doing today?'

'No.' Unless she had and he hadn't been listening.

'We're going to make a death plan.'

She's already planning to die, he felt like telling her, but he didn't. Instead he said: 'What's a death plan?'

'Very similar to a birth plan, really.'

'Which is?'

'When a woman goes into hospital to have a baby, she might write down her aspirations on how she'd like the birth to go.'

He looked at her doubtfully. 'Does that generally work?'

She laughed. 'Not all of the time, no. Not if the birth happens extremely quickly, or if medical intervention is required to save the child. Or sometimes you might get an unsympathetic midwife. But you're lucky.' She smiled at him. 'Because you have a very sympathetic midwife.'

He nodded out of politeness, still dubious. 'So what kind of thing would you include in a death plan?'

'All sorts of things. Where the patient would like to die – at home or in a hospital or hospice. Who they'd like with them when it's happening – or not as the case may be. The right to refuse certain treatments. Anything the person likes, really. It's to facilitate them in having as dignified and as natural a death as possible.'

'What do you mean, natural? She'll still get pain medication?'

'Of course. I work alongside medicine, not against it.'

'Okay, then. Will I go and see if she's awake?'

'Let's have that cup of tea first. You need a few more minutes for your face to go back to normal.'

'Oh. Thanks.'

Chapter 47

It had taken them twice as long as usual to walk to the cove. She'd had to keep stopping to sit on whatever happened to be handy. A doorstep. A bollard. The bonnet of a car. Maia had squealed with impatience, tugging her with size-defying strength. Or maybe it was just that Sarah was so weak now. At times it felt as if her legs were about to go from under her. But she managed to keep walking. Just.

She was sitting now. On her collapsible chair. The collapsible woman. Wrapped up in so many layers over her wetsuit, as if it were a winter's day. And still she couldn't keep the heat inside her bones. It was warm. She knew this logically. She saw the sun shining in the sky and the bathers out in their swimsuits. But she couldn't feel it herself. It was almost as if she were witnessing a scene in which she had no part. Or observing a painting.

Star was there too, Maia splashing close by. She held the image of the dolphin's perfect symmetry in her mind's eye. Her own body used to be perfectly symmetrical. Not any more. She was lopsided now. But not for much longer. In a short time – a breathtakingly short time – she'd have no more use for this body. She concentrated on her breathing as the fear threatened to overwhelm her. In. Out. In. Out. After a while, it worked. And she was left with a gentle feeling of peace. And an extraordinary sense of freedom. For the first time she felt it was good that she wouldn't need this body any more. This body that had ultimately betrayed her. Had looked so good on the outside, when all the time it had had an innate malfunction. To be free of her body was a good thing. Her spirit soared – up to the blowy blue sky, where the gulls floated on the air currents.

All of a sudden, Aidan was standing in front of her, dripping, the hair on his body plastered against his skin in its wetness. 'Are you coming in?'

She smiled up at him. 'I don't feel strong enough today, Aidan.'

'Rubbish.'

Without another word, he unwound all the material from around her, picked her up like the bag of bones she was, and strode across the sand – one arm supporting her back, the other gripping the backs of her knees. Sarah looped her arms about his neck and grinned, absorbing his delicious body heat. They were both oblivious to the stares of the people they passed.

Aidan was in the water now. Up to his ankles. His knees. Towards the place where Maia and the other children were playing. The water was barely at his waist here, so he sank to his knees, plunging her into the Atlantic. She gasped, the breath knocked out of her by the cold. Then her body acclimatized and so did she. She bobbed on the water, Aidan supporting her, Star swimming beyond her, her daughter laughing beside her. Her daughter. Laughing. Who'd have thought she'd see the day? But she had. She felt grateful. She felt privileged. She felt part of it all.

'Let's take the dinghy out tonight. We'll get Bridget to babysit,' Sarah said.

'You feeling up to it?'

'Yes. It's meant to be a clear night. And there's a full moon.'

He knew they were both thinking that she might not be here for the next one.

'All right, then.'

It felt wonderfully clandestine. Aidan prepared a moonlight picnic, in the vain hope that she might eat some of it. Then Bridget arrived and they left, Sarah barely visible beneath her layers. They linked one another and walked along slowly. So incredibly slowly that Aidan was worried she wasn't up to it. Perhaps they should have taken the car. But when he saw Sarah's face, tilted towards the moon, he stopped worrying and started enjoying. Perhaps 'enjoying' was the wrong word to describe the situation but it was the closest one he had. He was finding it increasingly difficult of late to find words to match his experiences, his emotions, so he just went with it – he had no other choice.

Their baby steps finally carried them to the harbour where they'd first met, less than five months ago. Their former lives smashed to smithereens now. It didn't seem to matter tonight. Tonight existed only for itself.

The rigging clanged on the breeze, a thousand bells ringing, a thousand stars above their heads. Aidan placed his hands on either side of Sarah's waist and lifted her into the boat, swinging her down in an arc. She was a feather. A piece of driftwood. Then he fastened the life-jacket over her multi-layers. Her body looked comical. Her face, rising above it, was luminous.

They sailed away from the harbour, away from all the other boats. Away from civilization as they knew it. Tonight it would be only them and the elements. Just the way he liked it. Sarah was looking as if she'd never stop smiling and his final misgivings floated away. She had been right. This had been the right thing to do. And in spite of it all, in spite of the madness and the pain, the strain he was under, the sadness that threatened to overwhelm him at times, there was nowhere else he'd rather be. This was where he belonged. With Sarah. In this moment.

This perfect moment. It was as if his entire life had been leading up to this single point. He was in it, inhabiting it with every ounce of his being. He felt that she was too.

They went out to where they thought Star might be, to where the mouth of the harbour opened out into the ocean. The wild Atlantic, calmed tonight, rippling gently beneath the boat, bobbing it along, working in unison. Aidan switched off the engine and they floated. Not a sound. It was eerie almost, the silence huge. It swelled and filled his head, his entire being. He was part of it and it was part of him. He'd forgotten what it was like – being out at sea at night. How could he have done?

They were between two worlds, depending in which direction you looked. One way was the harbour, the streetlights, the house-lights – lighting their way home if that was what they chose. That way was comfort and familiarity. The other way was nothing, yet at the same time everything. The sea, the sky, the stars, the moon. All of creation laid out for them. Calling them. Tempting them. This was the way they both chose to look.

And, suddenly, she was there, Star, part of it too, giving herself away with one of her gigantic sighs.

'Starboard,' said Aidan.

They turned their heads but she was gone again. Sarah smiled at him, the exact same smile she had given him on the first day. As if she was lit up from within. But this time, she seemed almost translucent. He knew it was partly the moon that was causing this effect – but only partly. There were times lately when he felt he could see right through her. And now, her eyes gigantic with moonshine, liquid and limpid like rock-pools, it made her seem like some otherworldly creature. And he realized that that was what she was. She had one foot in two separate worlds, straddling them with increasing ease. And although they were sitting in the same boat, he had the strangest sensation that she was drifting away from him. He had to fight the urge to pull her back from where he couldn't follow.

'This is just so . . .' She gestured around her, shaking her head.

'I know.'

Star circled the boat. Stars above them, below them and all around them. And suddenly there were two. Aidan thought he was imagining it at first. He knew how swiftly a dolphin could move – could appear to be in two places at once.

'There are two of them, Aidan – look!'

Sarah stood unsteadily and pointed. Sure enough. Two dorsal fins together at the one time didn't lie. They rose and fell in perfect unison, as if instructed by a choreographer. An elegant underwater ballet. Disappearing under, then emerging to breathe. It was a meditation just to watch them. Then they separated and began to play, gentle at first, then increasingly rough.

'Are they playing or fighting?'

'I don't know. It's hard to tell.'

'Where do you think the other came from?'

'Could be anywhere. There are a good few lone dolphins along this coast now.'

'Are there? You never told me that.'

'Did I not? I assumed you knew. Star is the friendliest anyway. Or this one could have come from the open ocean on its way to the Caribbean. Or on its way back to the Mediterranean. Came in to see what was going on.'

'What a life. Being free to go wherever you choose, do whatever you want. Completely in synch with your own environment.' Her voice was filled with an intense yearning. 'I'm coming back as a dolphin,' she said.

He smiled at her.

'How long do they live anyhow?'

'Up to forty years in some cases.'

'Same as me, then.'

The other dolphin had positioned its body along the side of the dinghy. Sarah reached down and grazed her fingers on its back. 'It's letting me touch. Look.'

Sure enough, the dolphin seemed to be relishing Sarah's caress. It turned over and allowed her to stroke the tender skin of its underbelly.

Aidan watched her. Her face was ecstatic. She closed her eyes. 'I can't believe this is happening,' she murmured.

He could.

Star was on the other side of the boat. Without warning, she reared out of the water and, for several seconds, her body was actually in the boat. Sarah ran her hand along Star's back and the dolphin plunged back into the water. They laughed, breathless with excitement.

The dolphins stayed with them for a couple of hours. Then they swam off into the deep blue yonder. Aidan started the engine and turned the boat to shore. Sarah seemed entirely spent and wildly happy. He saw her mouthing something at the retreating forms of the sea creatures. He knew it was 'goodbye'.

Chapter 48

The hospice nurse had come and gone. She had wanted to connect Sarah to a morphine drip. Sarah had refused. Right now, the drip stood impotently in the corner of the room. Sarah resented its presence. 'I won't use it, you know.'

'You might need to.' Her tablets were proving increasingly ineffective.

'I won't. I want to remain lucid. If I'm going to have hallucinations, I want to be able to tell the difference between real ones and artificial ones.'

It wasn't really the drip that was the problem. The problem, as they both well knew, was that being connected to it was tantamount to admitting that she couldn't venture out any more. She couldn't really anyway. But without the drip, she could retain the illusion of mobility.

Sarah sighed and lay down on her side, turning her back to Aidan and her eyes to the wall. Aidan left the room and joined Sheila in the kitchen. The woman appeared to be washing crystals in the sink. He didn't ask, just slumped wearily into the nearest chair.

'Is she upset?'

'Wouldn't you be? She can't even go outside.'

'Then you'll have to bring the outdoors to her. Bring her the things she loves from outside. Flowers, shells, stones. If you help me, we can move her bed closer to the window so she can see outside all the time.'

Aidan nodded. He could do that. He wished he didn't feel

a hundred years old. He felt Sheila move up behind him. She laid her hands on his shoulders. 'May I?'

'May you what?'

'Give you a healing massage.'

'I thought you were supposed to do that to the patient.'

'And caregivers too. Wherever the need arises.'

He shrugged. 'Okay.'

He wasn't sure about the healing part but a massage sounded good. As she worked on his shoulders, ironed out the kinks in his neck, Aidan felt the tension flowing out of him, and was suddenly overwhelmed by his own tiredness.

'I could sleep for a week,' he said.

'It's no wonder you're tired. You need to look after yourself, Aidan. You're going to have to be on top form to deal with what's coming next.'

He didn't ask for details. He decided he'd rather not know.

'I think I'll go out for a walk,' he said.

'Good idea. Buy her some flowers while you're at it. I'll go up to her for a while.'

Aidan nodded and got up. 'Thanks for the massage.'

'You're welcome.'

He wasn't sure if he felt healed. But he felt marginally better. Flowers. He didn't think he needed to collect shells. Maia had tons of them in her room – although they were so meticulously arranged that she would probably notice if he removed even one. The beach it was, then.

Tommy had spent a magical morning surfing. The September sea was increasingly rough and he'd ridden beneath the curve of more than one wave that morning. He felt elated as he stepped out of the water. He saw his father before his father saw him: Aidan was walking along slowly, peering at the sand

and bending every so often to pick something up. Odd. Tommy approached him. 'Dad.'

'Tommy!'

'What are you doing?'

'Here. What do you think of this shell?'

'It's a shell.'

'Is it pretty?'

'I don't know. I suppose so.' What had got into his dad? They must be for the little girl.

'I'm glad I bumped into you, Tom. I need to talk to you.'

'Yeah?'

'The dolphin tours. I'm probably going to have to knock them on the head for a while.'

'Why?'

'It's Sarah. She's not great.'

Tommy nodded. It embarrassed him to talk about her.

'So she's going to need me around a lot more. I might get out the odd afternoon, but that's about it.'

Tommy looked at his father as his father glanced away. He could have sworn he hadn't had as much grey hair the last time he'd seen him. 'I could cover for you.'

'What? Do the tours on your own?'

'Yeah. Why not?'

'It'd be too much for you, Tom.'

'No, it wouldn't.' Tommy was growing indignant. 'I know what to do. I've watched you hundreds of times.'

Father looked at son thoughtfully.

'I can do it. I know I can. And, besides, we have to squeeze the last of the money out of the tourists.'

His dad laughed. 'You're your mother's son.'

'I need the money too, you know – to squander when I'm in college.'

'You're on. I'll come out when I can, but other than that,

you're on your own. You can start this afternoon, if you like.'

'Magic. You won't regret it.'

'You make sure I don't.' He smiled. Then the smile faded. 'How's your mother?'

'She's doing all right. She said you came to see her.'

'I did. She threw a cup of tea over my head.'

'You got away lightly.'

'I did.'

'She'd been talking about using the nutcrackers on you.'

His father made a face. 'I've got to be getting back. Let me know how you get on this afternoon. Oh – I almost forgot.' He took something out of his pocket and tossed it to Tommy. 'The keys to the kingdom. Use them wisely.'

'I will.'

His father moved away. Tommy watched him walk on a few steps, then bend and pick up another shell. He examined it for a few moments, then put it into his pocket. Poor Dad. He was losing it. Maybe that was the explanation for his uncharacteristic behaviour over the past few months. He was actually going insane. He certainly looked half cracked. Maybe he had a brain tumour. You heard about that kind of thing. Tommy shook his head. It was meant to be him going through all the adolescent angst. Who would have thought he'd grow up to be the most sensible member of his family?

Chapter 49

Sheila was massaging Sarah's feet. She sat at the edge of the bed, Sarah's foot in her lap, and applied the rose-scented oil as Sarah drifted in and out of consciousness. She seemed altered. Her energy level had dipped considerably. Sheila drifted away herself as she worked, humming a lullaby from long ago.

'Sheila.'

She was jolted back. 'I'm sorry, my dear. I was miles away. I thought you were asleep.'

'What was that you were singing?'

'I don't know. Something from my childhood, I expect. It's amazing what's buried inside.'

'What's that smell?'

'I'm burning geranium oil.'

'I don't like it.'

Sheila got up immediately, blew out the tea-light and took the burner out of the room. Then she returned. 'Is there anything else I can do for you?'

'I could use some extra pillows.'

Sheila went over to the armchair, picked up two spares and approached the head of the bed. The two women looked candidly at one another.

'I don't think I can sit up.'

'Not to worry.'

Sheila hoisted her tenderly by the armpits. Sarah began to cry. 'I was always able to sit up before. What's happening to me, Sheila?'

'Your body is preparing itself for its journey.'

'I don't want to go on a journey. I want to stay here.'

Sheila clasped Sarah's hands as the other woman sobbed uncontrollably. She waited patiently for the storm to subside. When it did, she began to speak in a soft, gentle voice. 'All you're doing, Sarah, is returning to your source. You're going back to where you came from. Back to where you belong.'

'Back to God?'

'Straight back into the loving arms of God.'

'Do you really believe that?'

'Yes, I really do. I've been there now for so many people as they've died. Had the privilege to be there. And every now and then you catch a glimpse of the other side. You get to accompany them for a small part of their journey. Hold their hands as they cross to the other side.'

'What have you seen?'

'Peace. Joy. Pure love.'

'That doesn't sound too bad.'

Sheila smiled and squeezed her hand. 'It isn't.'

'Are you afraid of dying, Sheila?'

'No. Not one bit.'

Sarah looked intensely into the other woman's eyes. 'Do you really mean that?'

'Yes, I really mean that, Sarah.'

Sarah continued to stare for several seconds longer. Then her eyes fell away and her body relaxed. 'I believe you,' she said.

'When you spend so much time around death you lose your fear of it. You see the joy on the faces of the dying as their loved ones come to meet them and act as their spiritual guides. Their psychopomps.'

'Psychopomp!' Sarah sounded excited. 'I know that word.'

Sheila nodded. 'Well, that's how I see myself too. A spiritual guide.'

'Psychopomp.' Sarah rolled the word around in her mouth. 'Aidan doesn't believe in any of that stuff. He thinks we just rot in the ground and that's it. We're gone.'

'That's what happens to the physical body, but the soul soars as it's released. He'll find out when his time comes. Because it comes to all of us. Your time has just come a little earlier than most.'

Sarah nodded.

'Would you like to do a guided visualization?'

'Yes, please.'

'Okay. Close your eyes and get your body as comfortable as possible.'

'This bedspread is annoying me.'

'I'll take it off you.'

Sheila removed it and smoothed the remaining sheet over Sarah's limbs. She sat in the chair beside the bed and closed her own eyes. 'You're in charge of this journey, Sarah. You decide where you want to go and who you want to have travel with you. It can be a beautiful garden, a rainbow bridge, a body of water . . .'

'The sea. And I want Star with me.'

'Star is the dolphin?'

'Yes.'

'Okay. So close your eyes and breathe with me.'

Sheila placed her hand over Sarah's heart and the room fell into silence. Their breaths became deeper and one began to match the other. Sheila's voice entered the silence. 'You're walking along a cliff path on a beautiful summer's day. The sun is high and the sky is cloudless. Endless. Everywhere you look there are flowers, flanking each side of the path. The only sound is the rhythmic lapping of the waves against the rocks.'

She paused between each sentence. And the silences grew even louder.

'The path begins to spiral downward. Down and down you go. Down. Down. Until you reach a secluded cove. The sand is golden. The sea is sapphire blue. The sunlight dances on the water like so many diamonds. The cliffs are made of the blackest onyx. The path ends and your feet sink into the sand. It's the softest sensation you've ever known. You feel as if you're walking on clouds. Resting on the shoreline, where the sea meets the sand, there is a little blue boat. You know that someone has left it for you. Taking your time, you walk over and see that it's tied to a rock. You undo the knot and it falls away easily. You give the boat a push and it floats effortlessly into the sea. You step on board.

'It's a tiny wooden vessel. Just the right size for one. The perfect fit for you. You begin to drift, you and the boat, out to sea. The sea is calm and you feel perfectly safe, knowing that nothing bad can happen to you here. You float along, giving yourself over to the sensation of being carried by the water, by the boat. You move with the ebb and the flow of the waves. And after a while you realize that your little boat is travelling by itself, with no effort on your part. Yet you are not afraid. And you are not alone. Star is swimming alongside the boat. She's there to guide you. To help you on your way. She'll be with you until your journey's end and beyond. As the boat drifts away. Further from the shore. Further. And further. Away.'

Sheila opened her eyes. She exhaled and peered at Sarah. Her face was closed, her mouth slightly open. She was fast asleep. Sheila got up and left the room as quietly as possible.

Aidan was downstairs. He had evidently just got in. He was standing at the coffee-table, emptying shells from his pockets, handfuls and handfuls. Several bouquets also lay on the table.

Sheila gestured towards them. 'You did well.'

He nodded. 'How is she?'

'She's sleeping.'

'Good. She seemed very tired.'

'Aidan, you need to ring her sister.'

Aidan dropped the last of the shells onto the table. Several heartbeats passed between them. 'Why?'

'It's time.'

Chapter 50

That night the very portals of hell opened up for Aidan. He was woken up at four a.m. by a high-pitched keening. It was as if some animal were in the room with him. But it was Sarah, curled up foetally, her hands clutching her belly, the pain escaping her in a series of whimpers and moans.

He switched on the bedside lamp and pulled back the covers. Her face was contorted, her teeth bared. For a second he thought she was still asleep, in the throes of a nightmare, but then he saw that she was fully awake, her eyes wide open and glistening, wild.

'Are you in pain?'

She nodded between moans.

'Why didn't you wake me?'

The question was rhetorical. She was unable to speak.

'Oh, Jesus. The drip.' Aidan walked rapidly to the stand and began to fiddle ineffectually with it. Then he rattled it violently. It was the equivalent of thumping a broken appliance. 'I'll phone the nurse.'

He sat on the side of the bed and dialled, his foot tapping furiously. Then he got up and began to pace, too agitated to stay still. The phone went automatically to message minder. Shit. He left a short, curt message and hung up. Maybe she'd ring him straight back. Maybe she wouldn't. He didn't have the luxury of hanging around to find out. So he rang the out-of-hours GP service. He got through immediately and described the situation in urgent terms. The doctor on call would be there directly. Thank you.

He crawled into the bed beside Sarah. She had stopped making sounds. Her lips were no longer visible, her mouth a thin, pinched line. Her eyes were screwed shut. She was rocking herself as if she were her very own baby. Aidan thought he'd never seen a human being so wretched. He had never before been so closely involved in the process of someone dying. His mother had died at home, of course, but he had always been one step removed from the visceral process of death; his sisters had done all that. Dying was traditionally women's business. Probably because men weren't up to it. He knew that women were the stronger sex. He'd always known it. It had been evident in his parents' marriage. Blindingly obvious in his own.

'The doctor will be here soon, love. Can I do anything for you?'

It was a stupid question. Of course there was nothing he could do. Only watch as she writhed in agony. He'd never felt so helpless in all his life. There had to be something. 'I'm going to call an ambulance,' he said.

Her eyes flew open. He registered the panic in them as she shook her head manically, almost as if she were having a fit.

'No.' The word was barely audible, the meaning unmistakable. Sarah didn't want to die in hospital. On this she had been adamant.

'You don't have to stay there. Just till they sort you out. You can come straight back home.'

'No.' The word escaped in an outbreath.

Aidan got up and began to pace again. Then he ran downstairs to find her painkillers and prayed to a God in whom he didn't believe that she'd be able to swallow them.

Fiona woke up abruptly from an extraordinary dream, with the feeling that she didn't know where she was. But she was at home, in her ex-marital bed, her mobile buzzing furiously beside her. It vibrated right onto the floor and she hung precariously over the side of the bed to retrieve it. 'Hello.'

She listened carefully, aware that her mind was still groggy. What she heard made her doubt that she was fully awake. She sat up properly. 'I'm sorry. Could you repeat that?'

There it was again. She *had* heard right. She *was* awake. She put down the phone and considered ways to get out of it. There *was* no way. She'd have to go. She was a doctor. A professional. It was her duty.

Fully awake now, she got out of bed and put on socks and runners. Then she went downstairs, picked up her bag and put on her jacket. She paused and looked at her face in the mirror on the way out of the door. 'You can do this, Fiona,' she said out loud.

Aidan let her in, wearing a T-shirt and boxer shorts. His feet were bare, his demeanour frantic. 'She's upstairs,' he said.

Fiona moved past him wordlessly and headed for the stairway. She was hyper-aware of him one step behind her the whole way. 'In here?'

He nodded and she pushed open the bedroom door. Their bedroom door.

A twisted figure was writhing under the sheets. Fiona dropped her bag and glanced at the drip. 'Why isn't that connected up?' She looked briefly at Aidan, who was standing at the end of the bed, the lower part of his face covered with his hand.

'Sarah didn't want it. She said she wasn't going to use it.'

'Well, that was bloody stupid, wasn't it?' Fiona bent over Sarah's supine form. 'Sarah. It's Fiona.'

Sarah's eyes flickered open.

'I'm going to give you an injection. It'll take away the pain. See you through until the morning.'

Sarah was trying to say something. Fiona bent her head until her ear was directly above the other woman's mouth. She listened for a few seconds. 'No,' she replied. 'I won't.'

'What did she say?' asked Aidan.

'That I'm not to let you take her to the hospital.'

'Oh, I won't, love. I promise,' said Aidan.

Fiona made the necessary preparations, and plunged the needle into Sarah's skin. The effect was almost immediate, like the pressure released from a valve. Almost instantly Sarah's body became still and her breath slowed.

'Jesus,' said Aidan, behind her. 'Can I have some of that?'

Fiona turned to him. 'My pleasure. Trousers down.' She smiled grimly. Except it wasn't a real smile. Aidan's was, as he approached the bed and took Sarah's hand in his. Fiona's heart constricted.

'Are you all right?' he said.

Her husband's voice, soft and tender as he stroked Sarah's forehead. She saw her nod, then turned away to pack up her things as quickly as she could. She felt movement behind her and knew that Aidan was repositioning Sarah in the bed. She turned back to them. Sarah was looking directly at her. The two women took each other in. Fiona nodded and turned to go.

'Wait!'

She stopped. Should she just keep walking? She'd done her duty. The woman was no longer in pain. What if there were other medical issues? She sighed deeply and turned back. Sarah's head was propped up on a couple of pillows, which was likely the only way she could hold it up. Her eyes, perhaps the only part of her that showed any life, were boring into Fiona's.

'Can I . . .?' She began to speak, her voice a croak. Then she choked. Aidan immediately tilted her forward, cradling her body and patting her upper back. When the spasm had subsided, he placed a tumbler of water at her lips. Sarah sipped with apparent difficulty. Then he lowered her again. Who could have known, thought Fiona, that Aidan would make such an attentive nurse?

In sickness and in health.

Sarah tried again. 'Can I talk to you, Fiona?'

Fiona stared at her. She wasn't prepared for this. Twenty minutes ago she'd been sound asleep. But how did one prepare for such a moment anyhow? To confront the dying woman who stole your husband. Hardly a chapter in your standard book on etiquette. She wanted to walk away – run away. Yet how could she, and live with herself afterwards? Accept her lack of courage. Her dearth of compassion.

So Fiona stayed. And she sat in the chair provided for visitors. Sarah inclined her head slightly towards Aidan. 'Do you mind?' She widened her eyes and looked towards the door.

Aidan's eyes widened in response. 'You want me to leave?'

'Yes.'

'Are you sure?'

'Just do as she asks.' Fiona's voice was low. Authoritative.

Aidan's worried gaze moved from one woman to the other. Then he left.

It took some effort on Fiona's part to look at Sarah. Not because of anger or resentment or, God help us, jealousy. But because it was painful to see her. You could trace the skull beneath the skin. It was almost eerie. On the one hand her beauty was magnified. The perfect bone structure, the symmetry of her face. On the other, it was like staring point-blank at death. Death had its mark on her. It was all around her, like a shadow. A dark cloak masking the person she used to be. Her eyes were huge. Beautiful. Horrifying. Fiona stared into them unflinchingly. She wouldn't let herself down. She just wouldn't. 'What did you want to talk to me about?'

'A lot of things, Fiona. First, I want to say thank you for tonight.'

Fiona inclined her head in acknowledgement.

'It must be a great feeling. Having the power to heal.'

'We can't heal everything.'

'Don't I know it.'

Fiona instantly regretted her words. The silence began and rapidly built up in its intensity.

'You must really hate me.'

Fiona's exhalation was audible. She wished herself any other place. 'I don't hate you, Sarah. Not any more.'

'You mean not after tonight.'

'Not for a little while now.'

'But you did before. I don't blame you. I would have hated me too. Betrayal is a very ugly thing. Painful. Damaging. But now I guess I'm just pathetic.'

Fiona chose her words carefully. 'Sympathy does tend to get in the way of hatred.'

Sarah gave her a half-smile. 'Inconvenient that, isn't it?'

'It can be.'

'I'm not going to do anything so mawkish as to beg for your forgiveness, Fiona, but I am going to offer you my apology. I'm sorry for all the hurt I've caused you.'

Fiona couldn't bring herself to speak. It was hard enough not to cry. For whom, she didn't know. For herself. For Sarah. For the whole sorry mess. She could feel Sarah's ethereal eyes trying to fathom her. She couldn't even fathom herself. There was only one thing she knew for sure. The dying didn't lie. This was the truth. The pristine truth. And she was grateful to be at the receiving end of it.

'I'm not telling you this,' Sarah continued, 'to avoid going to hell. I don't believe in hell. But perhaps you feel I deserve to be punished.'

'I think,' said Fiona, 'that you've suffered enough already.'

'We both have. It would mean a lot to me to know that you're all right, Fiona.'

'I will be.'

'Yes, I think you will. You're so strong. Not like me. I've always been so weak. Always needed a man to lean on.'

'I don't think it's possible to be the single parent of an autistic child and to be weak.'

Sarah smiled. 'There is that. I did something right there, I suppose. And maybe it was a blessing all along, Maia being autistic.'

'Why do you say that?'

'Because she won't miss me.'

'Surely . . .'

'Not like a normal child would. She'll be disturbed at first by the change in her routine. She won't know where I've gone. Won't comprehend any of it. But she'll have Aidan. She'll be all right.'

'Maia's staying with Aidan?' Fiona was clearly amazed.

'Didn't he tell you?'

'We don't chat much any more.'

'Of course. Stupid of me.'

They were both quiet. Sarah seemed to be giving Fiona the time she needed to take it in. Gathering her strength for what she needed to say next.

'I was really only borrowing him, Fiona.'

Fiona looked sharply at her. 'That's not what it felt like.'

'But that's what it was. Essentially. Borrowing him for my borrowed time. I wasn't strong enough to do it on my own. But he's always been yours, Fiona. Always will be.'

'I don't want him any more.' Her words sounded vicious, even to her own ears.

But both women knew the hurt that lay behind them.

'Maybe you don't. But all I can say is I hope you don't always feel that way.'

Fiona examined Sarah's face closely, as a doctor might. She could see that she was battling to keep her eyelids from falling. She got up. 'You're exhausted. After what you've been through you need your rest. I shouldn't even have let you have this conversation.'

'I needed it.'

To Fiona's horror, Sarah grabbed her hand. 'It's been a huge relief for me to be able to say these things to you. Thank you, Fiona. Thank you so much. I know I've been a crap friend but you were a very good friend to me. Even now. It's been a privilege to know you.'

Sarah released her grip and closed her eyes, her head lolling gently to the side as she slipped comfortably into sleep.

Fiona took up her bag and moved towards the door. Then she stopped, went back and kissed the other woman on the cheek. It might have been her imagination. It might have been an involuntary muscle spasm. But she could have sworn she saw Sarah smile.

Aidan was sitting at the bottom of the stairs. He leaped to his feet as soon as he heard her. His eyes were full of questions that she didn't have the energy to answer. She fished a few sachets out of her jacket pocket. 'If she experiences any more pain before the morning, try to get these down her. They're soluble. She won't be able to manage anything else.' She was Dr Fiona. 'And get that fecking drip sorted first thing.'

Aidan took the sachets from her. 'Thank you. I'll do that.'

Fiona shook her head. 'Look after her.'

Aidan regarded his wife silently.

'And, for God's sake, take care of yourself. You look terrible. Try to get some sleep.'

By the time he'd recovered from the shock, she was gone.

Fiona abandoned her car until the morning, choosing instead to walk home along the beach. Or, rather, her legs seemed to choose for her.

She was wrestling with the wind and with her unwilling epiphany: that the other woman needed her husband more than she did. She who had life and everything to live it for. For all Sarah's beauty, all her talent, all her plaudits, Fiona was far, far luckier than her. Because she had life. And ultimately nothing else mattered.

And in that moment she saw, with blinding clarity, that Aidan, her husband, had done the right thing. He had made the right choice. And it no longer mattered that he hadn't chosen her.

She sat on the beach all night, revelling in this revelation. This gift.

Chapter 51

It was a strange thing, dying. At times, he could see the life force gently ebbing out of her. At others, she seemed to rally, energy and vigour replenished. And you could never tell from day to day, from hour to hour, how it was going to be.

Helen arrived on the evening after the hellish night-time episode. She dropped her bags by the front door and all but ran up the stairs. Aidan followed, two steps at a time, knowing she expected to find her sister drawing her last breath. Instead, she found Sarah sitting up in the bed and – of all things – eating. 'Helen!' she said. 'Have you come for the party?'

And the odd thing was that, at these times when Sarah was well – her energy levels up, her mind lucid – there was what could be described as an air of celebration in the room. As if some magnificent party was indeed about to take place. A strange kind of anticipation.

Sheila had turned Sarah's room into a haven of hospitality. An abundance of fresh flowers on every spare surface, fresh sheets every day, heavenly harp music playing in the background, sometimes replaced by chanting monks. Her bed was by the window now, and when she felt up to it, she sat propped up, watching the children walk to school, the shoppers come and go, the sea licking the shore at rhythmic intervals. And she was happy. The room felt happy, a pleasant place to be. The kind of place that would draw you.

Aidan had left the sisters to it for a good hour. Eventually, he heard the bedroom door closing. Helen came down the stairs and entered the kitchen. Aidan saw the renewed hope written between the lines of worry on her face. 'How about a cup of proper Irish tea?'

'There's nothing in the world I'd like more. Make it two sugars. I've earned them.'

She sat down and sighed, watching him.

'You know,' she said, 'I was expecting her to be . . . really bad. The way you sounded on the phone, I thought it was only a matter of days.'

'It is only a matter of days.' She looked so stricken that he regretted his bluntness. He sat close to her. 'She's continually up and down. You got her on an up, and I'm glad you did. But the ups are less and less frequent and each down seems to be further down.'

He watched her slump. 'I'm sorry, but that's the truth of it. I wish it wasn't.'

Helen was nodding. 'It was that way with my mother too. Only she was a lot older. Oh, God. Why is this happening?' She put her head into her hands.

Aidan watched mutely. He had no answers for himself or anyone else. Ever since the first moment he'd met Sarah, he'd felt buffeted by forces far greater than himself. Her death was no exception.

He waited patiently for Helen's tears to subside, rubbing her shoulder intermittently. And it occurred to him how accustomed he'd become to tears. Other people's and his own. To the point where they didn't embarrass him any more. Odd, that.

Sarah became irritable later on that day, her buoyancy collapsing in on itself. Aidan watched passively as Helen attempted to move mountains to please her sister. He was getting used to feeling helpless. It didn't bother him as much as it used to. But the newly arrived Helen still thought it was possible to exercise some control. Sarah requested eggs. Helen made eggs. Sarah refused eggs. She couldn't stand the smell: it made her feel sick. The eggs were removed. Other foodstuffs were produced with similar results. Sarah's eyes continually watered, although she wasn't crying. It was as if she was leaking. Another sign of her body's betrayal.

It was the following day. Mid-morning. Aidan knocked gently on the bedroom door.

'Come in.'

He entered, bearing a plate of strawberries. Helen was curled up asleep on the armchair. Sarah was sitting upright in bed, her arms around her knees, looking out of the window. As Aidan walked in, she gave him a smile of such radiance that he was transfixed. It was as if the sunlight was shining right through her. Through her eyes. Her smile. Through her very being. And it was this light-filled image of her that he was to hold before him in the darkness of the months that followed.

'It's a beautiful morning,' she said.

'It is.' Once he'd recovered himself he sat on the edge of the bed, the plate of strawberries between them. 'Will you try one?'

'Maybe later.'

'How about if I mash them up for you?'

'Okay.'

She was humouring him. He knew this. But he still couldn't stop himself.

'I was watching the tree change its colours.' She nodded to the sycamore outside the window. 'Every day it's different. Every single day. New colours. Golds. Some leaves missing. And on a day like today, with the breeze stirring things up and the light shining through, it's so breathtakingly beautiful.' She smiled at him again. 'It's a beautiful world we live in,' she said. 'I'm lucky to have been part of it for a while. Remind yourself of it, Aidan, won't you, after I'm gone, when you're sad and missing me? Remind yourself of all the beauty in the world. Will you do that for me?'

Aidan nodded and stared at the tree.

They sat in silence for a long while. Sarah. Aidan. The tree.

'Peter rang again,' he said at last. 'Will I tell him to come? Would you like to see him?'

She looked a little sad. 'I don't think so. I've said my good-byes to everyone, really. I think the time for visitors is over. I have you and I have Helen and I have Maia. That's all I want now.'

'If you're sure.'

'I am.' She reached out her hand and stroked his hair. Her eyes filled with tears. 'Thank you, Aidan. Thank you for the countless things you've done for me. You're the most wonderful man. Trust me to meet my soul-mate when I only have a few months left to live. My timing's always been lousy.'

She smiled at him again and he tried to smile back. His smile was weak. Watery.

'But I feel like the luckiest woman alive to have known you at all.'

There she was, calling herself lucky again. Aidan could hardly bear it.

'And to know that Maia will be well cared for. And safe. And loved. It's the only thing that really matters to me now. And you've made it all right. You've made everything all right. You've made my last months on earth so special. You've made it possible for me to die at home, on my own terms . . .'

'Don't go, Sarah.' The emotion spilled out of him. He was trembling with the force of it. She wrapped her arms around his neck and pulled him to her chest. She stroked his hair and kissed his crown and murmured sweet nothings. As if he were a child.

Later that evening, Sarah's body became as parched as the desert. Her lips were cracked, her bedclothes kicked to the floor. Aidan and Helen took turns to wet her lips, cool her brow. They met each other's eyes helplessly across Sarah's restless body, both wishing her peace, of one form or another. She woke from time to time, her mumblings nonsensical. Then, shortly before midnight, she opened her eyes and it was clear that full lucidity had been restored.

'My feet are cold,' she said, before closing her eyes again and returning to that strange netherland where neither of them could follow. They had both leaped up, so eager to help her. Helen won the race to the sock drawer – to find the cosiest, most comfortable socks there were to encase her sister's feet. She stood at the side of the bed and held them in front of her. 'Will these do, Sassy?'

Sarah opened her eyes and looked directly ahead. Unseeing. Helen suddenly remembered something she'd read. That people who are dying can lose their peripheral vision and can only see straight ahead, as if down a tunnel. She moved to the foot of the bed. 'Are these socks all right?'

Sarah looked straight at her, for the first time in hours, it seemed. She nodded and closed her eyes. Helen moved her chair to the end of the bed and began to put them on for her.

She didn't really believe her sister was dying. She still expected her to sit up and start talking again. Be the Sarah she'd always known. She'd done it before. Why not again?

Aidan remained where he was, stroking Sarah's hand, not even knowing if she was aware of his touch any more. He began to talk urgently, as her breathing became ragged. 'I love you,

Sarah. I don't regret a single moment that we spent together, you and me. It was worth it. All the pain. It was worth it.'

Should she leave the room? Helen wondered. Give them some privacy? But she didn't want to leave. And Aidan seemed barely aware of her presence. No more so than her sister was.

She closed her hand around Sarah's cocooned foot and rested her head against it. Sarah didn't flinch. Sarah of the oversensitive feet. Sarah who could be tortured with tickling. Her little sister was trickling away. She could feel it. And nothing she could do would bring her back. No words. No force of will. No wishing. Sarah's breath was terrifying now, rasping. At times she seemed to skip a breath. Helen squeezed her eyes tightly shut and prayed that her sister would live. That her sister would die. That this torture would be over soon.

As she opened her eyes, so did Sarah. She stared straight upward and her face melted into smiles. 'Daddy,' she said. 'Helen, Daddy's here.'

Helen and Aidan looked up at the empty space into which Sarah was staring. They saw what she saw only through the expression on her face. Sarah held out her arms, as if awaiting an embrace. Then her eyes closed again and her arms fell by her sides.

Helen was on her feet. 'Is she . . .?'

'She's still breathing.'

Helen came to where Aidan was sitting. She leaned in and listened. Sure enough, Sarah's chest still rose and fell, barely discernible beneath her white cotton nightdress. Helen returned to her seat and reflected on the strangeness of it all. How the separation between this world and the next was nothing but a breath. As fragile a thing as a breath. That if we stopped breathing, we stopped living. It was as simple and as final as that.

'Do you really think my father was here?' she said.

'I don't know, Helen.'

She shivered, as another bodily function grabbed her attention. 'I need to use the bathroom,' she whispered. 'I'll be right back.'

Aidan couldn't tell if Helen was talking to Sarah or him. He doubted she knew herself. Alone with Sarah, he could feel her slipping away from him, as if she left her body at intervals, then came back. As if she was as yet uncertain. Dipping her toe in the water. He whispered into the shell of her ear, 'It's okay, you know. You can go. I'll be fine. Maia will be fine. It's safe to let go, Sarah. It's safe to let go.' He stroked her hair, then leaned back in his chair. He blinked as he looked down her body: her feet appeared to be lit from the inside. Was it his turn to have hallucinations? He watched transfixed, as the light travelled upwards, through her shins, past her knees and upwards to her thighs. Her pelvis now. Her belly. Aidan thought of someone going around a house at night, turning off all the lights. That was what it was like. The light was on her breast now, her neck, illuminating her ever so beautiful face. When it went out through the crown of her head, Aidan knew she was gone. The Sarah he had known and loved was gone, and all that was left was this husk. This casket for her soul. And that was what he had seen leaving her body. He was sure of it. He had seen the soul he didn't believe in leave the body of the woman he loved. He felt no sadness, only wonder. The door opened and Helen walked in. Unaware.

'She's gone,' said Aidan.

Helen clasped her hand over her mouth and approached the bed. 'Oh, God,' she said. 'Sassy. No.'

Then she started to sob and it was as if her tears activated Aidan's sadness. He lowered his face into his hands and felt the depth of his despair, its heaviness descending on him. She was gone and he was still there. He would gladly have taken her place. Gladly. And at that moment, his dearest, most heart-felt desire was to go with her.

Neither heard the door open. Aidan's first awareness of Maia's presence in the room was when she pushed his hands away from his head to gain access to his lap. She climbed in and turned to Sarah's form.

'Mama sleep,' she said.

'Yes, Maia. Mama sleep.'

Chapter 52

It had been a conundrum while Sarah was still alive but once she was gone the answer seemed obvious: of course she must go to the funeral. How could she not? She owed it to everyone involved, not least herself.

Closure.

Sarah's coffin wasn't closed. Not until the very last. With looks like hers, it made sense. Fiona hadn't gone to see her, hadn't gone to the 'viewing'. What an odd term. As if Sarah were some swanky apartment you were aspiring to move into.

Fiona's presence at the funeral caused quite a stir among the locals. She couldn't help that. They had come to gawk anyway. Between her and Robert Mitchell and the various illuminati of the Irish showbiz community, they were well served. She sat midway down the church, flanked on either side by her children, her eyes fastened on the back of Aidan's head.

He had come home to collect his one and only suit. She had bought it for him when his mother had died and it had languished in the back of the wardrobe ever since. He wore it now with sandals and no socks. His hair stood up in an odd peak on his crown. He reminded her of a homeless person who had just got a suit from a charity shop, one that had perhaps belonged to a dead person.

Maia sat sandwiched between Aidan and a blonde woman. Must be the aunt. The little girl looked impossibly small, impossibly vulnerable, incomplete without Sarah by her side. Was it a tragedy or a blessing that she couldn't fully comprehend what was going on?

Robert Mitchell sat at Aidan's right hand. He wore dark glasses and looked profoundly uncomfortable. Sarah's crowd were there – a colourful lot. One woman's hat sported shocking pink plumes. The effect was defiantly festive: *I may be sad but at least my hat is happy.*

Aidan didn't cry in the church. Not visibly. His head remained erect throughout. He didn't cry at the graveside either. His expression was of bewildered desolation. Fiona and Alannah exchanged a glance and Alannah went to stand with him while they lowered the coffin.

Sarah had chosen to be buried here, in her final home, her daughter's future home, in a windswept graveyard commanding magnificent sea views.

It was an odd, disjointed feeling, watching your husband act as chief mourner at a funeral that wasn't your own. It was as if she were being offered a glimpse of her own funeral from the other side. A rare opportunity to appreciate his subtle dignity.

The afters were a relatively humble affair, given Sarah's status – tea and sandwiches in a room in the local hotel. Just outside the entrance to the room there was a display of photos of the deceased. That was unusual. The stand had drawn quite a crowd but Fiona was uneasy about being seen studying images of the woman who had stolen her husband. On second thoughts she decided that, since she'd already confounded everyone's expectations, she might as well give in to her curiosity. So she waited for a parting to reveal itself. In due course a woman stepped aside to let her in. The woman was one of the Dublin crowd and smiled warmly at Fiona. 'And how did you know Sarah?' she said.

Fiona paused briefly. 'I was a friend,' she said.

Some of the photos were old. Sarah as a young woman – couldn't have been more than twenty – her hair thick and lush, her expression warm and vibrant. There was one photo of a child, whom Fiona initially mistook for Maia. Yet it had to be Sarah. It wasn't only the seventies garb that gave her away. It was the eyes. Alive with promise, mischief and life.

Engaging as they were, these early photographs didn't affect Fiona. But the more recent ones, of which there must have been about fifty, got to her. She could see that her husband had taken them and they created an intimate portrait of his, Sarah and Maia's life together, a life that had been built on her pain. She felt the first stirrings of jealousy since the night she had been called to Sarah's bedside.

One picture kept pulling her back. It was in the centre of the display and slightly enlarged. She couldn't take her eyes off it. Sarah was sitting at her kitchen table, the light shining through her sparse white curls. A jar of bluebells stood alongside her, dating the picture to late April or early May. *So it had already started then.* She hadn't known for sure.

Sarah was looking right into the lens and directly at the person behind the camera: Aidan. Except now she was no longer looking at him but at Fiona. Her eyes contained no subterfuge; her expression was frank and open. Her beauty, as always, was effortless.

'What are you trying to tell me, Sarah?' Fiona spoke softly and unselfconsciously. The people on either side of her glanced at her and then at each other. Subtly, they moved away from her.

She stood there for several minutes longer, trying to work it out. At last she got it.

'Goodbye. Goodbye, Sarah.'

Fiona left shortly after.

It was a week after the funeral. Everyone was gone. Helen had flown back to the States. Maia was back at school. And Sarah was still dead.

Aidan walked along the beach alone. The beach that had never felt so desolate. The autumn wind rang hollow in his ears. The sea was empty. Empty of life. Not a single surfer. Not even Tommy.

Aidan felt lost, so very lost – on this stretch of sand that he knew so intimately. But everything he'd once thought he'd known, he saw that he no longer knew. He didn't belong here any more. Didn't belong anywhere. He had no home in this life, on this earth. So he wandered. He stared out to sea at the ceaseless waves and wanted to go with them.

Another figure crossed the beach towards him. She was small. Her arms crossed her chest. Her steps were rapid.

'What are you doing?'

He stared at her, not knowing what to say.

'You'll catch your death out here in a T-shirt. Come with me.'

She linked him and ferried him along with her. He offered no resistance.

Back to the house they went. Up the worn stone steps and onto the deck. Through the back door, the black dog frenzied. Aidan stood in his home and looked around him as if he'd never seen it before. He found the sea through the window and fixed his gaze on it. Fiona steered him towards the sitting room. 'When's the last time you slept?'

When her husband didn't reply she walked him to the couch. 'Here. Lie down.'

He kicked off his sand-caked boots and did as he was told, curling up his long body to fit the limited space.

Fiona laid the throw over him, placing it beneath his chin and tucking it up under his feet. Aidan drifted off into nothingness.

Tommy got up half an hour later. He thundered down the stairs and stood stock still at the entrance to the sitting room.

The figure on the couch snored deeply and evenly. He walked into the kitchen. His mother was at the table, sipping her morning coffee. He didn't say anything, just made the first move towards getting his breakfast. Then he turned from the fridge to her. 'Is Dad staying?'

'I don't know, Tommy.'

Epilogue

Aidan and Maia were out in the dinghy. Star had been gone for a year now, since the week that Sarah had died. She had disappeared, just like that. How could a presence that filled your life to the brim just go, never to be seen again? He sometimes wondered if Sarah would have been so keen to leave Maia in the harbour town if she had known Star wouldn't be there. But those thoughts only came upon him in his darker moments. In saner times, he knew she would have done.

He turned off the engine and they started to drift. He had found that the motion of the water calmed Maia, made her less agitated. Fiona was good at doing that too, but it was to the sea he turned as always.

A splash. A rush of breath somewhere close by. Aidan and Maia turned their heads in unison. It could have been anything. A fish. A nothing. A wish. But it wasn't nothing. It was Star. He recognized her instantly from the distinctive nick on her dorsal fin. No other dolphin.

Maia laughed, the enchanting sound bubbling up her throat and out through her mouth. Aidan laughed too and then his laughter caught in his throat as he saw the other creature. Star was not alone: a baby dolphin swam at her side. Their over-water under-water dance one of perfect synchronicity, as if the baby was still attached to its mother by some invisible umbilical cord.

Pure elation filled Aidan's soul. She had come back to him. She had come home.

'Mama,' said Maia.

The dolphins stayed for the longest time. Then the ocean took them away and they never saw them again.

Acknowledgements

Many thanks to the following:

Patricia Deevy, my excellent editor at Penguin, for making me and my novel look better; all at Penguin Ireland, Michael McLoughlin, Cliona Lewis, Patricia McVeigh and Brian Walker; Keith Taylor at Penguin UK and all in the London office who worked on my book; Faith O'Grady, my fantastic agent; Hazel Orme, copy editor, another woman who makes me look better; Keith Talbot and Thomasina Quirk, for their invaluable insights into autism; all at the Irish Society for Autism, especially Denis Sexton, for sharing his story with me; Sara Phelan, for her legal advice; Dorothy Allen, for her medical advice; Ger and Margaret Kirwan, for telling me about the dolphin; Frank Callery, for sharing his experiences with me; Winnie O'Keane, for her recollections on fishermen and their ways; Rachel, for lending me the book about the pink dolphins; my family; my parents; Leo and Marianne, the funniest double-act I know; Rory, for everything.

Thank you, everyone.

read more

my penguin e-newsletter

Subscribe to receive *read more*, your monthly e-newsletter from Penguin Australia. As a *read more* subscriber you'll receive sneak peeks of new books, be kept up to date with what's hot, have the opportunity to meet your favourite authors, download reading guides for your book club, receive special offers, be in the running to win exclusive subscriber-only prizes, plus much more.

Visit penguin.com.au/readmore to subscribe